PRAISE

"Clipston's latest is a swee

—Rachel Hauck, *New York Times* bestselling author,
on *Finding You*

"Amy Clipston delivers swoon-worthy romance while addressing realistic issues of fame and long-distance relationships. Heather is a heroine to root for, and when she meets her opposite in Alex, humor and growth are the result. A thoroughly enjoyable love story."

—Lee Tobin McClain, *New York Times* bestselling author, on *Starstruck*

"*Starstruck* is a lovely story filled with wonderfully drawn, fully relatable characters and a charming community. Amy Clipston writes with warmth and heart."

—RaeAnne Thayne, *New York Times* bestselling author

"Music, love, and dreams all combine in perfect harmony in this sweet romance."

—Sheila Roberts, *USA TODAY* bestselling author, on *Starstruck*

"A rockstar and his 'Baker Girl' will warm your heart in this sweet, small-town, slow-burn romance!"

—Jennifer Snow, *USA TODAY* bestselling author, on *Starstruck*

"Applause for *Starstruck*! Amy Clipston has masterfully crafted an endearing story of hope and taking chances. Readers will be instantly captivated by the charm of Bookish Brownies and Chocolate Chunk Novel cookies! A definite must-read for those looking for a feel-good romance."

—Lacey Baker, *USA TODAY* bestselling author of *Snow Place Like Home*

"Hometown charm and swoon-worthy second chances make this a must read."

—Kristen McKanagh, author of *Snowball's Christmas*, on
Something Old, Something New

"Amy Clipston writes a sweet and tender romance filled with a beautiful look at how love brings healing to broken hearts. This small-town romance, with an adorable little girl and cat to boot, is a great addition to your TBR list."

—Pepper Basham, author of *Authentically, Izzy*, on *The View from Coral Cove*

"Grieving and brokenhearted, novelist Maya Reynolds moves to Coral Cove, the place where she felt happiest as a child. An old family secret upends Maya's plan for a fresh start, as does her longing to love and be loved. *The View from Coral Cove* is Amy Clipston at her best—a tender story of hope, healing, and a love that's meant to be."

—Suzanne Woods Fisher, bestselling author of *On a Summer Tide*

"*The Heart of Splendid Lake* offers a welcome escape in the form of a sympathetic heroine and her struggling lakeside resort. Clipston proficiently explores love and loss, family and friendship in a touching, small-town romance that I devoured in a single day!"

—Denise Hunter, bestselling author of the Bluebell Inn series

"A touching story of grief, love, and life carrying on, *The Heart of Splendid Lake* engaged my heart from the very first page. Sometimes the feelings we run from lead us to the hope we can't escape, and that's a beautiful thing to see through the eyes of these winning characters. Amy Clipston deftly guides readers on an emotionally satisfying journey that will appeal to fans of Denise Hunter and Becky Wade."

—Bethany Turner, award-winning author of *Plot Twist*

"Amy Clipston's characters are always so endearing and well-developed."

—Shelley Shepard Gray, *New York Times* and *USA TODAY* bestselling author

"Revealing the underbelly of main characters, a trademark talent of Amy Clipston, makes them relatable and endearing."

—Suzanne Woods Fisher, bestselling author of *On a Summer Tide*

"Clipston's heartfelt writing and engaging characters make her a fan favorite."

—*Library Journal* on *The Cherished Quilt*

FINDING YOU

OTHER BOOKS BY AMY CLIPSTON

CONTEMPORARY ROMANCE

The Heart of Splendid Lake

Something Old, Something New

The View from Coral Cove

Starstruck

THE AMISH LEGACY SERIES

Foundation of Love

Breaking New Ground

Building a Future

The Heart's Shelter

THE AMISH MARKETPLACE SERIES

The Bake Shop

The Coffee Corner

The Farm Stand

The Jam and Jelly Nook

THE AMISH HOMESTEAD SERIES

A Place at Our Table

A Seat by the Hearth

Room on the Porch Swing

A Welcome at Our Door

THE AMISH HEIRLOOM SERIES

The Forgotten Recipe

The Cherished Quilt

The Courtship Basket

The Beloved Hope Chest

THE HEARTS OF THE LANCASTER GRAND HOTEL SERIES

A Hopeful Heart

A Dream of Home

A Mother's Secret

A Simple Prayer

THE KAUFFMAN AMISH BAKERY SERIES

A Gift of Grace

A Life of Joy

A Promise of Hope

A Season of Love

A Place of Peace

YOUNG ADULT

Roadside Assistance

Reckless Heart

Destination Unknown

Miles from Nowhere

STORY COLLECTIONS

Amish Sweethearts

Seasons of an Amish Garden

An Amish Singing

STORIES

A Plain and Simple Christmas

Naomi's Gift included in *An Amish Christmas Gift*

A Spoonful of Love included in *An Amish Kitchen*

Love Birds included in *An Amish Market*

Love and Buggy Rides included in *An Amish Harvest*

Summer Storms included in *An Amish Summer*

The Christmas Cat included in *An Amish Christmas Love*

Home Sweet Home included in *An Amish Winter*

A Son for Always included in *An Amish Spring*

A Legacy of Love included in *An Amish Heirloom*

No Place Like Home included in *An Amish Homecoming*

Their True Home included in *An Amish Reunion*

Cookies and Cheer included in *An Amish Christmas Bakery*

Baskets of Sunshine included in *An Amish Picnic*

Evergreen Love included in *An Amish Christmas Wedding*

Bundles of Blessings included in *Amish Midwives*

Building a Dream included in *An Amish Barn Raising*

A Class for Laurel included in *An Amish Schoolroom*

Patchwork Promises included in *An Amish Quilting Bee*

A Perfectly Splendid Christmas included in *On the Way to Christmas*

NONFICTION

The Gift of Love

FINDING YOU

Amy Clipston

THOMAS NELSON
Since 1798

Finding You

Published in Nashville, Tennessee, by Thomas Nelson. Thomas Nelson is a registered trademark of HarperCollins Christian Publishing, Inc.

Thomas Nelson titles may be purchased in bulk for educational, business, fundraising, or sales promotional use. For information, please email SpecialMarkets@ThomasNelson.com.

Library of Congress Cataloging-in-Publication Data

Names: Clipston, Amy, author.
Title: Finding you / Amy Clipston.

Description: Nashville, Tennessee: Thomas Nelson, 2024. | Summary: "Both of them want a relationship - but is beginning it a big mistake?"--Provided by publisher.

Identifiers: LCCN 2024000383 (print) | LCCN 2024000384 (ebook) | ISBN 9780840708984 (paperback) | ISBN 9780840709004 (e-pub) | ISBN 9780840709042

Subjects: LCGFT: Christian fiction. | Romance fiction. | Novels.

Classification: LCC PS3603.L58 F56 2024 (print) | LCC PS3603.L58 (ebook) | DDC 813/.6--dc23/eng/20240109

LC record available at https://lccn.loc.gov/2024000383

LC ebook record available at https://lccn.loc.gov/2024000384

Printed in the United States of America

24 25 26 27 28 LBC 5 4 3 2 1

For my super-awesome husband, Joe,
with love and appreciation.

I'm so honored and humbled to have had the opportunity to donate a kidney for you as a paired donor so you could receive your second kidney transplant.

I love you and this amazing life we've built together!

AUTHOR'S NOTE

Dear Reader,

When I was a little girl, I learned that my best friend's father donated a kidney to his sister. I really didn't understand what it meant at the time, and little did I know that kidney disease would become a huge part of my future.

In 2000, my husband, Joe, went to an urgent care facility for swelling in his legs. A simple test showed protein in his urine, which meant his kidneys were damaged. He was diagnosed with kidney disease, and unfortunately, his disease was fast-moving. After participating in a trial for an experimental drug, he faced dialysis. I remember the day he called to tell me he was going to start dialysis; we sobbed on the phone together, and after we hung up, a coworker whisked me off to the ladies' room to help me calm down.

Joe received a kidney from his brother on March 29, 2004, after a year of suffering on dialysis. Unfortunately, he experienced rejection eighteen months later. Though his doctors were able to save his transplanted kidney, he never regained full function.

In 2008, Joe's transplanted kidney began to fail. He was told to go back on dialysis and urged to register for the list to receive a matching kidney from a deceased donor. By the time he went back on dialysis, he was so ill that he wound up in the hospital. Since he had already endured one rejection, his body had built up antibodies, and none of the friends and family members who came forward to be tested as donors matched him—not even his mother.

Around this time I found out about the Paired Donor Network—a system for willing donors to exchange a kidney on behalf of their loved one. I immediately felt called to register as Joe's paired donor. And, after three long and arduous years on dialysis, Joe was finally able to receive a kidney.

On June 14, 2011, I gave a kidney to a woman in the morning, and later that afternoon, her husband gave one to Joe. What a miracle that we matched with another couple. It was also my privilege and honor to help not only my husband but also another person who had suffered with this terrible disease. Thankfully, they are both doing well and enjoying a healthy life free from dialysis.

I've shared our story many times over the years, and although I've written a memoir titled *The Gift of Love*, I hadn't yet composed a novel featuring a kidney transplant patient as the main character. When my editor suggested a storyline with a kidney transplant, I was nervous to write about something that was so personal to me, but once I started creating Darcy and Carter, it seemed I couldn't type fast enough. The characters came to life in my mind, and soon they were telling me the story. In fact, I had a difficult time moving on from this novel after finishing it. I still carry Darcy and Carter around with me since I poured a lot of Joe's experiences and my emotions into the book. I hope their story touches your heart.

Butterflies are the symbol for organ transplants. I hope that after reading *Finding You*, every time you see a butterfly, you'll think of people like Joe, Darcy, and Carter, who have been blessed with the precious gift of life.

Blessings,

Amy

CHAPTER 1

"YOUR LABWORK LOOKS FANTASTIC, DARCY." DR. MONA REYES SMILED and sank down onto the round rolling stool across from the exam table. "I can't believe it's been two years since your transplant. Your kidney numbers are perfect."

Darcy forced her lips into a smile and hugged her arms over her green shirt. "Time has flown," she said. She wanted to believe those words, but in truth, time had stopped eighteen months ago when her fiancé, Jace, died.

She sat up taller, steeling herself against the wave of grief that always seemed to lurk at the back of her mind, waiting to drag her under. She would never forgive herself for what happened to him.

The sound of Dr. Reyes scooting her stool over to the exam table jerked her from her thoughts. She took Darcy's hand in hers. "What's on your mind?"

With her dark hair, bright hazel eyes, and flawless, creamy skin, Dr. Reyes had become like a second mother to Darcy since she'd been diagnosed with kidney disease. Darcy was grateful for their heart-to-heart talks, which always helped settle her nerves and give her a new perspective on things.

"I always think of Jace when I think of the transplant. I'm so grateful for him." She sniffed and swiped the back of her hand over her eyes.

Dr. Reyes patted her hand. "That's natural. You'll always miss him and love him. Just remember that he would be happy for your good health too."

"I know you're right." Darcy tried to clear her throat past the lump that swelled there.

"Do you want to talk about how you're feeling?"

Darcy shook her head. She was certain her doctor had better things to do—such as seeing more patients—than to hear about Darcy's holding pattern of grief, regret, and guilt.

She held her breath, then released it as the truth spilled out of her. "I've been thinking about finding my biological mother."

"I remember when you shared with me that you're adopted."

"My parents never hid that from me. And even though I love them and am so thankful for everything they've given me, I can't help feeling that something is missing in my life. I wonder if I wouldn't feel so hollowed out if I found my mother." She fidgeted with the hem of her top.

Dr. Reyes nodded. "I know you're anxious to find out if your kidney disease is hereditary."

"Exactly."

"Well, I might be able to help you." Dr. Reyes wrote something on a piece of paper and then handed it to Darcy. "My best friend is adopted, and she contacted this not-for-profit agency when she wanted to find her parents."

"Thank you." Darcy studied the piece of paper, where Dr. Reyes had written down a website for an organization called Lost and Found. "I want to know where I came from, but I just don't know how to talk to my parents about this without hurting them."

"I think they'll understand."

Darcy leaned over and hugged her doctor. "You're the best."

"Back at you." Dr. Reyes grinned. "Now, do you need any refills?"

They discussed the cocktail of medications Darcy would take for the rest of her life in order to keep her transplant viable. She often got tired of taking the medications, but she was grateful that they kept her new kidney healthy. Darcy thanked her doctor once again before heading toward the exit.

She stopped at the front desk to schedule her next six-month checkup before pulling on her suit jacket, shouldering her purse, and hurrying out toward the parking lot in front of the sprawling medical complex.

Her high heels clacked along the sidewalk, and the cool, early April breeze lifted strands of her long blonde hair off her shoulders. Birds sang in nearby trees while daffodils smiled up at the sun shining in the cloudless blue sky.

Darcy tried to shake off her murky mood, but it clung to her like a second skin as she weaved past the rows of cars on the way to her sedan. She pulled her phone from her back pocket and found no missed calls or messages waiting for her. She considered calling her mom to tell her about her appointment, but instead she pocketed her phone, not ready to talk to her mother just yet. She was on the way to an important meeting and had to mentally prepare herself.

Thoughts of Jace swirled in her head as she approached her royal-blue late-model Lexus LS 460 sedan. She unlocked the door using her key fob and climbed in, dropping her purse on the passenger seat. As she hit the push-button start, she tried dismissing her late fiancé from her mind, but she could still see his handsome face. His brilliant smile and those sky-blue eyes seemed impossible to forget.

She and Jace had made so many plans. They were going to be married right before Thanksgiving almost two years ago, and thanks to her good health, she'd hoped they would soon start a family. Being a mom had been her dream since she was a little girl playing with her first baby doll. In fact, when her friends had moved on to playing with Barbies, Darcy had stuck with her baby dolls instead of joining them.

Click. Click.

Darcy's attention snapped back to her car. She hit the start button again.

Click. Click.

"No," she whined. "No, no, no. Not now . . ." She pushed the button again.

Click. Click.

Darcy leaned forward on the steering wheel, grimaced, and mashed the button.

Click. Click.

She rested her hand on her forehead. Her parents were at their beach house in Coral Cove, which meant she couldn't call her father for help. And her best friend, Haven, was already at work. Besides, Haven was a guidance counselor at a middle school located nearly thirty miles away, so Darcy wouldn't dream of asking her for help. That left her one option—calling a roadside assistance service.

Darcy glanced at her watch, a bead of sweat trailing down the back of her neck. It was after nine, and she had a public relations presentation to make to the board in under an hour. She hated policies-and-procedures stuff, but it was part of her job, and she didn't want a month's worth of work to go down the drain.

Unlocking her phone, she shot off a message to her manager, Meredith.

DARCY: Hi! Just left my doctor's office, and I'm having car trouble. Calling for roadside assistance now. I'll keep you updated.

Conversation bubbles appeared almost immediately, and her gut tightened. While she appreciated her understanding boss, she always dreaded the possibility of letting Meredith down.

MEREDITH: Oh no! Let me know if we should reschedule the presentation.

That was the last thing Darcy wanted to do. She'd been preparing for this for weeks, and her bonus depended on it. She had to get to her office *soon*.

She pushed the button one last time, praying for it to start.

Click. Click.

Darcy's frustration came out in a growl. "You had to let me down today of all days, car?"

Yanking her wallet from her purse, Darcy began rooting through multiple pockets for the roadside information card. She'd never used it before. What did it even look like? When a tap sounded on the windowpane, she gasped and jumped with a start.

Turning, she found a man peering in her window.

"Sorry." He lifted his hand. "I didn't mean to scare you." He pointed toward the hood of her car. "Need some help?"

She pushed her door open. "It won't start."

"I heard the clicks." He grinned, and she couldn't help but notice how handsome he was. His light-brown hair was cut short and covered with a dark-blue ball cap, and his eyes reminded her of the dark-roast coffee Dad loved to drink. He wore faded blue jeans, a black t-shirt, and a dark-blue work jacket. The outfit, coupled with the stubble on his chin, gave him a rugged look. She realized she was staring, and her cheeks heated.

The man lifted his eyebrows and nodded toward the hood of the car. "Sounds like a dead battery. I can jump it for you."

She sagged against the seat. Why hadn't she put that emergency roadside kit Dad had given her for Christmas in the trunk of her car instead of on a shelf in her garage? "Thank you, but I don't have jumper cables."

"You're in luck. I always carry a set just in case." He jammed his thumb toward the other side of the lot. "I'm just parked over there." He tipped back his cap.

She noticed the logo on the front: Barton Automotive. Hope lit in her chest. What were the odds of her knight in shining chrome being a mechanic? "Oh, that would be amazing."

"I'm Carter, by the way."

"Darcy."

"Nice to meet you." He stepped to the empty parking space in front of her car and pointed to the ground. "Do me a favor and try to stop anyone from parking here while I bring my truck over."

"Got it."

He pulled a set of keys from his pocket, causing them to jingle. "Hang tight. Be right back."

Darcy stood in front of her car and peered across the parking lot. A few moments later, a loud engine rumbled to life, and a black Chevrolet Suburban slowly crept down the aisle and came to a stop in front of her car. Country music sang from a radio inside of the SUV, which looked as if it had been lifted a couple of inches to accommodate the huge tires. Her father, a car enthusiast, would be impressed.

Carter killed the engine and then popped the hood on his SUV before he hopped down from the driver seat and moved to the rear of the vehicle. The tailgate opened and slammed before he sauntered toward her holding a set of jumper cables.

She drank in how his jeans hugged his trim waist and how his dark t-shirt stretched over a wide chest. Those dark eyes were captivating. She had to crane her neck to take in his full height.

Oh, I love a tall guy.

Carter raised his eyebrows, and she realized she was staring at him—*again*. Surely her face was going to catch fire.

"My dad would love your SUV." The words slipped out of her mouth before she could stop them.

He lifted the hood on the Suburban. "I guess he's into old Chevrolet trucks?"

"Old?"

He grinned, and like nearly all hot guys, he showed her a crooked smile. "It's a 2005, so I wouldn't consider it new." He pointed one of the clamps toward her car. "Can you pop your hood?"

She slipped back into the driver seat and did as she was told before rejoining him at the front of her car.

He tilted his head and scanned her car. His focus moved back to the engine, and he nodded. "This is a beautiful Lexus."

"Thanks." Heat prickled her neck, and she felt the strange need to explain how she could afford such a nice car. "It was my mom's. She wanted to trade it in for a newer vehicle, and I offered to buy it since my Honda needed a lot of work."

"Has it given you trouble before?"

"Yes." She grimaced as more embarrassment filled her. "It didn't want to start a few days ago. I meant to stop by the auto parts store to have them test the battery, but I had this big project at work, so I forgot." Just like she forgot to mention it to her dad before her parents left for the beach on Saturday.

Carter connected the positive clamp to the Lexus's battery terminal before connecting the positive clamp to his battery terminal. He followed the same procedure with the negative clamps and then climbed into his SUV. His engine came to life, and another country music song serenaded her. Then he turned off the radio and came to stand next to her. "Want to try starting it?"

"Here goes nothing," she whispered as she returned to the driver's seat. She closed her eyes before hitting the button. But instead of her engine purring to life, she only heard the Suburban continue to rumble. She looked toward Carter, who was frowning.

Darcy checked her watch. It was already nine thirty. Nerves now swarmed her stomach. She was running out of time before her presentation.

Carter killed his engine and removed the jumper cables from the vehicles before tossing them into his back seat. He joined her at the driver's side door of her car and crouched down beside her. "My guess? It's either the battery or the starter."

"And you can only know for sure by testing them," she finished.

"Right." He tapped her door. "Do you want me to have it towed for you?"

"I don't have a choice, do I?" Darcy pinched the bridge of her nose.

He shook his head. "I'll call the tow truck driver we use for our shop. He lives around here. If he isn't on another job, he can be here quickly."

"That would be perfect, because I have an important presentation to give at work in under an hour. I need to get there as quickly as possible."

"Where would you like it towed?"

Anxiety pressed down on her shoulders, and she tried to think. Once the car was towed, she'd still need another car, and the only way to get one would be to use a car service or call her parents and ask to borrow one of theirs.

"My parents are on vacation and probably took my mom's car with them. I could have my car towed to their house, but then I'd be stuck there." She wrung her hands. "I'm not comfortable driving my dad's cars." She took a deep breath. "I mean, he has a brand-new Corvette Stingray or his Porsche Cayenne. And you know how

Charlotte rush-hour traffic is. Plus I'd be mortified if someone dinged his doors in the crazy parking garage at work." Why was she sharing so much information with a complete stranger? *Shut up, Darcy!* "Anyway, I need my car fixed right away."

"I can look at it for you today, if you want."

Her gaze snapped to his. "You can?"

"Sure. We're not that busy at our shop. I'm not trying to pressure you though. If you have a mechanic you prefer and trust, go with them. You won't hurt my feelings."

"The only mechanic I know is my dad." She studied Carter's earnest expression, and for some strange reason she trusted him.

She shook herself. She didn't even know this man!

She looked at her watch again, and her heart lurched. She needed to figure this out *fast*. "Let's have it towed to your shop."

He chuckled. "Well, it's not exactly *my* shop. My brother-in-law and his folks own it, but I'm one of the mechanics."

"Where is it?"

"On Main Street in Flowering Grove."

"My best friend's boyfriend is from Flowering Grove. I love Treasure Hunting Antique Mall."

"The shop is close to that store." He stood and pulled his phone from his pocket. "I'll call the driver now." He leaned on the grill of his Suburban, dialed the phone, and began talking. When his eyes met hers, they seemed to twinkle.

Darcy's phone buzzed with a text, and she found a message from her manager.

MEREDITH: How's it going?

Darcy poised her thumbs over her phone, but her fingers froze in place while she debated what to tell Meredith. A tow truck was on the way, but how long would it take? She had expected her doctor's visit to be quick, but she'd never imagined getting stranded before her big meeting.

"Fred will be here soon."

Darcy lifted her chin as Carter leaned on the driver's side door. "Thanks."

"Is there someone who can pick you up?"

She moved her fingers over the steering wheel. She could reach out to Haven's boyfriend, but he worked forty-five minutes away. "No." She held up her phone. "I can call for a rideshare."

"Where do you work?"

"Uptown Charlotte. Not too far from here."

"I can drop you off."

Darcy studied Carter's expression and once again was surprised by how much she trusted him. At the same time, she could hear her mother's admonishing voice in her mind:

You got in the car with a stranger, Darcy Jane Larsen? Didn't I teach you better than that? It's a wonder you didn't wind up on the news!

And yet . . . it would be foolish to turn him down, considering her time crunch. "You sure?"

He shrugged. "It's not out of the way for me."

"I appreciate it. I'll reimburse you for gas."

He shook his head. "No need." His phone rang, and he examined it. "I'm sorry. It's my brother-in-law." He held it up to his ear. "Hey, man." He listened as he walked over to his SUV and leaned on the fender. "I'll be on my way soon. What do we need from the store?"

She shot off a text to her manager:

DARCY: My car is dead, but a tow truck is on the way. I also have a ride set up. Hope to be there in less than thirty minutes.

MEREDITH: Sounds good. See you soon.

She slipped her phone into her purse before retrieving her laptop bag. She climbed out of the car just as Carter wrapped up his call and slipped his phone into his back pocket. When he smiled, she felt a strange flutter in her stomach.

"Gage is sending me a shopping list."

"Your brother-in-law?"

"Yeah. He's been married to my sister for six years now." He rubbed his chin. "Time sure does fly."

"Right," she said, even though she had just been thinking about how time *didn't* fly. Instead, it had frozen for her when Jace had died. How odd that Carter would comment on something she had just thought of less than an hour ago. She held out her key fob. "I guess you need this."

"Thanks." When Carter took the key, her fingers brushed against his warm skin. His eyes drifted over her face. "So what do you do besides get stranded in parking lots?"

She laughed and felt some of the knots in her shoulders release. "I actually work in the communications department at one of the big banks."

"Really?" He looked intrigued.

"I handle public relations—employee communications, media relations, that sort of thing—for East Coast Banking and Trust." Darcy shook her head. "It's really not that impressive."

"Sounds like it to me." He opened his mouth to say something but then stopped as a tow truck steered into the parking lot. "Fred's already here."

Darcy adjusted the strap of her laptop bag on her shoulder, grateful they would be on the road heading toward her office soon.

CHAPTER 2

AFTER CARTER MOVED HIS SUV, HE HELPED THE TOW TRUCK DRIVER load Darcy's Lexus. She pulled out her phone and snapped a photo of the portly, middle-aged man with the bushy gray beard as he pulled her car onto the flatbed.

Then she sent the photo to her best friend, along with a text: How's your Monday going so far?

As if on cue, her phone rang with a call from Haven. "What in the world happened? Are you okay?"

"I'm fine. The Lexus isn't." Darcy frowned. "Aren't you working today?"

"I have a few minutes before my next meeting. Guidance counselors do get breaks every once in a while. Do you need a ride?" Her best friend sounded concerned. "Tell me where you are, and I'll be there as soon as I can."

Darcy moved over to the Suburban. "I'm fine, but thank you." She explained how Carter had approached her and not only offered to have her car towed to his shop to fix it but also insisted on giving her a ride to her office. She moved to the back of his SUV and read his license plate to Haven, then asked her to write it down since she had accepted a ride from a stranger.

"Carter, huh?" She could hear Haven's grin through the phone. "How old is he?"

Darcy glanced at him while he helped Fred secure the car with chains. When his eyes met hers, his lips lifted. And that man had one gorgeous smile. "Late twenties, maybe?"

"Cute?"

Extremely! But if Darcy admitted just how handsome he was, Haven would nag Darcy incessantly about trying to date this stranger. "He's all right."

"Single?"

"How should I know?"

"Is he wearing a ring?"

"My dad never wears his when he works on cars."

Haven expelled an impatient breath. "Then you'll just have to ask him."

Darcy lowered her voice. She'd pass out from embarrassment if Carter overheard their conversation. "I really don't have time to talk about this—"

"And if he's unattached, get his number. Girl, we're both twenty-seven, and we should be enjoying life. Maybe Carter will be your new boyfriend."

Darcy rolled her eyes and swallowed a groan, recalling the disastrous blind dates her best friend had set up for her. Haven was determined to get Darcy to date again. She knew Haven meant well, but Darcy just wasn't ready to move on and probably never would be.

"You need to start living again," Haven insisted. "Stop blaming yourself for what happened to Jace. It wasn't your fault." She paused. "So is Carter nice?"

Darcy's cheeks warmed as Carter started toward her. "I have to go."

"I want details. Call me later."

She hung up and put her phone in her purse. "Ready to go?" Darcy asked him.

"Yup," he said, and she was once again drawn into those dark eyes. He opened the passenger-side door for her as the tow truck exited the lot with her car sitting on the flatbed.

She set her purse and bag on the floor. Then she wondered how she was going to climb into the tall SUV without falling and embarrassing herself.

"Need some help?" He held his hand out toward her.

"Thanks." Grasping his strong hand, she hoisted herself up with the help of a handle and the running board. "That wasn't so bad."

His expression was sheepish. "My sister always complains about having to climb up in this thing, especially in heels."

She laughed. "No problem." Then she glanced down at her high-heeled shoes. While she enjoyed dressing up for work, she rarely wore pumps. Today, though, she'd chosen heels in order to look her best for the presentation.

Darcy settled in the passenger seat and inhaled the lingering woodsy scent that she assumed was Carter's cologne. He appeared beside her and folded his long frame into the driver's side. Soon they were on their way, with another country music song singing softly through the speakers. She gave him directions before a comfortable silence settled over them.

She snuck a glance his way as he slowed to a stop at a light. "I really appreciate this."

"I don't mind. I would hope someone would do the same for my sister." He drummed his fingers on the steering wheel in time with the song.

Darcy looked down at her watch. It was almost ten. She was running out of time . . .

As if reading her mind, he said, "I'll do my best to get you there in time."

She smiled. Not only was he handsome, but he also seemed so kind and thoughtful. Surely he had a girlfriend.

Not that it's any of my business. But Haven would be so disappointed in her for not asking him if he was single.

"Does your dad work in a shop nearby?"

Darcy felt her brow furrow.

He chuckled. "You said your dad was the only mechanic you knew."

"Oh. No, he's not a mechanic by trade. It's more of a hobby."

Carter clicked on the blinker. "Does he have any project cars?"

"He has a 1958 Dodge truck that took years to restore." She adjusted herself in the seat and let her tense muscles loosen. "It's a Power Wagon."

"What color?"

"Red."

"Wow." Carter shook his head, grinning. "Those trucks are so cool."

"Yes, they are," she agreed. "It took him a while to find it. He said he was looking for the perfect truck. He hired someone to handle the bodywork and paint, but he did most of the engine work himself."

"Impressive."

"Do you have a project car?"

"I do."

"Well, don't leave me hanging here," she said, and he laughed again. "What is it?"

"A 1970 Plymouth Road Runner. My grandfather's pride and joy."

She gasped. "Those cars are gorgeous. Is it close to being finished?"

He adjusted his hat on his head. "It's on hold right now. You know how sometimes life just happens."

"I can relate to that." She turned toward him. "What color is it?"

"Orange."

"That's the best color for a Road Runner."

His eyes crinkled at the corners as he studied her.

"Why are you looking at me like that? Did I say something wrong?"

"Not at all. You just seem to know a lot about cars."

"And that surprises you," she finished.

"Well, I mean . . ." He shrugged. "Kinda."

She rested her hands on her hips and pretended to be offended. "So women can't know anything about cars, huh?"

"I wasn't saying that."

"Yeah, you were," she joked. "You think that just because I'm wearing heels and a suit, I don't know how to check my oil and tire pressure."

A smile broke out on his face. "I would never accuse a woman of not knowing her way around a car."

"And I'll have you know that when I was younger, I hung out with my dad in his garage and learned a little bit. I can't rebuild an engine, but I can carry on an intelligent conversation about a car."

"That's actually very cool." He stopped at another red light and glanced over at her, his eyes dancing with what looked like amusement.

"Thanks. It was how I bonded with him. My mom and I watched movies, and my dad and I hung out in his garage."

"I bet you have some nice memories." He tapped the steering wheel. "You mentioned your parents are on vacation. Where'd they go?"

"Coral Cove."

"My grandparents took my sister and me there once, and we had a blast." He looked over at Darcy. "Where do they stay?"

Darcy fiddled with her suit jacket as another wave of embarrassment hit her. "They have a house there, and since they've both retired, they go down there frequently to enjoy it." She wondered if he thought she was spoiled, but his expression showed no evidence of shock. She almost felt compelled to tell him that her parents were retired orthodontists who had run their own practice and invested in real estate before they retired, but she decided to keep that information to herself. "Did you always want to be a mechanic?"

"Yes. I started handing my grandfather tools when I was four. I inherited my love of cars from him." He merged into the left lane to pass a slow-moving vehicle, then motored through an intersection, heading into Uptown Charlotte.

"So you're close to your grandparents?" she asked.

He moved his hands over the steering wheel. "I was. They're both gone now, but they pretty much raised my sister and me after my mom passed away when I was ten. My dad had already skipped out by then."

She grimaced. "I'm sorry. I didn't mean to be nosy."

"It's okay. I mean, I don't normally talk about my family. But I guess you're easy to talk to, huh?" When he smiled at her, it seemed sincere. "How about you? Any siblings?"

"No, I'm an only child, and since my parents are older, I never got to know my grandparents." Darcy didn't want to pry more about Carter's family, so she changed course. "How long have you worked at the shop in Flowering Grove?" she asked.

"Eleven years. I started there right after I graduated from high school. The Bartons are like family to me."

He steered through Uptown Charlotte toward her building. When he came to it, he parked at the curb.

She angled her body toward his. "I appreciate your help today. I'll find a ride out to Flowering Grove."

"Wait." He held up his phone. "Can I get your number?"

"Oh. Uh, well, I . . ." Darcy stammered. "I think you're really cute, Carter, and I really appreciate the ride." She held a hand up. "I really, really do, but I'm not really dating right now."

A strange expression flitted over his face. "Oh, I meant that I need to text you about the car." He grinned. "But I think you're cute too."

Heat traveled up Darcy's neck, and she was certain she might pass out from embarrassment. "Right." She took his phone and then created a new contact, adding her first and last name along with her number before handing it back to him. "Here you go."

He sent a quick text, causing her phone to chime. She glanced at her screen and read: This is Carter Donovan.

"I hope your presentation goes well," he said.

"Thank you." She gathered up her laptop bag and purse before climbing from the SUV.

"You're welcome. I'll be in touch."

As the SUV motored away from the curb, Darcy hurried into the building. Time to change gears and focus on her presentation.

* * *

WHISTLING ALONG WITH A BRAD PAISLEY SONG, CARTER PARKED AT THE back of the lot behind Barton Automotive. He unloaded a large box from his trunk, then started across the lot toward the building. The sound of meows caught his attention, and he spun as Smoky—a large gray tabby and the shop's unofficial mascot and greeter—trotted toward him.

"Hey, buddy," Carter called as the cat approached. Smoky walked in circles while rubbing against Carter's shins.

Carter set the box on the ground, and when the cat lifted his head, Carter rubbed his chin. Smoky purred his approval. "How are you this fine Monday?"

"Look who decided to finally show up at work today," Gage teased from the open bay door.

Carter snickered while he continued to pet the cat. He was so thankful that Shauna and Gage had gotten together. Not only had Shauna gained a thoughtful and supportive husband, but Carter had gotten an older brother. He enjoyed his easy banter with Gage. "I had nothing else to do today, so I figured I'd see if you needed any help," he joked.

"Fred said you rescued a damsel in distress and convinced her to have her car towed here." Gage pushed his hand through his thick, curly dark hair as he walked toward Carter and Smoky. He pointed toward Darcy's royal-blue Lexus parked near the shop.

Carter stood up to his full height. "All true."

Gage gave a low whistle. "Nice car." Then he grinned. "Fred mentioned the damsel was pretty too."

"Yes, she was." Carter couldn't deny it. Darcy was pretty—*really* pretty—with long blonde hair falling past her slight shoulders and the greenest eyes he'd ever seen. They reminded him of the bright-green grass in Flowering Grove Park, where his mother and grandmother used to take him and Shauna to play on swings every Sunday afternoon. And then there was Darcy's lovely smile, which lit up her beautiful face.

She'd looked embarrassed when she explained that she had purchased the car from her mom, and she seemed sheepish when she mentioned her parents' vacation home at Coral Cove. He wondered what her parents did for a living that enabled them to afford a beach home—not to mention her father's Porsche Cayenne and brand-new Corvette Stingray.

Carter also noticed that she wasn't wearing any jewelry on her left hand, which meant she wasn't married and possibly was single.

He shook himself. What was his problem? Considering his financial situation, the last thing he needed right now was a relationship. Besides, Darcy was clearly out of Carter's league. With her looks, her corporate job, and her money, what could a mechanic with grease-stained nails and no 401(k) really offer outside a few dates? He could never be good enough for her.

"Car wouldn't start, huh?" His brother-in-law's question yanked him from his thoughts of Darcy. The cat tapped Gage's shin with his paw to gain his attention, and Gage kneeled to take a turn rubbing Smoky's chin.

"I was on my way to my truck when I heard the clicking. I tried to jump it for her but didn't have any luck. I figured I'd test the battery first and then go from there."

"Sounds good."

"I picked up shop towels, disposable gloves, soap, brake parts cleaner, and carburetor cleaner." Carter lifted the box and started toward the open bay doors. "I guess I'd better get to work before my boss starts yelling at me."

Gage walked beside him with Smoky at his heels, the cat still meowing as if sharing a list of jobs they had to complete today. "Hang on. How'd your appointment go?"

"Fine."

"So your kidney levels are still good?"

"Yup. They're perfect." Carter tried to shove down the familiar regret and frustration that gripped him when he thought about the years he had struggled with kidney disease.

Gage patted Carter's shoulder and nearly knocked him off-balance. At six feet four, his brother-in-law was two inches taller than Carter and looked as if he'd spent every spare minute at the gym. "That's awesome, brother. What a blessing."

It was now. When he went on dialysis three years ago, he had despised the burden he'd been on his family. The kidney disease wasn't hereditary, and while doctors insisted it could have been environmental, the reason his kidneys had failed remained a mystery. His illness and medical bills forced him to leave his apartment and full-time job and move in with Shauna and Gage. But he didn't want a handout from them or anyone else. He paid them a fair price for rent, including his portion of utilities, and he also chipped in for food. Shauna suggested they ask their church to hold a fundraiser for Carter, but he insisted there were other people in their community who needed help more than he did.

He'd finally undergone a transplant two years ago. Shauna insisted on donating her kidney as a paired donor for Carter so he wouldn't have to wait on the transplant list. He had been against Shauna's donating, worrying the risk was too great—but since she was his nurturing older sister, she wouldn't take no for an answer.

And now, two years later, Carter cherished his good health but longed to climb out of his debt and move to a place of his own. If only he could pay off his consolidation loan early so he wouldn't be so reliant on Shauna and Gage. He could never repay their generosity though. That reality gnawed away at his insides.

"It *is* a blessing," Carter agreed as he crossed to the side of the bay where he worked. The familiar smells of tires, brake dust, oil, and cleaning solution hovered over him, along with the sound of country music playing from a nearby radio. He shucked his work jacket and plain black t-shirt before changing into a dark blue shirt emblazoned with the Barton Automotive logo.

The door that led to the office and showroom opened, and

Glenda, Gage's mother, shuffled out with a wide smile on her face. Although she was petite, it was easy to see that Gage had inherited his dark, curly hair and honey-brown eyes from her. The curls were threaded with gray—"sparkles," she called them—and her eyes were lined with wrinkles, but she was still young at heart.

"There you are!" Glenda sang as she hurried over to him. "I thought I heard your truck pull into the parking lot."

"That behemoth is hard to miss, Mom," Gage called from his side of the large bay.

Carter shook his head and finger-combed his short hair. "You're just jealous that it sits taller than your pickup."

Gage snorted before opening the box of supplies and pulling out the disposable gloves.

Glenda rested her hand on his bicep. "Did your appointment go well?"

"It did. My kidney numbers are going strong."

She gave his arm a gentle squeeze. "Well, son, you need to embrace your good health! It's time you started dating again. You're going to be thirty in June, and you'll have no trouble finding the right woman. You're a great catch."

Carter fixed a smile on his lips as memories of his ex-girlfriend filled his mind. He'd been certain that Gabrielle would be the one with whom he'd share a home and a family, but she'd bailed on him when his health had deteriorated and he started home dialysis. Three years later, he still hadn't recovered from that heartbreak.

Besides, what woman in her right mind would want to get involved with a man in debt up to his eyeballs and who lived with his sister and her husband? Gabrielle dumped him not only because he was ill, but also because he wasn't "living up to his potential." Or so she insisted. More than once she told him that he needed to find a higher-paying job, and she tried to talk him into working for her father's race team. She couldn't understand that he liked working for Ernie. And even after he finally agreed to work for her father, she still dumped him.

Darcy's beautiful smile flashed in his mind, and he remembered their fun conversation about his project car. But then he shook his head.

No, he wasn't a catch at all.

Glenda patted his cheek. "Carter Donovan, you're too handsome to spend your life alone."

Gage hooted from the other side of the garage.

"You hush over there, Gage," Glenda called with a grin.

"Enough talk about my nonexistent love life. I'll go pull the battery from the Lexus and test it." With a resigned sigh, Carter got to work.

CHAPTER 3

I'M SO SORRY I COULDN'T LEAVE WORK EARLIER." HAVEN STEERED HER HONDA CR-V through the rush-hour traffic on Interstate 485. "I had my usual middle school drama today." She rolled her eyes. "For one, there was a seventh grader who thought it would be a great idea to bring water balloons to the assembly. Then he dropped them all. What a mess!"

Darcy cupped a hand to her mouth to cover a snort. "You have the best stories."

"Yeah, but the call to the parent wasn't all that fun," Haven said. "Anyway, I had hoped to pick you up at four thirty, but my calls went late and then the principal wanted to discuss a few things."

Darcy looked down at her phone. "It's okay. Carter said he'd wait for me at the shop."

"He said he'd wait for you, huh?" Haven's smile was mischievous. "Carter. That's a nice name."

"It is." Darcy scanned their text message exchange from earlier this afternoon. He'd told her the problem had turned out to be the starter instead of the battery. She agreed to the cost of repair, and he said the car would be ready before the shop closed at five thirty.

Darcy glanced at her watch. Almost five thirty. The traffic in front of them crept along the highway. "I'll let him know we're running late."

DARCY: We got a late start, but we're on our way. Traffic is pretty heavy on 485.

The conversation bubbles appeared right away.

CARTER: No worries. Take your time.

"So tell me about this handsome mechanic who saved the day." Haven's baby-blue eyes sparkled.

Although her best friend worked as a middle school guidance counselor, Darcy always thought Haven could have strutted down runways at fashion shows with her gorgeous strawberry-blonde hair, flawless ivory skin, long legs, and perfect figure. She'd always secretly been envious of Haven's height of five feet nine. It often astounded her that Haven was so humble and down-to-earth despite being drop-dead gorgeous, and she never seemed to notice how she attracted men's attention when she walked past them.

"There's not much to tell really. He's a mechanic and he fixed my car." Darcy stowed her phone in her pocket. "I'd rather you tell me more middle school stories. Were there any food fights in the cafeteria today?"

Haven lifted one of her perfectly shaped strawberry-blonde eyebrows. "Nice deflecting, Larsen. I, for one, can't wait to meet Carter." She merged into the right lane, preparing to exit. "But I've also been dying to tell you that Derek has someone for you to meet."

Darcy couldn't stop her glower. Haven and her boyfriend constantly tried to set her up on blind dates, and they'd proved to be one disastrous evening after another. "I'm not in the mood for a blind date."

"This guy is different."

"Sure he is," Darcy deadpanned. "Different from the guy you set me up with who talked about Star Wars the entire night and kept showing me photos of himself in costumes at sci-fi conventions? Or different from the one who showed me pictures of his five grandchildren? Or how about the man who never let me get a word in edgewise? Or the one who had a tan line on his ring finger?"

Haven negotiated the exit ramp and stopped at a light before holding up her hand. "I'm sorry about those dates, but I promise this will be different."

"How can you guarantee that?"

Haven's smile faded, and Darcy braced herself for a lecture. "Darce, you really need to keep an open mind. It's time for you to start dating again, okay? Derek insists this guy is great."

Darcy sighed. She knew Darcy's longtime boyfriend, Derek, was a good guy. After Jace died, he and Haven brought her meals, listened while she cried, checked on her daily, drove her to appointments, and literally held her up at the funeral. Even months later, when other friends had gone back to their normal lives, Haven and Derek continued to be Darcy's emotional support. She was thankful that Haven had such a wonderful man in her life. Hopefully she would have a relationship like theirs someday.

"Fine," Darcy grumbled. "I'll go on the blind date."

"Yay! We're going to have so much fun. I love double dates. I just know it will be a blast."

Darcy's eyes narrowed as she looked over at her best friend. "He'd better not have a wife and family."

Haven shook her head and turned onto Main Street in Flowering Grove. "He doesn't. Derek said this guy is single and has been for a while."

Darcy took in the stores lining Main Street and smiled. "I love this little town."

"Me too. Derek loved growing up here."

The sign for Barton Automotive came into view, and Haven steered into the lot in front of a one-story cinderblock building with six garage bays and a glass front boasting the business's name and logo.

Darcy saw her Lexus parked in front of the building, and it seemed to glisten in the sunlight. "Looks like my car got a much-needed bath." She gathered up her laptop bag and purse, noting the time on Haven's dashboard. "It's after six now. I feel awful for making him stay late for me."

"From as nice as you've made him sound, I doubt he minds. After all, he said he'd wait."

They crossed the parking lot to the entrance. When Darcy pulled open the front door, a bell rang and the smell of rubber hit her. She took in displays of tires that led to a long counter. Carter sat behind it, flipping through a magazine.

When he smiled, Darcy couldn't help but notice how handsome he was with his chiseled cheekbones, angular jaw, and those dark-brown eyes.

Haven made an appreciative noise under her breath.

You got that right. She did her best to ignore her thoughts as they approached him.

Just then a large gray tabby cat came bounding toward them while singing a chorus of meows. Darcy crouched to pet the cat's head. The feline responded with a loud purr that reminded her of a car engine.

"That's Smoky," Carter announced. "He's our unofficial shop manager and mascot."

"Hi there, Smoky." Darcy began rubbing his ear, and the cat lifted his head higher while closing his eyes.

Haven bent down and stroked his back. "It's a shame he's not friendly," she quipped.

Suddenly bored with the affection, Smoky took off behind a tower of tires.

Darcy moved to the counter. "I'm so sorry I'm late."

"Honestly, it's not a big deal. My only plans were to watch reality TV."

"You watch reality TV?" Haven's expression held a mixture of shock and fascination.

"Not really." His lips twitched. "That was a joke."

"Oh!" Haven laughed.

Darcy grinned as she set her laptop bag on the floor and then touched Haven's arm. "Carter Donovan, this is Haven Morrisette."

"Thank you for not leaving my best friend stranded today," Haven said.

"It was no problem at all." Carter turned his attention to Darcy. "How'd your presentation go?"

A ribbon of warmth unfurled deep inside of Darcy as she took in the sincerity in Carter's eyes. "It went great, and my boss and the board members were really impressed. Thanks for asking." She pulled her wallet from her purse and retrieved her credit card. "I can't tell you how much I appreciate your help today."

He handed her an invoice. "I'm just glad I could get it fixed for you."

Darcy perused it and then handed him her card. "My car looks clean. Did you wash it?"

"I just took it through the car wash down at the gas station while I had it out on a test drive."

"I didn't see a charge for that on the bill."

He shook his head. "It's on the house."

Out of the corner of her eye, Darcy spotted her best friend grinning, and she ignored her. "Thank you, Carter." When he set her receipts and card in front of her, she signed one receipt and handed it to him. "I'll recommend this place to all of my friends."

"We appreciate your business. Call or text me if you have any trouble."

"I will." She stuck her card and receipt in her purse and then shouldered her laptop bag.

He handed her the key fob. "Be safe going home."

"You too." She mentally kicked herself for not thinking of something better to say as she walked with Haven toward the door.

Haven bumped Darcy's shoulder as they crossed the parking lot. "You should totally text him. Maybe you can disconnect your battery and then say, 'Come and rescue me again, Carter!'"

"Shh!" Darcy spun toward the door, hoping he hadn't overhead her friend. Thankfully, he was nowhere in sight. "He's probably married."

Haven's pink lips lifted in a wicked grin. "I'm sure his wife enjoys him if he is."

"Stop it," Darcy hissed. Then she pulled Haven in for a hug. "But thanks again for the ride."

"You know I'd help you anytime, and you would do the same for me." Haven's expression became serious. "I'm so glad your kidney numbers are great. I worry about you."

"Thank you for worrying about me, but I promise I'm fine. I'm always careful to keep up with medications and appointments. My goal is to do what I'm supposed to so I stay healthy. I'll see you soon, Haven."

"Yes, you will." Her best friend strutted toward her SUV.

Darcy unlocked her car and set her bag and purse on the passenger seat. She glanced up as Carter stepped outside and locked the shop door. He waved, and she waved back before climbing into her car.

As she nosed her car toward the parking lot exit, she wondered if she'd ever have a good reason to see Carter Donovan again.

* * *

AN APPETIZING WHIFF OF SPICES FILLED CARTER'S SENSES AS HE STEPPED into Shauna's kitchen later that evening.

Still dressed in her pink Disney princess scrubs, Shauna delivered a platter of taco shells to the table while Gage brought over a tray containing ground beef and all the fixings.

"Oh, you made my favorite," Carter said while scrubbing his hands at the sink.

Shauna grinned at him. "Anything for my favorite baby brother."

Although they shared the same dark eyes, he'd always thought his sister resembled their mother with her dark-brown hair, button nose, and tall and slender stature. From all accounts, he'd been told he looked like their father with his light-brown hair and height, but he didn't like to think about that. He didn't want to be anything like their absent dad.

Carter brought three glasses of soda to the table and sank down into his usual seat across from Shauna. He was proud of his sister, who had put herself through school to live out her dream of becoming a pediatric registered nurse. "How was work?"

Shauna took a sip of her drink. "It was busy. You know it's the start of allergy season, so we saw patients all day long." She held her finger up. "Oh, we did have one interesting case."

"Do tell," Gage said as he picked up his glass of Coke.

"A little boy decided to eat a ball bearing."

Gage grunted, and Carter lifted his eyebrows.

"What did Dr. Moore say to do for him?" Carter asked.

"She said it'll pass on its own."

Carter laughed.

Gage grimaced before turning his attention to Carter. "How'd it go after I left? And did your damsel in distress pick up her car?"

"I worked on that Hyundai." Carter added salsa, shredded cheese, and sour cream to his taco. "And, yes, she got her car."

Shauna held up her left hand, her small diamond ring glittering in the kitchen light. "Whoa now. Damsel in distress? You're not going to sneak that one past me. I want details."

Carter explained about Darcy and the car.

Shauna's eyes widened. "Oh my goodness! I completely forgot you had a checkup today. How did it go?"

Carter swallowed a bit of taco and wiped his mouth with a paper napkin. "Fine."

"Your numbers are good?" Shauna's eyes scrutinized him, looking for any signs of a lie.

"Yes, Nurse Shauna," he insisted. "My numbers are great. Dr. Brenner doesn't want to see me for another six months."

"Wonderful!" Shauna reached across the table to pat her brother's hand. "Now—back to this damsel in distress. Was she pretty?"

Carter sighed and took another bite of taco.

"Do you think she liked you?" His sister leaned forward as if Carter were one of her girlfriends sharing juicy secrets.

Carter shrugged. "She was friendly, and we had a nice chat on the way to her office."

"You should ask her out."

Carter looked to Gage for help, but his brother-in-law kept his eyes focused on his plate while he scooped refried beans with his spoon.

"Don't look at Gage." Shauna wagged a finger at him. "You know I'm right. If you liked her, then you should ask her out." She tilted her head. "Did you get her number?"

Gage finally looked up. "Of course he did. He had to send her the estimate."

"Thanks, man," Carter groused.

Gage shared a winning smile. "No problem, brother."

"Text her, Carter." Shauna's expression became serious, and he felt his shoulders stiffening in preparation for another one of her lectures. "I know Gabby hurt you, but that was three years ago. You're well now, and it's time you put yourself out there."

His lips flattened into a straight line in response to his ex-girlfriend's name.

Yeah, no.

Darcy was cute and seemed nice, but they were from different worlds. He'd only end up in the same situation as he had with Gabby: nursing a broken heart.

"You have to take chances."

Gage nodded. "She's right."

Carter did not agree, but sometimes caution was the better part of valor when his sister was set on something, and he didn't need another pep talk about how much he had to offer a girlfriend. "I don't want to be creepy by misusing her phone number."

"There's a car show on Main Street coming up," Gage said.

"When?" Carter jumped on the change in subject and took another bite of his scrumptious taco.

"Next Saturday night. First car show of the year," Gage said.

Carter relaxed as their conversation moved on to upcoming events and mutual friends.

When they finished eating, Carter offered to do the dishes. He carried the plates to the counter and began rinsing them off before filling the dishwasher.

As he worked, he peered out the window above the sink toward the detached garage, where he kept his toolboxes along with his grandfather's pride and joy. Carter had dreamed of rebuilding the

Road Runner's engine and driving it to local car shows, but his kidney disease had derailed all of those plans.

His thoughts turned to Darcy and their conversation from the morning. He smiled, recalling how she'd said that orange was the best color for his car. He found himself wondering if Darcy ever attended car shows with her father. Would they come to Flowering Grove together in his classic truck? And if so, would Carter be lucky enough to run into them and spend the evening talking to them?

As if struck by lightning, he felt a jolt of excitement at the thought and laughed out loud at himself. Why was he bothering thinking about a beautiful young woman like Darcy? She would probably never think about him again. She had a successful corporate job, and he was just a mechanic.

Carter finished filling the dishwasher and started it before wiping down the table. The hum of the dishwasher filled the kitchen, and while he worked, he imagined finding a place of his own—a small house with a garage. That was all he needed. If only he could find a way to pay off that consolidation loan, then he could start living his life for real.

But it wasn't only about living his own life. He also wanted to get out of his sister's way. He hated taking up so much space day in and day out. Shauna and Gage had been married for six years, and Carter knew she had dreamed of starting a family. Carter didn't want to be underfoot or in the way of those precious plans.

He had hoped to be on his own before he turned thirty, but his thirtieth birthday was looming only two months away. That would be impossible unless he won the lottery, but considering he didn't even play it—

"Carter?"

He tossed the dishcloth into the sink and pivoted toward his sister. She stood in the doorway clad in a pair of jeans and a faded Trisha Yearwood concert t-shirt.

"Yeah?" he asked.

"You know I only want what's best for you, right?"

"You've been like my mom since I was ten, Shauna. Why would I doubt that?"

She leaned on the back of a kitchen chair. "Whenever I mention that you should start dating, you clam up. You know Gabby was the one with the problem, not you."

He busied himself with straightening the salt and pepper shakers.

"Carter, it hurts my heart to see you so lonely. You should really think about texting the woman you met today."

He swept his hand over his mouth while choosing his words. "Darcy drives a late-model Lexus, a very nice car, and she mentioned that her parents were retired and own a beach house. *And* her dad has a brand-new Corvette Stingray *and* a Porsche SUV. Her father bought a very nice classic Dodge truck, which probably cost him more than this house to restore. She was dressed in what looked like a designer suit and expensive heels. She also was carrying one of those high-end designer purses, the kind you and your friends go nuts over, when I dropped her off at her job at one of the big banks in Uptown." He folded his arms over his chest. "Darcy could do a lot better than someone like me."

"You're wrong." His sister shook her head as her face clouded with determination. "You're thoughtful, kind, generous, and giving. And you're handsome."

He snorted. "Whatever."

"Seriously, Carter. My friends always used to tell me how hot you were, and I'd tell them to stop talking about my baby brother that way since it made me very uncomfortable."

"I appreciate the compliments, Shauna, but I don't think my path will ever cross Darcy's again."

"You never know, and if it does, she would be blessed to have you in her life. You just need to start believing that." Shauna tapped his arm and then disappeared into the family room.

Carter stared at the doorway and wondered if Shauna was right. Should he take a chance with a woman as beautiful and successful as Darcy Larsen?

He pulled out his phone, opened his text conversation with Darcy, and poised his thumbs over the keys. Then he shook his head. He was wasting his time. He had so many strikes against him—his terrible financial situation, his dependence on his family. Most of all, his precarious health. While his numbers were good now, they might take a nosedive in the future. What woman would want to be saddled with that? Gabrielle sure hadn't.

CHAPTER 4

Darcy pushed the start button on her dishwasher and leaned against the counter while scanning the kitchen of her three-level townhouse. Darcy's parents had bought the home for her and Jace as an early wedding gift. It was supposed to be their home to share after the wedding, and she and Jace had appreciated her parents' generosity.

They loved the house's large kitchen and family room, three bathrooms, three bedrooms, two-car garage, balcony, deck, and small backyard. It was the perfect starter home for them since Jace was an architect by trade and dreamed of designing his own house once he was established in his job.

But now the spacious townhome was just a large reminder of everything Darcy had lost the day a man in a pickup truck had run a red light and stolen her bright future.

It was also a reminder that Jace never got a chance to fulfill his dream of designing a home for them. The guilt of that continued to weigh heavily on her.

After Jace died, Darcy had contemplated selling the home and starting over somewhere new. But then she realized that if she sold the home, she'd be letting go of Jace—the man whom she'd loved for five years, the man who had risked his life donating a kidney for her as her paired donor, the man who had loved her unconditionally, the man whom she could never repay for all he'd done for her.

Tears filled her eyes, and her body felt heavy with grief. She missed his warm smile, his radiant sky-blue eyes, his warm hugs, his contagious laugh, his sweet kisses, his easy sense of humor, his kind and generous heart, and his quiet support.

How could she move on when he had given so much of himself for her?

Her phone began to sing with an incoming call, and when she swiped it from her pocket, she found her mother's smiling photo on her screen. She dabbed her eyes with a paper towel and sniffed before answering the call.

"Hi, Mom. How's the beach?" Darcy hoped she sounded more chipper than she felt.

"It's cool out, but we're enjoying it," Mom said. "But that's not important. I've been impatiently waiting to hear from you all day. Tell me all about your appointment. Oh, and how was your big presentation today? I'm sure you knocked it out of the park."

Darcy couldn't stop her smile. Her parents were her biggest emotional support—always cheering her on and telling her that she could do anything she set her mind to. She couldn't imagine life without them.

"Both went great." She meandered into the family room and sank down onto her sofa while sharing the details of her appointment. "My kidney numbers are perfect, and Dr. Reyes doesn't need to see me for a while."

"Oh, Darcy. I'm so relieved to hear that. And how was the presentation?"

"It went well, but I was almost late because my car wouldn't start when I walked out of the doctor's appointment."

"Your car broke down?"

Then she heard her father's voice in the background.

"Hold on, honey! Your dad wants to talk. Okay, now you're on speaker."

"Hi, Darcy," Dad's warm voice sounded through the phone. "What happened with the car?"

"I needed to have the starter replaced." She shared how Carter called for a tow and rescued her. "Haven drove me to Flowering Grove to pick up my car."

Her father clucked his tongue. "I'm sorry that happened, but I'm relieved someone was there to help you."

"I forgot to tell you last week that I'd had a hard time starting it. I also forgot to take it to the auto parts store to have the battery tested."

"All that matters is that it's fixed now," Mom said.

Darcy rested her feet on her coffee table. "Tell me about the beach." She reclined while her mother described the cool and overcast weather and the restaurant where they enjoyed lunch earlier in the day. She covered her mouth with her hand to shield a yawn.

"Sounds like you need to get to bed," Mom said.

Darcy peered over at the clock on the mantel. "I didn't realize it was almost ten. It's been a long day."

"We'll let you go," Dad said. "Call me if you have any more trouble with the car."

Or I can call Carter.

Darcy tried to push that thought out of her head, but Carter's smile filled her mind. She rested her arm on her forehead and slammed her eyes shut. She'd probably never see him again.

"Are you coming over Sunday?" Mom asked.

"Of course. Have fun and be safe driving home." She said goodbye to her parents and dropped her phone onto the sofa beside her.

Her eyes moved to her laptop sitting on the coffee table, and she considered her conversation with her doctor from earlier in the morning about the organization that could help her find her biological mother. She popped up from the sofa, then located her purse on the counter and the note with the website written on it.

She returned to the sofa and pulled her computer onto her lap. A familiar guilt clutched at her as she looked down at the piece of paper. She adored her parents. They were the most loving, giving, supportive people she knew, and she was beyond blessed that they had chosen her.

Yet the questions that had haunted her since childhood continued to echo in her mind. Where had she come from? Who were her biological parents? What would her life have been like if her biological parents had kept her?

And then the most urgent question of all: Did kidney disease run in her family? Darcy hoped to be a mom one day, and she needed to know if there was a chance she would pass the illness on to her future children.

Although Darcy felt like it was time to find her biological mother, fear mixed with her guilt. What if her birth mother didn't want to be found? Or what if her birth mother struggled with kidney disease and was no longer alive?

But most importantly, what if she hurt her adoptive parents—the ones who had raised her and loved her for all of her twenty-seven years?

Sagging against the sofa pillows, she studied the website name and then dropped the piece of paper on her laptop.

Darcy yawned as she turned off the lights and climbed the stairs to her bedroom. She'd tortured herself enough for one evening. She'd figure this out another day.

* * *

TWO WEEKS LATER, DARCY LIFTED HER CUP OF DIET COKE AND FORCED A smile to her lips. "Do you like the beach?" she asked, peering across the table at Mason Haines, Haven and Derek's latest blind date.

Mason looked up from his pulled pork barbecue special at the Barbecue Pit, a restaurant located on Main Street in Flowering Grove. "Not really. I'm more of a mountains kind of guy."

With dark hair, gray eyes, and a strong jaw, Mason was fit, and his broad shoulders and muscular arms led Darcy to believe he enjoyed going to the gym. Sure, he was attractive, but his near-constant frown seemed to be a sign of an unhappy or unimpressed person.

Or perhaps he was just as delighted as she was to be spending his Saturday on a blind date.

Darcy took a long drink and glanced down at her watch. It had been thirty minutes, and she hadn't found anything she and Mason could discuss. She snuck a gaze over at Haven beside her, and her best friend gave her an encouraging expression before clearing her throat.

Oh no.

"Mason is a software engineer who works with Derek at Byrum Consultants," Haven said a little too brightly.

Darcy licked her lips. "Oh, that's—that's great. So interesting."

Mason and Darcy shared an awkward look.

"And Darcy works in public relations," Haven added.

Mason swallowed a hush puppy. "Uh-huh." Then he glanced around the restaurant. "So this is supposed to be the best barbecue place in North Carolina, huh?" He snorted. "Could've fooled me."

Derek's honey-brown eyes flared with something that looked like annoyance as his mouth formed a thin line. Derek was a native of Flowering Grove, and it was obvious that his friend had hit a nerve.

Darcy popped a hush puppy into her mouth and wondered how Derek and Mason could be such good friends.

Haven reached across the table to rub her boyfriend's shoulder as if to calm him, then turned her blue eyes on Mason once again. "Are you a car fan?"

Mason shrugged and checked his cell phone.

"I think the car show is going to be fun tonight," Haven added. "Don't you, Derek?"

Her boyfriend pushed his hand through his dark hair and nodded. "Yeah. I saw a lot of cool cars out there."

Darcy had the same thought when they drove down Main Street and parked behind the restaurant. She had scanned the area for the big black Suburban that had come to her rescue two weeks ago, but she hadn't seen the vehicle or its owner.

She had tried to forget about Carter, but he still lingered in the back of her thoughts. She couldn't help but think of him every time she started her car. A small part of her had also hoped Carter might text her, but why would he? The idea that he might want to see her again was ridiculous. A man as handsome, kind, and thoughtful as Carter most likely had a steady girlfriend or a wife.

"Do you, Darcy?"

"Huh?" Darcy's attention snapped to Haven, who was watching her with something that looked like impatience. "I'm sorry. What did you say?"

Haven gave her a pointed look. "I asked if you need to use the restroom." Her words were measured, as if she were trying to send her a coded message.

"Yeah, I do." Darcy pushed her chair back. When she stood, she noticed Mason scrolling through his phone while Derek scowled.

Darcy followed Haven to the ladies' room, where Haven stood with her hands on her hips and stared down at her.

"Will you even try to talk to him?"

"Have you been sitting at a different table?" Darcy gestured toward the door. "He hasn't asked me a single question, and I can't seem to connect with him about anything. Now he's more interested in his phone. At least Star Wars guy maintained some eye contact with me when he wasn't showing me photos of himself dressed as a Jedi Knight."

Haven touched her shoulder. "I know this is hard for you, Darce, but I just want to see you happy, okay? I'm sure you can find *something* to discuss with Mason."

"I seriously doubt it. He just insulted the restaurant. How is Derek even friends with him?"

Haven's smile was a little too bright. "I'm sure he didn't mean it."

"He sure looked like it to me. He seems very unimpressed with the food *and* with me."

Haven pulled her in for a hug. "You look gorgeous tonight. If Mason hasn't noticed, then perhaps he is as arrogant as he seems." She frowned. "I was wondering what Derek saw in him too."

"Aha!" Darcy gave a victorious smile. "You *do* agree with me."

Haven looped her arm around Darcy. "Let's see if we can hurry up this meal and go walk around and look at the cars. Maybe that will loosen up Mason."

"We can only hope."

Darcy and Haven returned to the table, where the men were discussing politics. She finished her meal with the men's conversation as background noise. After the men paid the check, they headed out to the street. The delicious aromas from the restaurant mixed with the odor of exhaust and the smell from a nearby street vendor selling burgers, hot dogs, and fries.

As Mason held the door open for Darcy, his cell phone rang. He pulled it from his pocket, and his expression lit when he read the screen. "Oh, I need to take this. Excuse me."

Darcy turned toward Haven and rolled her eyes.

"I'm sorry he's being such a jerk," Derek muttered. "I thought he'd be different."

"It's okay," Darcy told him. She pivoted to face Mason and found him grinning while talking on the phone.

"No, it's okay, I can talk," Mason said, just loud enough for Darcy and the others to hear. "Yeah, I'm on a date too. How have you been?" he said into the phone. "Yeah, I miss you too. Your date is a disaster? Who's the guy? Well, there's no way he could be as charming and handsome as me, right? You said I was the best boyfriend you'd ever had." He chuckled.

Haven's mouth fell open. "Is he talking to another woman?"

Darcy shook her head and started down Main Street. She could count this as another failed blind date. She continued to wander, taking in the classic cars lining the road. She spotted a gorgeous blue Shelby Cobra, a purple 1969 Camaro, and a black late-model Dodge Viper. She noticed the Barton Automotive sign in the distance, and the memory of Carter's smile tickled her stomach. She once again wondered if he was somewhere on Main Street admiring the snazzy vehicles, and butterflies danced in her belly.

She silently scolded herself. What were the chances she'd ever see him again?

Darcy stopped in front of a baby-blue Ford Bronco that looked as if it might have been built in the 1960s. Her thoughts suddenly turned to Jace, and she wondered if he would be standing beside her admiring the cars if he were alive.

Surely she and Jace would have continued their double dates with Haven and Derek, since he and Derek had been close friends since college. Memories of their college years together filled her mind. While she and Haven had been roommates, Derek and Jace had met through their fraternity. The four of them were inseparable after Haven and Derek started dating and Derek introduced Jace to

Darcy. Although Jace wasn't a car enthusiast like her father, he enjoyed a car show every now and then. He just seemed to like being with her, regardless of what they did together.

She felt her eyes start to prick with tears, and she sniffed.

Don't lose it, Darcy. Not here.

"I always liked the 1968 Bronco, but if I were to pick a year, I'd have to say that 1978 is my favorite."

Darcy caught a whiff of woodsy cologne as she registered the familiar voice. The scent took her back to the ride she'd shared with Carter in his Suburban.

She turned to look up at him and couldn't stop her smile. She was once again struck by those dark-brown eyes, which were complemented by his tan t-shirt. A few days of scruff lined his jaw, and he somehow seemed taller and broader in the shoulders. His light-brown hair was hidden by a ball cap sporting a Chevrolet logo, and when he smiled, she felt sparking electricity travel through her body.

"Carter. Hi."

"Hey." His expression was open and friendly.

"My favorite year Bronco is definitely 1968. I saw one at a car show once and fell in love with it. I wouldn't mind having a pink one." She held her hand up. "And before you tell me that pink isn't a cool color, there was a pink one, and it was very, *very* cool."

"Huh." He chuckled. "Well, I'll agree that 1968 is a great year, but I'll have to take your word about the color pink."

She scanned their surroundings in search of his companion but found no one nearby. Folks moved up and down the sidewalk admiring the cars, but no one else seemed to be lingering. "Are you here alone?"

"Yeah." He rubbed the scruff on his jaw. "My sister and brother-in-law checked out the cars and then went to dinner with some friends."

"Why didn't you join them?"

He shrugged. "I had eaten something at the house earlier. I figured I'd walk around since all of the reality shows are reruns tonight."

"All of them, huh?"

"Oh yeah." He counted off on his fingers. "*The Bachelor*, *The Bachelorette*, the housewives shows, and *I Married My Brother-in-Law's Sister's Podiatrist*. All reruns."

She grinned. "*I Married My Brother-in-Law's Sister's Podiatrist*? Sounds riveting."

"Oh, it is—especially when they show the feet." And his crooked grin made its grand appearance.

A bubble of laughter escaped her throat. Darcy was drawn to his sense of humor. In fact, she wasn't sure she'd been this charmed by someone since the early days of dating Jace.

"You're easily amused if you laugh at my sorry attempts at a joke." His smile broadened, and those dark eyes twinkled.

She imagined getting lost in their depths, then shook herself back to the present.

"What do you really watch on TV if it's not reality TV?" she asked.

"I watch my version of reality TV, which is MotorTrend. It's a lot of rebuilding and restoring cars. That sort of thing."

"My dad watches that, much to my mother's dismay. She says it's like watching paint dry."

"Sometimes it actually *is* watching paint dry when they're painting a car."

They both laughed, and she felt a strange comradery.

"How about you? What do you like to watch?" he asked.

"Would you think less of me if I told you I love cooking shows?"

"I don't think I could ever think less of you." His smile made her insides melt as he came to stand beside her. "How's your car doing?"

"No problems—thanks to you."

"Good." Carter scanned the cars lining the street. "I haven't seen any '58 Dodge pickups tonight. I guess your dad didn't bring his truck, huh?"

"He didn't come tonight."

"Are your folks still at the beach?"

She studied him, surprised he recalled that detail about her life. "No, they came home last week, but he and my mom had plans with friends. Their social life is much more exciting than mine."

"Oh." He nodded slowly, as if contemplating what she'd said. "Do you attend a lot of car shows?"

"Not too often, but I used to go with my dad when I was younger. My friends dragged me here." She paused. "Not that it's painful or anything," she quickly added.

He laughed, and she relished the sound. And that smile.

"Did you work today?"

"No. Thankfully the shop is closed on Saturdays." He leaned on a newspaper dispenser. "What about you? Any other big weekend plans?"

"Usual Saturday stuff. I did some grocery shopping, a little bit of cleaning, a lot of sleeping in." She tilted her head. "Not necessarily in that order."

"Carter! Carter Donovan, is that you?"

They both spun toward where Derek and Haven headed toward him. Mason lagged behind, still talking on his phone.

"Derek McGowan." Carter's face lit up as he shook Derek's hand. "I haven't seen you since graduation."

"It feels like it's been a hundred years."

Darcy and Haven shared confused expressions.

"Carter and I went to high school together," Derek said, then looked between Carter and Darcy. "How do you and Darcy know each other?"

Haven placed her hand on her boyfriend's arm. "Carter is the mechanic who rescued Darcy a couple of weeks ago."

"I forgot you told me her car was towed to Flowering Grove," Derek said. "I didn't make the connection."

Carter nodded. "Small world."

"Where do you work?" Derek asked.

Carter jammed his thumb toward his shop. "Barton Automotive."

"So you're working for Ernie Barton?"

"That's right." Carter shoved his hands in his pockets. "I started right after high school. My sister married Gage Barton six years ago, so it's kind of the family business now."

"My dad always took his car and my mom's car there. How are Mr. and Mrs. Barton?"

"Ernie is slowly embracing retirement. He's doing more fishing than brake jobs, but he comes in just about every day. Glenda retired from the post office. She runs the office and does the books."

"That's cool." Derek patted Carter's shoulder. "You always said you'd be the fastest oil changer in Flowering Grove."

Carter blew on his fingers and rubbed them on his sternum. "I'm proud to announce I *am* the fastest."

They all laughed, and Haven shared a look with Darcy.

"Do you live nearby?" Derek asked.

Carter hesitated before nodding toward Main Street. "Yeah, just a few blocks from here. How about you?"

"I just bought a place out in Matthews, and I work in Uptown Charlotte." Derek pivoted toward Mason, who stood with his back to them while talking on the phone. He shook his head and mumbled something under his breath before addressing Carter again. "Would you like to join us?"

Carter glanced at Darcy as if for approval, and she smiled, hoping he'd say yes. Then he met Derek's gaze. "I'd love to."

"Great." Derek looped his arm around Haven's shoulder. "Lead the way."

CHAPTER 5

Carter had a difficult time keeping his eyes off Darcy while they walked side by side down Main Street, taking in the line of cars. She looked beautiful with her sunshine-colored hair fixed in a French braid, and she was clad in a flowing pink blouse and a pair of jeans that accentuated her slender figure. Just the right amount of makeup highlighted those gorgeous green eyes.

When he'd spotted her standing by the Bronco, he'd had to shake himself, certain he'd imagined her. After all, he'd thought of her on and off during the past two weeks, and a couple of times, he'd considered texting her. But what could he say that wouldn't seem creepy? The only texts he considered were:

Hey! It's Carter. How's your car? Want to go out with me?

Or:

Hi! It's Carter. Did you need me to check your oil or brakes? Want to grab a bite to eat?

Both were super dumb. Instead, he'd hoped that somehow their paths would cross. Maybe her dad would bring his classic truck to the car show and bring her along too. It blew his mind that part of his dream had actually come true.

When he'd approached her, his efforts at small talk made him feel like a doofus. But he sensed Darcy appreciated his goofy sense of humor when she played along with the banter and laughed. He relished the sweet lilt of her laugh, along with that dazzling smile.

And what were the chances that Darcy's best friend was dating one of Carter's buddies from high school? It all seemed too good to be true. Good thing he'd refused his sister's invitation to join her and Gage for supper. Had he gone with them, he wouldn't have bumped into Darcy. Carter was lucky to get a second chance with her, and he wasn't going to blow it.

He glanced behind them and saw a man following at a leisurely pace with his cell phone stuck to his ear. Carter's heart dropped. The guy broke out in a wide smile while he laughed and listened to the caller.

Questions rolled through his mind as Darcy kept pace beside him. Was the rude man Darcy's date? He certainly hoped not. She deserved someone much more attentive than that jerk.

"You need to see Darcy's dad's truck," Derek told Carter.

"I heard about it, but I haven't seen a photo yet."

"Oh, I have one here somewhere." Darcy pulled her phone from her fancy purse and stood still, scrolling through photos.

Carter moved closer to her, and the flowery scent of her shampoo or possibly her lotion filled his nostrils and made his senses spin.

"Here we go." She held out the phone for him to see. "My dad sent me this one after he cleaned it a few weeks ago. It's his baby."

Carter gave a low whistle as he took in the beautifully restored classic truck. "Too bad he didn't bring it here tonight. I'd love to see it in person."

"I'll have to find out if he plans to take it to any car shows." She slipped her phone into her pocket.

Haven divided a look between Carter and Darcy. "If he does, then the four of us will have to meet up at the show." An unspoken conversation passed between the women before Darcy smiled at Carter.

They started down the street, and Darcy stayed by Carter's side while they all pointed out their favorite cars. Derek and Carter also got caught up on their lives, and Derek talked about his work as a software engineer at a consulting firm in Charlotte. Carter wasn't surprised Derek had an impressive job since he'd always talked about going to college. He was successful and already owned a home. Carter was happy for his friend, but he clearly didn't fit into Darcy's or Derek's worlds.

When they came to Treasure Hunting Antique Mall, Darcy turned to him, her expression bright. "Do you like antiques?"

"Sure." He shrugged. "A couple of my high school classmates own this place. Christine and Brent Nicholson."

"No kidding! I love this store. I found an antique mirror for my living room the last time I was here with Haven." She took Carter's hand and yanked him toward the door, and he enjoyed the feeling of her warm skin against his.

He allowed her to steer him through the aisles. Together the four of them investigated booths full of furniture, records, clothes, jewelry, tools, and knickknacks.

"Where's Mason?" Haven asked as she perused a stack of old magazines and comic books.

Derek pressed his lips together. "Would you believe he's still on his phone? I have no idea why he agreed to come tonight."

Carter snuck a peek over at Darcy. "Is Mason your boyfriend?" A sarcastic peal of laughter burst from her lips, and he smiled along with her. "I'll take that as a no."

"Blind date." Darcy leaned closer to him and lowered her voice to a conspiratorial whisper. "Haven and Derek have taken it upon themselves to find me a boyfriend. So far they've struck out. This guy has been the rudest of all."

Carter nodded slowly, basking in her flowery scent. So she *was* single after all.

They wandered out of the store, and Haven pointed toward Heather's Books 'N' Treats across the street. "Want to go look at the books?"

"Not really." Derek shook his head. "I'm in the mood for ice cream."

"I'm always in the mood for ice cream," said Darcy. She looked up at Carter. "How about you?"

"Never met a flavor I didn't like." They started down the sidewalk toward the Flowering Grove Creamery. "Did you know the owner of Heather's Books 'N' Treats married a rock star?"

"Really?" she asked.

"Yup. Her parents own the Barbecue Pit, and she's married to one of the lead singers of Kirwan."

"I had no idea. Do you like Kirwan?" she asked.

"I'm more of a country music fan, but they're okay. My sister is a big fan." He waggled his eyebrows and gave her shoulder a gentle push. "Let me guess. You think they're dreamy, right?"

She laughed. "They're good-looking, and I like their music."

"Uh-huh," he teased. "Right. It's the *music* you like."

She giggled as he held open the door to the ice cream parlor. Then they took their place in line.

The little shop was decorated in a 1950s theme with a black-and-white checkerboard tiled floor, red vinyl booths, chrome high-top tables, and red vinyl stools. Photos of ice cream sundaes, banana splits, and cones dotted the walls. The shop buzzed with conversations as people enjoyed their sweet treats.

Carter looked out the parlor's windows to where Derek and Haven stood on the sidewalk talking to another couple. "Looks like Derek and Haven ran into someone they know."

"Oh?" Darcy peered out toward the sidewalk. "I can't see who it is from this angle."

"Do you want to wait for them?"

Darcy shook her head. "Let's get our ice cream, and they'll catch up with us."

They reached the counter, where she requested a pralines and cream cone and he ordered chocolate peanut butter. When they got to the cash register, she angled her body in front of him and pulled out her wallet.

"I got it," he said.

"Nope." She lifted her chin. "Consider this my official thank-you for rescuing me."

He thanked her as she paid for the ice cream, and they started toward a booth in the back.

Carter sat on the red vinyl bench seat across from her. He took a lick of his ice cream and enjoyed the sweet taste. "I can't remember the last time I was in here."

"If I worked nearby, I would find an excuse to come here every day." Her green eyes glittered. "Did you always want to stay in Flowering Grove?"

"Yeah." He wiped his mouth with a paper napkin. "My sister settled down here, so it made sense to stay close by to family."

Darcy seemed to study him over her ice cream cone, and he could almost hear the questions spinning through her mind.

"You look like you want to ask me something."

"I don't want to be rude."

He laughed. "Go ahead. I'm sure you're not rude."

"You said your grandparents raised you and your sister after your mom passed away. Did you know your dad?"

"He left when I was four, and my mom, my sister, and I moved in with my grandparents." He settled back in the booth.

Her expression was solemn. "I'm so sorry." Then her eyes glimmered. "Are you in touch with your dad?"

He shook his head. She looked like she had more questions but ate her ice cream instead.

"Now it's your turn. Tell me your life story, Darcy."

She shrugged. "There's not much to tell."

"What do your parents do?"

"They're older and retired now. They were orthodontists and owned their own practice. They also dabbled in real estate a bit."

"Oh." Now her beautiful car and clothes made sense. She'd grown up with all the advantages while Carter's grandparents had never owned their own home. He was definitely out of his league with this woman.

"Yeah, I know. It's impressive." Her shoulders sank. "I'm sure I disappointed them when I didn't go to medical school."

He shook his head. "I highly doubt you're a disappointment, Darcy."

She blushed and looked adorable.

"Sorry about that," Derek said as he and Haven appeared at the table, each of them holding a half-eaten ice cream cone. "We ran into a couple of friends from UNCC."

Darcy slid to the far side of the bench, and Haven joined her. "Carter and I saw you talking to someone on the sidewalk, but I couldn't see who out the window."

"It was Candi and Rick Benedict," Haven said.

"Really?" Darcy asked. "Candi and Rick got married?"

Derek nodded as he sat beside Carter. "And they have three-year-old twins."

"Wow!" Darcy looked embarrassed as she turned toward Carter. "I'm sorry to talk about people you may not know." She motioned between Haven, Derek, and herself. "We all met at UNC at Charlotte. In fact, Haven was my roommate all through school."

"That's right," Haven said. "Darcy thought I was stuck-up when we first met. We didn't even like each other."

Darcy snickered. "Well, any girl as pretty as you should be stuck-up."

"Speak for yourself," Haven countered.

Darcy shook her head, but Carter silently agreed.

"Anyway," Darcy continued, "we went to school with Candi and Rick."

Carter smiled and continued eating his ice cream while Darcy, Derek, and Haven talked about old friends from college. He found himself wondering if he could fit into Darcy's life. Was there a chance he could ever be good enough for a beautiful, successful woman like Darcy Larsen? After all, he hadn't gone to college.

When Mason strolled over to the table, Carter did his best to mask his frown. Mason was a real jerk for ignoring Darcy and spending their date on the phone. At the same time, he appreciated having the chance to get to know Darcy better. Mason's loss was definitely Carter's gain.

"Sorry about that." Mason had the nerve to look guilty. "An old friend needed someone to talk to." He glanced at his expensive-looking watch. "I didn't realize how late it was." His eyes flitted to Darcy's. "Do you need a ride home?"

Darcy's brow furrowed for a moment, then a sugary-sweet smile overtook her pink lips. "Thank you for the offer, but I think I'll ride home with Haven and Derek."

"Suit yourself." Mason nodded at Derek. "See you at the office."

Derek pressed his lips together. "Yup."

After Mason disappeared from the table, Darcy pinned Haven and Derek with a look. "Do me a favor and let me find my own dates from now on, okay?"

Derek cringed. "I'm sorry. When I talked to Mason, he said he'd love to meet you."

"Sounds like he'd rather get together with his ex," Haven pointed out.

They finished their ice cream and then headed toward the street, where the sun had begun to set and send a vibrant rainbow of colors dancing across the sky. The air was cool but held the promise of spring, and the streetlights cast a warm yellow glow on the few remaining cars lining the sidewalk.

Carter longed to find an excuse to keep Darcy in Flowering Grove longer, but when he glanced down Main Street, he saw that the little shops were now dark and their Open signs had been switched to Closed. He couldn't think of any other reason to convince her to stay.

Derek spun to face him. "We need to get together again soon, Carter. How about you give me your number?"

The air left Carter's lungs. Perhaps the double date that Haven had mentioned earlier could actually come to fruition!

"That's a great idea." He and Derek exchanged numbers before they continued down the street.

When they reached the Barbecue Pit's parking lot, Derek shook Carter's hand. "It was wonderful to see you again. Let's keep in touch."

"Absolutely," Carter said.

Haven waved before following Derek toward a line of cars at the back of the lot.

Darcy smiled up at him. "I really had fun tonight."

"I did too."

She opened her mouth, but then closed it as if debating what to say. Then she smiled. "You should text me sometime and tell me about those reality shows. I definitely want to hear more about *I Married My Brother-in-Law's Sister's Podiatrist*."

"Okay." He nodded. "I'll do that."

"I hope so." She shook his hand. "Have a good night, Carter."

As Darcy hurried off toward the far end of the parking lot, Carter tried to imagine himself on a real date with Darcy. The thought seemed almost too good to hope for.

* * *

THE QUESTION OF ASKING DARCY OUT FOLLOWED CARTER DURING HIS short walk home. The house was dark and quiet as he unlocked the back door and made his way upstairs to the room over the garage. He took a shower and then climbed onto his bed and opened his laptop.

While he checked his email, his mind whirred with thoughts of Darcy. His lips curved up in a smile while he recalled how beautiful she looked tonight and how conversation flowed so easily between them. He'd longed to spend the rest of the night just talking with her, learning more about her, laughing with her. She was so down-to-earth and humble, especially when she insisted that she was a disappointment to her parents. He couldn't imagine Darcy disappointing anyone.

"Hey."

Carter jumped with a start as Shauna appeared in his doorway. "I didn't hear you come in," he said. "How was dinner?"

"It was good. You should have joined us." She dropped onto the edge of the bed. "Did you go back to the car show?"

He nodded. "I ran into Derek McGowan from high school. He was there with his girlfriend and her friend." He didn't mention Darcy since he knew it would turn into a lecture about how he needed to get back out there on the dating scene. Carter longed to do that—if he could get his life back in order.

"Derek." Shauna tapped her chin. "Was he the one who lived over on Ridge Road?"

"That's right. His dad is a police officer."

"I remember his dad. He always liked to pull Gage over for speeding."

"That's right." Carter grinned. "He pulled over anyone who looked like they were under twenty-five."

"Derek was always friendly."

"He was a good buddy too. We talked about getting together again."

"Cool." She moved over to the chair by his desk. "I wanted to tell you something."

He angled his body to face her. "What's up?"

"I've decided I want to try to find Dad."

Carter sat up straight as confusion twisted through him. "Why?"

"I have a lot to say to him." She frowned. "I want to know why he disappeared on us."

"You're wasting your time. Remember when I tried to find him when I was in high school? It was like he disappeared into thin air."

"I know you couldn't find him, but I at least want to try. I have a lot I need to get off my chest with him." She moved to the doorway and tapped the doorframe. "I just wanted you to know."

He nodded. "I don't think you'll find him. If he wanted us to know where he was, he'd reach out."

"Well, we'll see. I'm glad you went out and had fun tonight. Have a good night."

Carter set the laptop on his nightstand, his mind churning with thoughts of his father and of Darcy. The last thing he wanted was to see his father—the man who had abandoned him, his mother, and his sister. But most likely, Shauna wouldn't find him. At least, he hoped she didn't. Their father was where he deserved to be, which was gone from their lives.

CHAPTER 6

Darcy sipped a glass of sweet tea while she sat on her parents' enormous back deck the following afternoon. She breathed in the fresh, warm, late-April air. Birds sang in the large trees lining her parents' property, and bees buzzed among her mother's colorful flowers. She looked out over the spacious backyard that included a large in-ground pool; a cabana house; her father's detached, three-bay garage with the apartment above it; and a shed—all surrounded by a privacy fence.

She shifted toward her parents beside her, and a familiar feeling overtook her. Not for the first time, she contemplated how she'd never felt like she fit into the family. She didn't resemble either of them. Both of her parents were tall—much taller than she was. At the age of sixty-eight, her mother still had gorgeous, creamy skin, along with glossy dark hair and deep-blue eyes. Very few wrinkles marked her complexion, and she had the warmest smile Darcy had ever known. Josephine Larsen stood at five feet ten, and while Darcy had always hoped she'd reach her mother's height, she had stopped growing when she'd reached five feet, six inches.

Dad had had salt-and-pepper hair and a matching goatee for as long as Darcy could remember. With broad shoulders and dark-brown eyes, Ross Larsen was still fit at the age of seventy. He was so kind and gave the best hugs. And Darcy would always consider him, at six feet tall, larger than life.

Darcy ran her fingers over the condensation on her glass as thoughts of her biological mother filled her mind. Had Darcy inherited her blonde hair and green eyes from her? If or when she found a photo of her biological mother, would she recognize her? Would her birth mother recognize her if they ever met?

Her lungs squeezed, and she tried to abandon those thoughts before turning toward her mother. "What is your book club reading this month?"

Mom's blue eyes lit with excitement. "Oh, it's the newest Kathleen Fuller book. Darcy, it's so good. Would you like to borrow it after I finish it?"

"Of course." She enjoyed talking about books with her mom. She still remembered curling up on her mom's lap every night as she listened to her read her favorite childhood stories.

Will Mom forgive me if I go looking for my biological mother?

Darcy turned her attention to her father. "Are you planning to take your truck to any car shows this year?"

Dad lifted a bushy eyebrow. "You haven't gone to a car show with me since you were in high school. Why the sudden interest now?"

Because of Carter. "I actually went to one in Flowering Grove last night."

"Is that right?" Dad grinned. "Did you go on purpose or stumble upon it?"

Darcy immediately regretted bringing up the subject since it would force her to talk about another failed blind date, but she pushed on. "Derek decided to set me up with another one of his friends. The date was a disaster, but the car show was fun."

"How was it a disaster?" Mom asked.

Darcy summarized how Mason spent the entire night on the phone with his ex-girlfriend. "But I still had a good time with Haven and Derek." She clutched her glass and then decided to share more details. "And I ran into Carter Donovan, the mechanic who rescued me when my car broke down."

"Oh, so *there's* the truth." Mom pointed a perfectly manicured finger at her. "You've met someone."

Ugh. "No, not exactly. We're just friends."

"Your dad and I started out as friends in dental school. Right, Ross?"

Dad gave Mom a sweet smile. "Yes, we did."

"So you and Carter could turn into more than friends," Mom sang.

Darcy shook her head. "I'm not ready for that."

"But you need to get to know some new people, Darcy," Mom continued. "You're too young to be alone."

"Josie," Dad began, "let's not push her. She's been through a lot for someone her age . . ."

Dad's words trailed off, but Darcy knew he was thinking of Jace. She swallowed as the familiar guilt and grief rose inside of her.

He placed his hand on Darcy's shoulder. "Take your time, sweetie. But if you feel like your friendship may lead to something special, then follow your heart."

Darcy smiled. Her dad always knew how to calm her. "Thanks. But back to the earlier question: Would you please let me know if you're taking your truck to any shows?"

"Yes, I will." The corners of his mouth lifted. "Are you asking me so you can invite Carter to join you?"

A flush overtook her cheeks. "Apparently, I'm pretty transparent."

"Only to us," Dad said.

Darcy laughed. She was beyond grateful for her wonderful parents.

But she still felt that pull toward the past—toward her biological mom and the answers to years' worth of questions. Darcy just hoped her parents would understand when she finally found the courage to find her.

* * *

SMOKY MEOWED AND RUBBED AGAINST CARTER'S SHIN BEFORE FLOPPING next to the Volkswagen sedan sitting in Carter's stall.

"I think he's saying you're taking too much time on that brake job," Gage called from the other side of the shop.

"No, he was just telling me I deserved a break." Carter took a long drink from his bottle of water.

The temperature had risen during the past week. This part of North Carolina usually tried to skip spring and barrel straight into summer, so even though it was only the second Thursday in May, it already felt more like mid-July. The humidity wrapped around Carter like a hot, wet blanket. If only the shop had air-conditioning instead of those big fans that only managed to move the hot air around instead of offering any relief.

Carter's phone buzzed with a text, and he sauntered over to his toolbox to read a message from Derek McGowan.

He thought back to the night he'd spent with Derek, Darcy, and Haven, then blew out a resigned sigh. It had been almost two weeks since he'd talked to Darcy. He had picked up his phone at least a dozen times with the intention of texting her, but such a move felt a bit too bold—and frankly, his skills in the dating department were rusty. Now he just needed to find a way to push through his thoughts, which seemed impossible since Darcy always seemed to linger at the back of his mind.

He opened Derek's text message.

DEREK: Hey Carter! Are you free Saturday night?

CARTER: Sure am. What's up?

DEREK: I'm having a housewarming party at my place. Would love for you to come. Nothing fancy. Just a bunch of friends coming over to eat.

CARTER: Sounds great. What can I bring?

DEREK: Just yourself. See you then!

CARTER: Can't wait.

Derek sent Carter the address and the time details for the get-together, then Carter set his phone back on his toolbox. If Derek was having friends over, then Haven would be there. And if Haven was there, certainly Darcy would come too.

He may have missed his chance with her, but he'd still get to see her. And that would have to be enough.

* * *

ON SATURDAY NIGHT, DARCY OPENED A BAG OF CHIPS AND POURED THE contents into a large bowl. She scanned Derek's spacious kitchen while Haven flittered around, gathering up a container of pasta salad and setting it on a tray, along with plates, utensils, and cups.

The delicious smell of the beef and chicken kabobs cooking on the grill wafted in from the deck through the open sliding glass door just behind the breakfast nook. Voices buzzed from guests milling around outside and in the family room beyond the kitchen.

"I need to find the tablecloth so I can set the table on the deck." Haven shook her head. "I should have done it earlier, but I was helping Derek with last-minute cleaning."

Darcy stepped toward the bar that separated the kitchen from the breakfast nook and spotted the disposable blue tablecloth. "I got it. I'll set the table." She reached for the tray.

"No, I can do it. Would you grab the pitcher of tea in the fridge though?"

"Sure." Darcy placed the tablecloth on Haven's tray and then retrieved the pitcher.

"Have you heard from Carter since the car show?"

"No." Darcy turned toward the counter, the large pitcher teetering in her hand. When she lost her grip, the cold liquid sloshed and spilled out from the open lid, dripping down her yellow shirt. Groaning, she set the container down, grabbed a paper towel, and rubbed it down her front. "Just great," she griped.

Haven clucked her tongue. "I'm sorry! Derek tells me that I always overfill containers." She rested her hand on Darcy's shoulder. "I have an extra top upstairs in the master bathroom. I was planning to change, but I ran out of time. Go get cleaned up, and I'll finish setting out the food."

"It's fine. It'll dry."

Haven shook her head. "You should get changed."

"Why?"

Haven smirked. "Carter is coming tonight."

Darcy's nerves jangled. "He is?" Then she studied her best friend. "Did you set this up like a date?"

"Just go freshen up. Feel free to use my makeup."

Darcy didn't move. For two weeks she'd hoped to hear from him, but his silence only proved what she'd presumed: that he wasn't available or interested in her. If he had been interested, he would have texted or called her.

Apparently she had imagined their mutual attraction. Darcy had tried to convince herself this was a good thing, since she wasn't ready for a relationship anyway. Still, she couldn't get Carter Donovan's handsome face, radiant smile, and delightful sense of humor out of her mind.

Haven exhaled a frustrated noise. "Will you go get changed already?" She gave Darcy a gentle push toward the stairs. "He'll be here any minute if he isn't already."

"But I don't think he—"

"Just go, Darcy," Haven interrupted with another nudge.

Stumbling forward, Darcy hurried up the stairs, which led to three bedrooms and two bathrooms. She jogged into the master bedroom past a queen-size bed, two dressers, a few unpacked boxes, and two closets.

She slipped into the bathroom, where a light-green peasant blouse hung on a hook on the back of the door. She pulled on the top and then scrutinized her reflection. She had applied minimal makeup and pulled her hair up in a ponytail. But now that she knew Carter was coming, she felt conflicted.

On one hand, she was tempted to braid her hair and add eyeliner. But why should she bother when Carter hadn't contacted her in two weeks? She thought they had bonded at the car show when he had spent the evening with her, but then again, he hadn't texted her even after she'd asked him to.

She felt a strange connection to Carter—something she hadn't experienced since Jace. And as much as she knew getting into a relationship would be a mistake, she couldn't deny that her heart seemed to come alive when she was with Carter.

Then it hit her. What if Carter was bringing a date? Just because Carter had attended the car show alone didn't mean he was single. For all Darcy knew, his girlfriend could have been busy or just not interested in cars.

Darcy frowned as she imagined Carter arriving at Derek's house with a gorgeous brunette on his arm. Then she shook her head. She had already developed a crush on a man she had spoken to three times. She really needed to grow up.

Still, Darcy located Haven's brush and quickly fixed her hair in a French braid before adding eyeliner and blush. She finished off her makeup with a little bit of lip gloss. Then she frowned as she took in her reflection.

"Well, here goes nothing," she whispered before ambling down the stairs and following the hum of conversations to the kitchen.

Darcy stopped by the kitchen counter and stared out toward the deck. There was Carter, standing beside Derek at the grill and laughing at something Derek said. Her stare raked over him, taking in the faded jeans settled on his hips and the blue t-shirt hugging his muscular chest and arms. His chiseled jaw was clean-shaven, and the sound of his laughter sent warmth stirring deep within her.

She had missed him, which was crazy. She hardly knew this man.

She scanned the deck, looking for a pretty woman who might be his date, but she didn't see anyone who would've fit the bill. Instead, groups of guests were spread out on the deck and in the yard by the tables and chairs.

"Instead of staring at him, why don't you go talk to him?" Haven appeared at Darcy's side and handed her a stack of napkins. "Here's your excuse for going out to the deck." Then she grinned. "You look gorgeous, by the way. Keep the top. It looks better on you."

Darcy chortled. "As if anything could look better on me than you."

"Whatever. Go talk to him." Haven nodded toward the open sliding glass door.

Squaring her shoulders, Darcy strode out onto the deck. When Carter's gaze swung to hers, his face lit up with a bright smile that nearly took her breath away.

"Hi, Carter." She hoped she sounded calmer than she felt. "Fancy meeting you here." *Oh, that was so uncool.* She inwardly cringed but forced her lips into a smile as she set the napkins beside the platters of food.

"Hi, Darcy." He gulped. "You look great."

"Thanks." Darcy's cheeks flushed in response to the compliment. Out of the corner of her eye, she spotted Haven watching her.

Derek turned the kabobs on the grill and then closed the lid. "They're almost done," he called out to Haven. "Thanks for setting everything up."

"You're welcome, but Darcy helped." Haven grinned at Darcy. "Why don't you give Carter the twenty-five-cent tour?"

Darcy gestured toward the house. "Would you like to go inside?" she asked him.

"I'd love to."

As Darcy led Carter into the kitchen, she held her head high. Even if he was dating someone else, she'd do her best to keep her wits about her. At the very least, maybe she could have a friendship with him. She didn't dare wish for anything more.

CHAPTER 7

CARTER FOLLOWED DARCY INTO THE HOUSE. HE HAD BEEN RELIEVED TO see her when she came out to the deck, not only because he liked her, but also because she was a familiar face. He felt like a fish out of water at Derek's place, surrounded by successful young professionals. It reminded him of why he and Derek had drifted apart after high school. While Derek had gone on to college and a professional career, Carter was a blue-collar mechanic who felt frozen in time due to his financial situation.

"This is the kitchen." She pointed toward the sink before stepping into the den, which was adorned with a large gray sectional, a huge flat-screen television, a couple of armchairs, a coffee table, and end tables. "And here's the family room."

She walked down a hallway. "There's a half bath here, a laundry room, and an office." She pointed toward a doorway. "That leads to the two-car garage."

Darcy started up the stairs, and when Carter followed her, he caught a whiff of her perfume or possibly her shampoo. She looked stunning again tonight. The color of her shirt seemed to bring out the green in her eyes, and he longed to touch her braid to feel how soft her hair was.

Although she smiled at him, she seemed more aloof than she'd been in the past. Perhaps she wasn't as thrilled to see him as he was to see her. Had she already met someone?

"And up here, there are three bedrooms and two bathrooms."

When he touched her hand, she stilled, and her eyes widened. "How have you been?" he asked.

"Fine. Great." Her manufactured smile didn't reach her eyes. Something was off. "You?"

He tilted his head and tried to interpret her unspoken mannerisms. "Have you talked to Mason since the car show?"

"Is that a joke?" She laughed, and relief filtered through Carter as she visibly relaxed. "Of course I haven't, and I really hope he doesn't come tonight." Then she scrunched her nose. "Oh, that was so snotty of me."

"Not snotty, just honest."

She leaned on the pony wall at the top of the stairs. "I'm glad Haven and Derek finally got the message that I'm not interested in any more horrendous blind dates." She studied him as if she were trying to figure out an intricate puzzle. "Are you seeing anyone?"

Surely that couldn't be hope he found in her gorgeous green eyes. "I've been single for a long time."

"Why?"

His brow crinkled, and his lips quirked. "Why am I single?"

"I'm so sorry." Her cheeks reddened, and she spun away from him. "That's really nosy of me. I'm . . . I'm just surprised you don't have a girlfriend." She moved down the hallway. "So the master bedroom is over here."

"Hold on." He touched her arm. "*Why* are you surprised?"

"Ah. Well." She seemed to search for the words as the sound of footfalls on the stairs filled the hallway. Then her eyes focused on something behind her, and she looked relieved. "Haven. Hi."

Haven stood at the top of the stairs and leaned on the banister. "I thought you two got lost. The kabobs are ready."

A knowing look passed between the friends, and curiosity gnawed at him.

"Great." Darcy pivoted toward him. "Let's get something to eat."

Back out on the deck, Carter and Darcy made their way down the food table. They filled their plates with kabobs, corn on the cob, pasta salad, and chips before picking up glasses of sweet tea.

"Would you like to find a quiet place to sit and talk?" he asked.

She nodded. "Yes."

They walked down a pathway through the yard that led to a fence lined with flowering dogwood trees. Balancing his plate and cup of tea in one hand, Carter opened the gate for her and then followed her to a bench at the edge of a pond. Other homes in the neighborhood surrounded the pond and enjoyed similar views. A prick of envy twisted through him as he took in the lovely two-story houses. He doubted he would ever be able to afford a home like the ones in this neighborhood.

"This place is incredible," he muttered as they sank down onto the bench together.

"I know. Derek got a great deal on it too."

Carter took a bite of a beef kabob and then craned his neck over his shoulder. The other guests of the party were sitting at tables throughout the yard and eating their food. Conversations wafted over them, along with the quacks from a group of ducks swimming in the pond.

"Do you know all of the people here?" He wondered if she felt as awkward as he did with the strangers.

She shook her head and swallowed. "Only a few, but I think some of them are Derek's and Haven's coworkers." She seemed to survey him for a moment. "So you're the same age as Derek?"

He nodded. "Yeah, we graduated together. I'll be thirty next month. How about you?"

"Twenty-seven."

An easy silence fell over them while they ate for a few moments. He felt himself completely relax for the first time since arriving at Derek's house.

"How are your folks?" he asked.

She seemed surprised by the question. "Great. How about your sister?"

"She's fine."

"You mentioned that she's been married for six years. Does she have any children?"

He shook his head. "Not yet."

She lifted an eyebrow.

"They're hoping to have kids, but she hasn't discussed it with me much." He recalled how his sister had mentioned wanting children, but he also had the impression that she and Gage were struggling. He looked forward to being an uncle someday soon. He'd love to have a niece or nephew to take to the park and teach how to ride a bike. Maybe Shauna and Gage would have a child who liked to work on cars too.

"I see." Understanding seemed to fill her face. "What does she do for a living?"

"She's a pediatric nurse, so she's great with kids. She always wanted to go to nursing school, and then she fell in love with pediatrics."

Darcy smiled. "I bet she has some great stories."

"Yes, she does." He chuckled.

"Is she older than you?"

He nodded. Darcy turned her attention to her food, and as she picked at her plate, she seemed to be working through something in her mind.

Carter waited a few moments and then leaned closer to her. "Is everything all right?"

"Yeah." She turned slightly toward him. "But can I ask you something personal?"

"Sure." He braced himself, unsure of how personal she planned to get. He reminded himself that she had no way of knowing about his past. About his illness, about his failed relationship, about everything that fell apart. After all, not even Derek knew about his kidney transplant.

Darcy's expression became somber. "You said you don't keep in touch with your father."

Carter's back went rigid. "He's never been around. I don't even know where he is."

She stared at the pond for a moment. "Have you ever wanted to find him?"

He blinked, certain he'd misunderstood the question.

Darcy cringed. "Oh no. I made it weird." She sat up straight and forced a smile. "So what's your favorite movie?"

On impulse, he put his plate down beside him and took her hand in his. When he moved his thumb over her palm, her eyes widened.

"Darcy," he began, "I was surprised by the question but not offended. The answer is no, I don't want to find my father, but my sister does. We don't agree on that subject." He glanced at their clasped hands. He'd meant only to reassure her, but since she wasn't letting go, he wasn't about to either. "As for your movie question, there are too many to list. I'll bore you to tears."

She opened and closed her mouth.

"You look puzzled." He lifted his eyebrows, awaiting her response, but she remained silent. "Go ahead and say whatever is on your mind, Darcy. I promise it's okay."

"Why do you and your sister disagree about your dad?" Her voice was soft, and her question was hesitant.

He raked his free hand through his hair. "Shauna wants to find him and demand to know why he abandoned our mom and us. I don't want to know, and I don't want to see him. It doesn't matter why he left us. He did, and his excuses won't mean anything to me. The past is the past, and he can't do anything to fix that now."

Darcy nodded. "I didn't mean to upset you."

"I'm not upset." He managed a half-grin and let go of her hand. "I'm just stating facts." He settled on the bench. "Now I have a question for you. Why are you so curious about my dad?"

She placed her plate of food on the bench beside her and then moved her finger along the hem of her shirt. "I'm adopted, and I want to find my biological mother. At least, I think I do."

"Oh." He hadn't expected that response, but it explained her interest. His lungs squeezed with compassion for her as he took in her serious expression.

"I hope to have a family someday, and I want to know about my family history. I also have other questions for her." She worried her lower lip. "Do you think that's bad?"

"Why would I think that's bad?"

"It's complicated. My parents adopted me in their forties. They had tried fertility treatments for years to have a child. Nothing worked. So when they adopted me, they were elated. All they ever wanted was a baby."

Darcy peered out over the pond again. "I adore my parents. I couldn't have asked for a better set if I had picked them myself. They're the most loving, giving, thoughtful, generous, amazing people on the planet." She rubbed her hands together and faced him again. "But I've always felt like I didn't fit in with them. I don't look like them, and I'm not smart like them. I mean, they graduated at the top of their classes in dental school, but I barely passed high school biology."

Her posture stiffened. "There's always been this hole in my heart that I can't explain. Does that make me sound unappreciative?"

"No, Darcy. I can't begin to comprehend how you feel, but from what I do know about you, you're not unappreciative."

"I have questions they can't answer," she said. "I want to know what my biological mother looks like. I know she was young when she had me—younger than eighteen. Do I look like her? Do I sound like her? Did she want to keep me? Did she have a choice? Do I have any siblings? Does she think about me? Does she worry about me?"

He nodded, encouraging her to continue.

"Someone told me about an organization that can help me find her. It's a nonprofit. I've thought so much about it, but I haven't even looked at the website yet."

"Sounds like you're afraid."

"Yeah. I think I am." Her lower lip trembled. "I don't want to hurt my parents." She sniffed, and the tears glistening in her eyes nearly tore him apart. "But I also want to know where I came from. I feel so torn." She shielded her face with her hands. "I don't know why I'm unloading all of this on you. You're the only person I've told about this. I haven't even told Haven."

Carter was so honored that he couldn't speak for a moment. Somehow, he had earned her trust. Perhaps Darcy liked him as much as he liked her. "Maybe you should talk to your parents about this. They sound like terrific people, so I'm sure they'd understand." He wanted to reach out and touch her again, but he held back.

Her hands dropped onto her lap. "I don't know if they will. They told me about my adoption when I was twelve years old, but we've never discussed looking for my biological mother. I only recently realized that yearning to know who I am is causing this emptiness deep inside of me." She shook her head. "I just feel like something is missing, and I can't explain it otherwise." Her eyes seemed to search his face. "You don't feel that way about your dad?"

He blew out a deep breath as he considered how much to share with her. Clearly, she was baring her soul to him. She deserved the same honesty she was giving him. "No, I don't. He threw away our family. He didn't want us, and I don't want him."

"I'm sorry he hurt you so deeply."

Carter was astounded by how compassionate and understanding Darcy was. She was such a stark contrast to Gabrielle, who only cared about herself.

But what shocked him even more was the connection he felt to Darcy. In an odd way, it felt like a deeper connection than any he had ever felt with anyone in his life. It was as if she was already a kindred spirit. He couldn't quite fathom the thought.

Then her beautiful smile returned. "Enough about family stuff. Let's talk about something fun. Now about those movies. You could never bore me to tears talking about them."

He laughed, glad for the change of subject. "My sister and I were raised by movie buffs."

"Tell me more." She pivoted toward him, folding her legs under her cutoff jean shorts.

"Saturday night was movie night when I was a kid. We watched all of the classics with our grandparents."

"Such as?"

"Oh, I don't know." He looked up at the puffy white clouds dotting the bright-blue sky as if they held the answers.

"Just tell me your favorites."

"Okay then . . . *Gone in 60 Seconds*, *Vanishing Point*, *Smokey and the Bandit*, and possibly *American Graffiti*. Oh, and you can't forget *The Fast and the Furious*."

"I see a pattern here—cars, cars, cars, cars, and cars." She counted off on her fingers. "Makes sense."

"You've got me figured out." He touched her shoulder. "How about you?"

She rested her elbow on the back of the bench. "My mom loves John Hughes's movies, and that has rubbed off on me. My favorite is *Pretty in Pink*."

"That's a good movie."

Her eyes narrowed with a mock dirty look. "You're just teasing me."

"I'm not," he insisted. "My sister loves it too."

Darcy placed a hand over her heart. "The best movie kiss is when he kisses her in the headlights of his Beamer." She sighed. "It gets me every time."

His gaze locked on her pink lips, and he leaned forward as if an invisible cord connected them. While she stared up at him, his mouth yearned to taste hers.

"Did you two want to join us for dessert?"

Carter sat back and turned to see Derek leaning over the gate, smirking at him.

"Yeah. Sounds good." Carter hopped up from the bench and balanced their plates and cups in one hand. Then he held his free hand out to Darcy.

She took it, and as he lifted her up from the bench, he thought he saw disappointment reflected in her eyes. Maybe it was the same disappointment he felt.

As they started toward the gate, Carter knew one thing for sure: He wasn't going to be able to stay away from Darcy Larsen now.

CHAPTER 8

DARCY WAS SURE CARTER WAS GOING TO KISS HER BEFORE DEREK interrupted them. And she had wanted him to.

A fresh buzz of excitement zapped through Darcy as Carter passed through the gate and held it open for her. She tried to stop her hands from trembling as they made their way into the backyard, where the guests were gathered around tables to eat cookies and continue their lively conversations.

Above them, the sun had begun to set, sending a kaleidoscope of colors across the sky. Derek moved from table to table lighting citronella candles.

"Darcy! Carter!" Haven called from a far table. "Come join us."

Carter dropped their plates and empty cups into a trash can, and Darcy followed him to the table. They sat in the two empty seats across from Derek and Haven.

Darcy picked out a chocolate chip cookie from a platter. Nearby, one of Derek's friends was sharing a story about his camping mishaps in the mountains last fall, but Darcy couldn't concentrate on his words. Her mind was whirring, replaying her time with Carter by the pond.

A tingle went straight to her toes as she recollected the spark in his dark eyes when they leveled on her lips. When he held her hand, she'd become so lightheaded that she thought she might pass out. He'd been a breath away from kissing her. Why on earth had Derek chosen *that* moment to pipe up?

She focused on the blue tablecloth and tried to slow her pulse. When she'd first seen Carter tonight, she'd been certain he wasn't interested in her. In fact, she had convinced herself he had a girlfriend, but now she was certain he *did* like her.

Beyond attraction, she felt a strange, special connection with him. She trusted Carter for some reason, which was why she found herself opening up to him and telling him her deepest secrets about her adoptive parents and her biological mother. She had the feeling he truly cared about her. It didn't make sense that a man she'd just met had become so important to her so quickly.

Surely she was setting herself up for heartache.

"You okay?" Carter had leaned close to whisper into her ear, sending a shockwave of heat rolling through her.

"Yeah. I'm fine."

He lifted a light-brown eyebrow.

"I promise I am."

He helped himself to a macadamia nut cookie. "These look good."

"They're all good," Darcy said. "I picked them up at a local bakery."

Carter took a bite and made a noise of approval.

When Darcy felt someone watching her, she peeked over at Haven, who had a smug look on her face. "Would you help me carry some of the empty platters inside?"

"Sure." Darcy pushed back her chair and followed her friend up the deck steps.

They gathered up the empty platters and bowls and carried them into the kitchen. Haven quickly closed the sliding glass door behind them.

"All right, Darcy." Haven stopped at the counter. "Spill it."

Darcy leaned against the sink and turned on the water. "What do you mean?"

"Please, Darce. You know *exactly* what I mean. You and Carter were sitting down by the pond for quite a while."

Darcy set the bowls and platters into the sink while she considered how much to share. "We had a nice talk."

"And?"

"And I like him a lot."

"Yay! You were right when you said you could find your own date. You found yourself a boyfriend all on your own."

"Whoa." Darcy turned to her and held up her hand. "He's not my boyfriend."

"But he will be . . . ," Haven sang while opening the dishwasher.

Darcy shook her head and wiped off the platters before handing them to Haven. "I like him a lot, but I'm nervous."

"What is there to be nervous about? It's obvious he likes you a lot too. He's handsome, and he seems funny and sweet. A total catch."

"He is . . ." Her mouth turned dry as familiar grief seeped through her. *Jace.* Here she was thinking about moving on when he'd sacrificed everything for her. It seemed too soon, too fast.

The sliding glass door opened with a whoosh, and Carter appeared in the kitchen holding a large pan, tongs, and a spatula. "Where can I put these?"

"I'll take them." Darcy reached for them. "Thanks."

"There are still a few plates out there, plus some leftover cups and cutlery. I'll bring them in."

"You don't need to clean up, Carter," Haven said. "We got it."

"I don't mind." He went back outside.

Haven placed her hand on Darcy's shoulder. "I think he's perfect."

"Stop it," Darcy hissed, but deep down, she agreed. Carter did seem perfect. Was he too good to be true?

For the next several minutes, Darcy, Haven, and Carter cleaned together in the kitchen. Guests came through waving their goodbyes, then headed out into the night. Soon only Derek, Carter, Haven, and Darcy were left in the house.

"Thank you for all your help," Darcy told Carter when they were done.

Carter shrugged. "You're welcome." He shook Derek's hand. "Thanks for inviting me. I had a great time."

"I'm glad we've reconnected. We need to do this again soon."

"Definitely."

As he and Derek chatted a bit longer, Haven nudged Darcy. "Walk him out," she said under her breath.

Darcy paused, but another nudge from her friend made her say, "I'll walk you out, Carter. I just need to grab my purse."

Carter grinned.

She jogged upstairs and fetched her stained blouse from the bathroom before zipping into the guest room for her purse.

When she returned to the hallway, she found Haven standing at the top of the stairs, grinning at her. "He's crazy about you."

Darcy shook her head despite the excitement buzzing through her.

Carter's and Derek's muffled voices sounded below them.

"I don't know if I'm ready for this," Darcy admitted, careful to keep her voice soft.

"You may not be, but it's obvious you two click. Just concentrate on being friends and see what happens. You can never have too many friends." She pulled Darcy in for a hug. "Go for it."

Darcy sighed. She was starting to believe Haven was right. But where did that leave her feelings for Jace? Would Jace understand? Would he want her to move on? Did she want to?

Haven released her. "And if you don't hear from him after tonight, maybe you should make the first move."

"What do you mean?"

"You ask him out. He probably won't expect it, and I bet he'll love it. You only live once."

Darcy considered her best friend's suggestion as they descended the stairs and met Carter and Derek at the front door.

"Glad you came," Derek told Darcy.

Darcy shouldered her purse and couldn't help but glance at Carter. "Me too."

She and Carter exchanged goodbyes with the couple before walking into the humid night air. The stars above them twinkled in the dark sky while frogs croaked nearby.

Darcy inhaled the scent of fresh flowers and the pond as they strolled toward the driveway. Her car was parked behind Haven's silver Honda CR-V, and Carter's SUV looked lonely sitting by itself on the side of the road.

She turned around and leaned against the driver's side door of her sedan. "I had fun tonight."

"I did too." He touched her arm, and her heart did a funny little dance. "Would it be okay if I texted you?"

Darcy conjured up a mischievous smile. "That sounds great, but do you have time for me in between all of those reality shows you watch?"

"Hmm." He flashed that crooked grin. "You're right. My schedule *is* pretty full, but I bet I can make time for you."

He held his hand out to her, and she hesitated as the urge to hug him overcame her. When her courage fizzled, she accepted his hand but held on a little longer than necessary.

"Good night, Darcy," he said.

"Good night." She opened her car door and dropped her stuff inside. Then she turned her head, unable to resist watching him walk away.

* * *

LATER THAT EVENING, CARTER WALKED INTO THE ONE-CAR, DETACHED garage and was greeted by the familiar smells of rubber, plastic, parts cleaner, and oil. He flipped on the lights, then hopped up on a stool and placed his laptop on the workbench beside him. Before him sat his grandfather's orange 1970 Plymouth Road Runner bordered by a row of toolboxes.

Memories of the hours he and his grandfather had spent working on the car together overtook his mind. "Wish you were here, Grandpa," he whispered.

Carter could sure use his advice right now while he tried to work through the conundrum of Darcy. He hadn't felt such a strong attraction to a woman before. Not even to Gabrielle.

But this was more than just attraction. What he felt for her was something deeper, more meaningful. He was stunned that she had trusted him with her secrets about wanting to find her biological mother. He trusted her in return, and even felt compelled to trust her with his heart. An invisible magnet seemed to be pulling them together.

But would he ever be enough for her? And what if his health failed again? Would that tear them apart like it did his relationship with Gabrielle?

Opening his laptop, Carter began searching for apartments in his price range and found nothing. Due to the cost of his monthly maintenance medications, he was out of luck until his consolidation loan was paid. He continued scrolling despite the gloom that filled him.

He was clicking through a page of overpriced one-bedroom places when the door opened with a creak.

Carter gave Gage a wave. "Hey."

His brother-in-law strolled in and pulled up a stool. "I was surprised when I looked out the window and saw the light on out here. What are you up to?"

"Not a whole lot."

"Are you finally going to start rebuilding the engine for the Road Runner?" Gage pointed toward the car.

Carter shook his head. "I was looking at apartments."

"You don't need to do that, bro." Gage crossed his arms over his wide chest. "This is your home."

Carter exhaled and closed the laptop.

"Why do you suddenly want to move out?" Gage's expression clouded with a frown. "Did we do or say something that upset you?"

"No, it's nothing like that. I feel like I'm in the way."

Gage scoffed. "Why would you think that?"

"Because you and Shauna don't have privacy when I'm around. I'm constantly underfoot." He rubbed his elbow. "I know you want to start a family, and you don't need me getting in the way of that."

"You're *not* in the way. You're our family."

Carter's posture drooped. "It doesn't really matter anyway, because I'm not going anywhere. All I can afford to rent is a room. Not even a whole place. Why move out of here only to be in someone else's way somewhere else?"

"Listen," Gage began, "we want you here. There's no reason for you to leave." He smiled. "Besides, if and when we're blessed with kids, we'd love to have Uncle Carter around to help."

"Thanks." Carter ran his finger along the edge of the workbench.

"Shauna said you went to Derek McGowan's place for a party tonight."

Carter rested his elbow on the workbench and his chin on his palm. "That's right. It was a housewarming party. He bought a place out in Matthews."

"I remember his dad." Gage snickered. "I've got the speeding tickets in my old Camaro to prove it."

Carter laughed. "He pulled me over a few times and a bunch of my friends too. I think he thought he was teaching us a lesson, but we just learned where he liked to sit and run radar so we could avoid those roads."

"How was the housewarming?"

"Fun." Carter grinned as a vision of Darcy's beautiful face filled his mind's eye.

Gage quirked an eyebrow. "Is that right?"

"It was nice to hang out with friends." Carter walked over to the front end of the Road Runner. He stared down at the engine, looking for a way to change the subject.

Gage joined him at the car. "What do you need to get started on this engine?"

"The time and the budget."

"Maybe I could help you," Gage offered before suggesting where they would begin.

While his brother-in-law talked on about the car, Carter once again thought of Darcy. He would keep his promise and ask her out. He just hoped he could be enough for her.

CHAPTER 9

On Friday evening Darcy kicked off her heels and dropped her laptop bag, purse, and medications from the pharmacy on the bench in her foyer. The week seemed to have moved at a snail's pace as she'd dealt with issue after issue at work.

Not only had she struggled to get the newsletter designed and distributed, but also her coworker had left for maternity leave the week before. Darcy wound up handling constant media calls after news had been leaked about their CEO's upcoming retirement. Although she was delighted for her coworker, who had welcomed a beautiful baby girl, she was relieved to have finally made it to Friday.

She'd stopped at the pharmacy on her way home to get another ninety-day supply of the medications that would help keep her kidney transplant healthy. She dreaded going to the pharmacy since it brought back memories of the day she'd lost Jace. If only she hadn't asked him to pick up her prescriptions for her, he'd still be here. And maybe they would be planning to welcome a baby girl or boy of their own. That familiar pang of wanting a family radiated in her chest.

Closing her eyes, Darcy stuffed those feelings down deep and focused on the present. She looked forward to making herself a frozen pizza and putting her feet up after the horrendous week she'd endured.

Darcy padded into the kitchen and yawned. Pulling her phone from the pocket of her slacks, she glanced down at the screen and once again found it blank. Disappointment bloomed in her. All week she'd hoped for a call or text from Carter, but she hadn't heard a peep. She'd thought they'd bonded at Derek's housewarming party, but she was starting to regret pouring out her soul about her yearning to find her biological mother.

She was certain he was attracted to her since he'd almost kissed her. A shiver raced up her spine at the memory of how close he'd been, how she'd felt his breath on her lips. If only Derek hadn't ruined that moment!

Then she reminded herself that Carter had asked if he could text her, and for the thousandth time this week, she wondered why he hadn't. Perhaps he'd had as crazy a week as she had.

With another yawn, Darcy yanked open the freezer door and searched for a pizza. She selected pepperoni and placed the box on the counter before preheating the oven. Just as she leaned down to collect her round pizza pan from the oven drawer, her phone rang.

Darcy popped up and grabbed her phone, hoping to see Carter's name on her screen. When she saw her dad's face instead, curiosity besieged her.

"Hi, Dad," she said as she answered.

"What are you up to?"

"Just got home." She leaned back against the counter. "I was getting a frozen pizza ready for the oven. How about you?"

"I'm sorry this is last-minute, but there's a car show in Mint Hill tonight. I didn't think I could go, but then your mom reminded me that she has plans with her book club. And you told me to let you know if I was planning to go to any car shows, so . . . wanna join me?"

Darcy bit her lower lip as Haven's advice about Carter from last weekend echoed in her mind:

You ask him out. He probably won't expect it, and I bet he'll love it. You only live once.

When she imagined asking Carter to meet her at the car show, her exhaustion evaporated and confidence surged through her. She squared her shoulders. "Yeah, Dad. I'd love to. And I'm going to invite a friend, if that's okay."

"Absolutely, Darcy. The more the merrier." He shared the details of when and where they would meet.

"I can't wait." Darcy disconnected the call. Her hands shook as she pulled up her last text message exchange with Carter, which had been the day her car had broken down.

"Here goes nothing," she whispered as she typed out a text.

DARCY: Hi. Do you have plans tonight?

She held her breath, hoping to see those wonderful conversation bubbles. After a few moments, they appeared, and her nerves fluttered to life.

CARTER: Don't think so. What'd you have in mind?
DARCY: There's a car show in Mint Hill. If you're not too busy watching reality TV, would you like to meet me there?
CARTER: Hmm. Let me check the TV listings. Oh, wow. They're all repeats tonight, even the podiatrist show. So, yeah, I'd love to.

Darcy danced around the kitchen for a minute, then pulled herself together and shared the details with him.

CARTER: See you soon. ☺

Darcy set her phone on the counter before shoving the pizza into the freezer, turning off the oven, and racing upstairs to change her clothes.

* * *

"WHAT'S THAT SMILE FOR?"

Carter glanced across the shop to where Gage watched him with interest. Smoky sat nearby, happily taking a bath on a box containing quarts of oil.

"Nothing." He tried to mask his excitement as he pocketed his phone, but it was impossible. Darcy had texted him and asked him out!

He had planned to see if he could take her out tomorrow, but she had beat him to the punch. Not only could he not wipe the silly grin off his face, but he thought for sure the adrenaline surging through him would cause him to float away. "I need to get going."

Gage held up a finger. "Hold on. You had the same look on your face Saturday night when you got home." He came to stand next to Carter. "Did you meet someone?"

Carter hesitated. He wasn't ready to tell anyone about Darcy.

"You can trust me." Gage's expression was earnest. "I won't say anything to Shauna if that's what you're worried about. I know she's always nagging you about getting back into the dating scene, and as soon as she finds out you're seeing someone, she'll hound you about a wedding date."

"It's not about her nagging. Honest. I just don't want to get Shauna's hopes up if it's not going to lead to something serious."

"Why are you convinced it won't work out?" Gage wore a serious expression that Carter rarely witnessed.

Carter sat on his nearby stool and pressed his lips together. "Because I have nothing to offer her. I have no house. I'm still crawling out of debt . . . What woman would want to get tangled up in my mess?"

"You're wrong." Gage tapped his shoulder. "You have plenty to offer, and the debt isn't permanent."

"The thing is, she has money. Her parents have money. When she finds out who I really am, she'll see that she can do so much better."

"No, she'll understand what you've been through and realize that your good health is a gift." Gage smiled. "That's the thing about love, man. It changes you. When you find it, your life will be transformed forever. Don't be afraid to let yourself experience it. It happens when you least expect it too. Shauna and I were acquaintances all throughout school, and then one day our junior year of high school, we sat at the same lunch table. Out of nowhere, I saw her in a new light. I thought she'd never even go out with me, but look at us now."

Carter swallowed. He couldn't imagine Darcy planning a life with him, but he also couldn't deny that his feelings for her were surprisingly strong. "I really need to get going," he said, setting his tools in his toolbox.

"Are you sure you're not just using money as an excuse? What are you really afraid of, Carter? Getting hurt again? Getting sick again?"

Carter swallowed, and his thoughts wandered to the last meal he'd shared with Gabby nearly four years ago. While he had believed they were just enjoying a date, Gabby had waited until their meals had been served to tell him she wanted to end their relationship. His illness was too much for her to handle, she had said. And she hadn't been pleased when he'd decided it was best for him to work in the office for Ernie and Glenda rather than make more money with her father's race team. She had made it clear he wasn't enough for her, and instead of standing by him as he faced his illness, she ended things.

Looking back now, he could see the fractures that were forming in their relationship long before she broke up with him. Their arguments had become more frequent, they had stopped speaking as often, and they had started living separate lives. Carter could also blame his permanent bad mood for pushing Gabby away, but if she had truly loved him, wouldn't she have been his support during his kidney failure and dialysis?

Carter examined his own heart. Was the real issue his fear of getting sick again and becoming a burden to Darcy? Or was he afraid of her rejection?

Carter shook his head, shoving those issues away.

"Is she the woman with the Lexus?"

Craning his neck over his shoulder, Carter met his brother-in-law's curious gaze. "How'd you know?"

Gage shrugged. "Just a feeling. You mentioned she had money, and that was a nice car."

Carter pushed the toolbox drawer closed. "Her name is Darcy, and I'm meeting her at a car show in Mint Hill."

"She's into cars and willing to go to car shows?" Gage pointed at him. "You need to propose to her right now."

"You sound like Shauna," Carter said with a laugh. "I'll see you later." He started toward the door.

"Have fun!"

Carter smiled. "I plan to."

* * *

A SHORT TIME LATER, DARCY TAPPED HER FOOT ON THE PAVEMENT. SHE sat in a portable camping chair beside her father at a strip mall in Mint Hall, scanning the parking lot full of classic cars and auto enthusiasts. Nearby, her father discussed the details of the impressive engine in his 1958 Dodge pickup truck with friends who were gathered around him.

She glanced down at her phone for what felt like the dozenth time in the last thirty minutes, hoping she'd missed a text or call from Carter. She inhaled deeply through her nose and tried to convince herself to calm down.

Carter said he'd come. He'll be here.

When her phone buzzed, Darcy jumped with a start, sending her phone crashing to the ground.

"You okay over there?" Dad asked with a chuckle.

"Uh-huh." She retrieved her phone, and her heart gave a kick when she found Carter's name on her screen. She clicked on the message.

CARTER: I'm here. Searching for your dad's amazing truck.

Darcy jumped up and examined the sea of people browsing the cars, and when she spotted him in the crowd, she couldn't stop her smile. She jammed her phone in her back pocket and started toward him.

Wearing khaki shorts and a plain black shirt that hugged his wide chest and muscular biceps, Carter waved and picked up his pace. Light-brown stubble lined his jaw again—the jaw that looked as though it had been molded from fine granite. He was just as handsome without the stubble, but the five o'clock shadow gave him a rugged look that stole her breath.

"Darcy!" He jogged toward her. "Sorry I wasn't here sooner. I was still at the shop when you texted, and I had to run home and shower."

She tried not to stare at him. "It's no problem. I'm just glad you're here." She reached out her hand, and without any hesitation, he threaded his fingers with hers. "Come meet my dad."

She led him through the knot of people, and when they came to her father's Dodge, Carter blew out a breath.

"Wow," he mumbled.

She grinned up at him. "He's used to that reaction."

"It's stunning."

Dad joined them by the truck. "Thank you."

"Dad, this is Carter."

"I've heard a lot about you," Dad said, and Darcy thought she might pass out from the embarrassment.

He released Darcy's hand to shake her dad's. "Nice to meet you, sir. Ah, Mr.—I mean—*Dr.* Larsen." As Carter stumbled over his words, a pink tinge rose on his cheeks.

Dad grinned. "Call me Ross." He patted Carter's shoulder. "Thank you for rescuing my Darcy when her car broke down."

"Happy to help." Carter smiled at Darcy, and her stomach flip-flopped. He pointed at Dad's truck. "She's a beauty." He took a step toward the front end. "What do you have in it?"

"A 1995 twelve-valve Cummins that came from a Dodge Ram 2500."

Affection billowed through Darcy while she watched Dad and Carter discuss the truck. As she took in their comradery, she imagined Carter accompanying her to her parents' house on Sunday afternoons, sitting in her parents' dining room on holidays, and visiting her parents' beach house with her.

Could Carter fit into her family? Would he want to?

A surge of warmth washed through her at the thought.

Dad beamed at the truck. "It was a labor of love."

"I can't imagine how long it took you to restore this." Carter touched the grill.

"Carter has a project car too," Darcy said. "Do you have a photo of your Road Runner?"

"I do, but it's been off the road for a few years." Carter looked sheepish as he pulled his phone from his pocket and began scrolling through photos.

Darcy leaned closer to him and peeked at his phone screen. She pulled in his familiar scent—teakwood, soap, and something else that was uniquely him. Then she tried to shake off the flutter in her belly.

He stopped at a photo, and a wistful expression overtook his handsome face. He angled the phone toward Darcy. "This was when the Road Runner was actually running."

Her mouth dropped open as she studied the picture of a stunning orange car parked on the side of the road. With the car stood a teenage Carter and an elderly man. Young Carter was gorgeous, with a shaggy haircut, worn-out jeans, and a faded concert t-shirt. Although his angular jaw didn't seem quite as pronounced, those dark-brown eyes were just as mesmerizing as they were now. He slouched against the car and grinned while giving a thumbs-up.

"How old were you in this photo?" she asked.

He shrugged. "Seventeen or eighteen. We were probably going to a car show that day. We went to a lot of them together."

She pointed to the elderly man in the photo. He was slightly shorter than Carter but shared the same muscular build and bright smile. "Is that your grandfather?"

"Yeah." He held the phone out to Dad, who put on his reading glasses. "This car was my grandfather's pride and joy. I promised to take care of it for him."

"I told you orange was the best color for those cars," she said.

The softness in Carter's eyes sent a tremor through her. "You're right. It is the best color, and you definitely know your cars."

Dad's salt-and-pepper eyebrows lifted. "That is one beautiful vehicle. Is it a 1970?"

"It is." Carter's smile diminished a little. "But I need to get the engine rebuilt. I've spoken to Zac out at Quality Auto Machine in Monroe."

"They do good work." Dad slipped his glasses into his pocket.

"Right. We send quite a few customers there," he said, putting away his phone. "I've had to put the project on the back burner. You know how life gets in the way sometimes."

Dad nodded. "I sure do. What does it have in it?"

"A four-forty."

Darcy rested her hands on her hips while Carter and her father discussed the engine in more detail. She smiled, enjoying how much Carter and Dad had in common. Once again, she imagined bringing Carter to her parents' house for suppers and barbecues. Maybe he would want to spend time with her as much as she wanted to spend time with him.

"Oh, there's Sam Malloy," Dad said, gesturing to a man standing by a deep purple Nova one row down. "Haven't seen him in ages. We'll catch up later, you two." He met Darcy's gaze and winked.

Darcy blanched, hoping Carter hadn't seen the wink. "So," she began, turning toward him, "did you want to walk around and look at the cars together?"

"I'll follow you."

She fell into step beside him, and they stopped to look at several well-kept cars along the line—a few Mustangs as well as a couple of Camaros and Firebirds—all beautifully restored and painted.

"Check out this Mustang," she cooed, pointing to a vintage muscle car painted candy-apple red. "It's gorgeous."

He nodded toward a robin's egg–blue Ford. "I like the Galaxie too. Someone did a nice job with that one."

The mid-May evening air was warm but comfortable, and having Carter at her side felt right.

"Check out that Volkswagen." Carter pointed to a classic white Beetle painted like Herbie in *The Love Bug*.

"That's cool."

He bent at his waist to peer inside. "Nice restoration work."

She studied his profile and longed to read his mind. Did he feel the same way about her, or was she imagining it? He had quickly responded to her text and seemed eager to join her tonight. When he turned and met her gaze, she realized she'd been staring and felt her face flush.

"You okay?"

"Yeah, of course."

They continued through the parking lot together, pointing out the cars they liked the best.

Carter turned toward her when they reached the last row of cars. "Your dad is great."

"He is, isn't he?" Happiness shimmered through her as she smiled at Carter. She gently jabbed his arm with her elbow. "It's obvious he likes you too."

The crowd was beginning to disperse, and the sound of revving engines indicated that the car show was coming to a close. But Darcy wasn't ready to say good night to Carter just yet. "Have you had supper?"

He shook his head. "I grabbed a pack of crackers on my way out the door." He nodded toward the far end of the parking lot. "Think it would be okay if we hop in my truck and go find something to eat?"

"Sure. Let's just say goodbye to my dad."

His smile sent a quiver through her. "Perfect."

CHAPTER 10

CARTER AND DARCY MADE THEIR WAY PAST THE LINE OF CLASSIC CARS toward her father's Dodge truck. Darcy had her phone tucked into the pocket of her light-blue jean shorts. A pink t-shirt and white sandals completed her outfit. Her blonde hair fell past her shoulders, and Carter wondered if he'd ever seen such beautiful hair on a woman.

As they came to the last row of cars, Ross stood by his truck smiling and nodding with another older man sharing a story. Ross spotted them and waved them over. "Terry, this is my daughter, Darcy, and her friend Carter."

Carter shook his hand as Darcy said hello.

"He works as a mechanic out in Flowering Grove," Ross continued.

Terry looked impressed. "No kidding. So you're a car fanatic too, huh?"

"Absolutely," Carter agreed.

Ross pulled a set of keys from his pocket. "Want to take her for a spin before I leave?" He jammed his thumb toward his truck. Then he tossed the keys to Carter.

Carter stared at the keys in his hand. Then he divided a look between Darcy and Ross, hoping for their silent approval.

"Let's go for a ride," Darcy said, looking eager.

"I promise I'll take good care of it." Carter jingled the keys.

Ross grinned. "Enjoy."

"Thanks, Dad. We'll be back soon." She beamed as she steered Carter toward the truck.

Carter held the passenger door open for Darcy, then hopped into the driver's seat. He ran his fingers over the pristine dashboard with reverence and suddenly recalled sitting in the driver's seat of the Road Runner with his grandfather beside him. "Grandpa would have loved this truck," he said. "It's incredible."

"My mom used to call it Dad's mistress."

Carter chuckled as he started the engine and carefully navigated out of the parking lot to the main road. He accelerated and shook his head. "Rides like a dream."

Leaning over she thumped his shoulder. "I knew you'd love it."

He laughed as he looked over at her, silently marveling at how beautiful she was. How had he managed to attract her attention? He didn't deserve a woman as lovely and funny as Darcy.

The skin between her eyes pinched. "Why are you looking at me like that?"

He slowed to a stop at a red light. "You know, I had been planning to see if you were free tomorrow night."

"Really?" Those gorgeous green eyes narrowed with fake disbelief. "Is that true, or are you trying to make me feel better for being the one to text you first after *you* said you'd text *me*?" She pointed to herself for emphasis.

"It's true. I was going to text you today and ask you to go out with me tomorrow." He held up three fingers. "Scout's honor." Then he lifted his eyebrows. "Are you free tomorrow?"

"I'll have to check the television lineup to make sure there aren't any reality shows premiering. You got me hooked on them, you know." Darcy pulled her phone from her pocket and unlocked it.

A bark of laughter escaped his mouth. He loved their easy banter. He couldn't remember a time when he'd felt so comfortable with a woman. His conversations were never this light or easy with Gabrielle.

Then Darcy's eyes danced with mischief. "Guess what? I'm free tomorrow."

"Thank goodness." He blew out a breath and pretended to wipe sweat off his forehead. "I was afraid there was a new episode of *I Married My Brother-in-Law's Sister's Podiatrist*."

She laughed. "That's what DVR is for." Then she held up her hand. "Or we could always watch it together."

"I like that idea too."

She smiled as she settled back in the seat. "So you said your grandpa would have loved this truck. Tell me more about your grandfather."

"What do you want to know?" He peeked over at her and she smiled.

"What was he like?"

"Well, he was soft-spoken—the opposite of my nana, who never ran out of things to say."

Darcy laughed. "They say opposites attract, right?"

"That's what I hear." He rested his left elbow on the door and steered with his right hand. "He always insisted that Shauna and I do our best in school, and he'd stay up late to help us with our homework if we needed him."

He stopped at a red light and turned on the right blinker. "Grandpa never hesitated to help a neighbor. I remember one time he fixed a leaky roof for the widow who lived up the street but then refused payment from her. Of course, he didn't turn down the loaves of banana bread she brought him."

"Banana bread. Yum!"

"I agree." He rubbed the scruff on his chin. "I'm named after him too."

"His name was Carter?"

"No, Anthony. That's my middle name."

"Carter Anthony Donovan." Darcy tilted her head. "I like that. I guess your mom was close to him if she gave you his name."

He nodded. "Yup. I don't think Shauna and I ever met my dad's parents."

"Did they live far away?"

Carter shook his head. "Supposedly they lived in Albemarle, but they didn't approve of my mom."

"Why not?"

"They were young when they got married. My mom was barely seventeen and my dad was eighteen when they got pregnant with Shauna." He waved the story off, not wanting to talk about his dad. "Anyway, I wish my grandfather could drive this truck. He'd be just as impressed as I am."

He motored around the block and then headed back toward the parking lot where the car show was petering out. After parking the truck in the same spot as Ross had earlier, Carter hopped out of the truck and met Darcy at the front end near Ross and Terry.

"So what'd you think?" Ross asked with a grin.

Carter blew out a puff of air. "What a great restoration! I love your attention to detail. It rides like a new vehicle." He held the keys out to Ross. "Thanks for the opportunity to drive it around."

"Anytime." Ross patted Carter's shoulder. "Where are you two headed now?"

"We're going for a bite to eat," Darcy said.

"You should go to Mike's Diner." Ross glanced at Terry, who nodded his approval. "They've got great food."

Carter shook Ross's hand. "Sounds good. Great meeting you."

"You too." Ross gave Darcy a kiss on the cheek. "See you soon, sweetheart."

"I'll call you and Mom tomorrow. Promise."

They said their goodbyes to Ross and Terry, then ambled toward Carter's Suburban.

* * *

CARTER SAT ACROSS FROM DARCY IN A BOOTH AND PEERED DOWN AT THE menu in Mike's Diner. The delicious scents of burgers and fries washed over him, and country music played on a nearby jukebox.

He snuck a peek at Darcy while she perused the menu. How easy it was to talk and laugh with her.

"What are you going to have?" she asked.

Carter scanned the menu once again. "The burgers smell amazing."

"I agree." Darcy grinned and closed her menu. "I want a bacon cheeseburger and fries."

Carter closed his menu. "I'll have the same."

Just then their server arrived with their drinks, and they shared their orders with her before she gathered up their menus and drifted off to another table.

Carter twirled a straw in his glass of Coke. "So I think it's your turn to tell me a few more things about you. Did you grow up in Charlotte?"

"I grew up in Marvin. It's near Waxhaw."

"I've heard of it." He tried to keep his face blank, but he was familiar with the area. The neighborhoods were known for ginormous houses tucked inside gated communities.

"My parents' house is near where their orthodontist practice was." She shifted in her seat. "Well, it's still there, but they sold it and retired about ten years ago."

"You've told me you like John Hughes movies, cooking shows, buying antiques in Flowering Grove, and hanging out in your dad's garage. What else is there to know about Darcy Larsen?"

She tapped her manicured finger on her chin. "Hmm. Well, I used to scrapbook when I was younger."

"Scrapbook?"

"Yeah." A sheepish expression flickered over her pretty face, making her look even more adorable. "Me and my friends would get together and have scrapbooking parties. We'd share supplies and design pages. I have scrapbooks that I've made for my dad with photos from car shows, and there's one all dedicated to our family trips to the beach."

She took a sip from her glass. "I've made others for our special family trips to Europe and the Caribbean. My mom says she loves them, and she pulls them out every once in a while to take a trip down memory lane. I loved taking the pictures, sorting them, and putting them together with little sticker designs." She shrugged. "I don't have time for it now." She twirled her finger in a lock of her hair, seeming engrossed in thought. Then her green eyes met his again. "Silly, right?"

"No, not at all." He imagined her sitting at a table working in her scrapbooks, and he smiled. "That's a great way to preserve those precious memories."

She nodded and took another drink.

"From what I saw at Derek's party, he and Haven seem to get along really well."

"They do. They met at a party in college and started dating right away, and they've been together ever since. I think it's been maybe eight years now." She studied the tabletop, looking lost in a memory. "It seems like only yesterday we were at that party. We were such clichés, actually. Haven saw Derek, and I saw . . ." Her voice trailed off, and a strange expression traveled across her face—maybe sadness or even regret. Then she visibly shook it off. "Now that Derek has a house, I think he's going to propose to Haven."

Carter's eyes snapped to hers. "Really?"

"Yeah. I've always thought they'd wind up together, but Derek was one of those guys who has a plan, you know?" She counted off on her fingers. "He wanted to be settled in a good, stable job, making a certain amount of money before buying a house. Then the ring, the wedding, the family, and the rest."

"Huh. Good for him then."

"What about you?"

The server appeared and set their food in front of them before leaving again, saving Carter from having to answer her. Hearing her talk about Derek and how well he was doing just hammered home how far behind he was.

"These look really good." Darcy smothered her fries in a lake of ketchup before handing the bottle to him. "So are you a plan kind of guy like Derek?"

Carter squeezed ketchup onto his plate. He had no choice but to answer now. "Not really. I like to keep my options open. Sometimes things happen when you least expect them, and they change the entire course of your life."

Something resembling understanding rippled across her face. "That is so true. I used to have a plan, but not anymore. I can't even figure out what to do about finding my birth mom."

"Have you reached out to that organization you told me about?"

"No." Her mouth formed a thin line. "You think I'm chicken, right?"

"I would never pretend to know how you feel, and I definitely don't think you're a chicken."

Darcy wiped her fingers on a napkin while continuing to frown. "You've just seen how warm my father is, and my mother is the same way. What if I tell them what I'm doing, and it breaks their hearts? I would never be able to live with myself if I hurt them deeply."

"If your parents are truly loving and supportive, then I believe they'll understand your need to know where you came from. They'll also understand that you'll never stop loving them even if you find your mom and cultivate a relationship with her. In fact, they may even want to meet her so they can thank her for giving them the chance to adopt you."

"Thank you." When she wiped her eyes with a napkin, his gut twisted.

"I'm so sorry," he said. "I didn't mean to upset you."

Darcy sniffed and shook her head. "You didn't upset me. You're giving me the courage to take the plunge." She smiled. "Thank you, Carter. I'm glad I shared this with you."

"I am too." He was grateful to see her feeling better about the situation. "How about we share a piece of turtle cheesecake for dessert?"

"Yes, please."

Carter ordered the dessert, and soon the server brought it over.

"How's Smoky?" Darcy forked a bite into her mouth.

Carter shook his head, almost certain he had whiplash from her subject change. "Smoky? The shop cat?"

"Yes, the shop cat. How is he?"

He studied her. "He's fine. Why?"

"I needed to lighten the mood."

"Oh." He forked a bite of cake. "Would you believe that he's a stray who adopted us, but he's pickier about food than any human I've ever met?"

"Really?" Her grin was wide.

"Yes, really. He doesn't like certain brands of food. If we try to feed it to him, he turns his nose up and struts away."

Darcy laughed.

They continued to discuss light subjects until the cake was gone. After Carter paid the bill, they walked out to the parking lot. The evening air was warm and smelled like honeysuckle, and the stars above them seemed to sparkle in the sky only for them. Carter wished the night would last forever.

When they reached his truck, he unlocked it and then wrenched open the passenger door for her.

"Thank you," she said before hopping up into the seat.

Carter jogged around the front end and jumped into the driver's seat before turning over the engine. "I'm glad I got to spend time with you tonight."

"Me too." She patted her abdomen. "Dinner and dessert were amazing."

They drove to the lot, where only a few cars remained. He parked next to her Lexus and then met her by her driver's side door.

"Are you still free tomorrow?" he asked.

"Absolutely." Closing the distance between them, Darcy wrapped her arms around his waist and rested her head on his sternum.

Carter froze in place. For a moment he thought he'd imagined the gesture, but it was as real as the feel of her arms entwined around him. He held her close, soaking in her warmth and rubbing her back. He rested his chin on her soft hair, inhaled her floral scent, and closed his eyes.

Darcy shifted, and he lifted his head. She looked up at him, and his eyes focused on her pink lips. For a moment, he imagined brushing his mouth against hers and drinking in her taste. The thought made his lips burn with desire.

She smiled. "Drive safely."

"You too," he whispered.

She released him and unlocked her car with her key fob. "I'll text you my address so you can pick me up tomorrow." She climbed into her driver's seat and started the engine.

Carter returned to his truck and followed her car out of the parking lot. As he relaxed into the seat, he wondered if he was floating on a cloud. He was falling for Darcy—fast.

But would the details of his financial situation bring everything to a quick end?

* * *

WHEN DARCY ARRIVED HOME, SHE BLEW OUT A HAPPY SIGH AS SHE STEPPED into her foyer and dropped her keys and purse on the bench. She spun in a circle, recalling how it had felt to be held in Carter's sinewy arms, her body pressed against his.

She hadn't planned to launch herself at him, but she'd been so overwhelmed by their conversation at supper that she felt the need to touch him. She felt safe and protected in his embrace with her head resting on his hard, muscular chest and his heartbeat sounding in her ear.

Being with Carter felt natural, a feeling she hadn't experienced since . . .

A vision of Jace's handsome face overtook her mind, stopping her dead in her tracks. Her feet became cemented to the floor, and her shoulders slumped.

Unlocking her phone, she scrolled to the last selfie she and Jace had taken together. They sat on the townhouse deck and smiled, the sunset lighting the perfect backdrop. Her eyes filled with tears as she took in Jace's handsome face, his dark hair, bright-blue eyes, and that smile that always sent a fluttery feeling through her.

"I miss you, Jace," she whispered. "I'm so sorry. It's all my fault that you're gone."

Guilt threatened to drown her. How could she find joy in being held by Carter when Jace was gone because of her? It was her fault that he was turning into the pharmacy parking lot when his car was broadsided.

Thoughts of the past would always cause her pain, but it was time to start living in the now and looking toward the future. Finding the courage to look for her biological mother would be a big step toward that future. She crossed the room and dropped onto the sofa. Her eyes focused on her laptop sitting on the coffee table. She grasped the piece of paper from Dr. Reyes and stared at it.

Then Carter's encouraging words from their conversation earlier in the evening echoed in her mind:

If your parents are truly loving and supportive, then I believe they'll understand your need to know where you came from.

Darcy opened her laptop. She wrung her hands before typing the web address into the search bar. With her heart hammering, she perused the Lost and Found site and created an account. She clicked a few boxes and added in all of the information she knew—her birth date, the name of the hospital where she was born, and the only information she knew about her biological mother, which was that she was sixteen or seventeen years old when she gave birth to Darcy.

With her heart trying to beat out of her chest, she submitted the information and then withered on the sofa.

She tried in vain to stop her emotions from spilling down her cheeks, and she longed for someone to talk to, someone to share this momentous occasion with. After years of considering it, she had officially started the search for her birth mother. She craved Carter's empathetic ear and warm hug to help soothe her soul.

Darcy sniffed as she reached for her phone and opened her texting app. Then she froze. How could she possibly put into words the feelings swirling in her gut like a cyclone? It wasn't possible. She needed time to process what she had done. Instead, she texted:

DARCY: Thanks for coming to the car show. I had a lot of fun.

Relief coiled through her when text bubbles appeared within moments.

CARTER: Thanks for inviting me.
DARCY: I'm glad you were free.
CARTER: You were lucky since I'm such a busy guy. ☺

Darcy laughed.

CARTER: What time should I pick you up tomorrow?

They agreed on a time, and she sent him her address.

DARCY: I don't live far from Derek in Matthews. I can't wait.
CARTER: Me too. Good night, Darcy.
DARCY: Good night.

After hitting Send, she closed her laptop and started up the stairs toward her bedroom. After such a long and exciting week, a good night's sleep would calm her busy mind.

CHAPTER 11

THE FOLLOWING AFTERNOON, CARTER SEARCHED THE SHELVES IN THE two-car garage attached to the house. He rooted around coolers, Christmas decorations, cleaning supplies, and a shop vacuum, grumbling all the while.

The large picnic basket that his mother and grandmother would pack when they took Shauna and Carter to the park was nowhere in sight, and he was running out of time. He growled in exasperation. It was nearly time to pick up Darcy.

"It has to be here somewhere," he muttered.

The door leading to the laundry room opened, and his sister appeared in the doorway. "What are you doing out here?"

"Have you seen Mom's picnic basket?"

Shauna's brow creased. "Why? Do you need it?"

"I'm taking a friend on a picnic."

"Carter!" She clasped her hands together. "Do you have a date?"

He purposely ignored the question. "If we don't have Mom's basket, do we have anything else we can use for a picnic?"

"Yes, but first you have to answer me."

Here we go.

"Who is she? Your date?"

"Right now, she's just someone I'm getting to know. We're sort of seeing each other."

"Seeing each other, huh? Interesting . . . And who is this woman you're 'seeing'?" She grinned and made air quotes with her fingers.

"Someone I met recently."

Shauna nodded slowly, as if putting pieces together in her mind. "Gage said you went to a car show in Mint Hill last night. Were you actually at a car show, or were you on a date?"

Carter lowered himself down onto a stool. He was impressed that his brother-in-law had kept his promise, but now he would be forced to tell Shauna about Darcy. "Both are true," he finally said.

"What do you mean?"

"I went to a car show in Mint Hill to meet someone. She invited me."

"Huh." Shauna descended the steps into the garage and leaned back on the quarter panel of her husband's project car, a hunter-green 1966 Ford Mustang fastback. "I thought it was strange that Gage said you went to a car show, but he didn't ask me if I wanted to go too. Normally when there's a car show we all go together." She paused as if waiting for him to elaborate.

A few seconds ticked by between them, and her lips pressed down into a deep frown. "Carter," she began, "why are you reluctant to tell me about this woman? Have I done something to make you not trust me?"

Guilt stabbed long and hard. He knew his older sister wanted the best for him, and not sharing the truth about Darcy would break Shauna's heart. "It's not that I don't trust you. I know you want to see me in a happy, long-term relationship, but I also don't want to get your hopes up. That may not happen for me."

"Why would you think that?"

He scratched his cheek. "Her name is Darcy. I met her in the parking lot after my doctor's appointment."

"The one with the broken-down Lexus." Shauna's lips tipped up again. "You're dating *her*?" The joy on her face reminded him of a child on Christmas morning.

He shook his head. "I hate to burst your bubble, but she's not my girlfriend."

"But you went on a date with her last night, and you're taking her out today."

Carter rubbed the stubble on his chin. "Please don't make a big deal out of this. We're getting to know each other. Nothing is official, so don't send out any wedding invitations."

"Listen to me, okay?" Her expression became serious once again. "I know you've been through a lot, and I know Gabby hurt you when she broke up with you."

"Shauna, don't—"

"Please, Carter, let me finish."

He nodded, preparing himself for another one of her speeches.

"When you got sick, you shut everyone out. You stopped seeing your buddies. You stopped going to parties. You stopped living. And even after your transplant and your recovery, you still haven't gone back to a normal life."

He pursed his lips. "I live a normal life, Shauna. I go out with you and Gage all the time."

"But you don't see your friends anymore." Her eyes studied his. "When was the last time you talked to Mark, Jovan, or Todd?"

He shrugged. "I don't remember. We lost touch a long time ago."

"They've been your friends since kindergarten, Carter. They called you constantly when you were on dialysis, *and* they came to the hospital after the transplant."

Irritation rushed through him. He wasn't in the mood for her analysis of his life, even if it was all true. He had shut himself off when he was ill, but how could he relate to any of his friends now? They'd all gotten engaged and then married. His buddies had moved on without him.

He started searching the shelves again. "Do you know where the picnic basket is or not?" He felt a hand on his shoulder, and his neck tightened.

"Carter, if you care about Darcy, then you should go for it." Shauna patted his shoulder. When he didn't say anything, she beckoned him. "Come on. I'll get the basket for you."

He walked behind her into the house, and she gathered up the large picnic basket from the hall closet. She also handed him a blanket and disposable plates, napkins, and utensils.

"What are you going to eat?" she asked.

"I'll stop by the deli on my way to pick her up. Then I'm going to bring her back to the park here in Flowering Grove. I thought we could talk and maybe even sit on the swings."

Shauna's pretty face lit up. "That is so sweet. You should ask her to officially be your girlfriend while you swing. And then—"

"Shauna . . . ," he warned.

"All right, I'll stop." She gave his arm a playful punch. "Can I at least meet her? You can invite her to your birthday barbecue."

He didn't answer.

Her smile withered. "Why would introducing her to me and Gage be the worst idea in the world?"

"Shauna, I'm not embarrassed by you or Gage. You're my family." He set the basket on the kitchen counter. "I just don't know how to tell Darcy that I'm almost thirty years old and don't have my own place. She'll think I'm a loser, and I'll never see her again."

Shauna frowned. "No, she won't. She'll understand what you've been through."

"I don't want her pity." He picked up the basket. "Thanks for finding this for me, but I really have to go."

Shauna placed her hand on his bicep. "It's not pity. It's understanding. Besides, you'll be back on your feet in no time."

"I'm going to be late." He balanced the basket in one hand and pulled his truck keys from the hooks by the back door.

Once outside he hit the button on the key fob. Then he loaded the basket into the unlocked trunk. He turned to Shauna, who was standing in the open doorway. "See you later, sis." He hopped up into the driver's seat and started the engine before rolling down the driver's side window. Shauna still watched him with annoyance on her face. "I'll consider the birthday party suggestion," he said.

Her smile was back. "Thanks, Carter." She waved and went back inside.

Carter pulled his phone from his pocket and texted Darcy. Hi! I need to make a stop and then I'll be on my way.

DARCY: Awesome! What are our plans?
CARTER: It's a surprise.
DARCY: I love surprises. ❤

He grinned and steered out of the driveway. For now, he would forget about the past and his current problems. All he wanted to focus on was Darcy.

* * *

THE LOUD RUMBLING OF AN ENGINE DREW DARCY'S ATTENTION TO HER driveway. She opened the door just as Carter jogged up the front steps, looking gorgeous in shorts and a gray t-shirt. The mid-May air was warm, and the sun was bright in the cloudless blue sky.

He stopped at the top step, and his dark eyes scanned her townhouse. "Nice place." He pivoted and took in the surrounding neighborhood. "How long have you lived here?"

"A little over two years. My parents bought it for me."

Carter's eyes widened with surprise.

She jammed a thumb toward the foyer. "I just need to grab my purse. Would you like to come in?"

"Sure."

Carter stood by the front door while she gathered up her purse and her phone. She walked over to him as he rocked back on his heels and took in the family room and the kitchen.

An unreadable expression tinged his face before he smiled. "It's a beautiful home."

"Thanks." She hesitated, and her lips twisted.

He pointed toward the door. "We should get going."

"Right," she said, following him to the door.

* * *

CARTER HUMMED ALONG WITH THE BLAKE SHELTON SONG SERENADING him and Darcy through the truck speakers. She angled her body toward Carter's and studied his profile while he drove. She took in the scruff-lined jaw and those dark roast–colored eyes.

Her stomach tightened as she recalled the surprise on Carter's face when she mentioned that her parents had gifted her the townhouse. She couldn't shake the feeling that Carter thought she was entitled. She had to explain the situation with the house. But first she had to find the courage . . .

Carter began singing the words to the song, and Darcy joined in. Together they were just slightly off-key. She met his gaze, and they both started laughing.

"We sound awful," she said.

"Speak for yourself." He chuckled. "Do you like country music?"

"I do. I like all kinds of music. I guess it depends on my mood. Sometimes I listen to country in the car. I especially love country from the nineties and early aughts. You know, old Tim McGraw, Faith Hill, and Shania Twain."

"I love country from the nineties. Tracy Byrd is one of my favorites," he said. "Do you sing in the car too?"

"Yes, but I do my best singing in the shower."

He laughed again.

"When do you do your best singing, Carter?"

"Well, I can tell you about when I did my worst."

She angled her body toward him. "I'm listening."

"When I was in the seventh grade, I remember my voice dropping in the middle of a choir concert. I wanted to melt into the auditorium risers."

"Oh no." She covered her mouth with her hand in an attempt to stop her laughter.

"That was horrible. My buddies never let me forget about it." He hit a button on his radio and tuned in to an older country station.

When Tim McGraw's "Red Ragtop" started to play, Darcy sat up straight. "I love this song!" She began singing along with it, and Carter grinned.

When Carter steered his truck down Main Street in Flowering Grove, he darted a glance over to her. "How do you feel about picnics?"

"I love picnics, but I haven't been on one in a long time. My mom used to take me when I was little."

"Good answer."

"Whew." She wiped pretend sweat off her forehead. "I was worried I was in trouble for a second there."

He laughed again, and she enjoyed the deep sound. Talking and joking with Carter was so easy, so natural. Already it was like they'd known each other for a long time.

He steered the truck into a parking spot at Flowering Grove Park, then killed the engine. They met at the back of the SUV, where he unloaded a large picnic basket and a blanket.

"Would you like to pick out our picnic spot?" he asked.

"I'd be honored."

Darcy carried the blanket, and he toted the basket as they entered the park. The sweet scents of grass and flowers mixed with the delicious aroma of burgers cooking on a nearby grill. She looked out toward the swing sets and slides, where children played and a cluster of young women sat on benches and talked. She spotted a toddler with blonde pigtails walking hand in hand with a young woman, and she felt that familiar longing swelling in her chest. Maybe someday . . .

Dismissing the thought, she turned to where a pair of chipmunks scampered past and then disappeared into a cluster of bushes.

She chose a quiet spot away from the playground and spread out the blanket. Then they sat down beside each other, and Carter began unloading the basket.

"I hope you don't mind sandwiches," he said. "I picked up some rolls, lunch meat, cheese, potato salad, chips, bottles of water, and cookies for dessert."

"I do love a good sandwich." He'd even chosen provolone, her favorite kind of cheese.

He smiled and handed her a plate. They built the sandwiches and then began to enjoy their meal.

Darcy looked up at the bright-blue sky and then took another bite of her sandwich. When she turned toward Carter, she once again contemplated his reaction to her townhouse. She felt the urge to explain herself, to amend the impression he might be forming about her. "I need to tell you something."

"Okay."

Her heart thudded as she tried to gather the words to tell him about Jace.

Carter tilted his head. "Take your time."

"My townhouse. I want to explain why my parents bought it for me."

He held his hand up. "You don't need to explain anything."

"I do actually. I told you the townhouse was a gift, but it was more than that." She took a deep breath. "The house was a wedding gift. I was engaged. I moved in first, and my fiancé was going to join me after the wedding."

He nodded slowly. "Oh."

Her hands trembled as she searched for the courage to tell him what happened. "My . . . my fiancé passed away about eighteen months ago. His name was Jace." A wave of remorse and grief for Jace engulfed her, and she tried to push past it.

Don't cry, Darcy. Keep it together.

Carter opened his mouth but closed it as concern seemed to overtake his expression. "I'm so sorry, Darcy." He rubbed her shoulder. "What happened to him?"

He took her hand in his, and the feel of his warm skin against hers encouraged her to continue. "He was on his way to the . . ." She hesitated. She wasn't ready to share about her kidney transplant. Not yet. "I was working late that day, and we had plans to meet at the townhouse for supper. He ran an errand for me—an errand I should have run for myself—but I was so distracted . . ."

She sniffed, and he gave her hand a gentle squeeze. "Jace had the green light to turn, and a man in a pickup truck wasn't paying attention and broadsided him." She swallowed as the details of that day filled her mind. "Jace's car rolled." She took a shaky breath. "His seatbelt failed, and he died on impact."

"Darcy, I'm so sorry that happened to him. And to you." He looped his arm around her shoulders and pulled her against him.

She closed her eyes for a moment and enjoyed the feeling of his warmth mixing with hers. "Thank you. It was difficult. I felt like

I was living in a bad dream or a fog for a long time. I leaned on my parents and Haven and Derek. They got me through it."

"I'm so glad you had them to take care of you."

She looked out toward the swings where children pumped their legs and floated up toward the sky. "After Jace died, I almost put the house up for sale, but it felt like I would be betraying him by moving. At the same time . . ." Her voice trailed off.

She found him watching her with a warm expression, and she felt itchy under his stare. But his sympathetic eyes calmed her. "It's difficult to explain why I stayed. When I'm there, I feel like he's still with me sometimes. But I know he's gone."

He nodded slowly, and embarrassment warmed her neck.

"That was a lot to unload on you, Carter. I'm sorry for doing that again."

"No, no." He rubbed her arm, and comfort rolled through her. "I'm sorry for your loss. I know what it's like to lose someone you love. They leave a hole in your heart that can't ever be filled."

She sniffed and gave a little laugh. "That's true." She turned toward the swings again. "Did you come here often when you were a kid?"

Carter nodded and looked out toward a group of adults. They laughed while they played a game of Frisbee on the lush green field of grass. "My mom and grandmother used to bring me and my sister here on weekends." He pointed at the playground. "Shauna and I would play on those swings for hours while my mom and nana sat on the bench and talked."

"What do you remember about your mom?"

He set his plate down, bent his knee, and rested his arms on it. "She passed away twenty years ago. I was about ten, and Shauna was fourteen." He scratched the back of his neck. "She was beautiful. Shauna looks like her—tall and slender. She had dark-brown hair, but her eyes were hazel. If I concentrate, I can still hear her voice and her laugh. She always read to me at night. She loved books and encouraged us to read, even though I wanted to be in the garage with Grandpa."

"May I ask what happened to her?" Her question was soft.

"She hadn't been feeling well." He studied his half-eaten roast beef sandwich as if the scene were reflected on the bread. "It was a Friday night. Nana kept trying to get her to go to the doctor, but she was worried about bills. My dad rarely paid support. She'd taken him to court and had his checks garnished, but I'd heard her telling my grandparents that he didn't make much money. What she got was hardly enough to cover food, which was why we moved in with my grandparents after he left."

A muscle ticked in his jaw. "I remember nights when I'd hear her crying, talking about how hard it was without him and how she still loved him." He shook his head. "Anyway, she was really sick, and my grandparents wound up calling an ambulance for her. Grandpa stayed with us while Nana rode to the hospital with her. That was the last time I saw her." He leaned back on his hands and stared out toward the Frisbee game.

Her lungs pinched with grief for him. "What was wrong, Carter?"

"Her appendix had burst, and it was too late."

"I'm so sorry," she whispered.

Carter gave her a sad smile. "Thank you. It really destroyed us. I cried myself to sleep every night for a long time. She definitely left a hole in my heart—in all of our hearts. Shauna changed. It was like she grew up overnight. She suddenly became my mom. She would irritate me at times, but even though I was only ten, I understood why she felt like it was her job to take care of me. I often heard her crying at night too, and it would tear me up inside."

Darcy rubbed his arm, hoping to comfort him. Her heart went out to him. They were kindred spirits, both understanding what it was like to lose someone they loved. But while she'd lost Jace, he had lost three people he loved—his mother *and* his grandparents. And then there was his dad, who had walked out on him and his family . . .

"My grandparents tried to be strong for us, but I would catch my nana crying in the kitchen or my grandpa wiping away tears in the garage when they thought they were alone," he continued. "They lost their daughter and suddenly had two kids to take care of without extra financial support. I know they didn't mind doing it. But they shouldn't have had to."

He frowned. "Shauna is convinced that we need to find our dad, but I can't forgive him for abandoning us when I can still remember how Mom cried for him and struggled without him. Then he didn't even come to her funeral. After she died, I kept asking my grandparents if Dad would come back now that Mom was gone, and they would frown and change the subject. I used to believe he'd show up on my birthday to surprise me, but of course, he never did. I never understood what I did to make him go away, but when I got older, I began to see it wasn't my fault. He was just a coward. He didn't want to be a father and a husband."

He paused and then added, "How can I forget how he went on and lived a new life without giving us a second thought?"

A hush blanketed them while they stared down at their plates.

"Thank you for trusting me with your story," she said softly.

He met her gaze and nodded.

"You're so strong, Carter."

He looked unconvinced. "Why would you say that?"

"You haven't let what happened turn you into an angry person."

He lifted an eyebrow. "That's not entirely true. I'm angry with my father."

"But you're still kind, friendly, and fun." She pointed her bottle of water at him. "And you're a really good singer."

He laughed.

They were silent again for a moment, and he rubbed his ear. "I'm surprised I shared so much with you. It's not easy for me."

"I feel the same way. I'm surprised I told you about Jace."

When they shared a smile, Darcy felt closer than ever to Carter. It was as if their relationship had become something deeper in the span of a conversation. Excitement zipped through her.

Darcy took a long drink from her bottle of water and turned toward him. "I owe you a big thank-you."

"For what?" His light-brown eyebrows lifted.

"For inspiring me to take the plunge and look for my biological mother." She pulled at the label on the bottle. "I registered on that website last night after I got home from the car show."

He bumped his shoulder against hers. "Good for you."

"Thanks." She tore the label. "I uploaded all of the information I know—my birth date, where I was born, how old my parents were when they adopted me . . . That kind of thing."

"And now they'll look for her?"

"Well, the people who run it will try to find her. If they do, and if she wants to be found, then they'll give me her information." Adrenaline flooded her at the thought of finally meeting her birth mother. She looked down at her lap.

"Keep me posted, okay?"

"I will." Darcy peered toward the swings, finding that the children had left. "The swings are empty," she said, giving Carter a mischievous smile.

He stood and held out his hand to her. "Shall we?"

CHAPTER 12

Carter sat on a swing beside Darcy and pumped his legs. He felt a strange sense of relief after sharing his feelings about his parents. He was stunned by how compassionate Darcy was when he talked about his mother. She was so different from Gabby, who had never seemed interested in hearing about Carter's past at all. He was aware that Gabby just wanted to parade Carter around her friends—but only after she'd convinced him to work for her father and make more money. Darcy, on the other hand, had opened her heart to him, sharing her heartbreak of losing her fiancé. He was honored that she had revealed so much to him.

They continued to swing, hooting and giggling as they moved back and forth. He couldn't recall the last time he'd been on a playground.

Darcy looked up toward the sky as she swung back and forth. She was so lovely. And after their revealing conversations today, he was drawn to her more than ever. Could a real relationship between them work? What kind of future could he offer her?

He dragged his sneakers along the ground and brought the swing to a stop as the gravity of his situation pulled him back down to earth. She had called him brave, but he sure didn't feel like he was.

"Penny for your thoughts?" Darcy's gentle voice broke through his reflections.

Carter clutched the chains. As he stared into her beautiful green eyes, he wondered if he was selling her short. What if he did tell her everything? His history with kidney disease, the year he spent on dialysis, the story of his transplant, and his current financial situation. What if she was okay with all of it?

And what if she's not?

"I was just thinking about how ice cream would be a great treat." He pointed toward the ice cream truck parked at the other side of the park. "What do you think?"

"Let's go, Donovan. Now," she teased.

Carter grinned and shook his head. He knew one thing for sure: He would be blessed to call Darcy Larsen his girlfriend.

* * *

CARTER WALKED DARCY TO HER FRONT DOOR LATER THAT EVENING. SHE looked up at the stars in the sky and wished the evening wouldn't come to an end after such a wonderful day.

After enjoying the swings and an ice cream from the truck, they had loaded up the blanket and basket in his SUV and walked around Main Street. They perused the local stores and talked about their childhoods. Later, they ate a snack at Heather's Books 'N' Treats before returning to the park to sit and watch the sunset.

It had been such a fun day, but it was late. Darcy longed to invite Carter to sit on her deck and talk with her until the sun came up, but she assumed he wanted to get home.

"Thank you for today," she told him.

"I'm glad you had fun." He touched her cheek. "I promise I'll text you this week."

She shook a finger at him. "You'd better, and I expect an invitation to your birthday party too."

"I'll see what I can do about that."

He held his hand out to her, but she pulled him close and hugged him instead. With her arms around his neck, she rested her head against his chest, listened to the rhythmic cadence of his heartbeat, and drew in his familiar scent.

Carter rested his hands on her hips and his cheek on the top of her head. His warmth surrounded her, seeping into her skin. She closed her eyes and basked in the feel of his arms around her.

When she released him from the hug, his dark eyes focused on hers with an intensity that sent her pulse galloping. He swallowed and licked his lips. "I like you, Darcy."

"I like you too."

"I mean, I *really* like you." He paused. "I'd like to see where this goes."

She nodded. "I would too." She touched his hand. "Can we take it slow?"

He blew out a puff of air, and his expression relaxed. "That would be perfect."

Happiness billowed through her.

"I'll text you." His handsome face lit with a smile.

She unlocked her front door and pushed it open. "Drive safe."

"I will," he promised. "Good night, Darcy."

"Good night." She stood in the doorway while he jogged down her steps and climbed into his SUV.

* * *

CARTER'S THOUGHTS SPUN LIKE A CYCLONE AS HE DROVE HOME. HE HAD relished every moment with Darcy today. He'd finally found the courage to tell her that he liked her, but he felt torn.

Darcy had a house, and her parents were comfortable—*very* comfortable—while Carter was crawling out of debt.

Still, when Darcy hugged him, he didn't want to let go. In fact, he wanted to tilt her chin up and kiss her until she was breathless.

Yet attraction could only go so far. He had nothing to contribute to her life except for debt. The cost of his routine medications alone was enough of a hardship for him. It would be unfair of him to even consider dragging her into the mess of his life. How could he expect someone else to take that on?

He was starting to care for her. And that scared him.

Carter rested his elbow on the door and steered with his other hand while he stared at the road ahead. His thoughts wandered to her fiancé and the pain he'd witnessed in her eyes when she talked about him. Carter couldn't imagine the depth of her grief, and her fiancé hadn't even been gone for two years.

Everything felt so hard right now. Darcy, his recovery, his finances, his dad . . . He frowned, recalling how he'd opened up to Darcy about his father. He had to find a way to convince Shauna to not waste her time looking for Dad. The last thing he needed was his father returning to disrupt their lives.

Carter parked his truck in the driveway, climbed out, and gathered up the basket and blanket. He was still deep in thought as he hit the button to open the garage door and sauntered into the house. He hung his truck keys on a hook by the back door.

The sound of a movie echoed in the kitchen from the family room. He padded through the house, waving to his sister and brother-in-law on his way toward the hall closet, where Shauna had kept the basket and blanket.

When the television muted, Carter pressed his lips together.

"Sooooo, how'd it go?" Shauna asked with a grin.

Carter nodded. "Fine," he said, opening the closet door.

"Details, please!" his sister demanded as he slipped the basket and blanket onto the top shelf.

He frowned, not in the mood for an interrogation. "We had fun. We had a picnic and walked around the park. We wandered around town, and then I took her home."

"And?"

"That's it." He spun to face his sister. "Shauna, I want you to stop looking for Dad."

His sister blinked. "Why?"

"Because we don't need him in our lives."

"He needs to answer for why he hurt us." She swallowed. "I want to know why we didn't mean more to him. We're his children."

"It doesn't matter. There's nothing he can say to make up for the past, so let's leave the past where it belongs—behind us."

Her eyes narrowed, and she shook her head. "No, that's not good enough."

"It has to be, Shauna. I don't want to see him, and I hope you'll respect my feelings." When she didn't respond, he added, "Please, Shauna. I'm begging you not to do this. Please don't hurt me this way."

Shauna swallowed, but then a manufactured smile overtook her lips. "Did you ask Darcy to be your girlfriend?"

"Why are you deflecting?"

"I'm not deflecting, Carter," she said. "I genuinely want to know. Darcy sounds perfect for you."

"For once in your life, stop smothering me and treat me like the adult I am. I need you to listen to me. Don't look for Dad, all right?"

She nodded, but deep down, he knew she wasn't going to listen to him.

Turning, he headed up the stairs to his room over the garage.

* * *

"NOW, DARCY," MOM BEGAN THE FOLLOWING AFTERNOON, "YOUR DAD MENtioned you have a new friend. His name's Carter, right?"

Taking a sip of sweet tea, Darcy peered out over the deck toward her parents' pool while she considered how much to tell her mother. *Thanks, Dad.*

Mom gave her a knowing smile. "Let me guess. You think your dad already clued me in on everything, and I'm just fishing for info."

"You said it, not me." Darcy felt her lips twitch.

Mom laughed. "Now tell me, Darcy. Your dad said he really liked him. He said he was very friendly and respectful. Apparently he looked completely flummoxed when your dad handed him the keys to the Dodge."

"Yeah, I think Dad likes him."

"You know he doesn't give the keys to his truck to just anybody."

"That's true." Darcy set her glass on the table and smiled. "He took me on a picnic yesterday."

"A picnic? How thoughtful."

"Yeah, it was, and we had a lot of fun." Darcy filled her in on their afternoon.

"Do you like him?" Mom asked.

"Yes." *A lot.* She paused. "I guess you could say we're seeing each other."

Before falling asleep last night, Darcy recalled how they'd poured their hearts out to each other, held hands, sat close together, laughed on the swings . . . And that hug . . .

Then she had thought about Jace, and the familiar guilt set in.

Darcy pulled her phone from her pocket and checked it again. Carter still hadn't texted her.

Slow down, Darcy! You saw him less than twenty-four hours ago!

"So he's your boyfriend, huh? Good for you!"

"No, Mom," Darcy insisted. "He's not my boyfriend. We're talking. Getting to know each other."

"You need to invite him over for supper so I can meet him."

"I will," she promised. "Eventually. I don't want to rush anything." She picked up one of her mom's homemade lemon bars and took a bite. "Yum. You still make the best lemon bars."

"Thank you, but don't try to change the subject. I want to hear more about him."

"He's sweet and easy to talk to."

Mom placed her elbow on the table and her chin on her palm as if they were two girlfriends sharing secrets. "Handsome?"

"Very." She moved her hand over her glass. "But he's so much more than that. I feel this connection with him that I can't explain."

Mom's blue eyes glimmered. "I'm so glad to hear that, Darcy. I know you've struggled since you lost Jace, and I'm thrilled that you've met someone. That is the best way for you to heal." She patted her daughter's hand. "You'll never forget Jace, but it's perfectly right for you to fall in love again. He would've wanted you to meet someone else."

Darcy sniffed as a vision of Jace filled her mind.

"Oh no." Mom scooted her chair closer and rested her arm around Darcy's shoulders. "Sweetheart, I'm so sorry."

Darcy dabbed her eyes with a paper napkin. "It's okay."

"No, it's not. I didn't mean to make you sad. I just wanted you to know it's okay to fall in love again."

Darcy shook her head. "I'm not ready to fall in love again."

"But that's when it happens. I met your dad after my long-term boyfriend broke my heart. I had convinced myself to just concentrate on school and give up on love. And then—boom! Your dad and I bumped into each other at a party, and the rest is history." Mom rubbed Darcy's back. "You deserve to be loved, honey. Don't forget that."

Darcy sniffed and nodded, but she didn't believe the words. She couldn't imagine ever forgiving herself for Jace's death. She rested her head on her mom's shoulder. "Tell me about book club. You always hear the best gossip there."

"Oh yes. Did I tell you that Doris's son was dating that woman who has eighteen cats?"

Darcy nodded. "You did."

"Well, turns out Doris's son is allergic. How is *that* relationship going to work out?" she asked with a laugh.

As Mom shared the latest news about her book club friends, Darcy considered bringing up the Lost and Found website. *Not today,* she decided. She would save that news until she was able to tell her mother something, and who even knew if that would happen?

CHAPTER 13

THURSDAY MORNING, CARTER LOOKED UP FROM THE 2013 HONDA Accord he was working on just as Glenda approached the doorway. Smoky scampered in and disappeared behind the row of toolboxes before she closed the door behind her.

Carter swiped his hand over his sweaty forehead and once again wished they had air-conditioning in the shop. The late-May air was humid and heavy.

"Mrs. Deese is here and says she hears a noise in her car again," Glenda announced.

Carter shook his head and focused on the Honda. "I'm in the middle of changing these spark plugs."

"Can't Dad take a look at it?" Gage came around from the side of a green Ford pickup truck. He'd been changing the CV joints.

"He ran to the pharmacy to pick up his prescription." Glenda held up her arms. "Look, I know she's a lot, but I need one of you to help her."

Gage pointed at Carter. "It's your turn."

"Please, no," Carter groused. "The last time she came in, she insisted her wiper blades were off-center by one-sixteenth of an inch. I spent thirty minutes trying to convince her they were just fine."

"It's because she has a crush on you, Carter." Gage waggled his eyebrows. "She finds any excuse to bring her car in just so she can lay eyes on you."

"She's at least seventy-five, Gage," Carter retorted.

Glenda moved to stand in the middle of the shop. "Look, I need one of you to help her, okay?" She turned toward Carter. "Please."

Pouting, Carter wiped his hands on a red shop rag and followed Glenda out to the storefront. Mrs. Deese stood in front of the counter wearing what looked to be her Sunday best. She was a petite woman with gray hair cut in a bob and thick glasses in purple cat-shaped frames sitting on her little nose, magnifying her golden-brown eyes. Her bright-red lipstick seemed to clash with her purple hat and pink dress. She had been a widow for as long as Carter could remember. The older woman looked up approvingly at him, and he shifted his weight on his feet.

"Good morning, Mrs. Deese. How can I help you?" he asked.

"Why, Carter, aren't you a sight for sore eyes?"

He swallowed back his frown. Maybe she *did* have a crush on him. *Oh boy.* "Glenda mentioned your car is making a noise."

"That's true, honey. Would you please take a look at it?"

He forced his reluctant lips into a smile. "Of course, ma'am."

"Thank you, Carter." Glenda patted him on the back before he followed Mrs. Deese out to her blue 2018 Ford Focus.

She handed him the keys, and he started the car. Then he popped the hood and listened to the engine for several moments.

"Ma'am," he finally said, "I don't hear anything unusual."

Mrs. Deese pointed to the driver's side. "Why don't we take it for a ride then?"

He didn't have time for this. His eyes scanned the line of cars waiting for his and Gage's attention. The shop had been so busy all week that he'd come in early every day and worked late every night.

He'd been so exhausted by work that he'd shared only a few texts each day with Darcy, even though she'd been a constant thought in his mind since he'd left her house Saturday night. He couldn't wait for the weekend when he could finally see her again.

"Yes, ma'am," he agreed before closing the hood and climbing into the driver's seat.

Carter steered out onto Main Street and drove toward the Barbecue Pit. He kept his eyes on the road while concentrating on the engine, which sounded completely normal. "I don't hear anything unusual, Mrs. Deese."

"It's a knocking sound." She pointed toward the hood. "Just listen, honey. I know it will do it again."

For the next five minutes Carter drove around town, hearing only perfectly normal engine and road noises.

"Ma'am, I'm sorry, but I don't hear a knocking noise. It sounds just fine to me." He steered into the parking lot of the shop. "Why don't you bring it back when it starts acting like there's something wrong."

Mrs. Deese shook her head. "I'm telling you, sweetheart, something's wrong with my car. I'll leave it with you and call my sister to pick me up. You can take another look at it when you have time." She patted Carter's thigh.

Carter's eyebrows shot up at the intimate touch.

She pulled her flip phone out of her humongous purse and started dialing.

Carter sucked in air, pulling all of his patience up from his toes. He was taught to respect his elders no matter what, but he was struggling to keep his frustration in check.

"Hi, Mildred?" Mrs. Deese spoke loudly into her phone. "Can you pick me up at Barton Automotive? I'm having car trouble again."

When he spotted Ernie crossing the parking lot, he jumped out of the car. "Ernie!" He trotted after him. "Hey, Ernie!"

Gage's father pivoted to face him. "Carter. Good morning."

"Mrs. Deese is back. She insists her car is making a noise, but I don't hear anything. Can you help? Gage and I are loaded up. I need to get four tune-ups done today."

Ernie nodded. "Sure thing, son."

"I can help!"

Carter and Ernie turned just as Old Man Dwyer strode across the parking lot. At the age of eighty-seven, he was known for his fedora and dungarees, along with his bushy white handlebar mustache. Wilford was a retired mechanic who enjoyed spending his days chatting with Ernie and giving advice, even though he hadn't worked in a mechanic's shop for at least twenty years. More often than not, he just got in the way.

Ernie muttered something under his breath while Carter bit back a laugh.

"Good morning, Wilford!" Ernie called. "So good to see you."

"I figured you missed me. Last week I went to Raleigh to see my sister, but I'm back and ready to help." He pointed to Mrs. Deese's car. "Would you like me to look at Rowena's car for you?"

"Absolutely. Thank you, Mr. Dwyer." Carter grinned at Ernie and then hotfooted it to the shop—back to the spark plugs in the Honda.

"Hey, Carter," Gage called as he walked over. "How did it go with Mrs. Deese?"

Carter rolled his eyes. "You know how it went. There's nothing wrong with her car, but she's insisting on leaving it here. Old Man Dwyer showed up, and he says he'll take a look at it."

Gage snorted, then returned to the Ford pickup in his stall.

Carter pulled out his phone and glanced at it. So far he hadn't officially planned a date with Darcy yet, though he couldn't wait to see her again. It felt good to get out and have some fun. And he couldn't think of anyone he'd rather be with more than her.

* * *

LATER THAT AFTERNOON HAVEN JOINED DARCY IN HER OFFICE AT THE bank. "I'm so surprised you got out early today and actually felt like driving to Uptown to see me."

"Thank goodness for an early dismissal day. Plus I didn't have any meetings, so it worked out perfectly," Haven said. "Now, tell me everything about your dates with Carter."

Darcy couldn't stop her smile. "We went to a car show Friday night, and then he took me on a picnic at Flowering Grove Park on Saturday."

"A picnic?" Haven gushed. "That's so romantic."

"It was fun." She smiled at the memory of the hug they'd shared, and a shudder rippled through her.

Haven crossed her legs. "I talked to Derek, and he really likes Carter. He said he's always been such a great guy. I'm glad you two are hitting it off."

"I am too." Darcy twirled a pen in her hand and considered their short text messages all week.

"Have you made plans with him for the weekend yet?"

Darcy shook her head. "Not yet. We've texted back and forth, but that's it." She rested her elbows on her desk. "Are you and Derek still painting rooms in his house?"

Haven brightened. "We finished the bathrooms last weekend. He's talking about changing the flooring in the laundry room, but I don't think it needs replacing yet."

Darcy nodded while Haven talked on about Derek's plans for his house. She was sure they would be engaged soon, and Haven would begin making wedding plans. Darcy smiled, imagining her beautiful friend as a stunning bride walking down the aisle.

When Darcy's phone suddenly pinged with a text message, she jumped and lifted it from her desk. Excitement sizzled through her when she found Carter's name on the screen. She opened the message and found a photo of the Flowering Grove Movie Theater marquee. It read: "Totally '80s Series—*Pretty in Pink*."

Then came Carter's message: Any chance you're free tomorrow night?

Darcy grinned.

Haven leaned forward on Darcy's desk. "Is it him? What's he saying?"

"He invited me to a movie tomorrow night." She angled the phone toward Haven so she could see the photo of the marquee. "My favorite movie is playing in Flowering Grove."

"Tell him yes."

Darcy held her hand up. "Calm down. I'm going to." She poised her thumbs over the phone: Let me check my planner.

CARTER: 😆

DARCY: Looks like I'm free.

CARTER: Great. I'll check the times and let you know when I'll pick you up.

DARCY: Can't wait.

CARTER: Me either. Talk to you soon.

"Has he kissed you?"

Darcy met her best friend's curious gaze. "No, but we've hugged twice now."

Haven's expression became mischievous. "Are *you* going to kiss *him*?"

Darcy shook her head. "We agreed to take things slow. Remember, this isn't easy for me."

"I'm sorry, Darce." Haven frowned. "That was really thoughtless of me. I'm just glad to see you smiling again."

Darcy nodded. "I am too."

* * *

"DO YOU LIKE BARBECUE?" CARTER ASKED FROM THE DRIVER'S SEAT OF HIS Suburban Friday night.

Darcy smiled over at him while they drove toward Flowering Grove. Country music played through his speakers, and he drummed his fingers on the steering wheel along with the beat. "Sure do," she said.

"Have you been to the Barbecue Pit?"

"Yes, I have, and I like it." She pushed a lock of her hair behind her ear.

"Did you know there's a Wall of Fame in the restaurant with photos of celebrities who've eaten there?"

"I noticed it, but I didn't pay much attention to it."

"It's mostly photos of NASCAR drivers and other athletes, but of course there's an autographed photo of the band Kirwan since the owners' daughter married one of the lead singers."

"I'll have to check that out."

"I thought we'd get something to eat there and then go to the movie. Sound good?"

"Absolutely," she said. His bright smile sent her heart beating in a staccato rhythm.

"Have you heard anything from the website?"

She shook her head. "Nothing yet." She moved her fingers down her jean shorts. "I also haven't told my parents about it. I figure there's nothing to tell until I find her—if I ever do. So why get them upset?"

"I agree." He took her hand in his. "And if and when it happens, I'll be here for you."

Appreciation for this wonderful man expanded in her chest. "Thank you, Carter."

* * *

"YOU HAVEN'T BEEN VERY TALKATIVE ON TEXT THIS WEEK. HOW'S WORK?" Darcy asked Carter at the Barbecue Pit. They had already given the server their order and received their drinks.

He rubbed his clean-shaven chin. "*Crazy* busy. Our parking lot is full of cars that need attention."

"That's good, right?" She moved her straw around in her Diet Coke.

"Yes, but it's stressful." He shook his head. "And we had our usuals stop by too."

"Usuals?"

"There's an older woman named Mrs. Deese who comes by at least twice a month insisting there's something wrong with her car. But there's never anything wrong." He explained how he'd once spent thirty minutes trying to fix her windshield wipers, but they weren't broken.

Darcy laughed. "That's crazy. What was it this time?"

"She told me her engine was making a noise, but it wasn't. She ended up leaving her car with us. Thankfully Old Man Dwyer showed up and said he'd help. He doesn't work at our shop, but he likes to hang around. I think he just wants something to do since his wife passed away a few years ago."

She frowned. "I'm sorry to hear that."

"Yeah, I feel bad for him too." Carter unwrapped a straw and dropped it into his glass of Coke. "Mr. Dwyer worked as a mechanic for a long time, but cars have really changed in the past twenty years. Anyway, he comes by and talks to Ernie all day, and sometimes he likes to help. When he offered to look at Mrs. Deese's car, I was relieved."

"Did he fix her car?"

Carter shook his head. "He convinced her there was nothing wrong with it, but I'm sure she'll be back next week with another complaint."

"It sounds like you have a lot of interesting characters who come by your shop."

"That's true." Carter took a sip of his Coke and then grinned. "One time Mrs. Deese insisted that her blinker was too slow, and she wanted me to speed it up."

Darcy studied him. "Is that an issue that a car can have?"

"Not exactly." He rolled his eyes. "Gage says she has a crush on me since she often asks for my opinion."

"Well, I can't blame her there." The words rushed out of Darcy's mouth, and her cheeks began to flush.

Carter's eyes widened. "Is that right?"

Just then the server arrived with their food—and Darcy had never been more grateful to be interrupted by a barbecue sandwich.

CHAPTER 14

After they finished their meals, Carter paid the check. Then he and Darcy headed out to the sidewalk. Crowds of people moved up and down the block, where vendors had set up booths to sell different items during the Flowering Grove Memorial Weekend Festival. The air was warm and smelled like popcorn mixed with funnel cakes and nachos.

"Carter! Look at those," Darcy exclaimed. She grabbed his hand and pulled him over to a vendor selling custom keychains.

He relished how natural it seemed for Darcy to hold his hand, and he loved the feeling of her warm skin against his.

"There are keychains for all of the local cities," she pointed out. Then she dropped his hand.

Never mind.

"Here's Matthews, Mint Hill, Monroe . . . Oh! There's Flowering Grove."

She was adorable as she fluttered around the displays, pointing out the ones she liked.

"Carter?"

He turned just as Jovan Rodriguez, one of his best friends since childhood, approached him. His sister had just brought up his friends, and now he'd run into one of them. "Jovan." He extended a hand to him. "How are you?"

"I'm great." Jovan's dark eyes seemed to study his. "But how about you? I haven't seen you since the transplant." He gestured toward Carter. "You look fantastic."

Carter turned toward Darcy, relieved she was still on the other side of the booth examining a display of keychains. He had to keep this conversation short or he'd risk Darcy overhearing. "Thanks, Jovan."

"What have you been up to?"

Carter snuck another peek over toward Darcy, who was talking to the vendor by the cash register. "Work, mostly. Gage and I are staying busy at the shop."

Jovan's dark eyebrows careened toward his hairline. "You're back to work full-time now?"

"Yeah. Have been for a while."

"I'm so happy to hear that. Me, Mark, and Todd worried about you when you just seemed to drop off the face of the earth, but we understood you were going through a tough time. I'm glad life is back to normal for you. How's Shauna?"

"Staying busy working for Dr. Moore over on Sunset."

"That's good, and she didn't have any complications with donating?"

"Nope." Carter shook his head. "How's Julia?" He recalled receiving their wedding invitation, but he'd been too ill to attend.

Jovan grinned. "We're expecting our first in a few months."

"Congratulations, man. That's amazing."

"Thanks. I'm still working for my dad's company, so if you need an electrician, you know who to call."

Carter chuckled. "I'll remember that." Out of the corner of his eye, he saw Darcy approaching him. "Jovan, this is Darcy."

"Hi," Darcy said.

Jovan gave Carter an approving smile, then turned his attention back to Darcy. "Nice to meet you." He faced Carter again. "We should all get together sometime. Mark and Todd would love to see you. It's been too long, buddy." He shook Carter's hand.

"Tell them hello for me."

As Jovan walked away, Carter rested his arm on Darcy's shoulder. "We'd better get going so we're not late for the movie." Then he steered her toward the sidewalk.

She looked up at him. "How do you know Jovan?"

"We've been friends since kindergarten."

"You should invite him and your other friends to your birthday barbecue. Then they can tell me stories about your youth." She laughed and bumped her shoulder against his side. "I bet you were wild and crazy, huh?"

Carter forced a smile. If he invited them to his barbecue, then Darcy for sure would hear about his transplant—and he wasn't quite ready to share that yet.

She stopped walking, her smile fading. "Is something wrong?"

"No, no." He nodded toward the theater. "We don't want to miss the previews."

"Okay, but just wait one second." She handed him a small bag. "I got you something."

"A present?"

She nodded, and her expression was sheepish. "Open it."

Carter pulled out a wooden keychain with the words *Flowering Grove* engraved on it.

"It's kind of silly, but this way you won't forget where we hung out the first time—in Flowering Grove at a car show."

Warmth surged in his chest. He couldn't help but pull her into a hug. "I love it."

She gave him a tight squeeze before releasing him. "I'm glad it means that much to you."

He pulled his keys from his pocket and slipped the keychain on the ring with his truck, shop, and house keys. "Let's go get our movie tickets."

They made their way to the Flowering Grove cinema, and Carter purchased two tickets to the movie.

When they stepped inside, Darcy pointed toward the concession stand. "Do you like popcorn?"

"Who doesn't?"

She pulled her wallet from her purse and started toward the counter.

"Whoa," he said. "I can get our snacks."

"Nope, I'm getting the popcorn."

"Fine. But I'll get the drinks."

"Deal," she agreed.

After purchasing a tub of popcorn and two sodas, they strode into the theater and found seats in the center.

"I'm so excited to see this movie on a big screen," she told him. "My mom always loved '80s movies, and we used to watch them when I was in high school. I haven't seen it in at least five years."

"When I saw it on the marquee yesterday, I thought of you."

A few more people joined them in the theater, and soon the lights dimmed. When the trailers for upcoming movies began rolling on the screen, Carter settled in the seat and stretched his arm across the back of Darcy's chair.

She smiled up at him and held up the bucket of popcorn. He slipped his hand into the bucket at the same time as she did, and their fingers touched. He waited for her to pull her hand away, but she didn't. Instead, he placed the bucket on the seat next to him, and they held hands for the rest of the movie.

Carter tried to concentrate on the story, but he was too aware of how well Darcy's hand fit in his. He adored the sound of her laughter as she enjoyed the comedy in the movie, and he noticed her wipe her eyes during a few scenes.

When closing credits filled the screen, she released his hand and turned toward him. "That was so much fun. Thank you, Carter."

"You're welcome."

They exited the theater, depositing their bucket and cups in the trash on their way out the door. The street vendors had closed for the night, and the stars above them were bright in the sky. Only a few couples milled about on Main Street. He threaded his fingers with hers.

"When exactly is your birthday?" she asked as they walked toward the parking lot.

"Next Saturday."

"Am I officially invited to your birthday barbecue?"

Teasing her, he lifted his eyebrows. "Well . . ." A smile played on his lips. "Yes, of course you'll be invited, Darcy. I'll find out what Shauna has in mind and text you details."

"Good. And let me know what I can bring."

"Just yourself," he told her as they approached his truck. He hit the button on the key fob and opened the passenger door for her. Then he helped her climb inside.

As he jogged around to the driver's side, he wished the evening could last forever.

* * *

DARCY AND CARTER STOOD BY HER FRONT DOOR, AND SHE LOOKED UP AT him with a smile. "I had a really great time tonight. Thank you for planning a night you knew I would enjoy."

"You're welcome." He trailed a finger down her cheek with a featherlight touch, making her blood sizzle in her veins. His dark-brown eyes became intense, and she shivered as they focused on her lips.

This is it! He's finally going to kiss me!

The air froze in her lungs as he leaned down, and she closed her eyes, awaiting the feel of his mouth against hers.

Instead, his lips grazed her cheek before he pulled her into his arms. Her eyes fluttered open, and she swallowed back her disappointment.

"I'll text you," he promised as he released her and took a step back. "Sleep well tonight."

"You too," she managed to say. Then she unlocked the door and stood in the doorway while he backed out of the driveway.

After setting her purse and keys on the bench, she jogged up the stairs to her bedroom and pulled out a framed photo of Jace and her. Nearly two years ago, her father had taken the photo on the beach. She took in his handsome face and their bright smiles. She closed her eyes and tried to recall the sound of his voice when he said her name, the taste of his lips, the feel of his warm embrace.

Her eyes moved to her left hand in the photograph, and the large diamond she had worn until six months after Jace passed away. Opening her jewelry box, she pulled out the ring and stared at it. After he died, she had offered the ring to his parents, but they insisted that she keep it. Her eyes filled with tears as she recalled their plans for a life together—living in the townhouse, starting a family, growing old . . .

"I'm sorry, Jace," she whispered to the empty room.

Darcy flopped back on her bed and stared up at the ceiling. Her mind replayed the wonderful time she'd had talking and laughing with Carter tonight—holding hands as they walked down the street and enjoyed the movie. If only he had kissed her.

Her mind spun. To feel remorse for moving on from Jace while hoping for a relationship with Carter left her conflicted and confused.

She pushed up from the bed and wandered into the bathroom to take a shower. She couldn't make heads or tails of her complicated feelings, but she knew one thing for sure: She was falling for Carter Donovan. She just hoped he felt the same way about her—and she had a strong inkling that he did.

* * *

THE FOLLOWING MORNING DARCY AWOKE TO THE SOUND OF HER PHONE ringing. She reached over and grabbed it off the nightstand and hit the speaker button.

"Hello?" Her voice sounded hoarse.

"Darcy," Mom sang through the phone.

Rubbing her eyes, Darcy sat up. "What's up?"

"Great news but terrible news. Our friends, the Pfeiffers, canceled. Remember how they were supposed to spend the Memorial Day weekend at the beach with us? Anyway, we'd love to see you since we're freed up. Come out and have some fun."

"Like . . . right now?" she asked.

"Yes, as soon as you can. Bring your new boyfriend, who isn't really your boyfriend, with you. Oh, and invite Haven and Derek too. We have plenty of room and plenty of food."

"Um . . . ," Darcy hedged. "I don't know."

"Why not? The weather is beautiful. Call Carter and tell him you're heading to Coral Cove for the remainder of the weekend. It's only Saturday. You can enjoy almost three days down here."

Darcy considered what could happen if she invited Carter to spend the weekend with her parents. Her mother might start talking about the kidney transplant, or she might talk too much about Jace. Either way, Darcy would wind up crying. She couldn't let that happen. "I'll invite Carter, but you need to make me a promise."

"Anything."

"Don't mention the kidney transplant. I haven't told him about it, and I'm not ready. Tell Dad too."

"Mum's the word, and I'll instruct your father not to say anything either. Now get your butts down here. The weather is too beautiful to waste."

"I'll call you soon with an update," she said before disconnecting. She opened her last chat with Haven and shot off a text message:

DARCY: Hey. Wanna go to the beach?

After a few moments, the chat bubbles appeared.

HAVEN: Right now?
DARCY: Yup, now.

Her phone rang with a call from Haven.

Darcy answered the call. "Is that a yes?" she said.

"Let me get this straight," Haven began. "You want me to pack and go to the beach *now*?"

Darcy leaned back against her headboard and folded her legs under her. "My mom just called and asked if you and Derek want to come. There's plenty of room."

"You should invite Carter."

Excitement shimmied through her at the idea. "My mom said that too, but I don't know . . ."

"Aren't there five bedrooms?"

"Yes. We'd each have our own room."

"And you had fun last night, right?"

"We had a blast." She summarized everything from dinner to the movie to the kiss on her cheek at the end of the night. She gnawed her lower lip. "I just don't know if it's too soon to invite him to the beach since we're not officially dating."

"Darcy, I know you wanna take things slow, but he might feel your hesitation. Maybe if you invite him, he'll see you're ready to date and ask if you want to make it official."

An image of kissing Carter on the beach filled her mind, and a sudden rush of desire pulsed through her body. "Okay. I'll invite him, but I told my mom not to talk about the kidney transplant. I'm not ready to tell him yet."

"Why not?"

Darcy cupped her hand to her forehead. "I'm just not. I already told him about Jace and don't want to overwhelm him. I'll explain everything else to him eventually. Would you please tell Derek not to talk about the kidney transplant?"

"I will. Now call Carter and then text me. In the meantime, I'll call Derek and tell him to get up and start packing for the beach. Bye." Haven disconnected the call.

Darcy's hands trembled as she hit the button to dial Carter's number. Why was she so nervous? Turning toward her nightstand, she cringed when she realized it was only eight thirty. She hoped he was awake.

"Darcy," Carter said through a yawn. "Hi."

She covered her face with her free hand. "Oh no. I woke you."

His chuckle rumbled through the phone. "It's okay. What's up?"

"Wanna go to the beach?"

Silence filled the phone line.

"Right now?"

"Yeah. My parents are at their beach house for the weekend, and they told me to invite friends down. I know it's last-minute, but Haven and Derek are coming too, and you can have your own room. We can come back on Monday. If you're not busy . . ." Her voice trailed off.

More silence filled the line, and she bit her lower lip as worry coursed through her. Was it too soon for them to do something like this? After all, they'd only known each other a few weeks.

Oh no . . .

"I'd love to," he finally said, sounding fully awake. "What do I need to bring?"

"Your swimsuit." She felt her cheeks heat thinking of him in his suit. "Oh, and other clothes, of course. Whatever you want to wear."

"What time should I pick you up?"

"Whenever you're ready to leave."

"Great," he said. "I'll pack and head your way. See you soon."

Darcy hung up and gave a little screech of happiness before texting Haven: Carter said yes! He's going to pack and head my way ☺

HAVEN: I talked to Derek and he said yes too. We'll meet you at your place soon.

Darcy danced out of bed and started packing.

CHAPTER 15

AN HOUR LATER DARCY DASHED OUT THE FRONT DOOR AND DOWN THE steps to where Carter stood in the driveway. He was already talking with Derek and Haven next to Haven's Honda CR-V.

Carter turned and grinned as she joined them. "There's the woman who woke me up this morning."

"She woke me up too." Haven laughed.

"And this one," Derek began, wrapping his arm around Haven's waist, "woke *me* up."

"I'm so sorry." Heat bloomed in Darcy's cheeks as she set her backpack and rolling suitcase down beside the CR-V.

Carter grinned at her. "You can wake me up early anytime, especially if you're inviting me to go to the beach with you."

Haven and Derek agreed.

Darcy met Haven's bright smile. "Are we ready to go?" she asked.

Carter pointed to his Suburban. "Wanna take my truck?"

"That reminds me," Darcy said. "I've been meaning to ask you something. Why do you always call your SUV a truck?"

"Well, it's a truck to me. It hauls all my stuff, but nothing gets wet in the back. Plus it will tow a trailer." Then his crooked grin appeared. "And, you know, big vehicles are more manly, so that's why they need to be called trucks."

Darcy laughed. "If you say so." She shrugged and handed him her key fob. "How about we take my car instead of your *truck* to save on gas? You can drive."

"Sure." Carter shrugged. "You know my Chevy is a gas hog."

"We'll drive Haven's car in case we decide to head home early," Derek said.

"All right," Haven exclaimed. "Let's go to the beach!"

Carter popped the trunk with the key fob, and he and Darcy set their bags in before he pushed it closed. They climbed in the car, and Carter adjusted the seat for more legroom.

"Do you know how to drive this thing?" Darcy teased as he hit the start button. "Or do you only know how to drive manly vehicles?" She couldn't stop her grin.

Carter's light-brown eyebrows rose as he met her gaze. "Boy, you wake me up early and then you pick on me, huh?" She spotted a flicker of humor in his eyes. "You're awfully full of yourself today."

She laughed and turned on the radio as he backed out of the driveway. "How about a country station?"

"Whatever you want to listen to is fine with me."

Darcy found a country satellite station and turned the volume up before settling back in the seat and taking in his handsome profile. "What exciting plans did I keep you from this weekend?"

"Hmm. Let's see." He tapped the stubble on his chin. "Sleeping in, doing some laundry, seeing if you wanted to hang out again, and sleeping in some more." He gave her a quick glance. "No matter what, I hoped to see you again." He held his hand out to her, and she took it. "Thank you for inviting me."

"I'm just grateful you could fit me in your schedule."

He laughed, and the sound warmed up her insides. This weekend at the beach would be one to remember.

* * *

NEARLY FOUR HOURS LATER, A GASP ESCAPED CARTER'S MOUTH AS HE nosed Darcy's Lexus into the driveway of a sprawling light-pink beachfront home. He blinked as he took in the two stories sitting on stilts. With its large windows and white shutters, the house was at least twice as big as Shauna's, he guessed, if not more so. He couldn't imagine how much a home like that cost, and he couldn't fathom ever being able to afford something so impressive.

"Endless Summer," he finally said, reading the sign on the side of the home. "What a great name for a beach house."

Darcy pushed the door open. "My mom loves it here. Well, they both do, and they couldn't wait to retire and have their endless summer. Come on inside."

Carter opened the trunk and slung her backpack and his duffel bag over his shoulders before lifting her small suitcase.

"I can take that," she insisted.

He shook his head. "You just lead the way."

Derek and Haven parked beside the Lexus, then climbed out of her CR-V. They gathered up their own luggage and met Carter and Darcy at the stairs to the front entrance.

The sky above them was clear, the sun was bright, and the air was humid. Seagulls flew by while calling to each other, and the sound of the waves pounding the shoreline echoed around Carter.

"You're not going to believe this place," Derek said as he and Carter started up the stairs behind the women.

Carter shook his head. "I'm already overwhelmed."

"Just wait until you see the inside, man." Derek grinned. "It's enormous."

Carter's posture sagged. What if he didn't fit in? He still remembered the feeling of not being at home in Gabby's world.

"Come on!" Darcy stood by the open door and bounced on the heels of her sandals.

Derek and Carter stepped into the foyer, and Carter's mouth dropped open as he took in a large family room that stretched all the way to a wall of sliding glass doors leading to a deck. The room had white walls and was decorated with light-blue accents. One wall featured a mural of a beach at sunset, complete with dunes, beach grass, and the sunset reflected on the rolling waves. A light-blue sectional sofa sat in the middle of the room alongside two matching recliners, all facing a huge flat-screen television attached to the far wall.

He walked over to a credenza sprinkled with family photos. Most included Darcy on the beach as a little girl, posing with her parents at different ages.

Darcy placed her hand on his bicep. "Leave the luggage here. I want to show you the deck."

He set the bags and her suitcase down, and she took his hand and yanked him out onto the sweeping deck. The two-story deck stretched out over the dunes toward a set of stairs leading down to the beach, where knots of people were out enjoying the perfect afternoon.

A group of young people played volleyball, while others bobbed in the water. Some lounged in chairs or on towels in the sand, and others walked along the shoreline. He spotted sailboats boasting colorful sails moving in the distance, along with a few Jet Skis. The light breeze brought with it the scent of salt air mixed with cocoa butter.

Darcy steered Carter to the far end of the deck, where her parents sat at a table drinking glasses of lemonade.

Her mother popped up from her chair and hurried over to meet them. "You made it!" She pulled Darcy in for a hug.

"Mom," Darcy began, "this is Carter."

Carter shook her hand. "It's so nice to meet you, Mrs.—oh, um—*Dr.* Larsen."

"Call me Josie." She gave him a once-over and then smiled at Darcy before turning her attention back to him. "We've heard *so* much about you."

Darcy frowned and rubbed her forehead. "Mom."

He laughed. He didn't think she could be any more charming than she already was. "Likewise. Thank you for inviting me. Your house is phenomenal."

"Thank you," Josie said.

Ross shook his hand next. "Welcome, Carter." Then he looked past Carter to Derek and Haven. "We're so happy to have you all here this weekend."

"Have you eaten lunch?" Josie asked. "We have plenty of lunch meat and rolls."

"Thanks, but we stopped to get something on the way," Darcy said.

"Well, you all get settled and then come back out here. Carter, Darcy will show you to your room." Josie waved them off. "Haven and Derek, you already know your way around. Make yourselves comfortable."

"Let me give you a tour." Darcy escorted them back into the house. "The kitchen is over there," she said, pointing to her left. "Beyond it is a utility room, laundry room, and my parents' suite." She pointed to her right. "The other bedrooms and the stairs are over this way. You and Derek can stay in the rooms upstairs, and Haven and I will be down here."

Carter picked up his luggage. "Lead the way."

They walked through the tremendous family room to the hallway, where Darcy pointed out two bathrooms and two bedrooms. Then they climbed a set of stairs, and Darcy motioned to the doorways. "There are two bedrooms up here with a bathroom between them."

Carter entered the first bedroom while Derek and Haven headed into the second one. After dropping his bag on the queen-size bed, he took in the room, silently noting that it was at least twice the size of his room at Shauna's house. It was decorated in a nautical theme with a life preserver and a painting of sailboats hanging on the wall, blue-and-white sheets and blankets, a shelf housing miniature boats, and a mirror decorated with anchors. The blue walls were adorned with a border peppered with starfish.

Carter pushed open the sliding glass door in his room and stepped out onto the deck. He leaned on the railing and looked down on the beach and the magnificent Atlantic Ocean. He drew in a deep breath and blew it out. He felt as if he were living a dream.

He didn't belong here. If Darcy and her parents knew his situation, surely they'd agree.

Darcy appeared beside him. "Mom said this view is what sold her on the house." She made a sweeping gesture. "She said she knew that with the house at this angle, she could see the sunrise *and* get an impressive glimpse of the sun setting in the west."

She turned and pointed behind her. "From here we can also see the bay side of Coral Cove. If we turn toward the bay, we can see the entire sunset stretched across the sky."

He studied Darcy's beautiful profile, taking in her high cheekbones, her gorgeous lips, and those green eyes. His palms itched with the desire to kiss her. He touched her shoulder. "This is really nice, Darcy. I'm so glad you invited me."

"I'm grateful you're still talking to me after I woke you up at eight thirty this morning."

He looped his arm around her waist and towed her to him. "I meant it when I said you could wake me up at any time."

The waves lapped against the shore as their gazes met. She rested her hands on his shoulders. Her eyes seemed to sparkle as her expression became serious.

His blood heated as he moved his hand over her cheek, and he thought he heard her breath hitch. The urge to kiss her nearly overcame him. "Darcy," he began, his voice sounding rough, "I wanted to—"

"Carter!" Derek bellowed from inside the house. "Are we hitting the beach or what?"

Darcy spun out of his arms and started toward the door. "That's a really good idea."

Carter bit back a groan. He should have just told her how he felt about her and kissed her, but the moment had been stolen by Derek—*again*!

He was determined to gather up his courage this weekend to tell her what she meant to him—and if she felt the same way, he would kiss her. But he had to find that perfect moment.

Darcy stood in the doorway and beckoned him. "Come on, Carter. We shouldn't waste this perfect beach day."

He joined her in the bedroom and unzipped his duffel. "You're right. I'll change into my suit."

"See you downstairs," she sang before disappearing through the door and closing it behind her.

He dug out his suit and a t-shirt, then hid his daily pill holders in a dresser drawer. He planned to keep the medications tucked away so he wouldn't have to explain why he took so many.

He changed into black swim trunks and a white t-shirt sporting a Chevrolet logo. As he jogged down the stairs, Darcy's and Haven's voices floated toward him from the kitchen.

He took in the pine cabinets, white-and-gray granite, matching white-and-gray backsplash, and stainless-steel appliances. A long oak table surrounded by six chairs sat in a nook, and through the sliding glass door, he spotted Darcy's parents still sitting on the deck.

Darcy and Haven were at the large island in the center of the room, filling a cooler. He couldn't keep his eyes off Darcy, clad in a modest, vintage-style black two-piece bathing suit under a sheer floral cover-up. Her blonde hair was styled in a long French braid that fell to the middle of her back. She turned toward him and smiled.

"Give me something to do," he said.

Haven pointed toward the doorway. "You could go tell my boyfriend to get moving. He was in such a hurry to go swimming, but now we're waiting on him." She wore a large sun hat that matched the pink lacy cover-up hanging loosely over her pink bikini.

Carter jammed his thumb toward the doorway. "I'll light a fire under him."

"Hey, no need for that," Derek announced before walking into the room in gray swim trunks and a tank top. He rubbed his hands together. "Are we ready?"

Darcy closed the top of the cooler. "Let me just grab some towels and a blanket."

"Is the umbrella still in the utility room?" Haven asked.

"Yup."

Derek crossed the kitchen. "I remember where it is."

While Darcy collected a blanket and towels, Derek grabbed the umbrella, and Carter carried the cooler as they stepped out onto the deck.

"Enjoy your time at the beach," Josie said.

Ross pointed to the large grill near the table. "I'll grill up some steaks for us later."

"Thanks, Dad," Darcy said, and everyone chimed in their own thanks. Then they started down the length of deck that stretched out over the dunes.

"Is this your parents' beach, or is it public?" Carter asked.

"It's a public beach," she told Carter. "They only own the lot where the house sits."

Carter, Haven, and Derek followed her down the steps to the sand. Carter enjoyed the feel of the warm sand between his toes as they strolled out toward the crashing waves. They passed groups of people lounging on chairs and soaking up the hot afternoon sun. Two small boys built sandcastles, while a couple of older children flew kites shaped like dragons in the sky.

Darcy stopped near the water. "How's this spot?"

"This works." Haven took the blanket from her and began to spread it out. Then she pointed to Derek. "Don't just stand there. Put up the umbrella."

Derek eyed her with feigned annoyance. "So bossy."

Carter put the cooler down and helped Derek set up the umbrella. When he turned toward Darcy, he did a double take when he realized she had already removed her cover-up. She rubbed sunscreen over her legs, arms, chest, and abdomen. His mouth dried as his eyes raked over her curves.

She pulled her braid over one shoulder and held up the bottle of sunscreen. "Havey, could you put some lotion on my back?"

Her best friend glanced over at Darcy and Carter before shaking her head and pulling a tube of lotion out of her bag. "Sorry, but I need to put lotion on myself. Why don't you ask Carter?"

Darcy hesitated and gave Carter a sheepish look. "Would you help me?"

"Uh, yeah. Sure."

She turned around, and he poured a copious amount of sunblock onto his hand. Then he moved his hand over her back, rubbing it in and enjoying the feel of her soft skin. He took his time, doing his best to prolong it. When he finished, he handed her the bottle.

"Thanks," she said before pointing the bottle at him. "Would you like me to rub it on your back too?"

He nodded a yes, then reached behind his neck, pulled off his shirt, and dropped it onto the blanket. When he turned around, he was surprised to find her staring at him. He peered down and hoped she wouldn't notice the dimpled scar beside his belly button. He would bear that scar for the rest of his life due to the tube he'd endured during his year spent on peritoneal dialysis. Thankfully, his swim trunks covered the larger scar farther down on his abdomen from his transplant.

When she continued to study him, he swallowed. "Is something wrong?"

"No, of course not." Darcy moved to stand behind him and began rubbing the lotion onto his back. He glanced over at Haven and found her grinning at Darcy. As Darcy's hands moved over his skin, his mouth turned to cotton and his body came to life. Passion rippled through him—down each limb, all the way to his fingers and toes.

Darcy slathered more lotion on his shoulders and down his biceps before handing him the bottle. "You might want to put some on your chest and legs before we swim."

"Good idea." He quickly finished applying the lotion, and when he peeked over at Darcy, she was staring out at the ocean. Had she liked what she'd seen? He felt like a teenager again, all awkward limbs and body, hoping the pretty girl at the pool thought he was cute. Carter thought hard and couldn't remember the last time he was in a swimsuit like this out in the open. Not since his surgery. It felt good—scary, but good.

Haven took Derek's arm and towed him in the direction of the water. "Let's swim!"

"Are you ready?" Carter asked Darcy.

She ran past him. "Race you!"

They bolted into the water, both of them hooting as they rushed out past where the waves crashed.

Darcy splashed him and laughed as he splashed her back. She dove under the water and then popped back up beside him. Happiness overtook him as he smiled at her.

She floated on her back, and when he yanked her leg, they crashed into each other. Laughing, she grabbed him, and they held on to each other longer than they needed to, hugging in the water. Carter stared into her eyes, and his pulse rocketed.

As they bobbed in the water together, he looked out toward her parents' enormous beach house. His spirit languished at the sight of it. He could never give Darcy the kind of life her family had given her—but he also couldn't deny that he was falling in love.

CHAPTER 16

HAPPINESS FIZZED INSIDE DARCY LATER THAT EVENING WHILE SHE SAT beside Carter on her parents' deck. The aroma of steak and roasted corn on the cob lingered in the air.

She smiled at Carter while he talked about car projects with Dad and Derek. She had relished every moment they had spent at the beach earlier that day—playing in the waves, resting on a blanket, and watching kids build sandcastles while the colorful sails of the boats fluttered in the distance.

Although she had been attracted to Carter since the moment she'd met him in the parking lot, she'd marveled at his gorgeous broad shoulders, muscular biceps, wide chest, and sculpted thighs. Heat shimmied up her spine as she recalled the feeling of his warm, strong hands massaging the sunscreen into her back and then holding her close in the water.

But she wasn't only attracted to him. She knew she was falling for him hard and fast. *Really* fast. That truth of it sent a mixture of excitement and fear skittering through her.

When she realized she'd been staring at his profile, Darcy blinked and tried in vain to stop the blush that was seeping into her cheeks. She glanced across the table at Haven, who watched her with an amused smirk spreading on her pretty face. Darcy examined her hands in her lap and hoped her blush would dissipate.

"So, Haven," Mom began, "you always have the funniest stories about your students. What have they been up to lately?"

Haven put down her drink. "Oh, there are so many stories. School will be out soon, and everyone is counting down. So a group of sixth-grade girls decided to celebrate the end of the year by coming to school dressed in different vacation themes. One day they wore beach cover-ups and sun hats and carried around beach bags."

"No kidding," Darcy exclaimed while Mom grinned.

Haven shook her head. "No kidding! They didn't get too disruptive until one of them blew up a beach ball and thought it would be a good idea to toss it around the cafeteria."

"Oh no." Mom laughed. "I assume you took care of that."

"I did since I was on cafeteria duty, but then they all wore parkas the next day to fit their skiing theme."

Mom scrunched her nose. "Did their parents see them leave the house dressed like that?"

"The principal and I asked that question too. I suppose their parents didn't notice they had large coats shoved in their backpacks. Apparently the heat got to the kids on parka day though. Once they started sweating, they regretted their decisions."

Darcy and Mom laughed.

"How about a game?" Dad suddenly asked.

Carter nodded. "Sure."

"What game?" Derek asked.

Dad gave Mom a knowing look. "Well, Darcy may have told you that Uno is a tradition during Larsen family beach vacations."

Carter turned toward Darcy, who nodded.

"That's true," she said.

Dad looked around the table. "What do you say?" he asked, and everyone nodded.

Darcy pushed back her chair. "Why don't you find the cards, and we'll clean up the dishes?"

"I'll help." Carter began stacking empty bowls from the gelato they'd had for dessert.

While Darcy filled the dishwasher, Mom wiped down the table and Haven and Derek refilled everyone's sweet tea.

Once the dishwasher was whirring, they returned to the table and played a couple of rousing games of Uno. Darcy was amazed at how well Carter fit in with her parents and her closest friends as they laughed and teased each other during the game.

When their second game came to a close, the sun began to set, sending a rainbow of colors across the sky and reflecting off the ocean.

Dad gathered up the cards, and Mom pushed her chair back and stood.

"How about we watch a movie?" Mom suggested.

Haven shook her head and covered her mouth with her hand. "Thank you, but I think the sun wore me out. I'm ready to head to bed." She leaned over and kissed Derek. "I'll see you in the morning." Then she popped up from her chair and waved. "Good night, everyone."

Dad pointed to the family room. "I'll look for a movie, and you're all welcome to join us."

Mom and Dad gathered up the remaining glasses, and Haven opened the sliding glass door before they filed inside.

Derek pulled out his phone. "I'm wide awake. I think I'll just sit out here and enjoy this beautiful night."

Carter turned toward Darcy, and his expression seemed hopeful. "Would you like to go for a walk?"

"I'd love to."

* * *

DARCY AND CARTER LEFT THEIR FLIP-FLOPS ON THE DECK BEFORE THEY descended the deck stairs to the beach. The air was warm with a comfortable breeze blowing off the water.

She relished the rhythmic sound of the waves, the sand between her toes, and the feeling of Carter walking by her side. The remnant of the spectacular sunset reflected off the water as darkness began to close in around them. A few other couples remained on the beach while others walked along the shoreline.

"I hope my parents aren't too much," Darcy said.

"Are you kidding? They're great." His gaze toggled toward the beach homes behind the dunes. "I can't get over this place. You must love coming here."

"When I was a kid, we came a few times a year, and my parents rented it out when we weren't here. They stopped renting it out when they retired." She looked up at him. "Do you like the beach?"

"I do, but I haven't had the chance to enjoy it as much as you have." He pushed his hair back from his forehead. "I remember my grandparents bringing Shauna and me to Coral Cove once after my mom died. Someone let us stay at a condo for free. My grandparents were working-class. My grandfather was a mechanic in a little shop like Barton's, and my nana was a housekeeper at a country club. They rented the same house for probably forty years or so. We didn't really go on vacations, so being at the beach that one time was a treat." He smiled. "We didn't have much, but we had love."

Darcy nodded, and thoughts of her biological mother spun in her mind. What would life have been like if she'd been raised by her instead of by the Larsens? What would her family have looked like?

Carter's smile was sheepish. "I didn't mean to make you uncomfortable."

"No, no," she said quickly. "You didn't make me uncomfortable. I'm glad to learn more about you."

The boardwalk appeared ahead of them, and Darcy picked up the pace. "Would you like to sit and watch the waves?"

"Definitely."

They found a bench on the boardwalk and sat down to look out toward the waves crashing on the beach. The delicious scents of pretzels, nachos, and popcorn from nearby vendors wafted over Darcy, and she peered down the boardwalk toward where people moved in and out of the small shops.

"I could get used to being here," Carter said softly.

"You'll have to come down here with me more often."

"You won't have to twist my arm."

They sat in a comfortable silence for several moments, taking in the sounds of the waves.

Then Carter sat up and turned toward her. His gaze roved over her features and lingered on her lips before returning to her eyes.

Her body began to tremble with anticipation as she stared up at him. Her lips ached for his touch. *Please kiss me, Carter. Please!*

"Darcy," he began, his voice sounding strained. "I really like you. I mean, I like you a *lot*."

"I'm glad it's mutual."

His dark eyes became intense. His fingers moved over her cheeks before cupping them. Then he leaned down, and his mouth covered hers.

Desire plunged through her as she lost herself in the feel and taste of his mouth. She wrapped her arms around his neck, and he rested his hands on her shoulders.

Carter's lips began a slow exploration, and she lost track of everything as the world around them fell away. Her hands moved to the nape of his neck, and her fingertips combed through his soft hair. When he broke the kiss, she pulled in air, working to slow the shockwaves still rocking her body.

His eyes studied hers as if searching for an answer. "I've been wanting to ask you something."

"What?" she asked, her voice sounding throaty.

"I would like to make things official between us." He paused and took a breath. "What I mean is, I would be honored to be your boyfriend. How would you feel about that?"

Relief skittered through her. "I thought you'd never ask."

"Good." He smiled and then his lips were caressing hers again, and she felt as if she were gliding above the ocean, like a kite that had been released on the wind.

He gently pulled away, then turned back toward the water. She rested her head on his shoulder. When Carter kissed the top of her head, Darcy's toes curled in the sand.

* * *

LATER CARTER AND DARCY WALKED HAND IN HAND BACK TO THE HOUSE. Stars sparkled in the dark sky and the steady cadence of the waves continued to serenade them as they approached the stairs leading to the Larsens' gorgeous home. A strange light glowed on the deck as they approached the dark house.

When they drew closer to the top step, Carter realized the light came from Derek's cell phone, which he held to his ear while leaning on the railing. Derek gave them a wave and then moved to the far end of the deck, where he continued to talk softly to someone on the other end of the line.

Darcy held Carter's hand and led him to the back door. "Thank you for the most amazing evening ever." She touched his cheek.

"I enjoyed it too."

She traced a finger along his jaw before balancing up on her tiptoes, wrapping her arms around his neck, pulling him closer, and kissing him. As she deepened the kiss, every nerve ending inside of him caught fire, and he knew to the depth of his bones that he was crazy about this amazing woman. He breathed her in and relished the taste of her.

When she pulled away, he came down to earth. She held on to his shoulders as if for balance. "Good night, Carter," she whispered. "I hope you sleep well."

"You too." He took her hand in his and gave it a gentle squeeze.

She stepped through the doorway, then faced him again. "Are you going up to bed?"

He shook his head and pointed toward the far end of the deck. "Not yet. I think I'll sit out here and talk to Derek for a while."

"Okay. See you in the morning." She gave him a little wave before closing the door and disappearing into the dark house.

Carter leaned over the deck railing, his mind racing. He knew he was falling for Darcy, and he was thrilled she returned the feelings. But it was easy to ignore reality in an idyllic place like this. How could he even imagine a future with her when they were so different? They had been raised in different worlds, and he would never be able to give her a beach house. A house was even questionable at this point. She might like him now, but what about in the future? How long would she be content with diner burger dates and movies before she realized her career would be their primary income if they got more serious?

"Sorry about that." Carter turned and saw Derek sauntering toward him.

"No problem."

Derek slipped his phone into his pocket. "My brother called, and we don't get to talk that often. He's always traveling to some exotic place for his job." Derek came to a stop beside Carter and leaned on the railing. He peeked over his shoulder and then looked out toward the ocean again. "I have some news," he said softly.

Carter rested his elbows on the railing and lifted his eyebrows. "Yeah?"

Derek looked back toward the door once more and then lowered his voice. "I bought a ring."

Darcy's words about Derek from the night of the car show in Mint Hill suddenly echoed in Carter's mind:

I've always thought they'd wind up together, but Derek was one of those guys who has a plan, you know?

Carter wondered if he would ever get the chance to plan a future with Darcy. When would he ever have a chance to offer her a future, buy her a ring, support her?

When he realized Derek was watching him, he yanked himself from his thoughts and grinned. "That's . . . that's great, Derek," Carter said, careful to keep his voice low. "Congratulations." He shook his friend's hand. "When are you going to ask her?"

Derek huffed. "I'm not sure." He folded his arms on the railing. "I need to figure out the best time."

"You look nervous."

Derek laughed. "Of course I am."

Carter scoffed. "Please. I don't think you have anything to worry about."

Derek shook his head. "I hope not. I fell head over heels for her when we met in college." He grinned. "She wasn't that interested in me at first. I had to convince her to go out with me, but once she did, we fell in love."

Carter swallowed against his dry throat and considered his blossoming feelings for Darcy.

Derek patted Carter's shoulder. "Did I see you kiss Darce good night?"

"Yeah, you did." Carter turned his attention out toward the waves.

"I suppose that means you two are official. We all knew it was only a matter of time."

Carter nodded. "We are." He pressed his lips together.

Derek cocked his head to the side. "Why don't you look happier about it?"

"I don't see how it will work out between us."

"What do you mean?"

Carter rubbed at a spot on his cheek while considering how much to share. "I don't fit into her world."

"Why would you think that?"

Carter gestured toward the house. "I can't compete with this."

Derek snorted. "None of us can, Carter. I'm sure you remember the modest house where I grew up."

Carter looked down at his bare feet.

"Why do you feel like you have to compete with her parents?"

"I don't even have my own place." He checked the door and then lowered his voice just in case Darcy had her window open. "I haven't told her this yet, but I live with my sister and her husband." Shame nearly choked him as empathy filled his friend's face. "I went through a tough time a few years ago. An unexpected medical issue." He hadn't expected to say this much to Derek, but he suddenly felt the need to tell him.

Derek blinked, then opened and closed his mouth. "I'm so sorry."

"Thanks. I'm a lot better now, but it destroyed me financially. I had to move out of my place, move in with my sister, and depend on her and her husband's family for a while. It was completely humiliating."

"But you got through it, and you're healthy now?"

"Yes, but I'm still digging out of debt."

"We all go through hard times, Carter." Derek seemed to study him. "Why would you believe that would interfere with your relationship with Darcy?"

Carter frowned. "I have nothing to offer her. I can't promise her a bright future. I've been nothing but a leech on my family. Why would she want a man like that?"

Derek gave him a knowing look. "My girlfriend is best friends with your girlfriend. I've known Darcy for a long time too. She's not shallow."

He hadn't thought Gabby was either.

"Darcy understands hard times. She had . . ."

Carter looked at him. "She what?"

Derek cleared his throat. "She lost her fiancé, remember?"

They were silent for a moment as they looked out toward the dark beach. Thoughts of Darcy's late fiancé filled his mind, along with questions.

"She told me a little bit about him. Did you know Jace?"

"Yeah. I knew him well—*really* well. He was one of my best friends." Derek moved his hand over the deck railing as if wading through memories in his mind. "Jace was a good guy. We all met in college, and he and Darcy started dating around the same time I started dating Haven."

"What did he study in school?"

"He was an architect. He treated Darcy great—always took care of her."

Carter rubbed the back of his head. He could never live up to that either.

"They got engaged on Valentine's Day and were going to get married around Thanksgiving."

Carter nodded slowly. "She told me he was in an accident. Some guy ran a red light and broadsided him."

"Yeah." Derek shook his head. "Darcy took it hard. She still blames herself."

Carter hung his head. He couldn't imagine the depth of her grief.

"You're the first guy who has gotten her attention since Jace passed away."

Carter looked up at him. "I am?"

"Yes, Carter, you are." Derek's words were measured. "You shouldn't sell yourself short. Darcy sees something special in you."

Carter was grateful for Derek's words, but Darcy didn't know the full story. When she found out, she'd see he wasn't special at all.

CHAPTER 17

DARCY YAWNED THE FOLLOWING MORNING, THEN TURNED TO FACE THE clock. It was only seven thirty, but she felt refreshed and happy—so very happy—as the memories of last night filled her mind. Holding hands and walking on the beach with Carter, and then those kisses . . . Oh, those kisses! The memory sent a flush of bashful pleasure through her cheeks and made her lightheaded.

She stretched and rolled over, assuming her boyfriend and friends were still asleep, but she was wide awake and ready to take on the day. When a delicious whiff of coffee drifted into her room, she rose and dressed.

"Good morning," Mom sang from the counter as Darcy padded into the kitchen. "Would you like a cup of coffee?"

"Yes, please. Are you the only one up?"

"Your dad is in the shower." Mom retrieved a shell-patterned mug from the nearby cabinet and filled it with coffee, cream, and sweetener.

Darcy joined her at the table and took a long sip. "This is delicious."

"I remember how you like it." Mom smiled across the table at her. "Carter is a very nice young man. I see why you like him."

Darcy tried to hide her smile by taking another sip of coffee.

"He's so handsome and friendly." Mom leaned forward. "It seemed like you were having fun at the beach while we visited on the deck last night. How are things going?"

Darcy nodded. "He asked if he could be my boyfriend last night."

"I'm so happy for you, Darcy. And I'm proud of you for taking a chance and moving forward after all you've been through."

Darcy felt her lips flatten. She couldn't allow herself to think too long about Jace. It was just too painful to let the memories back into her mind. She pushed herself up from the table. "I need a bite to eat so I can take my medication." She dropped a slice of bread into the toaster.

"What are your plans for today?" Mom asked.

Darcy leaned back against the counter. "I thought maybe we'd visit the boardwalk. Haven loves going into the different stores there."

"Oh, how fun. Has Carter been to Coral Cove before?"

"Once when he was a kid."

Mom smiled. "I'm sure this is special for him."

The toast popped, and Darcy buttered it before sitting at the table once again. She took a bite and drank more coffee. "Do you think we could make pancakes and bacon for everyone?"

"What a great idea." Mom stood. "I have pancake mix, and your dad picked up bacon yesterday."

Darcy took the last bite of toast. "I'll go take my meds and be right back." She carried her cup of coffee to her room and found her pill organizer. She took her pills and returned to the kitchen, where her mother had two large frying pans warming while she mixed up the batter.

Mom prepared the pancakes, and Darcy began cooking bacon in the microwave. Soon the kitchen was filled with delectable aromas.

"Pancakes and bacon?" Dad rubbed his hands together and kissed Mom on the cheek. "What a wonderful smell. Want me to set the table?"

Darcy loaded the bacon onto a platter. "Yes, please."

Dad opened the utensil drawer and counted out forks. The table was set and more coffee was brewing by the time Haven and Derek wandered in.

"I can't think of a better way to wake up than to the smell of bacon and coffee," Derek said, and everyone agreed.

Haven sidled up to Darcy and snatched a piece of bacon from the platter. "How can I help?"

"Pour the coffee?" Darcy asked.

Derek moved to the cabinet. "I'll get mugs."

Darcy carried the platter of bacon to the table and kept checking the doorway for Carter.

"He was in the shower when I came down," Derek said, answering her unspoken question.

Darcy nodded, then brought the butter and syrup to the table.

Mom plunked two large platters of pancakes in the center of the table. "I think we're ready."

"Let's eat," Dad announced before they sat down.

With her parents on either end of the long table, Darcy sat down across from Haven and Derek. Footfalls sounded in the family room. Then Carter appeared in the doorway, looking handsome with his light-brown hair wet and his face clean-shaven.

His expression was full of chagrin as he sat down beside Darcy. "I overslept. I'm sorry."

"Not at all." Darcy gave his hand a squeeze. "Good morning."

"Hi." His warm smile sent a shiver of delight dancing down her back.

Dad picked up the pancakes and piled a few on his plate before passing the platter to Carter. "Here you go, son."

"Thank you." Carter added a few onto his plate. "What's on our agenda today?" he asked as he slid a couple of pancakes onto Darcy's plate.

"I thought we could enjoy the boardwalk," Darcy said.

Haven's face lit up. "I love those little stores."

"Does that sound okay?" Darcy asked Carter.

He smothered his pancakes in butter and syrup. "Of course it does."

Derek swiped a piece of bacon from the platter. "We should have lunch at the delicious pizza place. What's it called?"

"Yes!" Haven snapped her fingers. "A Slice of Heaven."

Carter swallowed a piece of pancake and wiped his mouth with a napkin. "I might not be hungry again until tomorrow after these delicious pancakes."

Everyone chuckled in agreement, and Darcy shared a smile with her mother. She was so grateful that Carter was officially her boyfriend and that he seemed to be enjoying his time at her beloved Coral Cove.

* * *

LATER THAT AFTERNOON CARTER CARRIED DARCY'S SHOPPING BAGS INTO the house. They had spent the morning at the boardwalk, wandering through the beachfront stores that sold everything from t-shirts to beach towels to toys to funny little gifts. After a pizza lunch, they ventured into more stores, including CeCe's Toy Chest, Beach Reads, and the supermarket. For dinner they had purchased hamburger patties, buns, chips, and baked beans, along with cupcakes for dessert.

"How was the boardwalk?" Josie asked from the doorway leading to the family room.

Darcy slipped the burger patties into the refrigerator. "Fun. We picked up supper."

"You didn't need to do that." Josie clucked her tongue.

Haven set her bags on the counter. "We wanted to do something for you and Ross since you've been so generous to us."

"That's thoughtful of you." Josie rubbed Haven's shoulder. "What are your plans for the rest of the afternoon?"

Darcy picked up her bag from the bookstore. "The beach, of course." She rested her hand on Carter's strong bicep. "Should we go get changed?"

"Sure."

"Okay. I'll see you in a few minutes."

Carter jogged up to his room and changed into his black swimming trunks and flip-flops. Back out on the deck, Darcy's parents sat and read books.

"Sit with us, Carter," Josie said, tapping the chair beside her.

He joined her at the table.

"Darcy said you grew up in Flowering Grove," Josie said. "I assume you went to school with Derek."

Carter rested his forearms on the table. "That's right. We became good friends in high school after suffering through geometry together."

Ross chuckled while Josie grinned.

"My older sister and I were pretty much raised by our grandparents." He shared how his father left when he was young and how his mother passed away when he was ten.

Josie shook her head. "I'm sorry to hear that."

"Thanks. My grandfather taught me everything I know about cars, and I work with my brother-in-law at his parents' shop in Flowering Grove."

"Family is important," Ross said.

"That's true." Carter moved his hands over the smooth tabletop, wishing he could read her parents' minds. Did they believe he was good enough to care for their only daughter? If not, would they encourage her to break up with him?

His stomach twisted at the thought of losing Darcy. Guilt filled him as he considered how he wasn't yet being completely honest with Darcy about his health history or his financial situation. He also wondered in that moment if he should put some emotional distance between himself and her parents. After all, if their relationship didn't last, he would have to face even more heartache if he got attached to her parents too.

"I'm so glad Darcy met you," Josie said. "It's been a long time since we've seen her smile so much." She reached over and touched his arm. "You are an answer to our prayers."

"Josie's right," Ross chimed in. "Darcy has had a hard time the past couple of years, and we were worried she wouldn't ever recover. We're thankful she found you."

Carter tried to mask his surprise as more guilt nagged him. He didn't feel worthy of their praise. "Thank you. She means a lot to me."

The sliding glass door opened with a whoosh, and Darcy walked out wearing another vintage suit and cover-up. "What are you three talking about?"

"How amazing you are," Carter quipped.

"Uh-huh." She graced him with a beautiful smile. "Are you ready to swim?"

"I've been waiting for you," Carter said.

Darcy held her hand out to him, and together they headed down from the deck and toward the water.

* * *

LATER THAT EVENING, DARCY AND HAVEN SAT ON BEACH CHAIRS AND watched Carter and Derek throw a football back and forth near the shoreline. After swimming all afternoon, Darcy and her friends had grilled burgers and served supper for her parents on the deck. They had enjoyed the meal and cupcakes before cleaning up the kitchen and returning to the beach.

Carter threw the ball to Derek, who jumped up in the air only to miss it and fall down on the sand. When Carter bent at his waist to laugh, Darcy admired his golden tan, his muscular legs, his sun-streaked light-brown hair, and his perfect nose. He was the most gorgeous man she'd known . . . well, since Jace.

Haven leaned over and tapped Darcy's arm. "Earth to Darce."

"What, Havey?" Darcy shot her a look.

"From the way you and Carter have been acting today, I take it that you two are official now, huh?"

"Yes, we are."

"And he kissed you?"

Darcy smiled. "He sure did."

"And?" Haven pushed her sunglasses farther up on her petite nose.

Darcy bit her lip. "A lady never tells."

"That good, huh?" She nudged Darcy. "I'm really happy for you."

Darcy turned toward the water just as Carter threw the ball again. His gray t-shirt lifted and shared enough of his taut stomach for her to spot a dimple of a scar near his belly button. She had noticed that scar the first day at the beach. What could have caused the scar? She thought of her own scar from the kidney transplant, but it was lower down on her abdomen. She was careful to wear modest bathing suits to hide it, and she was grateful that vintage bathing suits were in style.

Could Carter's scar have been caused by an injury or a surgery? The thought dissolved when Derek threw the ball back to him and he caught it.

Soon the guys headed over to a blanket spread out on the sand, then dropped down onto it. Carter pulled a bottle of water from their cooler and took a long drink. Then he stood and pulled off his shirt before taking Darcy's hand and lifting her to her feet.

"Swim with me?" he said.

She moved her finger over his jawline. "How can I ever say no to you?"

He lifted his eyebrows before tugging her toward the water, and she laughed.

Darcy let him pull her to the waves, and they ran in together, splashing just beyond where the waves met the shore.

When they came to a stop, he towed her over to him and kissed her until she was breathless. Darcy lost herself in the kisses that nearly buckled her knees.

When he released her, he splashed her, and she laughed. Then he pulled her against him and kissed her again.

* * *

CARTER SPENT THE FOLLOWING MORNING WITH DARCY AND HER PARENTS on her father's impressive sailboat. Derek and Haven had left after breakfast, leaving the four of them to enjoy the day together.

The sky was bright-blue and cloudless, and the air of the Coral Cove bay was warm and sweet. Carter and Darcy talked and laughed with her folks, but even though her parents clearly went out of their way to make him feel comfortable, he couldn't escape the notion that he didn't belong with her. He also couldn't stop his secrets from burning his insides. He had to tell her the truth himself before it ate him alive.

Carter looked out over the bay toward a group of seagulls calling out to each other. He owed Darcy the truth, and if she decided to break up with him after he told her, he would be left gutted. Yet as much as the idea of losing her scared him, he couldn't continue to live this lie. It would be better to get the truth out in the open before he and Darcy got in too deep.

"Hey." Darcy's voice was close to his ear. "Are you okay?"

"Everything's fine."

Her green eyes were wide with worry. "You don't look like everything is fine."

"I promise it is." He kissed her cheek. "In fact, I'm having the time of my life with you."

She smiled, and relief filled him. "I am too." She linked her fingers with his.

He kissed her, and when she rested her head on his shoulder, he hoped she'd still care about him when she found out his truth.

CHAPTER 18

When they arrived back at the beach house after sailing, Josie and Ross disappeared into their bedroom on the far side of the house. Then Carter took Darcy's hand and pulled her into the family room.

"Could we go for a walk before we leave?" he asked, anxious to get his secret off his chest.

"Sure." Darcy's eyes seemed to search his. "Are you sure you're okay?"

"I need to talk to you, and I don't want to do it while I'm driving."

She nodded slowly. "I'll let my parents know where we're going, okay?"

When they reached the boardwalk, Carter was relieved to find their bench empty. They took a seat, and he brushed his sweaty hands down his shorts.

"Carter, what's going on?" she asked.

"I, uh . . . I just need to tell you something."

"Okay." She placed her hand on his, and the warmth of her skin gave him strength to move forward.

He looked out toward the waves and tried to find the right words. "I live with my sister." He snuck a glance at her, but she only shrugged.

"Okay."

"There's more to it. I went through a tough financial period a few years ago. I had some unexpected medical costs come up, and

I had to move out of my apartment. My brother-in-law's parents kept me on the payroll even though I couldn't do much in the shop. My sister helped me out tremendously." He paused and considered talking about being on dialysis and having a kidney transplant, but he realized he wasn't ready to share that piece of himself with her—at least not yet.

She touched his cheek as concern filled her face. "Are you okay?"

"I'm fine now, but the medical costs took a toll. I took out a consolidation loan, but it's taking me longer than expected to pay it off. I thought I'd be back on my feet by now, but it looks like it will be another two years or so before I can find my own place again."

She nodded and smiled. "That's okay."

He narrowed his eyes and searched hers for any sign of disapproval. "Okay?"

Her brow puckered. "Why are you looking at me like that? What did you expect me to say?"

"I-I don't know. I'm afraid of disappointing you."

She opened her mouth and closed it, then shifted closer to him. "Why would you think I'd be disappointed in you?"

He brushed his hands down his face. "Darcy, you're amazing, and your parents are amazing. I just can't give you what they can. I—"

"Whoa!" She touched his shoulder. "Carter, look at me."

He lifted his gaze to her, awaiting her admonishment.

"Carter, I care about you—*deeply*. I'm not concerned about how much money you make or what you have. I care about *you*." Her eyes searched his. "Do I give you the impression that I'm materialistic?"

He shook his head. "No, not at all."

"Then what are you afraid of?"

"That I'm not good enough for you." He cast his eyes down toward the boardwalk. "Some women may not be as understanding."

She lifted his chin and captured his lips with hers. He leaned into the kiss, and his thoughts became fuzzy.

When she pulled away, she gave him a mischievous grin. "You passed the test. You are really, *really* good for me."

A bark of laughter escaped his mouth.

"Carter, I care about you and want you in my life. I hope I've made that clear."

He shook his head. "Nope, not yet. But one more kiss might do the trick." Then he kissed her again and felt himself relax. Darcy was even more amazing than he had realized.

When they pulled apart, she placed her hand flat against his chest. "We'd better get on the road soon. We have a three-and-a-half-hour drive ahead of us and work tomorrow."

* * *

"I WISH WE COULD HAVE STAYED AT THE BEACH FOR ANOTHER WEEK," Darcy said later that evening as Carter carried her backpack and her suitcase up the steps to her front door. She pulled out her key and unlocked it.

He set her luggage on the small porch. "I agree." He leaned down, and his lips did things that made her knees feel like cooked noodles.

"*Now* am I invited to your birthday party?" she asked with a grin.

He folded his arms over his wide chest. "Why would I invite my girlfriend to my birthday party?" he teased before kissing her again. "I'll text you, and I hope to see you before then."

"You'd better."

Carter gathered her in his arms. "Have a good day tomorrow."

"I'll miss you until I see you again." She looked up at him. "One more kiss?"

"Yes, ma'am." After kissing her one last time, Carter handed her the key fob for her car and then loped down the front steps.

She smiled as he climbed into his truck and started the engine. He waved before backing out of her drive.

As she entered her house, Darcy contemplated their conversation on the boardwalk before they'd left Coral Cove. When he'd mentioned an unexpected medical problem, she'd been worried he would tell her he was still ill. She was relieved he was well now, but curiosity nipped at her.

She wondered what the medical issue was, but she also understood wanting to keep that information private. She would never pry or ask him questions he wasn't ready to answer. Even so, she hoped one day he would feel comfortable enough to tell her what he'd been through. Just like she hoped to share her own past one day.

Darcy placed her luggage on the bench by her door while she reconsidered Carter's worries about his self-worth. She hoped she could find a way to prove to him that she cared for him and didn't care about his financial situation.

As she locked the door behind her and picked up her luggage, Darcy knew one thing for sure: Carter had carved out a piece of her heart, and she trusted him to hold it.

* * *

CARTER WHISTLED A MONTGOMERY GENTRY TUNE AS HE WALKED INTO THE house. He was still thinking about kissing Darcy when he entered the family room, where Shauna was watching a movie and Gage was clicking through car videos on his laptop. He waved on his way to the stairs, but when Shauna paused the movie, he stopped moving forward and turned toward them.

"How was the beach?" Gage asked.

Carter nodded. "Great."

"Sit for a minute," Shauna said.

Carter pointed toward the stairs. "I really need a shower. I'll come back down after I'm changed." He started toward the stairs and then jogged up them.

"Wait, Carter." His sister trailed after him.

He set his bag on his bed and then turned toward her standing in the doorway. "What's up?"

"I want to hear more about your weekend."

Carter described Darcy's parents' beautiful house and boat, and he filled her in on the high points of their time there. "It was great to get away and relax," he said.

Shauna tapped the doorframe. "Are you and Darcy official now?"

He nodded.

"So I'll get to meet her on your birthday?"

"Yup."

Shauna lingered in the doorway, seemingly hesitant about something.

Dread pooled in his gut as he dropped onto the edge of his bed and pointed to a chair. "You look like you want to talk. Have a seat."

She sat down on the chair by his desk, and her serious expression sent a flare of worry through him.

"What is it, Shauna?"

She huffed a breath. "I think I found Dad."

"What?" His eyes narrowed. "I asked you not to look for him," he snapped. "Did you do this just to spite me?"

"Of course not, Carter," Shauna said.

"Why would you want to find him, Shauna? He was never there for us when we needed him most. What could you possibly hope to gain from talking to him?"

"Just calm down, okay?" Her voice implored him. "I haven't spoken to Dad yet, but I think he might be in Tennessee. I remember

Mom mentioning he had an uncle there. I've been searching social media, and then I found someone who is starting a private investigator business. He said he'd give me a discount if I let him help me."

"That's great," he deadpanned. His hands trembled, and he looked for something to keep them busy. He opened his bag and carried his toiletries to his small bathroom, where he set some on the counter and others on the shelf in his medicine cabinet.

Shauna appeared in the bathroom doorway, and he glared at her. "If our so-called father cared about us, then he would have been here a long time ago," Carter seethed. "He knew where Nana and Grandpa lived. He could have come at any time. Why are you insisting on finding him after what he did to us? What he did to *Mom*?" He swallowed as his eyes stung. "Don't you remember how much he hurt her?"

"I remember *all* of it." Tears glistened in her dark eyes. "You're right that he doesn't care, but I need to talk to him. I want to know why he abandoned Mom and us, and I want him to know what you went through with your kidney disease."

He shook his head. "Don't bother, Shauna. All he's going to do is hurt you again. You're wasting your time. If you talk to him, don't even mention me. If he asks how I am, tell him it's none of his business because he doesn't have a son. I don't want or need him in my life."

She shoved her hands in the pockets of her jean shorts and gave him a withering glare. "Then that's what I'll do." She backed out of his bathroom. A few moments later, he heard the door to his bedroom click shut.

Carter dropped down onto the lid of the commode and rubbed his hands down his face. Why hadn't Shauna respected his feelings and abandoned this ridiculous plan? If Carter came face-to-face with his father, he would turn and walk the other way—but if his father came looking for him, he would have to face Carter's fury.

CHAPTER 19

CARTER RUSHED AROUND THE HOUSE SATURDAY AFTERNOON, straightening the sofa cushions and the coasters on the coffee table. Then he hurried into the kitchen and lined up the canisters on the far counter.

"The house looks great," Shauna said. "We cleaned until midnight last night, Carter. You need to chill out."

He rested his hand on the back of his neck and faced his sister. He was relieved they had called a truce over the issue of their father. She hadn't agreed to stop looking for him, but she said she'd leave him out of the conversation if she found Dad. "You didn't see how immaculate her townhouse is or how perfect the beach house is."

"You must really like her." Shauna grinned. "I've never seen you like this about any woman before."

The doorbell rang, and he took off toward the foyer. Yanking open the door, he found Darcy standing on the porch holding two grocery bags and an aluminum pan. She looked stunning in a yellow sundress that made the most of her trim figure. Her long blonde hair was pulled up in a thick ponytail that spilled past her shoulders.

"Happy birthday!" Her eyes beamed with warmth and affection that soaked through his skin.

He took the pan from her and kissed her. "Thank you."

"I have something for you." She pulled a card from her purse and handed it to him.

He set the brownies on the bench beside him, then opened the envelope and found a beautiful poem inside wishing him a happy birthday. When he flipped the card open, he noticed she'd written "Love, Darcy" inside. On a separate piece of paper he found a printout of two tickets to see Tracy Byrd, one of his favorite country singers, at the amphitheater in Charlotte. His mouth dropped open.

"It's in two weeks. I hope you don't have plans that night." She arched an eyebrow and bit her lower lip.

Carter swallowed, overwhelmed by her generosity.

Memories of the expensive gifts Gabby had given him flashed in his mind—airfare and tickets to NASCAR races, an overpriced and engraved watch he never felt comfortable wearing, and rims and tires for his truck—all of them symbols of the social divide between them. He'd come to see them as bribes to get him to do things for her, such as quit his "lowly job" and work on her father's race team.

He shook off the memories and looked into his girlfriend's beautiful green eyes. This gift was perfectly tailored to him, and he was certain it had come straight from her heart. "Darcy, this—this is too much."

"No, it's not too much," she said. "In fact, it's not nearly enough considering how happy you've made me."

He pulled her to him. "Come here." He leaned down and kissed her until he heard someone behind him clear her throat. Turning, Carter found Shauna standing behind them. "Darcy, this is my sister, Shauna."

"Glad to finally meet you."

"Great to meet you too." Darcy's cheeks flushed bright red, and she held up her grocery bags. "I brought chips, dip, and macaroni salad." Then she gestured toward the aluminum pan. "I also baked some brownies."

"Brownies are always welcome in this house. Come on in." Shauna beckoned her farther into the house.

Carter picked up the pan and followed Darcy and his sister through the family room to the kitchen. Gage stood at the counter marinating chicken breasts to ready them for the grill.

"Darcy, this is my husband, Gage," Shauna said.

Gage nodded. "Welcome."

"Hi." Darcy waved.

Carter set the pan of brownies on the counter. "Wow. You made enough for two crowds."

"I didn't want to show up empty-handed." She glanced around the kitchen. "I love your house."

"Thank you," Shauna said.

The front door opened and closed, then Gage's parents joined them in the kitchen.

"Happy birthday," Glenda sang before hugging Carter. Then she handed him an envelope. "Here's a little something from Ernie and me."

"Thank you both." Carter slipped the envelope into his pocket, then made a sweeping gesture toward Darcy. "Darcy, these are my bosses and also Gage's parents, Glenda and Ernie."

Ernie nodded a hello.

Glenda's eyes widened with excitement. "Is this the young woman who's been taking up so much of my Carter's time?"

He turned toward Darcy, who gave him a sweet smile. Then he looked at Glenda again.

"Yes, she is."

"I'm so glad you're finally dating again." Glenda pulled Darcy in for an awkward bear hug.

Darcy patted her back. "Nice to meet you, Glenda."

Carter and Gage exchanged a grin, shaking their heads at Glenda.

Shauna touched Carter's arm. "Why don't you give Darcy a tour?"

"Good idea." Carter took her hand and guided her toward the doorway. "That was the kitchen."

She laughed.

"Over here is the laundry room and a half bath." He steered her through the family room. "Shauna and Gage's room is over there, along with two other bedrooms and another bathroom." Then he stopped in the hallway and dropped his voice to a whisper. "Glenda gets a little overly excited. Sorry about that."

"Don't be. She just cares about you." She peeked down the hallway. "This is really spacious," she said, and he shook his head. "You don't agree?"

"Your parents' beach house is at least twice the size of this place."

"But I like this house too."

He smiled and wondered what it would be like to have her in his life permanently—as his wife, his family—but first he needed to get his own life together.

"Where's your room?" she asked.

"Upstairs." He towed her to the staircase and up to his room. "I have a small bathroom of my own, which is nice."

Darcy walked around his room and stopped in front of his dresser. "Is this your mom?" She pointed to a photo featuring Carter with his sister and mother standing on a porch.

"Yeah. I was about eight."

She picked up the photo and examined it. "I recognize your smile." Then she tilted her head. "You resemble her."

"Thanks." He took in his mother's beautiful face and tried to conjure up the sounds of her voice and her laugh. "I was always told I looked exactly like my dad. It's a relief to hear I look like her." The frustrated words he'd exchanged with Shauna about finding their father echoed in his mind. He sat on the chair beside his desk. "Derek texted last night and said he and Haven would come today."

"I haven't heard from Haven today, which isn't like her." Darcy set the photo back on the dresser and picked up another one. "Your grandparents?"

He nodded. "That was also taken at their house."

"They look nice."

He grinned. "They usually were—unless Shauna and I were getting into mischief."

Darcy laughed as she examined photos from Shauna's wedding and a few more of his mother.

When she set the last photo down, Carter stood, pulled her into his arms, and kissed her. "I'm so happy you're here."

"Well, I've been trying to invite myself to your birthday party for over a week," she joked.

The sound of a car pulling into the driveway drew their attention to the window. Carter peeked out to see Haven and Derek climbing out of his late-model blue Jeep Wrangler.

Taking her hand, Carter led Darcy down the stairs to the front door just as Haven and Derek stepped onto the porch.

"Happy birthday, Carter," Haven sang out. Then she held up her left hand. "We have news." A huge diamond sparkled on her ring finger.

Darcy gasped and grasped her hand. "Haven! It's gorgeous!"

Derek shook Carter's hand. "Happy birthday."

"Thanks and congratulations to you."

Darcy hugged Haven. "I'm so happy for you."

"Thank you," Haven said. "I thought it was strange when Derek said we should go to breakfast this morning. After we ate, we drove to the UNCC campus and he asked me to go for a walk, which was even stranger. He took me to the very spot where he'd asked me out on our first date to propose." She took Darcy's hands in hers. "Will you be my maid of honor, Darce?"

Looping her arm around Haven's neck, Darcy led her into the house. "Of course I will. I can't wait to get started on your wedding plans."

Derek patted Carter's shoulder and handed him a card. "This is for you."

"Thanks," Carter said. "I was wondering when you would give her that ring."

"I finally came up with the perfect plan, but I had to find the courage first." He grinned. "I'm just glad she said yes."

Carter chortled and shook his head. "You knew she would." As they walked into the house together, he wondered if he'd have his own chance to plan a proposal, a wedding, and a future.

* * *

LATER THAT AFTERNOON DARCY SAT ON THE DECK WITH HAVEN, SHAUNA, and Glenda. She smiled across the small yard toward where Carter stood inside the detached garage with Derek, Gage, Ernie, and a few neighbors. They had eaten delicious grilled chicken along with the food Darcy had brought. Now she felt herself unwinding as she spent time with friends new and old.

"That ring is something." Glenda examined the huge diamond on Haven's finger.

Shauna took a sip of iced tea. "I agree. Were you surprised?"

"Yes." Haven's smile was as bright as the June afternoon sun. "He was acting nervous all day, and I kept asking him what was wrong. Then he got down on one knee." She sniffed. "I thought it would be another year or so before he'd be ready."

Darcy touched Haven's shoulder. "I think it's wonderful."

Haven had a strange look on her face as she stood. "Darce, how about we go inside and get your brownies?" She tilted her head oddly, as if trying to signal something to her friend.

"Sure." Darcy followed Haven into the house and to the kitchen. "What's up?"

Haven's expression became serious. "Darcy, I want to ask you something, and I need you to be honest with me."

Darcy was taken aback. "Of course."

When Haven looked down at the counter, Darcy's stomach tightened.

After a moment, Haven looked up once again. "How would you feel if I got married the last Saturday in October?" She placed her hand over Darcy's. "I don't want to hurt you, and I hope you'll tell me if it's too painful for you."

Darcy felt an ache in her chest. "It's your wedding, Haven. You need to do what you want." As she said the words, they stung—but she determined to push that feeling away. She would be happy for her best friend no matter how difficult it was to smile through her grief.

"No, I don't. I need to think of my best friend and her feelings first." She studied Darcy's face. "Is it okay if I have a fall wedding? I don't want to upset you or make you sad."

Darcy hugged her. "You are so sweet to think of me, but don't worry. I promise I'll be okay no matter what. This will be your day. Make it the wedding of your dreams."

"You're truly my best friend on the planet." Haven gave her one last squeeze and released her. "Let's get back outside then." Darcy cut up the brownies while Haven grabbed disposable plates and napkins. Back out on the deck, Haven and Darcy served up the dessert.

"So have you thought about a wedding date yet, Haven?" Glenda asked.

Haven nodded. "The last Saturday in October."

"That's only four months away," Shauna said. "You'll need to start planning now."

Haven swallowed a bite of brownie. "We're going to talk to Derek's pastor this week since we want to get married here in Flowering Grove, and we want to have the reception at the Flowering Grove Country Club."

"It's really nice," Shauna said. "I've been to a couple of bridal showers there."

"Derek had his high school reunion there, and I went with him. It was lovely," Haven added. "I talked to my mom this morning, and she's already in planning mode. She said she's been waiting for this." She gazed down at her ring, and her smile faded. "We have so much to do. We'll need a caterer and a menu, a good DJ, and a cake. Oh! Invitations. I guess the save-the-date postcards would have to go out soon."

Darcy turned toward the detached garage, where Carter sat on a stool and grinned at Ernie, who appeared to be sharing a story. At the thought of a future with Carter, excitement hurtled through her.

Yet it seemed too soon to daydream about those things. They'd only known each other for two months, and they'd been dating for barely two weeks. It seemed premature to imagine a lifetime with a person she'd known for such a short time. Yet she'd never felt such a deep connection with anyone so quickly—including Jace.

The sound of Shauna pushing her chair back pulled Darcy back to the present.

"These brownies are delicious. I think I'll grab the cake too," she said as she stood.

Darcy popped up from her chair. "Would you like some help?"

"Sure."

As Darcy followed Shauna into the house, she hoped this would be the first of many visits with Carter's sister.

* * *

LATER THAT EVENING, AFTER EVERYONE ELSE HAD GONE HOME, DARCY rested her head on Carter's shoulder while they sat on his sister's porch swing. She drew in the fragrance of freshly cut grass while the cicadas began their usual chorus and lightning bugs showed off their sparkling display.

Carter kissed her head, and she peered up at him and smiled.

"Did you have a nice birthday?" she asked.

He took her hand in his. "No, I had the best birthday in a long time because you were here." He touched her nose.

She snuggled deeper into his shoulder. "I enjoyed meeting your family."

"They liked you too."

"I was surprised you didn't invite Jovan and the rest of your friends from high school."

He paused for a moment. "Shauna and I agreed to keep it small this time, but maybe I'll have them over soon."

"Okay."

He was silent for a moment, and the sound of the swing creaking back and forth filled the porch. "Were you surprised by Derek and Haven's engagement?"

"Yes and no. I had a feeling it was coming, but I didn't know how soon."

"If I admit something to you, will you promise not to be angry?"

She sat up as curiosity gripped her. "What do you mean?"

Carter looked ashamed. "When we were at your parents' beach house, Derek told me he had bought a ring. He just wasn't sure when he was going to propose."

Darcy opened and closed her mouth while trying to gather a response. "Carter," she began, her words measured, "why didn't you tell me?"

"I'm sorry." He held his hands up in surrender. "I got the impression it was top-secret information."

She studied him, then cradled her arms to her middle. "Do you not trust me?" Her voice sounded thready.

He shook his head. "It's not that at all. I just thought he might want to keep the element of surprise. I never meant to hurt you, Darcy. I would never deliberately hurt you."

As Darcy took in the earnest expression on his face, she realized her feelings were displaced. Carter had given her no reason to be on edge. She'd just been daydreaming about having a future with him when she didn't know what he wanted for *his* future. Did he even want to get married and have a family one day?

Carter's thumb swept across her cheek, leaving a trail of heat. "I can tell you're thinking about something serious. You can be honest with me, Darcy."

"You can tell when I'm concentrating?"

He nodded. "I'm learning how to read you. What's on your mind?"

"What do you want?"

He arched a brow. "Can you be more specific?"

"For your future, Carter. What are your goals for your life?"

He trailed his fingers over the stubble on his neck. "Well, I eventually would like a home and a family, but it will be a while before I can have those things." He rested his hand on her shoulder. "How about you?"

"Well, for one, you already know I want to find my biological mother. But I haven't heard anything from the Lost and Found people yet."

He looked out toward the street as if avoiding her gaze. A dog barked somewhere in the distance, and an SUV drove by with the radio so loud that the bass reverberated in Darcy's chest.

She took in the frown darkening Carter's handsome face, and she touched his cheek. "Did I say something to upset you?"

"No, it's not you." His expression softened. "Shauna thinks she found our father."

"And you're not happy about it."

He snorted. "No, not at all. I told her to keep me out of it."

"But what if he wants to apologize and actually be a father figure to you and Shauna?"

"His words wouldn't mean anything to me. He wasn't there when we needed him, so why would we want him in our lives now?"

"I'm sorry." She leaned against him, and he pulled her close. She breathed in his familiar smell of soap and sandalwood and felt safe and protected in his strong arms. "You can vent to me anytime, Carter."

"Thanks. I didn't mean to dampen the mood."

"I can think of ways to lighten the mood."

He looked down at her, and his smile was wicked. "Is that right?" When he kissed her, her stomach swirled wildly.

My thoughts exactly.

Darcy sat up and wrapped her arms around his neck. Happiness blossomed in the pit of her belly, and as she melted against him, she lost herself in his kiss.

CHAPTER 20

"This is not my style at all." Haven stood in front of a mirror and frowned at her reflection. She wore a sleeveless tulle wedding gown with a low-cut neckline and a corset-style bodice. "I honestly didn't think I was this picky." She turned back and forth for another look, then shook her head as she met her mother's gaze.

It was Friday afternoon, two weeks later, and Darcy sat on a chair in the dressing room at the Fairytale Bridal Shop located on Main Street in Flowering Grove. She and Haven had taken the afternoon off from work since Derek's mother, Marcia, had managed to get an appointment for Haven. She insisted they come to the Fairytale Bridal Shop since Marcia's nieces had all gotten their wedding gowns there. Haven's mother, Lola, and Derek's younger sister, Kaylen, had also joined them.

"I agree." Lola touched her daughter's shoulder. "Let's keep looking."

Marcia gave Haven a sympathetic expression. "You need to feel comfortable on your wedding day. You're not picky, Haven. You just haven't found the right gown yet."

Dakota Jamison, the shop owner, tapped her chin. "I think I might have just the one." She disappeared into the back of the store while Haven and her mother slipped into a dressing room.

Darcy's mind wandered to the gown she had planned to wear to her own wedding. She had felt like a princess in that gorgeous dress with its beading, lace, and long train. After Jace had passed away, she'd tucked the gown away in the back of one of her closets, unsure of what to do with it.

If she were to get married, she couldn't imagine wearing that gown. She'd bought it while planning her future with Jace and no one else. She'd asked about returning it, but since it had been altered for her, the sale was final.

She'd thought about selling it or even donating it in hopes of another woman wearing it and feeling as beautiful as Darcy felt when she first tried it on—but she couldn't bring herself to do that yet. The idea made her feel like she was giving away her memories of Jace and all of their special plans.

Darcy's heart squeezed at the memory, but she banished it. Today was Haven's day, and she wanted to be as supportive to her as Haven had been while planning Darcy's wedding.

When Haven reappeared from the back of the store with Lola and Dakota in tow, she wore the new gown. She stood in front of the mirror, turning from side to side while scrutinizing her reflection. As if on cue, Lola, Marcia, Kaylen, and Darcy all gasped at once. The white sleeveless gown had a sweetheart neckline, a dropped waistline, and a chapel-length train. The full tulle skirt featured lace appliques, and the top included a matching short-sleeved removable jacket. The gown looked as if it had been designed especially for her.

"Oh, Haven," her mother whispered. "Honey, this is it."

Darcy moved to the wall of mirrors. "You're stunning." Her eyes filled with happy tears as she imagined her best friend walking down the aisle on her father's arm toward the love of her life.

"Breathtaking," Kaylen added.

Marcia nodded. "Absolutely."

Haven laughed before spinning in front of the mirror. "I love it."

Dakota clapped her hands. "Wonderful. Now, have you thought about shoes?"

Darcy and Kaylen exchanged smiles. Darcy had always thought Derek's younger sister was lovely with her dark hair and eyes that matched her mother's. At twenty-five, she was sweet and friendly, and she loved her job as a pet groomer.

Kaylen waved Darcy toward the front of the store. "The wedding will be here before we know it. We need to talk about the bridal shower."

"You're right," Darcy answered.

Kaylen nodded. "Let's plan a time to get together."

"There you two are." Lola joined them at the front of the store. "Darcy, I've been meaning to ask you about Carter. How are things going?"

Darcy blushed. "Great."

"I'm so glad to hear it." Lola clasped her hands together. "I know you've been through a hard time, sweetie, but Jace would want to see you move on and find happiness with another man who loves you."

Hearing her late fiancé's name never seemed to get easier for Darcy, but she tried to mask the sadness with a smile. "Thanks."

"Mom!" Haven called from the dressing room. "Come and tell me what you think of these shoes."

Lola motioned toward the dressing room. "Duty calls."

After Haven had settled on the gown, veil, and shoes, they all headed out to the sidewalk. The mid-June air was humid, and the sun was high in the sky. Darcy smiled at Haven as they started toward their cars. She couldn't wait for her best friend's special day.

* * *

THE FOLLOWING EVENING, CARTER LIFTED DARCY'S HAND. HE KISSED HER knuckles as they sat in his truck in her driveway after the concert. His heart felt full after sitting on the amphitheater lawn and watching one of his favorite country singers perform some of his favorite songs.

The concert had been amazing, and he'd had the time of his life. He grinned as he recalled the best part of the night—when he'd held Darcy close and slow-danced with her to "The Keeper of the Stars," a country song he'd always loved.

"From that smile on your face, I'm going to assume you had a good time tonight." Darcy's expression was coy.

"Try *wonderful* time."

She scrunched her nose. "I just wish I could've gotten you real seats instead of general admission, but those were already sold out."

"I don't think we could have gotten away with slow-dancing in the seats, so the lawn suited me just fine." He shifted closer to her. "Thank you for the best birthday gift ever." He brushed his lips over hers, and the taste and feel of her sent desire humming through his veins.

When he broke the kiss, he rested his forehead against hers. "Good night, Darcy."

She touched his cheek before pushing her door open. "Good night."

He started the engine but waited until she was safely in her house with the door closed before he began his drive home.

When he stopped at the entrance to her neighborhood, Carter found Tracy Byrd on his phone's music app and clicked on "The Keeper of the Stars" before turning it up loud. He sang along with the song and remembered their dance—the feel of holding her tight and swaying to the music with her. It was like heaven.

Carter rolled down his window and rested his arm on the door while he sang along with Tracy Byrd's music. During the whole ride home, he relived the evening. He couldn't remember a time when he'd been as happy as he was, and he owed it all to Darcy. He was so grateful she'd come into his life. He laughed to himself thinking about the first time they'd met. What were the chances that he'd walk by her car just as she was struggling to start it? He had definitely been in the right place at the right time, and he had her car to thank for that.

When he reached Flowering Grove, he drove down Main Street and turned onto Ridge Road before merging onto Zimmer Avenue. He pulled into the driveway and parked behind Gage's silver Dodge pickup. He killed the engine and was surprised to find Shauna sitting on the porch swing, talking on her phone.

Carter climbed out of his truck, shut the door, and locked it before starting up the path to the porch. When he reached the top step, he noticed that Shauna's brown eyes were red and puffy. Worry shot through him as he closed the distance between them.

"Shauna," he whispered. "What's wrong?"

She held up her hand to shush him. "Hang on a second, okay?" she told the person on the other end of the line. Then she hit the button to mute herself and wiped her eyes. "Carter, it's Dad."

Carter's entire body went rigid.

"Do you want to talk to him?" She held the phone out toward him. Her eyes seemed to beg him to say yes and take the phone from her.

His face twisted with a deep frown. "Hang up. He's upsetting you."

She shook her head, sniffed, and wiped her eyes again. "No, he's not. We were just talking about Mom."

"I'm going inside." He ground out the words.

"Carter, wait!"

Ignoring her pleas, he stalked up to his room and flopped down onto his back on the bed. The joy he'd felt earlier disintegrated the second Shauna mentioned their father. He rested his forearm on his forehead and tried to block the memories that swamped him—losing his mom, getting sick, becoming a burden on his family—but it all hit him hard. He felt like anvils had landed on his shoulders.

The truth felt like a blow to his chest, making it hard to breathe. Every time he discovered a little bit of happiness, it was snatched away. Dad left, Mom died, he got sick, Gabby abandoned him—and now Shauna was talking to the man who was the genesis of his pain. Of course Dad had to show up just as he'd found Darcy.

He stood and made his way to his bathroom, where he stripped and climbed into the shower stall and turned on the hot water.

When his anguish had dulled to numbness, he turned off the water and dried himself before dressing in shorts and a t-shirt. Then he stared at his reflection in the mirror.

Pushing the door open, Carter stepped into his room and froze in place. Shauna was sitting in the chair by his desk.

"I don't want to discuss him," he growled, throwing his dirty clothes in the hamper.

"Then you're going to listen to me. I told him what we've been going through, and he feels terrible that he hasn't been here. I told him about Mom and about you. He said—"

"I don't want to hear this! The damage is done." He nearly spat the words as he dropped onto the corner of his bed. "If he had been here, then maybe you wouldn't have had to go under the knife for me," he said, his voice cracking. "I hate myself for what I've put you and Gage through. I think there's something wrong with me—physically because of the transplant and emotionally because of all the losses I've experienced." He sniffed and wiped his eyes. Why couldn't he keep his emotions under control tonight?

"Hey." She sat beside him. "You're my brother, my only sibling, my family, and I love you, Carter. I would do it all over again without hesitation, and I know you'd have done the same for me if the situation had been reversed."

He wiped his nose with a tissue. Then he pushed himself off the bed and crossed the room before leaning against the wall. He needed to put some distance between himself and Shauna. "I don't want to talk to him."

Shauna nodded. "Okay."

"You shouldn't talk to him either."

Shauna's expression became fierce. "That's my choice, Carter, and I'm not done with him yet. I've only just begun saying what I needed to say to him. You need to trust me on this." She stood, walked to the doorway, and spun toward him. "I'm sorry for upsetting you. I didn't mean to make you feel bad. I just wanted you to know that I'm going to get through to Dad."

She wagged a finger at him. "And don't you ever say you're broken again. There's nothing wrong with you, Carter. You're my brother and my family." Then she turned and trudged down the stairs.

* * *

THAT SAME EVENING, DARCY BOUNCED UP THE STAIRS WHILE HUMMING "The Keeper of the Stars." She flounced into her bedroom and twirled around as the memory of Carter holding her close filled her mind. She couldn't remember a time when she'd been so happy. Not since . . .

A vision of Jace's handsome face came to her, and she froze with her arms outstretched. As it often did, her happiness evaporated as sorrow dragged her back down to earth.

Crossing the room, she opened her jewelry box once again and pulled out her engagement ring. She sat down at her vanity and turned the ring over in her hand, recalling the night she had received it. Jace had taken her out for a fancy dinner on Valentine's Day, and the server had brought them two glasses of champagne. The ring was in the bottom of her glass, and when she looked up with surprise, she saw Jace had gotten down on one knee.

Plans for their November wedding took over her life that year. Haven would be her maid of honor and walk down the aisle wearing a gorgeous navy-blue dress. Derek would serve as Jace's best man, and Haven would walk back down the aisle with Derek after the ceremony. Darcy planned to throw the bouquet straight to Haven in hopes that Haven and Derek would be the next couple married.

And just as Darcy had predicted, Haven and Derek's engagement day had come. They were the next couple to be married, and Haven was planning her wedding.

Actually, they would be the first to be married since Darcy and Jace never got their day. Their life together was not to be.

Darcy could still see Jace's face and hear his voice, his laughter, in her mind. She slipped the ring onto her finger, and it still fit like a glove. She sniffed as she placed the diamond ring back in her jewelry box next to the wedding bands she and Jace never got to wear, gently tucking them into their special spot at the bottom of the box. She closed the lid, wiped her eyes, and curled up on her bed.

When Darcy closed her eyes, Haven's mother's words from the day before at the bridal shop echoed in her mind.

Jace would want to see you move on and find happiness with another man who loves you.

Darcy shook her head. It was so easy for people to tell her that Jace would want to see her happy, but how could she be happy when she was the reason he died?

Darcy lifted her phone. When it automatically unlocked, a selfie of her and Carter at the concert filled the screen. She scrolled through her photos, finding more of her and Carter at the concert, at his birthday party, at her parents' beach house.

Darcy set her phone on her nightstand, and tears pricked her eyes. Would she ever find true happiness with Carter—happiness without guilt?

As her sorrow and regret spiraled, she found her mind shifting toward a new fear. What if something happened to rip Carter from her life? She couldn't imagine losing him like she'd lost Jace. Just the idea of another loss nearly broke her heart in two.

CHAPTER 21

A WEEK LATER IN FLOWERING GROVE, DARCY SAT ON A CAMPING CHAIR IN Vet's Field. She scanned the clusters of people sitting on chairs and blankets awaiting the July 4 fireworks. Although Darcy's parents had invited her to join them at the beach house, she had thanked them and instead chosen to enjoy a small-town July 4 holiday with friends.

In the morning she had sat in the Barton Automotive parking lot with Carter, Haven, Derek, Shauna, Gage, Glenda, and Ernie for the traditional parade. She had loved every moment of it, especially the Flowering Grove High School marching band. Local children had also decorated their bikes and ridden along the parade path. Afterward, they all went to Shauna's house for a barbecue and spent the afternoon eating and laughing together.

Now they waited with the rest of the town for the fireworks to begin. The appetizing smells from the food trucks selling baked pretzels, nachos, popcorn, and funnel cakes filled the air while a buzz of conversations rumbled through the crowd. Children with glow sticks danced around as darkness began to take over the sky.

"I can't believe it's July already," Haven said as she popped open a can of Diet Coke. "Our wedding will be here before we know it."

Darcy looked up at the stars beginning to dot the sky. The air was humid and still. The fireworks would start any minute now, and anticipation seemed to crackle in the air.

"My parents and I booked a caterer and a DJ this past week, and we signed the contract for the Flowering Grove Country Club," Haven continued. "It's all coming together."

"That's amazing, Haven." She glanced over at Carter, and her senses fluttered. She hadn't told him yet, but she knew for sure that she loved him.

"Your brother is going to be my groomsman, right, Havey?" Derek took his fiancée's hand in his. "He hasn't gotten back to me."

"Of course he will be. We'll have to get the family together for dinner to work out the details."

"Hey." Carter's voice was right next to Darcy's ear, sending waves of goose bumps down her arms. "You look beautiful tonight."

Leaning over, she kissed him. "Thank you."

Just then a *whoosh* sounded, followed by a boom. Darcy jumped, then laughed as fireworks exploded in the sky. Carter positioned his chair closer, and Darcy rested her head against his shoulder.

They oohed and aahed as the show continued to color the night sky. She lost herself in thoughts of what their future could look like—together.

* * *

CARTER GLANCED OVER AT DARCY IN THE PASSENGER SEAT WHILE HE DROVE her home later that night. He found himself smiling as she continued to talk about Haven's wedding plans.

"Kaylen and I bought our bridesmaid dresses earlier this week. Haven finally found the ones she wanted us to wear. Did I show you the photo I have?" she asked.

"No." He stopped at a red light a couple of blocks from her neighborhood.

She leaned over and held the phone toward him and revealed a photo of her in a greenish-colored short-sleeved dress. "The color is called peacock. What do you think?"

"The dress is stunning, and you look beautiful as always."

"You're sweet." She set her phone on her lap. "Kaylen and I are still working out the bridal shower. We have so much to do. I told you we're Haven's only attendants, right? Derek is having his brother, Liam, as his best man and then Haven's brother, Vince, as his groomsman, so I'll walk with Liam."

Carter nodded before motoring through the intersection.

Silence fell between them, and he stole a glance at her. She was now staring down at her lap. "Do you want to talk about whatever is on your mind?" he asked.

When she looked up, her eyes were filled with tears.

Alarm raced through him. "Babe, are you okay? Do I need to pull over?"

She sniffed and then gave him a sad smile. "No, no, I'm okay. I was just thinking about Jace and my wedding."

He swallowed, not sure what to say.

"Haven was supposed to be my maid of honor, and Derek was going to be Jace's best man." Her voice was quiet, almost reverent. "We were going to be married in November, right around Thanksgiving, but he died in September."

Carter nodded, his lungs constricting with grief for her. He longed to take away her pain.

"My gown is stored in the back of one of my closets. I didn't know what to do with it after he . . . after he died."

Reaching over, Carter took her hand in his and gave it a gentle squeeze, hoping to give her the strength to continue. He lifted her hand to his mouth and kissed her knuckles.

She sniffed again and wiped her eyes with the back of her free hand. "Anyway, I need to plan this bridal shower. My mom thinks we should have it at a fancy restaurant, but I'm not sure if Haven would care for a place like that. She's not a super-fancy person, you know?" She pulled a tissue from her purse and blotted her eyes and nose.

He remained silent.

"Does it bother you when I talk about Jace?" Her voice sounded unsure, almost worried.

He shook his head. "Jace was an important part of your life, and I want you to feel comfortable sharing anything with me."

"Thank you," she whispered.

When he found a safe place, he pulled over and parked the truck. Then he placed his hands to her cheeks, and leaning down, he swept his lips over hers. His body relaxed. She wrapped her arms around his neck, and he savored the thrill of her mouth against his.

When they gently pulled apart, she rested her head on his sternum. "I'm so glad my car didn't start that day."

He grinned and rubbed his hands up and down her back. "I am too, babe. I am too."

* * *

DARCY SAT DOWN AT HER DESK IN HER OFFICE AFTER A TEAM MEETING ON a Friday afternoon. She glanced out her window toward the Uptown Charlotte skyline and smiled as she reflected on the past month and a half. She and Carter had gotten even closer as they spent more time together. They had enjoyed going to ball games, playing cards and mini golf, attending more car shows, and talking late into the night over the phone.

She was certain she loved him, but she still hadn't found the courage to tell him. She supposed she was waiting for him to say it first, but perhaps he was just as hesitant as she was. She knew he cared deeply for her. She could see it in his eyes when they talked, and she felt it in his kiss. She sighed at the thought of his lips and how they made her melt.

Darcy leaned back in her chair and mulled over why she was afraid to tell Carter how she felt. Perhaps she wasn't sure how he'd react when he found out the truth about her past. Would he want a woman who'd received a transplant and had to take medications for the rest of her life? But more than that, what if she found her birth mother and learned her kidney disease was hereditary? Would he want to plan a future with a woman who could possibly pass that disease on to their children?

Releasing a deep breath, she tried to turn her attention to her work emails. But when she found nothing pressing in her inbox, she pulled her phone from the pocket of her blazer and scrolled through a few photos of Carter. In one recent favorite, he stood next to a light metallic green 1968 Plymouth Fury during a car show the previous weekend.

She'd begun to cherish their car show dates in particular. As they walked around looking at the cars, they talked about everything from their favorite makes and models at the show to their childhoods to their workweeks. She still hadn't found the courage to tell him about her kidney transplant, but she had shared a little more about Jace. She promised herself she would tell Carter everything someday soon.

When Darcy returned to her email app, she found a message from the Lost and Found website. Her hands began to tremble as she opened the message and read it.

Dear Ms. Larsen,

We have information regarding your biological mother. Please call us for more details.

As Darcy read the email over and over again, her entire body began to quake. *Maybe they found my biological mother!* Her mouth dried as she debated what to do. She needed encouragement. She needed to talk to Carter.

DARCY: Can you talk?

Her phone began to ring almost immediately, and Carter's name and photo filled her screen. "Hey."

"What's going on?" he asked. The sounds of tools and automotive noise faded into the background, and she imagined him walking out to the parking lot.

"You're not going to believe this."

"What? Is something wrong?"

"I . . . I got an email from Lost and Found." She swiveled in her chair as she read the email to him.

"That's good news, Darce." She could hear the smile in his voice.

"Is it?" Her voice creaked. "What if it's *not* good news? What if she's no longer living? Or what if she doesn't want to talk to me? What if she never wanted me? Was looking for her a mistake?"

"You won't know until you call. I understand that you're scared. It's your decision if you reach out or not, but you've come this far." He paused. "Do you want to call them and find out?"

Her eyes brimmed with tears. "I . . . I don't know. I'm scared, Carter. I'm not as brave as I thought I was."

"Hey, babe. It's okay. If you're not ready, then don't reach out. That doesn't mean you're a coward. You don't have to do anything that makes you uncomfortable."

Darcy plucked a tissue from the box on her desk and dabbed her eyes. "I'm a wreck." A nervous laugh escaped her throat.

"Tell me how I can help you." His voice was warm, smooth, and exactly what she needed. "Do you want me to come over tonight? I can sit with you while you make the call."

She smiled. How had she managed to find such a wonderful and supportive boyfriend? "That's sweet, but I need to do this alone. Thanks for listening."

"Anytime. Call me if you need me."

"I'll let you know as soon as I find out the news."

"I'll be waiting," he promised before they disconnected the call.

Darcy stared at the email for a few moments, then picked up her phone again and dialed the number.

* * *

LATER THAT EVENING, DARCY SAT ON HER SOFA AND STARED DOWN AT THE name and phone number the woman at Lost and Found had given her. The woman's name was Robyn, and her phone number was local—meaning this woman who might be her biological mother might also be living in the Charlotte area.

Darcy had stared at the phone number for the past thirty minutes. She had paced her family room, nibbled on her fingernails, made herself a snack, and then paced some more. At one point, she considered taking Carter up on his offer of sitting with her while she called the woman. But then she talked herself out of it.

You've waited your entire life for this moment, Darcy. Just dial the number!

"Okay, okay," she whispered. Then she laughed. "I'm actually talking to myself and answering myself. I'm truly losing it!"

She took a deep breath, picked up her phone, and slipped her earbuds in her ears before dialing the number. Her heart pounded against her ribcage as the phone rang.

"Hello?" a woman's voice asked.

"Um, hi. My name is Darcy Larsen, and I'm looking for Robyn." She hoped she sounded more confident than she felt.

"Hi, Darcy." The woman paused. "I know who you are." Her voice was warm and thick. "I'm Robyn."

"Oh." Darcy hesitated, and suddenly all of the emotion—longing, hope, worry, loneliness—she'd carried for so long welled up and poured out of her, stealing her words for a moment. "I've . . . I've . . . Well, um . . ."

An awkward pause stretched between them as Darcy wondered what to say. She'd always imagined this moment, but now she was tongue-tied. What if this woman wasn't really her birth mother? What if the folks at the website sent her the wrong information?

"So?" Robyn said. "How . . . uh, how was your day?"

Darcy nodded as if Robyn could see her face through the phone. "It was good." She bit her lower lip. "Yours?"

"Good."

They were silent again, and then they both laughed.

"I've dreamed of this for so long, and now I don't know what to say," Darcy said.

Robyn sniffed. "I know what you mean." She cleared her throat. "I dreamed of hearing your voice." She paused. "And now, well, now it doesn't seem real."

"Exactly." Darcy pulled on the hem of her shirt.

"But here we are."

"Right."

More silence hovered between them, and Darcy kneaded her temples. She was going to take the plunge and tell Robyn how she felt. She just hoped Robyn was truly her birth mother and wanted to know her too.

"I've always wondered what you sounded like. What you looked like." Her eyes filled, and she wiped them. *Keep it together, Darce!*

"I have some photos I was going to send to you. When Lost and Found told me you were looking for me, I started getting some things together. Can I text them to you?"

"Yes, please."

"Okay. Coming now. Here are a few photos of me in my twenties and then a couple more recent ones."

Darcy chewed her nails, trying to imagine what the woman looked like. Did Darcy have her eyes? Her nose? Her facial structure? She closed her eyes and tried to settle her frayed nerves.

After a few moments, Darcy's phone chimed with a text. She opened the message and scrolled through the photos. She gasped as she opened photos of a woman who looked just like Dàrcy—blonde hair, bright-green eyes, petite stature.

Darcy started to cry. An overwhelming feeling doused her when she realized she had, for the first time, found someone who looked like her, someone who was a part of her, someone who knew where Darcy came from.

Her biological mother.

Finally.

"Darcy?" Robyn asked. "Are you okay?"

"Yeah, I am. I'm better than okay." She swallowed as more tears streamed down her warm cheeks. "I finally found you."

Robyn sniffed.

"I'll send you some of me." She chose a few photos of her and Carter and then one of her alone standing on the deck at her parents' beach house.

Silence filled the space between them for a few moments, and she imagined the photos appearing on Robyn's screen.

"Oh, Darcy," Robyn gushed. "You're beautiful."

"Thanks."

"Is the handsome man your husband or boyfriend?"

"Boyfriend."

"He looks nice," Robyn said. "Tell me about your life."

"Well, I live in Matthews, and I work in Charlotte. How about you?"

"I live in Concord."

Darcy folded her legs under herself. "You're that close?"

"I never wanted to leave here in case you looked for me." She paused. "Darcy, I never forgot you." Darcy could hear her take a trembling breath. "I've always wondered about you. You've been on my mind and in my heart since the moment I found out I was going to have you." She sniffed. "I've always hoped you were okay."

Darcy stared at her front door.

"I worried that you had enough to eat, that you were warm, that you were happy, that you were healthy, and that you were loved—because, honey, I've always loved you."

Darcy bit her lower lip as her tears began to fall again. These words were music to her ears. "Thank you." She rubbed her fingers over her eyes. "Do you have a family?"

"Yes, I'm married and have two sons."

"I have brothers?" Darcy whispered.

"Yes, you have two half-brothers," Robyn said. "Hang on and I'll send you photos."

Once again Darcy tried to imagine what the photos would reveal. Would her brothers look like her? Would she feel a connection when she saw their faces? She wiped her eyes and tried to stop her body from trembling.

When the photos came through, Darcy took in the faces of her two half-brothers. Like her, they had blond hair, and she was certain of a resemblance in their smiles.

"I can't believe it," she whispered. "I've always been an only child. I thought I'd never have siblings." Darcy started to cry again.

"Did I upset you?" Robyn asked.

"No," Darcy managed to say. "I'm crying because it's really you."

Robyn chuckled. "Yes, and it's really you." She paused for a beat. "Now what else can I tell you?"

Darcy snuggled under a blanket and listened as her biological mother began to answer questions she'd carried around in her heart for as long as she could remember.

CHAPTER 22

Darcy ended the call and wiped her eyes. She felt as if she were spinning. For the first time in her life, she had just spoken to her biological mother—*her biological mother*—for almost four hours. After all of these years she'd finally found Robyn, and Robyn wanted to know Darcy in return.

She hugged her arms to her middle as another wave of happiness swept over her. She glanced at the time on her phone and found it was midnight, but she was wide awake. She felt like she might burst with excitement. She wanted to tell Carter everything, but most likely he was asleep. She recalled when he'd once told her she could text or call him anytime.

Taking a chance, she shot off a text to him: Are you awake?

Her phone began to ring with a call from him right away.

"I've been waiting for you to call or text. How'd it go?" he asked.

"I found my birth mother, Carter. I really found her." Her emotion bubbled up, and she started crying again. Would she ever run out of tears?

"Do you want me to come over?"

She sniffed and pulled herself together. "That's okay. It's after midnight."

"If you need me, I'll be there. I don't care what time it is."

Admiration glowed in her chest for this wonderful man. "I don't want you out driving this late."

"I'm wide awake and ready to come over."

"Are you sure?"

"Positive, Darcy. I'll be there soon."

She ended the call and hugged a blanket to her chest while her tears continued to flow.

* * *

CARTER KNOCKED ON DARCY'S FRONT DOOR FORTY-FIVE MINUTES later. As soon as they had hung up the phone, he had dropped his overnight essentials into a backpack and flown out the door. He glanced around her quiet neighborhood, taking in the warm yellow glow from the row of matching porch lights while the hum of car engines sounded on the main road behind her neighborhood.

He knocked again and then tried to peek through a sidelight window, but a privacy curtain blocked his vision. When he heard footfalls closing in, he stood up straight.

The lock flipped and the door opened, and Darcy stood before him dressed in light-green pajama pants and a matching shirt. Her hair was styled in a knot on the top of her head, and she looked adorable.

"Thank you for coming," she said.

He entered the foyer and locked the door behind him. "You don't have to thank me." He dropped his backpack on the bench by the door. "Would you like some tea?"

"How'd you know?"

"Lucky guess."

Carter located a tea bag and mug before adding water and then warming it in the microwave. Once it was ready, he brought it to her in the family room and set it on a coaster on the coffee table.

He sat down beside her on the large sectional. "When you're ready, tell me everything."

Darcy took a sip of tea and moved her fingers over the warm blue mug. "She was everything I hoped she'd be and more." She set the mug down, and her lips trembled. "Carter, I have two half-brothers. I'm not an only child."

When her tears began to flow, he gathered her into his arms, wishing he could soothe her. "It's okay," he whispered. "Let it all out, babe."

"She told me she loves me and never forgot me. Every January 22 she thought about my birthday, and she tried to imagine what I looked like and what I was doing." She snuggled against him, and he rubbed her back. "She lives in Concord, Carter. We're going to meet tomorrow."

"I'm glad she's close."

Darcy pulled her phone from her pocket. "Look at these photos she sent me."

He scrolled through the photos of a young woman who was the spitting image of Darcy. "That's her?"

"Yeah." She beamed. "Her name is Robyn Decker." She pointed to a photo of two young men. "Those are my brothers—Brayden and Keaton. They're seventeen and fifteen."

"Wow." He shook his head. "I see a resemblance."

"Me too."

"What did she tell you about your biological dad?"

"We didn't get into that yet," Darcy said. "I'm going to ask about him tomorrow. She wanted to keep me, but her parents said no. They arranged for her to come to Charlotte and stay with friends until she had me. She couldn't even hold me after I was born. All she knew was that an older couple who had tried to have a baby for years adopted me, and she prayed they would love me and give me a good life." She paused. "Her parents live in Florida. She also has a couple of younger sisters, so that means I have aunts, uncles, and cousins too."

When Darcy sniffed again, Carter closed his eyes. Listening to her cry was tearing his heart out, and he would do anything in his power to offer her comfort.

During the last month he had realized he was in love with Darcy, and his feelings for her were like nothing he'd ever felt for anyone before in his life. He needed her like he needed air to breathe.

She snuggled up to him. "I'm so glad you're here."

"Me too."

"I just can't believe I found her, Carter. It's like a dream come true." She wrapped her arms around his waist.

He kissed the top of her head.

Darcy covered her mouth to shield a yawn. "I think I've worn myself out." She drooped against the sofa cushions.

"You should go to bed."

She stood and picked up the cup of tea. "I can make up the guest room for you."

"No need. This sofa looks comfortable."

She eyed him with suspicion. "My guest room has an actual bed in it, Carter."

"I'll be fine here."

"Let me get you a pillow." She strode toward the kitchen, then he heard footsteps climbing a staircase.

He glanced around the family room and noticed a shelf packed with books and framed photos. He stepped over to it and found photos of Darcy with her parents posing on the beach and a few of Darcy and Haven dressed up at what looked like parties.

Questions about Jace filled his mind. He perused the shelf for snapshots of Darcy posing with a man, but he didn't find any. Perhaps seeing them every day had been too painful, so she had packed them up. He wouldn't blame her for that at all.

Footfalls sounded on the stairs, and he met her at the doorway leading to the kitchen.

"Here's a pillow and a blanket." She held them up. "I know it's the middle of August, but I still use a heavy blanket to keep warm in the air-conditioning."

He took the pillow and blanket from her. "Thanks."

They stared at each other for a moment, then she reached for his free hand. Carter set the pillow and blanket on the counter beside him.

"I don't know how to thank you, Carter." Her eyes filled again. "It means so much to me that you jumped out of bed and drove out here after midnight."

"Darcy, you should know by now that I would do anything for you."

"Thank you," she whispered. "I couldn't get through this without you."

Carter pulled her against him before placing a finger under her chin and angling it toward him. Longing tore through every cell of his body as he placed his palms on her cheeks, leaned down, and pressed his lips against hers. He closed his eyes while his lips massaged hers, and a quiver of wanting vibrated through him.

When he broke the kiss, she stared up at him. "See you in the morning," he said. Then he grinned. "Actually, later today."

"That's true. Sleep well, Carter."

She retreated up the stairs, and he turned off the lights in the kitchen and hallway before returning to the family room. He settled on the sofa and tried to get comfortable. Then he lost himself in thoughts of Darcy and waited for sleep to find him.

* * *

DARCY AWOKE TO THE DELICIOUS SMELLS OF COFFEE, SAUSAGE, AND TOAST later that morning. For a moment she was confused, wondering where the smells came from. Then the events of the night before came back to her in a rush. She had found her birth mother! And Carter had come over to hold her while she cried.

Carter!

She jumped out of bed and dashed into the bathroom. She brushed her teeth and chose a pleated green sundress with white flowers trailing the bottom of the skirt. After styling her hair in a loose French braid and applying minimal makeup, she pulled on strappy sandals and raced down to the kitchen.

"Hey, sleepyhead." Carter stood at the stove, scrambling eggs in a skillet. Sausage sizzled in the pan beside him, and toast popped up from the toaster.

He looked gorgeous dressed in his khaki shorts and a black t-shirt advertising a performance shop. His chiseled jaw sported a few days of scruff, and his light-brown hair looked as if he had wet it before running a brush through it.

Darcy recalled how safe and protected she had felt in his arms last night. Her lips tingled at the memory of that amazing kiss he'd given her before she'd gone to bed.

"This all smells fantastic," she said. "How about I set the table?"

He nodded toward the nook. "Thanks."

She gathered up plates and utensils, then quickly set the table. "How'd you sleep?" she asked, moving to the coffee machine to pour each of them a mug.

He shrugged. "Fine. That sofa is pretty comfortable." He carried the frying pan over to the table and scraped half of the eggs onto each plate. Then he served them both sausage and toast.

"You really didn't need to cook for me, Carter."

"Well, you cooked for me when we were at the beach." He motioned toward the chair. "Sit, please," he said, and she did as instructed. After grabbing butter and creamer from the refrigerator, he returned to the table to join her.

Darcy examined their breakfast and smiled up at him. "This is amazing."

"And you look beautiful. Now enjoy your breakfast. You need to leave soon to meet Robyn."

She pulled out her phone and checked the time. He was right. She had to be on the road in less than an hour. She fidgeted with the skirt of her dress. She couldn't be late to her first meeting with her birth mother!

"You have plenty of time." He rested his hand on hers. "Deep breaths."

Darcy nodded. "You're right. It'll be fine."

"Yes, it will." He tapped his fork on her plate. "Now eat."

Darcy buttered a piece of toast and sampled the eggs. "You're a good cook, Carter Donovan."

"I'll admit I make a mean piece of toast." He held up his half-eaten slice, and she laughed. "Are you excited or nervous to see Robyn?"

She frowned. "Nervous." She set her fork down. "We bonded on the phone, but what if it's awkward in person?"

"The first few minutes might be, but the ice will be broken once you start talking."

Darcy nodded and took a bite of sausage.

Carter's lips pressed down into a frown. "I don't think I ever told you that my sister found my father."

Darcy wiped her mouth with a paper napkin. "She did?"

"Yeah. The night we went to the concert I came home and found her sitting on the porch on her phone. She looked upset, like she'd been crying." He ran his tongue over his teeth. "She was talking to him."

Surprise spread through her. "Did you talk to him too?"

He shook his head with emphasis. "I refused." He clasped his mug. "I think she's trying to make him understand how badly he hurt us and Mom, but I'm not sure what she thinks she's going to prove. He obviously doesn't care about any of us. Why would he change now?" He glowered. "As far as I'm concerned, it's too late. She's wasting her efforts on him."

The pain in Carter's eyes nearly split her in two. She took his hand in hers. "I'm sorry he hurt you."

"Thanks." His expression warmed, and he swallowed a bite of sausage. "Let's talk about your day. Do you want me to go with you?"

She shook her head. "I appreciate it, but I need to do this alone."

"Are you going to call me as soon as you head home?"

"You know I will."

Carter held up his mug as if to toast her. "Good. I'll be waiting for your call."

They ate in silence for a few moments, and Darcy tried to think of something to lighten the mood. Then she recalled Carter's funny stories about the customer who harbored a crush on him.

"You haven't mentioned Mrs. Deese in a while. Has she been by to visit you lately?"

When Carter grinned, Darcy felt relief flutter through her. She had missed that glorious smile. "As a matter of fact, she came in yesterday insisting that her wiper blades were broken again."

"Were they?"

He shook his head. "She needed washer fluid. And I took care of it for her, of course."

They both laughed, and Carter shared more funny customer stories while they finished breakfast.

When their plates were clean, Carter carried them to the counter. "I'll clean up so you can get on the road." He opened the dishwasher.

"No." Darcy reached for the plates. "You did the cooking, and I also don't believe you slept well on the sofa."

He gave her a knowing smile. "I got this." He nodded toward the stairs. "Go."

She stilled and then rushed upstairs, where she took her daily cocktail of medications required to keep her transplant healthy. She brushed her teeth, fixed her makeup, and tucked a few flyaway hairs into her braid.

When she returned to the kitchen, Carter was washing the pans.

"You really don't need to do that," she said as she gathered up her purse.

"I don't mind." He set one of the pans on the drying board. "How should I lock up? Is there a keypad next to the garage?"

Darcy hedged.

Carter held up his hands. "Unless, of course, you don't want me to know the code, which I respect."

"It's not that." She moved to the end of the counter and opened the junk drawer. She found the spare key—*Jace's* spare key—and stared at it. To hand the key to Carter would feel like a big step in a new direction. She closed her eyes. Was she making too much of this? If not, then why were her insides tied up in a knot?

A hand on her shoulder brought her back to reality.

"Hey, I was kidding. I'll just set the bottom lock and pull the door closed. You don't have to—"

"It's fine," Darcy said, interrupting him. She held the spare key out for him. "Here's a key."

Carter's eyes widened. "Thanks. I'll give it back to you."

"No. Keep it." She kissed him. "I'll call you later. Thank you for everything."

"You're welcome," he called as she hurried out the door to meet her biological mother for the first time.

CHAPTER 23

DARCY FIDGETED WITH HER PURSE STRAP WHILE SHE STOOD ON OAK Street in Matthews. She scanned the nearby parking lot, looking for anyone who might possibly be Robyn. She paced back and forth, imagining all kinds of scenarios for how the meeting might go. What if she and Robyn had nothing in common? What if they sat awkwardly and stared at each other?

Or what if they bonded immediately, and Darcy walked out of there feeling complete for the first time in her life?

Darcy already felt guilty for looking for her biological mother because her adoptive parents had given her such a wonderful life. They had provided her with nothing but love and unending support. If she were to become close with Robyn, though, they might feel slighted or taken advantage of. Even worse, they might feel left behind. Betrayed.

She folded her jittery hands.

"Darcy?"

Turning, she came face-to-face with Robyn. She sucked in a breath as she looked into green eyes that reflected hers. Although Robyn's blonde hair had a few strands of gray, and though her lips had surely thinned with age, Darcy still knew she was looking into a face that resembled her own.

For the first time in her life, she was looking at her biological family. Darcy felt an immediate connection—something unexplainable, warm, and overwhelming.

"Hi," Darcy whispered.

Robyn clasped her hands together. "Oh, Darcy. You're absolutely beautiful!"

"Thank you," Darcy said. "Would it be okay if I hugged you?"

Robyn nodded, and her eyes glimmered as she opened her arms. Darcy stepped forward and wrapped her arms around the woman who had brought her into the world. She breathed in her scent—lavender mixed with soap—and couldn't stop her tears from flowing. She'd waited nearly her entire life for this moment.

"I'm so happy to meet you," Robyn whispered. "I've waited so long for this."

Darcy laughed. "I was just thinking the same thing." She stepped out of her embrace. "Thank you."

"Sweetie, you don't need to thank me." Robyn squeezed her shoulder. "Let's sit."

They found a bench in front of a line of stores and sat down. The August morning was hazy, hot, and humid as the sun beat down on Darcy's shoulders and neck. Birds sang in nearby trees, and the fresh scent of flowers from nearby planters floated over her. Darcy's heartbeat took flight as she looked at her birth mother, and questions churned inside her.

"So," Robyn said. "How are you today?"

Darcy laughed. "Great."

"Tell me about your parents," Robyn said. "All I know about them is that they were older."

"Their names are Ross and Josie. They were in their forties when they adopted me, and they had tried for years to have a child. They've given me an amazing life." Darcy shared how her parents had run their own orthodontic practice and then sold it about ten years ago. She talked about growing up in Marvin, spending vacations at the beach house, traveling around the world, and going to the University of North Carolina at Charlotte.

"Are you close to your folks?"

"Yes, very close."

Robyn nodded, and her expression seemed wistful. "I always prayed you had a good life. I'm grateful to hear that you do."

"I definitely do, and I appreciate everything they've done for me. I've always known they love and support me." She paused. "I just always felt like I didn't fit in. It's nothing my parents did or said. I just always felt different from them—like I didn't belong.

"They never pressured me to be like them. That was all pressure I put on myself. For example, I felt I should go into the medical field because that's what they did, but turns out, I'm not cut out for that. I know it's okay to be different. They love me for who I am, and I'm so thankful to have their love and support." She was silent again, trying to find the right words. "But I also think it's natural to wonder about where you came from. Something always seemed to be missing in my life, and I think that missing piece might have been you."

Robyn sniffed and blotted her eye with a tissue. "I begged my parents to let me keep you, but they insisted it would be best if I gave you up since I was only sixteen. Still, it broke my heart."

Darcy moved her finger over the edge of the worn wooden seat. "Would you tell me about my father?"

"Of course." Robyn folded her hands in her lap. "His name was Stuart Bost. I met him at a friend's birthday party. He was very handsome. He was tall, brown-haired, and had stunning blue eyes that reminded me of the Carolina sky. I was smitten the first time I met him." She shook her head. "He was a couple of years older than me, and we went out on a few dates. I thought I was in love, and . . . well, you know." A sigh sifted through her lips. "Next thing I knew, I was pregnant."

Robyn frowned. "I was terrified to tell my parents because I knew I had let them down." She fidgeted with her purse strap. "And then I couldn't find Stuart to tell him the news. I called the house, and his mother said he had left for boot camp."

"He joined the military?"

Robyn shrugged. "That's what his mother told me. I don't know if it was true or if she just said it to get me to stop calling. I dropped by the house, wrote him, and tried to track him down in the military, but I couldn't find him. Then I gave it another shot after you were born. I wanted him to know that you existed, but my efforts were in vain. I have a feeling his mother blocked me the best way she could, even though I told her about you."

"I'm sorry he hurt you." Darcy took Robyn's hands in hers.

She smiled. "Thank you, but it all worked out. I got my GED and then went to college, and that's where I met Graham. He's very supportive and loving, and we adore our two boys." She gave Darcy's hand a gentle squeeze. "I've waited a lifetime to find you, and now I have."

"I feel the same way."

"Tell me about Carter," Robyn said.

Darcy couldn't stop her smile. "He's wonderful." She shared a brief version of how they met and started dating. "We just seemed to click. Something about him just felt familiar." She sighed. "He's kind, sweet, easy to talk to, and has a great sense of humor." She chuckled, recalling how he'd joked about watching reality TV when she'd picked up her car at his shop.

"And handsome," Robyn added with a grin.

"Oh yeah, he's very handsome," Darcy agreed. "Will you tell me about my brothers?" Happiness whirled through her. "I'm so excited to have siblings."

"Well, they are very athletic, but they get that from their father," Robyn began. "They both play football on their high school team. They're very competitive."

Darcy listened while her birth mother discussed her brothers. Then she folded her hands as the question that had haunted her for more than three years rose to the surface.

"Does kidney disease run in your family?" She froze, waiting for the response.

"Kidney disease?" Robyn asked. "Well, uh, my mother told me my grandfather suffered with kidney disease. He was on dialysis for several years. He passed away when I was an infant." Then her brow creased. "Why do you ask?"

Darcy's limbs trembled as the words she'd feared rolled through her mind: Her kidney disease *was* hereditary. There was a chance she could pass it along to her children. She took a ragged breath as she stared down at her sundress. Then she met her biological mother's concerned gaze. "I had a kidney transplant a little over two years ago."

Robyn leaned toward her. "Oh, Darcy. What happened?"

"I wasn't feeling well, and when my symptoms seemed to linger longer than an ordinary virus, my doctor ran some tests. I thought I might have mono or something, but when the bloodwork came back, I found out the truth." She stared out toward the line of stores across the street as memories of the ordeal filled her mind.

Robyn touched her hand. "Take your time."

"My kidney function was declining, and the numbers weren't good. My primary care doctor gave me a referral to a nephrologist." She picked at a loose piece of wood on the bench seat. "Next thing I knew, I was told to start preparing for a transplant. My parents wanted to donate a kidney for me, but they both are older and weren't matches." She hedged as her eyes began to sting. "But my fiancé insisted on donating for me."

"Your fiancé?"

Darcy nodded. "Yes, I was engaged . . . His name was Jace Allen."

"Oh." Robyn's expression was full of curiosity.

"He wasn't a match for me, so he donated a kidney on my behalf. He gave to another man about his age, while I received a kidney from a man who was donating for his daughter. It's called a paired donor exchange."

"And you were engaged to Jace?"

"Yes." Darcy took a deep breath. "He passed away. It will be two years next month."

"Oh sweetie. I am so sorry." Robyn looped her arm around Darcy's shoulders. "That had to be devastating for you."

"Yes." Darcy looked out toward a group of young women walking into a boutique across the street. "I had forgotten to pick up my medications, and he offered to go pick them up for me." She released a tremulous breath. "He was turning into the pharmacy parking lot when a man ran a red light and broadsided him. He died on impact." She shuddered. "If I had only gotten my medication a few days before, he'd still be here. We'd be married and maybe even starting a family by now. But he's gone because of me."

"Don't say that, Darcy. It wasn't your fault."

"Yet I live with that guilt every day. And I don't know how to move on."

"But you are moving on. You're with Carter now."

"It's not that simple. I love Carter, but I don't know how to tell him. I also haven't told him about the kidney transplant yet." She hugged her arms to her middle. "I feel this invisible force holding me back. It's like I can't take that step with him. I can't fully let go of Jace because it's my fault he died. Jace gave up his kidney for me, *and* his life." She turned toward Robyn and sniffed. "I'm sorry. I didn't mean to unload."

"Don't apologize," Robyn said. "You deserve happiness, Darcy."

Although she nodded, she didn't agree. "So kidney disease does run in your family." Disappointment continued to rain down on her.

"Well, if my grandfather had it and now you have it, it seems to have skipped a few generations. I'm sorry you've suffered like that."

Darcy ran her hands down her sundress. "I had wondered if I might pass the disease along to my children—if I ever get married and have a family."

"I suppose there might be a chance, but I wouldn't allow that fear to stop you from having a family if that's what you want." Robyn touched her arm. "How are your kidneys now?"

"Perfect. I saw the doctor the day my car wouldn't start, which was the same day I met Carter. I'll need to take medication for the rest of my life, but hopefully I won't need another transplant."

"That is a miracle." Robyn rested her arm on Darcy's shoulder. "I'm sorry I couldn't be there for you when you were going through that."

Darcy smiled at her. "But you're here now."

"Yes, I am."

They sat on the bench and talked for another hour. Then they took a few selfies and walked to their cars sitting in a nearby parking lot.

"I don't mean to be forward, but I'd love to meet Graham and my brothers sometime," Darcy said. When Robyn hesitated, Darcy's stomach dropped.

"I need to tell you something." Robyn grimaced, and Darcy clasped her purse strap. "I haven't told Brayden or Keaton about you."

"Oh. Why?"

Robyn leaned back against her SUV. "I honestly don't know how to tell them."

Darcy blinked, trying to comprehend what Robyn had said. "So you don't want them to know about me?"

"I'm not sure they're ready yet. It will be a big shock to them to learn they have an older sister."

Darcy felt her heart begin to break, but she worked to keep her expression even.

"But when I do tell them, I'll be sure to get you all together." Robyn pulled her in for a hug. "I'll call you soon. I'm so glad I found you."

"Me too." As Darcy watched her birth mother drive away, she tried to fight the surging disappointment. She had finally found her family and some answers, but she was still part of a secret Robyn wanted to keep.

* * *

CARTER LOOKED AT THE TIME ON HIS PHONE LATER THAT EVENING. HE'D been waiting on pins and needles to hear news about Darcy's meetup with her biological mother. After she'd left her townhouse, he had cleaned up the kitchen, folded the blanket he'd used overnight, and left it on the sofa beside the pillow.

He'd left her house and spent the afternoon running errands and taking care of chores, repeatedly checking his phone and expecting a text or call from Darcy.

Worry and concern kept nipping at him, though he'd tried in vain to keep his mind occupied with something else. Once his other chores were done, he paced the detached garage and organized the tools in his toolbox to stay busy. He hoped Darcy and her biological mother were engrossed in a wonderful discussion and had lost track of time.

When his phone finally rang, Carter tripped over his floor jack and grasped the edge of his workbench to right himself. Lifting his phone, he found Darcy's name on his screen. His heartbeat trilled.

"Hey," he answered.

"Hey yourself, Donovan." He could hear road noise in the background, indicating she was driving. "Can you meet me at our spot in the park?"

Carter pulled his Suburban keys from his pocket. "Yup. Are you on your way?"

"Be there in about fifteen minutes."

He exited the garage and hit the code on the keypad to close the bay door. "See you soon."

Carter arrived at their favorite bench ten minutes later. He scanned the area, and when he spotted Darcy walking toward him, he closed the distance between them.

When she wrapped her arms around his neck and pulled him close, he closed his eyes and breathed in her comforting scent. "I guess it went well?" he asked.

"I know where I come from, Carter," she whispered, her voice wobbling. "It feels like a dream."

He rubbed her back. "I'm so happy for you."

"Me too." She rested her head on his shoulder. "Thank you."

He looked down at her. "For what?"

"For being you." She moved her fingers over the stubble on his chin.

He kissed her. "Are you hungry?"

She nodded. "I can't believe I skipped lunch. We were so into our conversation that I lost track of time. Let's get something to eat."

He took her hand and led her over to a nearby food truck, where they each ordered a chicken bacon wrap, chips, and a drink before returning to their bench. "Give me details," he said as they opened their wraps.

Darcy's eyes glistened as she held up her phone. "I look like her, right?"

He expelled a puff of air as he took in the photos. Darcy smiled alongside a woman who looked like she was in her forties. She had blonde hair and the same green eyes he adored. "Yup."

She sniffed. "We talked about everything." She opened her small bag of chips. "My brothers are fifteen and seventeen, and they're athletic, which she says they got from their dad. Her husband, Graham, works in IT. I guess he's my stepdad? My step bio-dad? My bonus dad?"

Carter nodded. "I guess so."

She ate a few chips before telling him about her talk with Robyn.

"There's just one thing that's bothering me about Robyn."

Carter turned to face her. "What?"

"She hasn't told my brothers about me." She frowned. "I asked if I could meet them, and she said she wasn't ready." She stared down at her bag of chips. "It hurts. I finally have siblings, but I can't meet them."

He gave her a side hug. "I'm sorry. Just give her time. I'm sure you'll meet them eventually."

"I hope so."

"When are you going to tell your parents about Robyn?"

Darcy cringed. "I haven't figured that out yet, but I will tell them soon."

They talked in the park until the sun began to set, and then he walked her to her car.

"I'm glad you had a good day with your birth mother." He skimmed his hands down her arms.

Darcy kissed him and then unlocked her car. "Thank you for meeting me. Good night, Carter."

"Good night." As he watched her drive away, he hoped someday he'd find the courage to tell her everything.

CHAPTER 24

"WHAT ABOUT YOUR 'SOMETHING BORROWED'?" DARCY ASKED HAVEN. It was a Friday evening two weeks later, and they were perusing a department store in Charlotte. "Are you borrowing something from your mom?"

Haven turned from a display of wedge sandals. "My grandma's pearls. I guess they count for something old *and* something borrowed." Her blue eyes sparkled. "I can't believe the wedding is only two months away."

Darcy nodded. "Time is going by so fast." In fact, it seemed like it was coming too fast. She and Kaylen had three weeks until the shower, and even though the invitations had been dropped into the mail, they still had details to iron out.

"What do you think of these?" Haven held up a pair of sandals. "Do they look like honeymoon sandals?"

Darcy faltered. "Um, I'm not sure what honeymoon sandals look like, but those are really cute."

"Then honeymoon sandals they are." Haven walked over to one of the sales associates. "Excuse me. Could I see these in a nine?"

The young woman took the shoe and disappeared.

"So, Darce." Haven leaned against the counter. "We haven't really talked much lately. I'm sorry I've been so distracted."

"Stop it. You're getting married."

"I know, but I miss you." Haven touched her arm. "How's Carter?"

"He's fine." Darcy frowned.

Alarm overtook Haven's face. "Oh no. Are you two having problems?"

"No, no." Darcy held her hand up. "It's not that. I haven't told you something that happened recently, and I feel really guilty."

Haven's strawberry-blonde eyebrows rose. "What?"

"I found my birth mother."

Haven gasped so loudly that a few customers wandering the shoe department turned and gave her and Darcy curious stares. "When?"

"A couple of weeks ago." Darcy placed a hand on Haven's forearm. "Please don't be angry. I'm sorry I didn't tell you. I started looking for her in May, and I kept it quiet in case nothing came of it. I found her two weeks ago, and we've been talking almost every day since."

Haven hugged her. "That's amazing, Darce."

The sales associate returned with the shoes, and Haven tried them on. After she paid for them, she and Darcy walked out into the mall.

"Tell me more about her," Haven said.

Darcy filled her in on Robyn, her stepdad and biological dad, and her half-brothers. "I want to meet my brothers, but Robyn isn't ready for that." She frowned. "And I haven't told my parents about Robyn yet because I don't know how." She sighed. "I almost told them last weekend, but I couldn't find the courage."

"What are you afraid of?"

Darcy looked down at her feet. "I don't want to hurt them."

Haven halted. "Darcy, you've always been close to your folks. I think they'll understand."

Darcy nodded.

"Let's go into Bath and Body Works. I need some new lotions." Haven took Darcy's arm and steered her into the store.

The delicious scents of the store washed over Darcy as they weaved through the crowd to the display of new lotions.

"Does Carter know about your birth mother?" Haven asked.

"Yeah, and he's been so supportive," Darcy said. "He came over after midnight the night I first connected with her just to hold me while I cried."

Haven clucked her tongue. "That's the sweetest thing I've ever heard."

"Meanwhile I still haven't told him about the kidney transplant."

Haven studied her. "Again, Darce, what are you afraid of?"

"I don't know. There's something holding me back. I'm afraid to tell him I love him too."

Haven shook her head. "Darcy, it's so obvious you two are in love. He wouldn't have come over at midnight to hold you if he didn't love you. Maybe you need to be brave and take the first step. Be honest with him."

Darcy nodded. "Maybe I should." But deep down, as much as she wanted to tell the truth, she worried that honesty with everyone she loved might come at a cost.

* * *

CARTER SAT AT THE KITCHEN TABLE THE FOLLOWING TUESDAY EVENING, staring at a bank statement. If only he could pay off his loan early, then he could consider starting a life with Darcy.

Every time he spoke to her on the phone or met her for a date, he longed to be completely honest about his battle with kidney disease—but his pride held him back. Well, not only pride, but also fear of hurt, rejection, and loss.

The sound of a truck pulling into the driveway drew his attention to the back door. He'd been surprised when Shauna had texted to tell him that she and Gage were going out to dinner on a weeknight.

Lately Shauna had looked exhausted after work. She had dark circles under her eyes, and she seemed to yawn nonstop before she went to bed early. She also seemed to have an upset stomach nearly every day, and the smell of the chicken Gage had made last night sent her running out of the room.

Carter was worried about his older sister, but whenever he asked her if she was okay, she insisted she was fine.

He closed his computer and slipped the bank statement back into its envelope as the back door opened and Shauna stepped in from the garage. She seemed to glow as she laughed at something Gage said.

"What are you up to, Carter?" she asked with a grin.

He shook his head. "Not much. How was dinner?"

"Great." Shauna and Gage shared a look. "I think we should tell him."

"Tell me what?" Carter asked.

Gage made a sweeping gesture toward her. "Go ahead."

"Well." Shauna clasped her hands together. "Gage and I have been seeing a fertility specialist, and it's finally happened." She sucked in a breath. "You're going to be an uncle!"

Carter jumped up from his chair, and excitement rushed through him. "That's fantastic!" He pulled his sister in for a hug and then shook Gage's hand. "Congratulations!"

"But that's not all of our news." She took a deep breath. "We're having twins!"

Carter's mouth dropped open. "Twins? That's amazing!" He hugged his sister again and patted Gage's back.

"Thanks." Gage pulled Shauna against him. "We've been praying for this for a long time."

Shauna nodded. "I was beginning to think it wouldn't happen. We wanted to wait until we were sure before telling anyone. Today I had a checkup, and we confirmed everything is looking good. We're due at the end of March, but twins usually come early."

"I'm so excited for you," Carter said, certain his joy would bubble over.

She hugged him. "Thank you. I couldn't wait to tell you, but our appointment was late, so we decided to grab something to eat first." She started through the kitchen. "And now I'm exhausted again. I'm going to take a shower."

Gage grabbed a can of Coke from the refrigerator and held it out to Carter. "Want one?"

"Sure." Carter accepted the can and sat down on his chair.

"I've been dying to tell you, but Shauna wanted confirmation first. We've had some heartbreaks in the past, so we didn't want to get our family excited only to have to tell everyone that something went wrong." He sat down across from Carter. "How was the shop this afternoon after I left?"

"Fine." Carter's mind spun as he considered what it would mean for Shauna and Gage to become parents. Carter couldn't wait to be an uncle, but surely he'd be in the way—especially when they brought home twins. Now he truly had to find a way to move out—and within six months.

Gage took a drink and studied Carter. "What's on your mind?"

"Just excitement."

Gage's smile was wide. "This has been such a long journey." His smile wobbled. "Seeing Shauna so distraught over it has been tough. I'm thankful it's finally happening for us."

Carter popped open his can. "When you came in, I was trying to figure out a way to pay off my loan early. Once I get my act together,

I'll find my own place. That way you and Shauna won't have an extra person around while you're taking care of babies."

His brother-in-law gave him a look of disbelief. "Please, Carter. You've never been in the way. I don't know why you think you are."

"It's not just that." Carter took a drink from the can. "I want a future with Darcy, but I don't know how to get out from under this debt."

Gage's expression brightened. "So things are going well with her."

"They are." Carter considered his options. "I was thinking maybe I should sell the Road Runner. I could get more for it with a rebuilt engine, but the car body is in excellent shape. I'm sure there's a collector out there—"

Gage held his hand up. "Whoa, Carter," he interrupted. "I know how much that car means to you. I'd hate to see you sell it."

"If it meant rebuilding my life, then I'd do it."

"I know you care for Darcy. I can tell by the way you talk about her, and it's obvious she makes you happy. You deserve to be happy, Carter." He paused as if working through something in his mind. "But if you let that car go, you'll regret it. I know how much your grandparents meant to you, and that car was a big part of your memories of your grandfather."

Carter nodded. "Right."

"Would you consider something else first?" Gage paused. "There might be another way for you to get back on your feet, but you need to listen."

"I'm listening."

"You know that Shauna found your father."

Carter felt every muscle in his body stiffen.

"Just hear me out, Carter. She's been talking to him. At first I think she wanted to find him because she needed him to acknowledge what he did to you, her, and your mom." He pressed his lips together. "Now that we're expecting twins, it's more than that. I think she wants him to learn how to be a grandfather so our children can have more family around."

Carter shook his head as frustration surged through him. "She's just going to get her heart broken if she's expecting our father to step up."

"Well, he wants to visit."

"I hope she tells him no."

Gage took a drink of his soda as if avoiding the response.

"You've got to be kidding me, Gage." He pushed his chair back and stood as his frustration morphed into fury. "You'd better tell me when he's coming so I can make sure I'm not here. I'll crash on Darcy's sofa until he's gone."

"I'm not done. There's more." Gage's expression seemed to plead with him. "Sit, Carter. Please."

He slowly lowered himself down onto the chair.

"How would you feel if your father wanted to do something to try to make it up to you?"

"Like what?"

Gage tapped the tabletop. "What if your dad wanted to help you financially?"

"I don't want anything from him." Carter nearly ground out the words.

"I don't think you should be so dead set on telling him no. You might be surprised by what he has to offer."

"There's nothing he can do to make it up to me. He can keep his money." Carter picked up his can of soda, his laptop, and the statement from the bank. "I'm going to bed. Congratulations again. I'm really happy for you and Shauna."

As Carter climbed the stairs to his room, his mind spiraled with thoughts of his father and the possibility of a visit from him. He had to figure out a way to move out of Shauna's house before coming face-to-face with him. Carter would never let that man back into his life, and no amount of money could change the past.

CHAPTER 25

DARCY RUSHED AROUND THE PARTY ROOM AT A FANCY RESTAURANT IN Charlotte on a Saturday two weeks later. She set the last centerpiece of teal-and-white roses on a round table, then stood in the center of the room. The tables were set with place cards along with elegant place settings.

In the corner she had arranged an area for guests to take selfies, complete with teal balloons, silver balloons, and a white neon sign spelling "McGowan"—Haven's soon-to-be last name. A table near the room's entrance was set up for cards and gifts. And the waitstaff was ready to deliver their lunch as soon as the guests and the guest of honor arrived.

"What do you think?" she asked Kaylen, Lola, and Marcia.

Kaylen placed her hand on Darcy's shoulder. "Everything looks gorgeous, and you need to relax."

"Are you sure?" Darcy held her breath as Lola scanned the room. If anyone was going to be critical, it would be Haven's mom. After all, this was her only daughter's bridal shower.

To her surprise, Lola smiled. "Darcy, it's beautiful. Haven will be overjoyed."

"I agree," Marcia said. "It's perfect."

Darcy felt the muscles in her shoulders begin to unwind. "Okay."

She glanced at her watch. They had fifteen minutes before everyone was set to arrive. She busied herself with straightening the balloons on the back of Haven's chair.

Lola sidled up to her. "How have you been, Darcy?"

"I've been so focused on this shower that I haven't really had a minute to think about anything else." She glanced over to where Kaylen and her mother, Marcia, talked by the gift table.

Lola seemed to study her. "I hope this isn't a breach of trust, but Haven told me you found your biological mother. I'm happy for you."

"Thanks. Robyn and I have been talking during the past month." Darcy was still hurt that Robyn wasn't ready for her to meet her brothers, but she hoped Robyn would introduce them soon.

While Darcy straightened the light-green napkin by Haven's plate, she considered the other question that had been haunting her for weeks. "I'd love your advice on something, Lola."

"What's that?"

"I don't know how to tell my parents that I found her. I'm so afraid of hurting them, but I also feel terrible for keeping this huge secret from them. What should I do?"

"Honey, I've known your folks since you and Haven were freshmen at UNCC, and I've always thought they were loving, supportive, and proud of you." Lola gave her a knowing look. "You need to be honest with them. They'll understand your need to find your biological mother, and they won't be angry."

"You don't think they'll feel betrayed?"

Lola shook her head, and her strawberry-blonde bob swished with the motion. "No. In fact, I bet they'll want to meet her. I'm sure your parents are grateful Robyn had you, and Robyn is grateful for the life they've given you."

"I'm sure you're right. I just need to find the courage."

Voices sounded at the doorway to the private party room as shower guests began to arrive.

"Well, here we go." Lola strutted to the doorway and began welcoming them.

Darcy took a deep breath and joined Lola. Soon the room was full of women who were friends and family members of both Haven and Derek. Darcy and Kaylen invited them to sign the guest book and find their seats.

"Everything looks lovely," Mom said as she walked over to Darcy.

"I feel like we've been planning this forever." Darcy glanced over to where Lola spoke to a few guests, recalling her advice about telling her parents the truth.

Mom touched Darcy's shoulder and nodded toward her dress. "You look beautiful. I've always said that green is your color."

"Thanks, Mom." Once again, she contemplated her conundrum.

"You okay, Darcy?"

She opened her mouth, but her words were cut off by a flurry of claps. She pivoted toward the doorway, where Haven stood. She was gorgeous in a gray pantsuit with a light-blue blouse. Kaylen scurried over and placed a pink sash with the word "Bride" over her, then Darcy hurried over with a tiara and placed it on Haven's head.

The party spent the next two hours playing games, laughing, and eating delicious food. Throughout the shower, Darcy couldn't help but ponder the possibility of her own future with Carter. But in order to have that future, Darcy had to be honest with him about her past. Would she ever be ready to share that part of herself with him?

When the shower was over, Haven graciously thanked the guests as Darcy, Lola, Marcia, and Kaylen began cleaning up. Then the hostesses piled the mountain of gifts onto a cart they had borrowed from the waitstaff.

"Oh, good," Kaylen said. "My brother is here." She waved Derek over. "You can load all of the gifts into her car."

Derek gave his younger sister a mock salute. "I'm here to serve." Then he smiled at Darcy. "How's it going, Darcy?"

"Everything went off without a hitch." Darcy began gathering the name tents from the tables. When she felt a hand on her shoulder, she jumped with a start.

Mom stood beside her. "Give me a task so I can help."

"Would you like to get the balloons together for Haven?"

"Happy to." Mom started toward the corner where Haven had posed for probably one hundred selfies with guests.

As she watched her mother, a surge of courage overcame Darcy. "Mom," she called.

"Yes?" Her mother pivoted to face her.

"Could we have lunch tomorrow?" she asked, her hands trembling.

Mom looked surprised. "Don't we always have lunch together on Sundays?"

"I just wanted to make sure you and Dad weren't busy."

Mom grinned. "We're never too busy for you. I'll make something special, and you should bring that handsome boyfriend of yours too."

"I will." Darcy took a deep breath and resolved to tell her parents about Robyn. Then she prayed they would forgive her for waiting so long to tell them.

* * *

"I COULD TELL YOU WERE TIRED LAST NIGHT WHEN YOU TEXTED. HOW WAS the shower?" Carter asked as he steered Darcy's car on Interstate 485 the following afternoon.

She turned toward him. "Great. We had a lot of fun. We played some games, and the food was delicious. Most importantly, Haven was happy. She called me this morning and thanked me since we didn't really get a chance to talk yesterday."

"Good." He gave her a sideways glance.

"How's Shauna feeling?"

"She told me her morning sickness is finally subsiding. She's tired, but she's pushing through with work."

"That's great," Darcy said. "I know you all are excited. How does it feel knowing you're going to be an uncle?" She could already see him playing with the twins, taking them to the play area in the park. He would be a wonderful uncle—and a wonderful father. The thought sent a thrill racing through her.

Something unreadable drifted over his face. "Like a miracle. They've been hoping for a child for so long, and now they're going to have two."

"I can't wait to meet those twins." She rubbed his neck. "Thanks for coming with me today. I'm planning to tell my parents about Robyn at lunch."

His eyes widened. "You are?"

She nodded, picking at the seam on her denim shorts and pondering the day ahead. While she dreaded sharing the news about Robyn, on top of it all was the fact that it was the two-year anniversary of Jace's death. She had almost forgotten what day it was until she'd looked at her planner this morning. Since she'd been so focused on Haven's bridal shower, the milestone day had hit her like a ton of bricks. How had Jace been gone for two whole years?

A cold chill washed over her as the memories returned to her mind. She still recalled the day like it was yesterday. How he'd been so considerate picking up her medicine. How he offered to cook dinner because she was so focused on a special project at work. How she couldn't reach him when she arrived home. How the house was empty. How his mother sobbed on the phone . . .

"Are you sure you're ready?" Carter's voice broke through her thoughts and transported her back to the present. "That seems like a private family discussion. Maybe I shouldn't have come."

Darcy tried to focus on her boyfriend beside her. “I wanted you here for moral support.”

“I understand.” He reached over and patted her thigh. “But if you want me to leave, just tell me, okay? You won’t hurt my feelings.”

She nodded, but she doubted she’d want him to leave. Not today. She couldn’t be left alone with her thoughts and the grief packed around her heart.

When they arrived at her parents’ neighborhood, Carter entered the code at the community gate. After it lifted, they followed the winding road down to her parents’ sprawling brick colonial. Carter steered the car into the driveway and parked behind Darcy’s mother’s black BMW SUV.

Darcy swallowed a deep breath. She met Carter at the front of the car, and he took her hand in his.

“You got this,” he told her before kissing her cheek.

She smiled up at him.

They ascended the steps to the front door, and before Darcy’s hand reached the doorknob, the door swung open.

“Come in! Lunch is ready,” Mom announced, smiling.

They followed her through the house to the large eat-in kitchen, where the table was set with chicken salad sandwiches, spinach dip, and pita chips.

“This looks amazing, Josie,” Carter said.

Mom looked proud. “Thank you.”

“What can I do?” Darcy offered, trying to steady her voice.

“I’m all set. You two sit, and I’ll call your father down. He’s upstairs on his computer.” Mom walked to the back staircase.

Carter and Darcy took their seats, and Darcy closed her eyes and tried to calm her racing heart. She was strong. She could make it through the anniversary of Jace’s death, and she was brave enough to tell her parents about Robyn.

Carter pushed a tendril of her hair behind her ear. "Darce, you look like you're going to pass out. Deep breaths," he whispered. "It's going to be fine."

She nodded.

Dad walked into the kitchen behind Mom. "It's great to see you both." He took his seat at the end of the table and shook Carter's hand. "How's the shop?"

"Busy," Carter said. "The lot's full right now."

Mom sat down in her usual spot. "Let's eat."

"What kind of jobs are keeping you busiest?" Dad asked before biting into his sandwich.

"Mostly state inspections and brake jobs."

Darcy stared down at her plate while she ate her sandwich and tried to figure out the best way to break the news to her parents. Carter's conversation with Dad about the shop became background noise as she silently went through conversation scenarios in her mind.

Her eyes stung, and she held her breath.

Don't cry! Keep it together, Darcy!

When she heard her name, Darcy's eyes snapped to her mother's across the table. "I'm sorry, Mom. What'd you say?"

Mom tilted her head and set her glass of sweet tea on the table. "Sweetie, are you okay?"

Darcy glanced around to where her father also watched with concern.

Carter touched her arm, and the gentle gesture gave her the courage to speak.

"Mom and Dad," she began, "I have something to tell you." Her heart thumped against her ribcage. "I've . . . I've been trying to figure out how to admit this to you for a while."

Her parents exchanged concerned expressions before returning their gazes to hers.

"You can tell us anything," Dad said. Mom nodded in agreement.

"In May I signed up on a not-for-profit website to try to find my biological mother." Her voice sounded thin and reedy. "And I found her last month."

Her mom's eyes rounded, while her father seemed to remain calm.

"I've been talking to her, and we're getting to know each other. She lives in Concord. She stayed in the Charlotte area just in case I ever tried to find her." Darcy's voice quavered, and Carter rubbed her shoulders. "I hope this doesn't upset you. I love you both, and I'm so grateful you're my parents. I just needed to find out where I came from. And I wanted to learn my family history."

Mom picked up a paper napkin and wiped her eyes. "Oh my goodness. I'm sorry you didn't feel like you could tell us."

"Please don't misunderstand me." Darcy reached across the table to touch her mother's hand. "I was afraid of hurting you. That's why I didn't tell you. I didn't want you to think I didn't love you, because I do."

"Maybe I should wait outside while you talk." Carter stood.

Darcy looked over at him and considered asking him to stay, but she realized he was right.

Dad pointed to the back door. "You can go out to my garage if you'd like, and I'll be out there soon."

Carter gave Darcy a reassuring look, then sauntered toward the back door and disappeared into the garage.

Darcy took her mother's hands in hers. "*You* are my mom. *You* are the woman who raised me, but I needed to get to know my birth mother. I'll never stop loving either of you."

Dad nodded. "We understand, Darcy, and you know we love you too."

"We love you with our whole hearts." Mom sniffed. "What's her name?"

"Robyn Decker," Darcy replied before telling her parents everything. She explained how they talked on the phone for hours and then met in person the next day. She shared the stories about her biological father, her birth mother's family, and her half-brothers.

Mom nodded slowly. "Wow."

"You have brothers," Dad said.

"I haven't met them yet, but I hope to soon." Darcy searched her parents' expressions. "Are you angry with me?"

Dad shook his head. "Of course not. You have a right to know where you came from." He came around the table and pulled her into a warm hug.

Darcy rested her cheek on his shoulder and shuddered as her tears broke free.

"It's okay," Dad whispered into her hair. "We knew you'd want to find her someday."

Darcy held on to her father until he loosened his grip. When she stepped out of his embrace, she found her mother beside her with her arms outstretched. "Mom?" She watched her mom's expression carefully. "Are you okay?"

"Of course I am." Mom pulled her in for a hug, and Darcy held on tight.

"Thank you for understanding," Darcy whispered.

"Of course we understand," Mom said. "You're our daughter."

When her mother released her, Darcy sat down at the table with her parents on either side of her. She wiped her eyes and gathered her thoughts. "I asked her if kidney disease runs in her family, and she said her grandfather had been on dialysis. So now I know it's hereditary."

"I'm sorry to hear that," Dad said. "But that doesn't necessarily mean you'll pass it on to any future children."

"I know," Darcy said, but the worry still haunted her.

"Did you get photos of her?" Mom asked.

Darcy pulled out her phone. "Yeah. I also have some pictures of her sons." She opened her photo app, and her parents each put on their reading glasses as she started scrolling through the photos.

"Oh my," Mom exclaimed. "You look so much alike."

"I know. And here are my brothers."

"They definitely look like they're related to you," Dad said.

She flipped through photos, and her parents looked with interest. "I would like you to meet her someday. Would that be okay?"

"Of course it would," Dad said.

"Thank you," Darcy said.

Mom chuckled. "Honey, she gave birth to you. We're thankful for that."

Darcy felt her heart lift and her shoulders loosen.

"I'm going to go check on Carter." Dad slipped his reading glasses into his pocket. "After you two talk, we can have dessert. Text me when you're ready for us to come in."

After her father walked out the door, Darcy held her mother's hands. "I also realized this morning that today is the two-year anniversary of Jace's death." She sniffed. "I'd been so wrapped up in Haven's shower that the date completely slipped my mind."

"I thought of that this morning too. Are you okay?" Mom's blue eyes searched hers.

Darcy swallowed. "I'm not sure how I feel."

Mom hugged her again. "If you need to cry, it's okay, sweetie."

Darcy rested her cheek on her mother's shoulder and closed her eyes as more memories rained down on her. She had to tuck those feelings away and not reveal them in front of Carter. She wasn't ready for him to see that side of her. She would cry with her mother and then keep this anniversary to herself.

As her tears broke free, Darcy didn't know when or if the pain would ever stop. All she knew was that she wasn't completely ready to let go of Jace.

CHAPTER 26

THE DOOR LEADING FROM THE HOUSE TO THE GARAGE OPENED, AND Carter looked up from where he sat on a stool to see Ross descending the steps. Ross's gorgeous silver Corvette Stingray, his white Porsche Cayenne, and his Dodge Power Wagon sat in a line surrounded by his toolboxes. Carter had peeked in the windows of the Corvette and Porsche, and he hoped someday he'd get a chance to drive them.

"Is everything okay in there?" Carter asked.

Ross nodded. "Yes, it's fine. Josie and I were a little emotional, but we knew this day would come. We understand Darcy's need to find her biological mother. It's only natural." He took a seat on a stool beside Carter. "Have you met Robyn yet?"

"No, not yet, but Darcy asked me to go with her when she does meet her and her family."

"You're a great help to her. She went through so much after . . ." Ross stopped. "I'm sorry. I'm probably saying too much."

"She told me about how her fiancé passed away."

"That was devastating. It was gut-wrenching to watch her suffer and blame herself." Ross's posture slumped. "Josie and I worried she'd never come out of it." His expression brightened. "But she met you, and she changed. She's living again. She's happy again. And we have you to thank for that."

Carter tried in vain to swallow back his shame. He hadn't been honest with her, and every time he was about to, he was terrified he would lose her. "She's made a huge difference in my life too." He faced Ross's classic Dodge truck along with the other vehicles. "I was just sitting here admiring your Porsche and Corvette. They're stunning."

"Thank you. Have you had a chance to work on your grandfather's Road Runner?"

Carter's gaze flitted to Ross's. "No." He paused. "I'm thinking about selling it."

"Selling it?" Ross looked shocked. "Why?"

Carter pressed his lips together, and the urge to admit the truth seemed to grab him by the shoulders. "In order to start a life with Darcy."

Ross's salt-and-pepper eyebrows lifted. "What do you mean?"

Carter told the story of going through a hard time three years ago and having to move in with his sister, leaving out the details of his kidney failure and transplant. "I'm fine now, but I'm still crawling out of debt. And now my sister and her husband are expecting twins. I'm happy for them, of course. They've been hoping and praying for children for a long time."

He rubbed his hands down his thighs. "I want to get my own place to get out of my sister's hair before the babies come, and I also want to be able to start a life with Darcy. Right now I have nothing to offer her, but if I can sell the car, I might be able to pay off the loan early and finally get a bit ahead in life. I've been stuck in a holding pattern for so long, and I'm tired of being a burden on my family."

Ross took a deep breath and rested his elbows on his lap. "I understand where you're coming from. My wife and I struggled when we were first starting out with our practice. We felt like we were drowning in debt and never going to come out of it. Everyone goes through those tough times. Believe me when I say that Darcy has had her fair share too. She was in a dark place after Jace died."

Carter nodded, waiting for him to continue.

"I can see how you're frustrated. You're ready to be on your own, and you're looking forward to starting a new chapter with my daughter. But I would hate for you to sell your grandfather's car. That's not something you can undo. When you told me about the car and showed me photos, I could tell it means a lot to you. Am I right to say that when you look at that car, you think of your grandfather and the times you shared together?"

"Yeah."

"I'm not going to tell you what to do, but I'll give you my opinion. Don't make a hasty decision you'll possibly regret. I wish I had kept one of my father's old trucks, but I sold them when I needed the money. I still think about those trucks and how I could've restored them."

He paused for a moment. "If you see an end in sight for your money problems, then be patient. This too shall pass. I have a feeling my daughter wants a future with you as much as you want one with her, and you two can figure out the details together."

The back door opened, and Darcy stood there smiling. "Who wants a piece of chocolate cake?"

"I do!" Ross held his arm up.

Darcy met Carter's gaze, and he lifted his eyebrows to ask if she was okay. She nodded, and relief sluiced through him. "Come have some cake, Carter."

He pushed aside his problems and went in the house.

Later he would talk to her. If Ross was right, maybe there was hope for him and Darcy after all.

* * *

DARCY ENTWINED HER FINGERS WITH CARTER'S AS HE BACKED HER CAR out of her parents' driveway. "Thank you for coming with me today."

He gave her a sideways glance and silently marveled at how beautiful she looked with her sunshine-colored hair flowing over one of her slight shoulders and her pink lips turned up in a smile. She looked relaxed for the first time in days, and she seemed to glow.

"That went well," he said as they motored out of the neighborhood.

"Yes. So much better than I imagined. My parents want to meet Robyn, and I feel like this giant weight has been lifted." She sighed. "I was so afraid I'd hurt them, but that wasn't the case at all."

"Awesome." He squeezed her fingers.

They were quiet for a moment while he drove. She pulled her hand back, and he placed both of his hands on the wheel.

When he felt her watching him, he glanced over at her. "Are you staring at me?" he asked with a chuckle.

"What were you and my dad talking about in the garage?"

He shrugged. "Cars."

"Really?" She leaned toward him. "You had a pretty intense look on your face when I opened the door and invited you in for cake."

Carter tried to act casual, but his laugh sounded nervous to his own ears. "Well, you know, Darce, cars can be pretty intense."

She smiled, and he relaxed. "It's cool that you and my dad get along so well."

"I agree." He rested his left arm on the car door and kept his right hand on the wheel.

Carter stared at the road ahead as the truth threatened to spill from his mouth. He was still keeping secrets, and the longer he waited to share the truth with Darcy, the more painful it would be to tell her.

But if he wanted a future with her, she needed to know everything.

* * *

DARCY WONDERED IF SHE WAS DREAMING. IT WAS A SATURDAY EVENING three weeks later, and she was sitting in the family room with Carter, her parents, and Robyn. They were all smiling and laughing while Mom flipped through a photo album on her lap and shared the story of Darcy's first day at kindergarten.

"When she got home that afternoon, Darcy said the best part of her day was when they went to art class and they *arted*," Mom said before guffawing.

Darcy rolled her eyes. "She loves telling that story."

"It's a great story." Dad beamed from his favorite wing chair across the room.

Carter winked at Darcy from his seat beside her. "I can't wait to hear more so I can tease you about it later."

The entire evening had gone perfectly. Darcy and Carter had headed over early to help Mom make beef Wellington and prepare the dining room. When Robyn had arrived, Darcy was nearly moved to tears to see her and Mom hug each other. She was certain she had imagined it, but now they were all here, laughing together.

"Oh, look at that haircut." Robyn clucked her tongue as she pointed to Darcy's first grade portrait.

Mom gave Darcy a knowing smile. "That was when she wanted to be like the other cool girls at school."

A flush crawled up Darcy's neck, and she gathered their empty glasses. "I'll start cleaning up the kitchen."

"I'll help." Carter popped up from his seat and picked up their dessert plates, which were dotted with crumbs from her mom's delicious chocolate chip cheesecake. Then he followed her into the kitchen. "They're getting along great in there."

Darcy opened the dishwasher and set the glasses on the top shelf while Carter placed the stack of dishes on the counter.

She pivoted and found Carter standing directly behind her. His nearness made nervous pleasure shimmy through her entire body. "It's going so much better than I imagined. Did you see them hug when Robyn arrived? I nearly sobbed right there."

Carter's dark eyes smoldered as he rested his hands on her hips. "Have I told you lately how beautiful you are?"

"No." She shook her head, and her lips quirked. "You definitely need to tell me more often."

His lips brushed against hers, and when Darcy leaned into the kiss, she felt dizzy and warm all over. He gently pulled back, and she held on to his muscular shoulders to steady herself. They were firm and solid under her palms.

"Thank you," she whispered..

His eyes seemed to search hers. "For what?"

"For being you, Carter."

His grin was wicked. "You could thank me by kissing me again."

"Okay," she whispered before his lips captured hers once again.

* * *

LATER CARTER STOOD OUT ON THE LARSENS' ENORMOUS DECK AND LOOKED out over their tremendous backyard. Above him the sun had started to set, bringing with it a cool mid-October breeze and a slight chill. The hum of traffic in the distance filled the air, along with the scent of a nearby wood-burning fireplace.

He tried to imagine what it would be like to have all of these things—a huge house with all of the amenities in a beautiful neighborhood, a loving wife, a family, a future. But it all seemed foreign to him.

Carter had enjoyed the evening with Darcy's parents and Robyn, and he felt a glimmer of hope when he thought of a future with this family. He was beginning to believe what Ross had told him—that somehow he and Darcy would work out the details of their life together. He smiled. He couldn't wait to move forward with those plans.

"Are you taking a breather from the photo album discussion?"

When Carter turned, he found Ross standing behind him holding two cans of Coke. He held one out to him.

"I thought the women could use some time alone." He grasped the soda. "Thanks, Ross."

The men both popped open their cans and then leaned on the deck railing.

Carter took a long draw of soda and then focused on Ross. "What do you think of Robyn?"

"She's great." Ross pivoted to face the sliding glass door that led to the family room, where the women were still gathered around a photo album and laughing. "I can tell she makes my daughter happy, and that's what matters."

Darcy's father looked out at his large pool. "My fear was always that her biological mother wouldn't be interested in her. Or that she wouldn't want to be found. I'm relieved and grateful it worked out for them both. It's obvious that she and Darcy care about each other very much. Robyn is a lot younger than Josie and I are, so Darcy will have her in her life when we're gone."

Carter took another drink of the cool liquid and peered through the sliding glass door to where Josie, Robyn, and Darcy laughed together. "I'm so glad to see Darcy happy with them."

"I feel the same way," Ross said.

* * *

"THANK YOU FOR A WONDERFUL EVENING," ROBYN TOLD DARCY AS THEY walked out to her car together.

Darcy smiled at her biological mother. "I'm so glad you came." She paused and thought of her brothers. "I really would like to meet Graham and my brothers."

Then she stilled, waiting for Robyn's response. Maybe now that Robyn had met her adoptive parents, she would change her mind.

"You will." Robyn opened her door and tossed her purse inside.

"Okay," she said, her hope deflating. "I know you need to take your time."

Robyn touched Darcy's arm. "This is new for me. I always prayed I'd find you, but now that I have, I don't know what the right timeline is for you to meet my sons."

"I understand."

"It's not anything against you, Darcy. They're young. I don't know how they're going to react." Her expression warmed. "I promise you that when the time is right, you'll meet them. Just be patient with me, okay?"

Darcy sniffed before nodding.

"Please know I don't mean to hurt you. You're important to me." Robyn licked her lips. "If you ever need me, text me. If it's four a.m. and you want to talk, I'm here for you." She leaned on the car door. "Keep in touch, Darcy."

"I will." Darcy stood on the pavement as Robyn drove away, wrestling with her disappointment. She hoped she could have Keaton and Brayden in her life sooner rather than later, but she understood that such a complicated situation would take time.

When she heard footsteps behind her, she pivoted to find Carter sidling up to her.

"It was a great night, huh?"

"Yeah, it was." She looped her arm around his trim waist. "I asked Robyn if I could meet my brothers again, but she said not yet."

"Maybe this is a difficult adjustment for her."

"I know it is. She told me so herself." She paused and huffed out a sigh. "I thought it would feel different, you know? That I'd meet my birth mother, and everything would be fixed, but it hurts to know that while I love her, Robyn is still a stranger in many ways." She linked her pinky with his. "You're pretty great, you know."

"You are too."

She stood up on her tiptoes and pressed her lips to his cheek.

* * *

LATER THAT EVENING DARCY STOOD IN HER BEDROOM AND HELD UP THE wardrobe bag that contained her wedding gown. She had found it in the back of her guest room closet and placed it on her bed. Then she gently set the gown inside a plastic storage container from the garage.

Moving to her jewelry box, she retrieved the wedding bands and her engagement ring and added them to the container. After closing it, she pushed it to the corner of her room and stared at it.

Resting her hand on her chest, she smiled. It was time to let Jace go. She would never forget him and the love they'd shared. He would always have a piece of her heart, but it was time to open herself up to Carter. She would tell him she loved him, and she hoped he would tell her that he loved her too. Her body felt relaxed and peaceful at the thought. Now she just had to find the perfect opportunity to share her truth.

* * *

"I CAN'T BELIEVE I'M GETTING MARRIED IN TEN DAYS, DARCY," HAVEN announced the following Wednesday evening. "Ten days. How'd that happen?"

Sitting across from her at Haven's kitchen table, Darcy gave her best friend an encouraging smile. "It's going to be fine, Haven. Now put me to work."

"Thankfully my mom loves all of this party planning stuff, and she finished the seating chart." She handed Darcy a printout of the table numbers and the names. "My mom's also handling table tents. She followed up with the caterer and the photographer. My cousin Allyson is the wedding coordinator, so she has the order of events and the schedule worked out. She's going to keep us all on task at the church and the reception hall."

Haven flipped through her notebook, which apparently had pages and pages of wedding plans. "Oh! Is Carter coming to the rehearsal dinner with you?"

"Yes, he is."

Haven looked up from the book and frowned. "Oh no. I'm a terrible friend. I never asked about your dinner with your birth mom and your folks." She grimaced. "Forgive me."

"It's fine, Haven." Darcy pointed to her notebook. "You kinda have a lot going on."

"How'd it go?"

Darcy smiled. "It went well." She shared how her mom and her biological mother hugged when they first met and how they spent hours going through photo albums and sharing stories. "They thanked each other. I was so happy and overwhelmed that I had tears in my eyes."

"I'm so happy for you." Haven gave her shoulder a squeeze. "And how's Carter?"

Darcy blew out a deep breath and rested her elbows on the table. "He's thoughtful, supportive, sweet, funny, and he knows how to kiss." She fanned herself as if suddenly coming down with a case of the vapors. "Oh my goodness, does that man know how to kiss."

Haven lifted an eyebrow. "Has he told you that he loves you?"

A quiver passed through her. "No, but I'm ready to tell him."

"I'm so happy for you, Darce." Haven pointed to her notebook. "Now, maid of honor, we have centerpieces to finish."

"Yes, ma'am." Darcy smiled, ready to help her best friend have the wedding of her dreams.

CHAPTER 27

THE FOLLOWING FRIDAY AFTERNOON, CARTER SCOOPED A LARGE SPOONful of canned cat food into the bowl while Smoky stood nearby and yowled.

"This stinks. You'll love it." He placed the bowl down on the concrete floor, and the gray tabby cat began inhaling it as if he hadn't eaten in a year. "Enjoy, buddy." He tossed the can and turned to face his brother-in-law, who was leaning over a car. "See ya later, Gage."

Gage stood and wiped his hands on a red shop towel. "You're heading out already?" Then he snapped his fingers as understanding lit in his eyes. "Tonight's the rehearsal dinner for Derek's wedding, right?"

"Yup." Carter grabbed his truck keys, and they jingled in his hand. "I'm Darcy's date. I need to clean up before I meet her. They're having the rehearsal at his church and then the dinner afterward. Derek's family rented out the entire Italian restaurant on Godwin Avenue. Darcy's riding over with Haven, but I'm taking her home."

Gage nodded. He drew his lips together, and Carter could almost feel him choosing his words carefully. "Listen, I know it's none of my business. But before you head out, I wanted to tell you that Shauna has been talking to your dad fairly often lately."

Carter's entire body went rigid.

Gage held his hands up as if to calm Carter. "Just listen, okay? I know you're angry with him, but that anger only hurts you, not him.

So if you have a chance to talk to him, it would do you some good to keep an open mind."

"You're speaking in code, Gage." Carter studied his brother-in-law as irritation sparked in his chest. "What are you not telling me?"

"Just keep an open mind," he repeated.

"I don't have time for games. I gotta leave or I'm gonna be late. Now give it to me straight."

"Don't be surprised if you have an opportunity to talk to your dad soon, and stay calm for your sake and also for Shauna's."

Carter stared at him, waiting for him to share more, but Gage shook his head.

"That's all I can tell you right now, okay?" Gage said.

"Fine." Carter headed for the door. "I'll be home late. See you tomorrow." As he hastened to his truck, he worked to shove away the black mood that thoughts of his father always ushered in. He tried to focus on Darcy, but irritation clung to him, refusing to be ignored.

* * *

DARCY PUSHED THROUGH THE DOOR AT BELLA ITALIA LATER THAT EVENING, and the delicious aromas of tomato sauce and garlic filled her nostrils. Right away she spotted Carter standing on the far side of the restaurant, examining his phone. He was even handsomer than usual dressed in khakis and a light-blue button-down. She felt a flurry of pride as she rushed over to him and kissed him. She breathed in the familiar musky scent of his aftershave and grinned. "Wow, Donovan. You clean up nice."

"You do too, beautiful." He dropped his phone into his pocket. "How was the rehearsal?"

"Good. Hopefully I'll walk down the aisle in those ridiculous shoes without tripping tomorrow." She grimaced. "At least I can hold on to Liam on my way back up the aisle."

"Hold on to him, huh? Just don't hold too tight," he teased. His lips tipped up, but his smile didn't quite reach his eyes.

She placed her hand on his hard chest. "Everything okay?"

"Yeah. Why?"

"You seem . . . preoccupied."

He took her hand in his and kissed her knuckles. "Everything's fine."

"No, there's something wrong." She studied his dark eyes. "You can tell me."

He shook his head. "It's nothing important."

She pulled all of her courage up from her toes and then said the words she'd longed to say for so long. "I love you, Carter. That's why I'm worried about you."

He blinked twice, then opened and closed his mouth as he stared at her.

"I love you, Carter," she repeated. "I really do."

His expression warmed, a genuine smile overtaking his lips. "And I love you too, Darcy." His voice was husky. Then he pulled her to him and kissed her with so much passion that she forgot where she was for a moment.

Bliss rushed through her veins as she wrapped her arms around his neck.

When Carter released her, he touched her cheek. Joy sparkled in his eyes. "You make me so happy, Darcy."

"Back at ya," she said.

His eyes focused behind her, where Derek and Haven were steering folks to tables. "I think we're being paged." Carter led Darcy toward the table where Derek's younger brother, Liam, and his girlfriend, Tonya, also sat.

After Derek and Haven took turns thanking everyone who had traveled for their wedding, the guests moved through the buffet line, filling their plates with the delectable offerings of lasagna, pasta, meatballs, eggplant parmigiana, breadsticks, and salad before returning to their seats.

After dinner and a delicious tiramisu dessert, Darcy and Carter said goodbye to the bride, the groom, and the other guests. Then they traipsed out to Carter's truck in the parking lot. The late October sky was clogged with gray clouds, and the air smelled like rain. She hugged her arms to her chest and wished she had grabbed a sweater.

"Oh no," Carter groaned as he pulled his keys from his pocket.

"What's wrong?"

"I can't believe I left my wallet at home. We're gonna have to stop by my place on our way to yours."

"No problem," Darcy exclaimed. "I haven't seen Shauna in a while."

Carter unlocked his truck, wrenched open the passenger side door, and held out his hand to her. She took it, and he lifted her into the seat.

As she watched him jog around the front of the truck, more excitement poured through her. She was so relieved and grateful that he loved her too. She couldn't wait to see what the future held.

* * *

"I HAVE TO BE AT THE CHURCH EARLY TOMORROW TO HELP HAVEN GET ready," Darcy explained.

Darcy's words about the wedding became background noise to his thoughts. He couldn't stop his smile. Darcy loved him, and he loved her! He couldn't remember the last time he'd been this happy.

Maybe he'd *never* been this happy. Ross had been right—Darcy did want a future with him, and now they could plan it. He had the Road Runner advertised, and as soon as he sold it, he would pay off his loan, move out on his own, and finally start his life. Oh, he couldn't wait!

"Carter? Carter!"

He blinked when he realized Darcy had been calling his name. "Sorry. What?"

She eyed him, and he shifted in the seat. He was aware of how well his girlfriend could read his expressions and his mood, and though he found it endearing at times, at this moment it was unnerving.

"What were you thinking about?"

He smiled, took her hand in his, and kissed her knuckles. "How much I love you."

She beamed. "I love you too."

"Good." He grinned. "Glad we agree on that."

Carter turned onto his block. When he neared the driveway, his eyes locked on a silver Ford Fusion with a Tennessee license plate parked behind Gage's pickup truck. He immediately recalled what Shauna had told him the night he had come home from the beach:

I haven't spoken to Dad yet, but I think he might be in Tennessee.

A ball of lead formed in Carter's stomach as he parked the truck. Gage had been trying to warn him about this.

"Oh no." Dread sank in bone-deep. "No, no, no, no. Not tonight . . ."

Darcy leaned toward him. "What's wrong? Whose car is that?"

Unable to speak, he shook his head, pushed his door open, and hopped out of the truck. The sky was packed with dark clouds, and the air held the threat of rain.

"Carter? Carter!" Darcy called after him.

He ignored her while squaring his shoulders and marching toward the house.

Darcy rushed after him, her heels clicking on the rock pathway that led to the front door. "Carter Anthony Donovan, please stop and talk to me!" Her voice shook.

He turned to face her, holding up a hand. "Wait in the truck, okay?" He worked to pronounce his trembling words as calmly as possible.

"No." Her eyes glittered, and she rubbed her hands over the sleeves of her dress. "You're worrying me, Carter."

"Please, Darcy, I'm begging you. I promise I'm just going to grab my wallet from my dresser. I'll be right back."

"Fine." Her brow puckered. She stared at him a moment longer before retreating toward the truck.

Carter grasped the door handle, pulled it open, and stepped into the foyer. Voices filtered out from the family room. He took in a deep breath through his nose and started toward them. When he reached the doorway, he froze and stared. A middle-aged man sat on the sofa across from Shauna and Gage.

He recognized the man from fuzzy childhood memories and photos his mother had stashed away. Though the man's brown hair was now mixed with gray, and though wrinkles lined his mouth and his dark-brown eyes, Carter knew he was looking into the face of Myles Donovan, the man who had once been his father.

Bile rose in Carter's throat, and the muscles in his neck tightened. He turned his glare on his brother-in-law. "You *knew* he was coming when you talked to me at the shop earlier." He pointed an angry finger at Gage. "Why didn't you tell me outright?"

"Carter, I'm sorry, but—"

"Save it!" Carter hollered before trudging toward the stairs.

"Carter!" Shauna yelled after him. "Carter, please wait. *Please.* You need to hear what he has to say."

"No, I don't!" Carter called over his shoulder. Anger and frustration ran through him as he searched his room for his wallet. He checked his dresser, his bed, and then the floor. He finally found it wedged between the wall and his bed.

He jammed it into his back pocket, and when he turned to the doorway, he found his sister blocking it with her hands held up. "Move," he growled.

"Carter, just listen."

He took a deep breath and heard the front door open and close. Hopefully that meant their so-called father was leaving.

Good! Don't come back!

"Carter—"

"Stop! I'm sick of your constant lectures about our father." His voice shook. "If he had been here, maybe you wouldn't have turned your life upside down for me when I went on dialysis. And maybe you'd still have two kidneys. If *he* had been here, maybe I wouldn't have imploded your life. There is no way he can make up for that. *Ever.*"

Shauna sniffed and wiped her eyes.

Carter made a sweeping gesture. "I'm taking Darcy home. He'd better be gone when I get back."

Shauna allowed him to pass. He stormed down the stairs, then froze. Darcy stood at the bottom of the stairs, her eyes wide, red, and puffy.

He felt a punch to his gut as he took in her horrified expression. "Tell me you didn't just hear that conversation," he said.

"Carter," she whispered. "You had a kidney transplant?"

He scrubbed his hand down his face.

"Answer me! Did you have a kidney transplant?"

He nodded.

She clapped her hand to her mouth as her eyes widened. "Carter, I . . . I did too."

Carter remained cemented in place. He turned toward the doorway to the kitchen, where Gage and his father stood.

The walls began closing in on him. He had to get out of there. He took Darcy's arm and led her toward the door. "Come on. We'll talk in the truck."

CHAPTER 28

Rain sprinkled the windshield. Carter sat ramrod straight in the driver's seat and steered the truck down the road. He and Darcy sat in silence, the only noise coming from raindrops, the hum of the wipers, and the truck's rumbling engine.

Darcy hugged her arms around her middle and tried to stop her body from shaking. Confusion, anger, and the cold fall air combined to chill her.

He stopped at a red light and reached into the back seat. His hand clasped a black hoodie with a Chevrolet logo on it, and he handed it to her. "I meant to get you a jacket when I was in my room," he mumbled.

She pulled the hoodie over her head, breathing in his scent as the thick fleece warmed her skin. But inside she was cold. So cold.

She studied his profile as he stared straight ahead at the traffic light. His mouth was a thin line, his brow furrowed. He seemed to clutch the wheel as if his life depended on it. "When I met you in the doctor's office parking lot, I was there for a checkup with my nephrologist," Darcy said. "Were you there for a checkup too?"

He swallowed, and his Adam's apple bobbed up and down. "Yeah." He remained silent as the light turned green, and he drove through the intersection.

She gripped the hoodie's cuffs, anger coursing through her. "Why didn't you tell me about your transplant?"

"I could ask you the same question."

Darcy wilted a little inside. They were both guilty of keeping the same secret. What were the odds of that? "I had a kidney transplant on April 3, two years ago. Jace was my paired donor, and he gave for me through a swap. I didn't tell you because—"

"You didn't trust me."

"Is that why you didn't tell me? Because you don't trust me?"

Something unreadable drifted over his face. "I was on dialysis for a year. Then Shauna donated for me."

She was silent for a minute. "What kind of dialysis?"

"Home. Peritoneal. Why?"

"That's why you have that dimpled scar by your belly button."

He stared at her. "How'd you know about that?"

"I saw it at the beach. I wondered what it was from."

"And you didn't ask me?" Before she could answer, he started talking again, his tone acid-laced. "Well, now you know why I'm broke. No insurance. Lots of bills. Expensive medications I'll have to take for the rest of my life. I'm a burden because I'm not a trust fund baby."

She scowled at him. "That was low, Carter. Really low."

"You said you loved me. How can you say those words and not trust me with . . ." His voice was ragged, as if he'd spent all night screaming at a concert. "Forget it."

She wanted to respond, to throw his words back in his face. But something stopped her. Her hypocrisy, for starters. They had both been holding back the one thing they should have been honest about long before now. Neither of them should have found out about their transplants like this.

"For what it's worth," she said, fighting the tremble in her voice, "six months after my transplant, Jace died going to the pharmacy to pick up my meds because I was too busy to get them myself." She pressed her hand against her chest, the heartache returning. "The reason I didn't tell you was because it has always been too painful to talk about. Maybe I was being selfish about not wanting to feel the ache that deeply again."

He continued to stare straight ahead, his jaw set in stone.

"One of the reasons I wanted to know about my family history was so I could know for sure if my kidney disease was genetic. I found out from Robyn that my great-grandfather was on dialysis."

"I'm sorry," he mumbled. "And I'm sorry about Jace. But you could have told me all of this. I would have helped you. I would have comforted you." His voice broke. "You held all that back from me."

"Because—"

"It doesn't matter why! Not anymore."

"It matters to me." She blinked away her tears. "And it matters that you wouldn't tell me why you've had financial problems. I could have helped."

"I'm not a charity case." He clenched the steering wheel again. "I don't want your money."

And you don't want me. He was making that as plain as day.

He was right: It didn't matter anymore what the reasons were. The bottom line was that they didn't trust each other, not enough to be completely honest.

When they reached her house, he nosed his truck into the driveway.

Darcy gathered up her purse from the floorboard and pushed open her door, ready to flee from this furious man. His rejection was worse than any pain she'd felt before. But she couldn't leave without telling him one more truth.

"I do love you, Carter," she said. "My feelings for you are real, and they're true. I'm sorry I didn't . . . I'm just sorry." She jumped out of the truck and ran into her house.

Only when she was inside did she let the tears fall. Collapsing on the floor, she hugged her arms to her chest as if to stop her heart from breaking.

Her thoughts spun as sobs tore from her throat, and memories of the pain she'd felt the night she lost Jace filled her mind.

After several moments, she pulled herself up from the floor and propelled herself up the stairs to her bedroom. Closing her eyes, she drew Carter's sweatshirt to her face and breathed in his scent, committing it to her memory. Their relationship was fractured, damaged beyond repair.

She turned toward her dresser, and her eyes fell on the storage container on the floor. She'd lost Carter on the very night she'd finally opened her heart and expressed her love for him. In the blink of an eye, everything they'd built had been torn down. She was alone—*again*. And now it had happened with Carter, just like when she'd lost Jace.

She dropped to her knees in front of the storage box and ran her hands over the lid. Maybe she had let go of Jace too soon. If she had held on to Jace's memory more tightly, she wouldn't be in pain now.

With tears clouding her vision, Darcy opened the box and peered inside.

* * *

At least something positive happened tonight, THOUGHT CARTER. WHEN HE arrived home, the sedan with the Tennessee tag was gone from the driveway. The last thing he needed after realizing his relationship with Darcy was over was a run-in with his father.

He dragged himself from his truck, the weight of his misery and grief bogging his steps toward the front door. When he reached his room, he collapsed on his bed.

Staring at the dark ceiling, Carter rested his arm on his forehead. Just as he had feared, he lost Darcy. Like everything else in his life, she was ripped away from him when he had finally found happiness. Surely his heartache would swallow him whole and he would become a shell of a man once again.

He thought he'd found his match, his soulmate, the love of his life. In the end, though, she had never trusted him.

But I didn't tell her my own truth either.

He rolled to his side and tried to calm down, but his body felt tied up in knots. Then the truth hit him in the face: He was just as guilty as she was. He'd been too afraid to tell her about his illness because he thought he'd lose her—but by not telling her, he'd lost her anyway.

Carter winced as he recalled their conversation in the car. How horrible he'd been to her. A real jerk. He'd even accused her of being a trust fund baby. He was sure his words had cut her to the bone.

He sat up as guilt saturated him. Darcy deserved better than the way he'd treated her. And despite his horrible words, she'd left him with an apology and a reassurance of her love.

He loved her more than he'd ever loved anyone in his life. He couldn't let it end like this.

He grabbed his phone from his nightstand and noticed that the battery only had 10 percent power. It was almost dead.

"Please work," he whispered, praying she would answer as he dialed.

"Carter?" Darcy's voice was soft and unsure.

"Darcy." Her name came out in a croak. "I'm sorry. I'm so sorry."

The line remained silent, and his heart pounded in his ears. Had she hung up on him—given up on him for good? His body trembled. He couldn't lose her! He loved her. He needed her.

When she sniffed, his body relaxed—slightly.

"I . . . I was awful to you." His eyes stung, and he swiped his fingers over them. "I shouldn't have said those horrible things. I didn't mean them. I was hurt and angry—mostly at my father." His voice sounded raw.

More silence stretched between them, and he leaned back on his headboard. "Are you still there?"

"Yeah," she whispered.

"Darcy, I love you," he began, his words scratching out of his dry throat. "And I don't want to lose you." He stared toward his window, taking in the dappled shadows created by the streetlights. "I'm sorry I wasn't honest with you either. I should have told you about my transplant."

She sniffed again.

"Will you give me another chance?" he begged her. "Please, Darcy. I want to work this out."

"I do too," she said, her voice breathy.

He heaved a sigh of relief. "Thank you. I promise I'll be completely honest with you from now on. No more secrets."

"Let's talk tomorrow at the wedding."

"Okay." The line went silent again, and he closed his eyes. "I love you, Darcy."

"I love you too, Carter. Get some sleep now. Good night."

"Good night." He set his phone on his nightstand before dropping back on his pillow. He tried to relax as he stared up at the ceiling again. Darcy still loved him and was giving him a second chance. Maybe, just maybe, they would be okay.

He rested his forearm over his eyes, trying to convince himself to go to sleep. But their conversation in his truck echoed through his mind. He could hear Darcy's voice as she said:

I had a kidney transplant on April 3, two years ago. Jace was my paired donor, and he gave for me through a swap.

"April 3, two years ago," Carter whispered. "April 3 . . ."

The realization hit him like a speeding train, and he sat up straight. His own transplant had also taken place on April 3, two years earlier. His swap had involved three donors and three recipients.

Shauna had given to a teenage girl. The girl's father had given to a young woman. And a young man—the woman's boyfriend or fiancé—had given to Carter.

Carter's breath came in short bursts. Jace had been Darcy's paired donor, which meant he'd given to someone else in exchange for a kidney for Darcy.

And Jace was Darcy's fiancé.

From what Darcy had told Carter, Jace had been the same age he was.

His mouth dropped open as the pieces came together in his mind.

His eyes stung as he realized the truth.

Jace had given him a kidney.

"No," he groaned. "No, no, no, no, no . . . This can't be true."

For more than two years, Carter had wondered who his donor was. He'd wanted to thank the man for generously giving him the gift of life.

Now Jace was dead. Carter could never properly thank him.

And Carter had fallen in love with his donor's fiancée.

Popping out of bed, Carter started to pace his room. It was hard to believe that Carter was walking around with Jace's kidney functioning in his body. The only piece left of Jace, the man whom Darcy still missed, still grieved.

And Carter would always be a reminder of Darcy's heartbreak.

He had to tell her. He had promised not to keep any more secrets from her, and he intended to keep that promise.

He halted, looked at his clock radio, and realized it was almost midnight. Too late to text her or call her. Besides, this was a conversation he needed to have with her in person.

Dropping back onto his bed, he imagined how painful the conversation with Darcy would be tomorrow. The news that Jace was his donor might destroy her.

And this time, Carter might lose her forever.

His eyes stung and his thoughts spun as he imagined how it all might end. It was going to be a long night.

* * *

THE FOLLOWING MORNING, DARCY CHECKED HER PHONE AND FROWNED. NO messages. She had hoped to hear from Carter, but maybe he was getting ready for the wedding.

Now she stood in the church's parlor with Haven, Kaylen, and Lola. She tried to keep her thoughts focused on her best friend as they made last-minute preparations. After all, this was Haven's day, and it was Darcy's job to be the best maid of honor possible.

Still, her heart seized whenever she recalled her emotional conversation with Carter on the phone last night. She'd been shocked to see his name appear on her phone screen. After all, she had convinced herself that he no longer loved her and their relationship was over.

When she'd heard his apology and the pain in his voice, her heart had come back to life. She'd been so overcome with emotion that she'd struggled to form words in response. She was so thankful he hadn't given up on her. If they both were completely honest with each other, she believed their relationship would have a chance.

More than anything, Darcy wanted to make it work. She loved him and couldn't imagine losing him now—especially after losing Jace.

She shot off a quick text to him:

Hi. Thanks for calling me last night. I'm ready to try again, and I promise no secrets. Can't wait to see you today and talk things through. Text me when you're on your way to the church. I love you, Carter.

Kaylen came to stand beside her. "Darcy?" she whispered. "Are you okay?"

Slipping her phone into her purse, Darcy smiled. "Yeah. I'm fine."

And she was. Carter still loved her, and they were going to work things out.

She snuck a peek at Haven, who was discussing her makeup with her mother. Then she turned back to Kaylen. "She's gorgeous."

"She sure is." Kaylen gave her a knowing smile. "From what I've witnessed between you and Carter, I have a feeling you'll be the next couple planning a wedding."

Darcy sighed. "I hope you're right," she said.

* * *

CARTER DRAGGED HIMSELF OUT OF BED LATER THAT MORNING. HIS ENTIRE body ached as if he had been hit by his truck. He rubbed his eyes and wondered if he'd gotten even two hours of sleep. He was certain he had stared at the ceiling and the wall for most of the night.

He stood under the hot water in the shower for longer than usual, trying to wake up and figure out how to have another difficult conversation with Darcy. It seemed there wasn't a gentle way to tell her about Jace. No matter how he imagined explaining it, he expected the news would rip her heart to shreds—and he could never forgive himself for hurting her again.

After his shower, Carter shaved and put on his only suit. He was just grateful it still fit. When he came downstairs to the kitchen, he ground his teeth together at the sight of Shauna and Gage sitting at the table.

"You look exhausted, man," Gage said. "You okay?"

Ignoring them, he slipped over to the pantry and grabbed a box of cereal. Then he silently pulled out a bowl, a spoon, and the half-gallon of milk.

Silence hung over the kitchen while he ate. Carter bet he could cut the tension with a knife.

After only a few bites, he carried his bowl to the sink, washed down the cereal, and slipped his bowl and spoon into the dishwasher.

Without saying goodbye, Carter loped out to his truck and climbed in. He pulled his phone from his pocket and frowned when he found the battery was dead. He'd forgotten to charge it last night after he called Darcy. He plugged it into the cable connected to his dashboard and heaved a deep breath. He was emotionally and physically overwrought.

Today just might be the toughest day of his life—and he didn't know how he'd get through it.

CHAPTER 29

DARCY CHECKED HER PHONE ONCE AGAIN. NOT FINDING ANY TEXT messages from Carter, she looked out the church parlor window toward the parking lot in search of his truck. He'd always responded to her texts. Why hadn't he answered her?

Worry clawed at her as she tried not to imagine what could have happened to him. Memories of Jace's accident overtook her mind, and she sucked in air. She then bit back annoyance and considered why he hadn't texted her. Maybe he was just running late? She hoped that was the case.

When she felt a hand on her shoulder, she turned toward Kaylen's encouraging expression. "I'm sure he'll be here. Maybe he overslept?"

"But why hasn't he bothered to text me?"

"Some guys just get so focused on one thing that they forget everything else."

Darcy nodded, hoping Kaylen was right.

The door to the parlor opened, and Lola stepped in. "Is Haven ready?"

The bride appeared from the restroom at the back of the parlor. "What do you think?" she asked. She resembled a princess in the gorgeous gown that looked as if it had been created just for her. Her beautiful strawberry-blonde hair was pulled back from her face beneath her tiara and veil, falling in waves past her shoulders. Her makeup was subtle but managed to accentuate her baby-blue eyes.

Darcy's eyes filled, and she rushed over to her friend. "You're positively glowing."

"You're perfect," Kaylen gushed. "My brother is going to flip."

Haven lifted her bouquet of white roses and baby's breath. "I hope so."

Lola clasped her hands together as her eyes also filled. "Oh, Haven. You're as pretty as a picture, and Kaylen is right. Derek is going to be stunned when he sees you." She took her daughter's hand in hers. "I'm so happy for you, honey."

"Thank you for all you've done to make this wedding a reality, Mom."

Allyson, Haven's cousin and the wedding coordinator, stuck her head into the room. "It's time, ladies. Let's roll."

Darcy and Kaylen picked up their bouquets and moved down the hallway to the sanctuary, which was packed with friends and family members of the bride and groom. Peeking into the sanctuary, Darcy scanned the pews in search of Carter. When she didn't find him, her heart felt heavy. Her shoulders slumped with the weight of her fear, irritation, and anguish.

Her gaze moved toward the altar, where Derek stood with his brother, Liam, and Haven's brother, Vince.

"All right," Allyson said, speaking barely above a whisper. "We all remember how we practiced, right? Take your time going down the aisle and don't forget to smile." Her face displayed an exaggerated smile.

Darcy took her spot behind Kaylen and waited while two of Derek's cousins serving as ushers seated Lola and Marcia. Haven's father, Bob, came to stand beside Haven, and the warm smile on his face sent happiness through Darcy. She could see the pride in his eyes for his beautiful daughter.

When the organ music began to play, Darcy's hands began to tremble. She turned to face Haven and smiled before mouthing, "I love you," to her best friend.

Haven pretended to kiss her fingers and held them out to Darcy before mouthing, "I love you too."

"Darcy," Allyson hissed. "You're next."

Turning toward the sanctuary, she spotted Kaylen moving down the aisle.

"Now, Darcy. Go," Allyson ordered.

Darcy began to walk down the aisle, forcing her lips into a smile. She felt her shoulders loosen slightly when her eyes found her parents sitting on the bride's side. Her mother waved while Dad held up his phone and snapped several photos. She hoped to see Carter sitting beside them, but he was nowhere in sight. She fought the urge to panic and kept moving. She finally reached the altar, where she took her spot across from the groom and his attendants.

Derek looked handsome in his traditional black-and-white tuxedo, and his younger brother resembled him with the same dark hair and honey-brown eyes. Vince stood beside Liam, and although he and Haven had similar baby-blue eyes, his hair was sandy-brown.

When the wedding march began, the wedding guests stood and turned toward the back of the sanctuary. Then Haven's father began escorting her down the aisle.

Once again Darcy scanned the crowd for Carter, and when she found him standing in the back, she almost fainted with relief. He was handsome in a black suit with a gray shirt and a darker gray tie.

When Carter's gaze finally tangled with hers, her heart stuttered. He nodded, and she returned the gesture, but worry and exasperation still lingered in the back of her mind.

Darcy turned her focus to her beautiful best friend. Haven seemed to float down the aisle toward her sweetheart. Love radiated in Derek's eyes, which were focused on his bride coming toward him.

As Darcy witnessed the affection beaming between the bride and groom, she couldn't help but wonder if Kaylen was right and she and Carter might be the next couple to stand in church. Would they have a chance to promise their futures to one another?

Haven and her father came to a stop at the end of the aisle, and Darcy whisked her thoughts of Carter out of her mind. Her beautiful best friend deserved every ounce of her attention today.

* * *

DARCY HELD LIAM'S ARM AS THEY PROCEEDED DOWN THE AISLE NEARLY forty-five minutes later. As they moved toward the back of the church, Darcy smiled over at Carter, and his lips formed a half-smile in return.

Liam led Darcy out to the vestibule, and Darcy hugged Haven. "Congratulations, Mrs. McGowan."

"Thank you, Darcy." Haven squeezed her. "I did it! I'm married."

Allyson clapped her hands, then took the bouquets from Haven, Darcy, and Kaylen. "Okay, people. Let's all take our places for the receiving line."

Darcy stood between Liam and Vince while the family members and friends of the wedding party began moving down the line, shaking hands and hugging each of them.

When Carter approached, Darcy felt a heady rush of emotions. He worked his way down to Darcy, and she swallowed a gasp as she took in the dark circles under his eyes. He looked as if he hadn't slept at all last night.

"Carter," she whispered. "Did you get my messages this morning?"

When he nodded, she felt her heart stutter. Was he having second thoughts about starting over? "Are we okay?" she asked.

"I'm sorry. My phone died after I called you last night, and I forgot to plug it in."

"Oh." She nodded. "Okay." But when she took in the sadness in his eyes, along with his distraught expression, her stomach clenched. "What's wrong?"

As if he hadn't heard her, he pulled her into his arms. "You're absolutely stunning."

"Carter, please tell me what's wrong." She stepped out of his embrace. "We promised no secrets."

"I know, and I meant it when I said it." He touched her sleeve. "I promise we'll talk later."

She shook her head. "I don't want to wait. Let's talk now."

"Not here." He jammed his thumb toward the receiving line. "You're the maid of honor. We'll talk at the reception."

Carter stepped over to Liam and shook his hand, and Darcy frowned. She didn't like having to wait, but he was right. She had to perform her duties as maid of honor.

As concerned as she was about Carter, she also feared her world was about to come crashing down around her.

"Hello, dear," an older woman said as she shook Darcy's hand. "I'm Derek's aunt Lydia."

Darcy forced a smile on her face. "So nice to meet you, Lydia." Time seemed to slow as she greeted stranger after stranger. She couldn't get to the reception fast enough.

* * *

CARTER STOOD NEAR THE BACK OF THE RECEPTION HALL AT THE FLOWERing Grove Country Club and waited for the wedding party to arrive.

The large room had been decorated with white fairy lights, and round tables were adorned with white candles and teal-and-white roses. A dance floor was set up at the far end of the room with a DJ nearby. In the corner, Carter spotted what looked like a photo booth set up for people to take selfies.

Beyond the large room was a balcony that overlooked a gorgeous golf course. It felt strange to attend an event at the fancy country club, especially since his grandmother had worked there as a housekeeper for years. Though he knew it was an irrational thought, he wondered if someone would assume he had snuck into the country club and ask him to leave.

He tried not to pace while mentally preparing what he was going to say to Darcy when they finally had a chance to talk. How gorgeous she had looked walking down the aisle in the teal dress—a color called "peacock," she'd told him—which seemed to make her eyes somehow greener. Her beautiful blonde hair was styled in a fancy twist, and her lovely face sported just the right amount of makeup. He couldn't take his eyes off her during the ceremony, and when she came back down the aisle on Liam's arm, he hated the ridiculous thread of jealousy that wormed its way through him.

He was aware that Liam was in a relationship, but he also knew that after today, Darcy would no longer be his girlfriend. Surely she would meet another man to sweep her off her feet and treat her the way she deserved to be treated. He couldn't stand the idea of another man holding her, kissing her, wiping away her tears, and spending the rest of his life by her side. But that was how it was supposed to be.

"Carter?"

He turned as Darcy's parents approached him, and he worked his lips into a smile. "Josie. Ross. Good to see you."

"Wasn't the wedding beautiful?" Josie placed her hand on her chest.

Carter nodded. "Yeah, it was."

"Darcy looked amazing in that dress," Josie continued. "It was as if Haven picked that color just for her."

"I thought the same thing." Carter took a sip of his Coke and then snuck a peek at the door. Was the wedding party ever going to arrive?

"We hate to leave the party early," Ross said, "but we're heading out for a cruise in the morning and have to drive down to Charleston tonight."

"Where's the cruise taking you?" Carter asked.

"Puerto Rico. When I booked it, I didn't realize it left the day after the wedding." Ross appeared embarrassed. "You should have seen Darcy's face when I broke the news to her. She was upset we'd have to miss the reception, but the cruise was nonrefundable."

"I told Ross to double-check the date," Josie said, "but he never listens to me."

Carter forced a smile as sadness filled him. He was going to miss Darcy's parents almost as much as he would miss her. He had enjoyed getting to know them and appreciated how kind they had been to him. It was a shame things wouldn't turn out differently.

"Are you feeling all right, Carter?" Josie asked.

Carter cleared his throat. "Yes, just a little tired."

Just then the DJ's voice crackled over the large speakers. "All right, folks. It's time to put your hands together for the new Mr. and Mrs. Derek McGowan!"

Claps, whistles, and hoots broke out around the room as Derek and Haven made their grand entrance and paraded to the center of the room.

"And now the best man and maid of honor. Let's give it up for Liam McGowan and Darcy Larsen!" the DJ called, and more claps, hoots, and whistles sounded.

Darcy held on to Liam's arm and beamed as they joined the bride and groom in the center of the dance floor.

Carter's heart squeezed as he watched his beautiful girlfriend. Her eyes seemed to search the room, and she smiled when she found him standing with her parents. Josie and Ross waved to her.

"And lastly, we have the bridesmaid and groomsman—Kaylen McGowan and Vince Morrisette!" the DJ exclaimed, and everyone clapped and cheered again.

"Now we invite everyone to please take your seats," the DJ said. "Dinner will be served shortly."

"It was nice seeing you, Carter," Josie said before taking Ross's hand. "We need to go say goodbye to Haven and Darcy."

Ross patted Carter's shoulder. "Don't be a stranger."

"We'll have you and Darcy over for supper as soon as we get back," Josie promised. Then they started over toward the crowd gathered around the bride and groom.

Carter lingered by the table while Josie and Ross said something to Darcy and each hugged her. Then Darcy whispered something to Kaylen before making a beeline to Carter.

She closed the distance between them and took his hand in hers. "No more waiting. We're going to talk. Now."

Holding his hand, she guided him toward the door. Carter wasn't ready for this. He felt his heart begin to crack.

* * *

DARCY'S STOMACH DIPPED AS SHE LED CARTER TO THE FAR END OF THE parking lot. While she waited for him to speak, he kept his dark eyes focused on something in the distance. She was sure he was avoiding her stare.

"Carter, please talk to me."

He finally turned toward her, and the pain in his eyes took her breath away. He cleared his throat. "I love you, Darcy. With my entire heart. I've never loved anyone as much as I love you."

She nodded, and her lip trembled. "I love you too, Carter." She took a step toward him as worry and confusion drenched her. "Tell me what's going on. I can't take seeing you so upset."

He studied his loafers. "I realized something last night."

"What?"

Carter's lips twisted. "When I told you I would be completely honest with you from now on, I meant it."

"Okay." A feeling of foreboding washed over her.

"Complete honesty, no matter what. No matter how difficult it is to tell you the truth." His eyes seemed to glisten, and when he finally faced her, he sniffed.

"Carter, what's wrong?" Her words were measured.

He faltered again.

"Carter, *please*," she said.

He rubbed his sternum. "My transplant was also April 3, two years ago."

"The same day as mine?"

"Right." He rocked back on his heels. "Shauna and I have incompatible blood types since our parents were different blood types. So she also gave a kidney for me as a paired donor through a swap. She gave to a sixteen-year-old girl."

"Okay . . ." Darcy tried to decipher what he was saying. She glanced past him just as her mother's BMW SUV motored out of the parking lot.

"Was your transplant at the main hospital in Charlotte?" he asked.

She nodded.

"Mine was too." He turned toward the main road and rubbed his eyes. "Did you receive a kidney from a man who donated for his daughter?" His words were gravelly as if he were trying to hold his swelling emotions back.

"Yes." She squinted in confusion. "How'd you know that?"

She waited for him to continue, but when he remained quiet, irritation wafted over her. "Carter? What aren't you telling me?"

"My donor was a man who was my age, twenty-seven. And he gave in exchange for his fiancée." His voice was strained.

The pieces began to fall into place, and Darcy clapped her hands over her mouth. She took a step back from him and felt as if the ground was crumbling beneath her and tilting the world.

"Darcy, do you understand what I'm saying?" His voice vibrated.

She was frozen, unable to respond.

"Shauna gave a kidney to a sixteen-year-old girl. You received a kidney from that girl's father." He sniffed again as his eyes became puffy.

She took another step away from him. Her thoughts were foggy.

"Darcy, we were part of the same kidney swap. My donor . . . my donor must have been Jace."

"No, no, no. That can't be." Her temples began to throb.

He shoved his hands into his pockets and remained silent.

"Are . . . are you sure?"

Carter took a shaky breath. "Who was Jace told he donated to?"

"A man who was his age."

"Right." He swiped tears off his cheeks. "I'm sorry, Darcy, but there's no doubt that person was me."

Darcy tried to mask the pain as her hands shook. "It's not possible . . ." But the truth stood between them like a chasm, waiting to swallow them whole.

Darcy rested her hand on her forehead. This was a nightmare. This couldn't be true, but it *was* true.

Another truth hit her. "You knew this last night but didn't tell me?"

"I didn't figure it out until after I called you and apologized. I was trying to fall asleep when I tied the threads together. I wanted to tell you in person." He wiped his eyes with the back of his hand.

She studied Carter as his words wrapped around her heart. Jace had been Carter's donor. He was walking around with a piece of Jace—the last piece of Jace—inside his body.

Darcy's chest felt as if it might implode. There was no way she could be with Carter and live in peace. Being with him would remind her of Jace's death every day, reopening the wound she thought Carter's love had healed.

Tears burned her eyelids.

"I'm sorry, Carter, but I can't see you anymore," she said, her words raspy.

"I know." His voice hitched as he swiped at his red eyes. "You'll always be reminded of Jace."

Tears poured down her face.

"I'm truly sorry, Darcy."

Carter pulled her into his arms, and his lips met hers. She held on to his shoulders as his mouth explored hers with a hunger and intensity she'd never felt before. Every cell in her body stirred to life, and with their tears mingling, they continued to share the most passionate kiss Darcy had ever experienced.

When he finally released her, her lips felt swollen, and she flushed with heat from the fire he kindled inside her. But Darcy's hope was shattered. This kiss was only a last grasp at tasting what could never be between them.

"I'll always love you, Darcy," he said.

He pulled his keys from his pocket and removed her house key from the wooden keychain she had bought him at the festival in Flowering Grove. He pressed it into her palm.

She closed her hand around it, frozen in place while he moved toward his truck.

Darcy had no choice but to watch Carter drive out of her life, taking her heart with him.

CHAPTER 30

Carter felt as if his soul had been ripped into shreds as he made the short drive from the country club to his home. His mind kept replaying the pain he'd witnessed in Darcy's beautiful green eyes when she realized what he'd been trying to tell her. She had taken the news just as hard as he'd imagined, and he hated himself for causing her so much agony.

He knew someday she'd meet someone better than him—someone who wouldn't be a daily reminder of everything she'd lost. She would fall in love, get married, and have a family with him, the family she'd always wanted, and her relationship with Carter would be a distant memory—something she'd never even think about.

But Carter, on the other hand, would never recover. Darcy was the love of his life, and no other woman would ever make him feel the way she had.

He'd lost her.

When he reached his house, he steered down the rock driveway to the detached garage where he kept his tools and his grandfather's Road Runner. The Suburban's tires crunched along until he parked in front of the bay door.

Carter dragged himself from the driver's seat and entered the garage. He hopped up on a stool, and his truck keys fell out of his pocket, jingling as they landed on the floor in a heap. He picked them up and ran his fingers over the wooden keychain. He recalled the day Darcy had given it to him and what she'd said:

It's kind of silly, but this way you won't forget where we hung out the first time—in Flowering Grove at a car show.

A knot of grief clogged his throat. No, he would never forget that day. In fact, he would never forget Darcy. She was imprinted on his heart, mind, and soul.

And every time he took his medication or thought about his transplant, he'd remember Jace and the woman who had loved them both.

He closed his eyes as his emotions threatened to boil over.

"Carter?"

He swiveled on his seat toward the door and spotted his father standing there, looking hesitant. Carter blinked—and as if someone released a valve, the fury drained out of him before numbness seeped in.

Then Gage's words from yesterday echoed in his mind:

Just listen, okay?

"Can I come in?" his father asked.

Carter shrugged and tried to clear his throat past the ball of grief that blocked his ability to talk.

His dad took two steps inside the garage and then stopped. "Is it all right if I talk to you?"

"Why not?" Carter snorted. "My life has already imploded today, so I have nothing left to lose."

"What happened?"

They stared at each other in silence for a moment, the only sound coming from a car driving by in the distance.

His father pointed to the Road Runner. "I remember when your grandfather used to drive that car around town. It was gorgeous. Anthony would enter it into car shows and win every single one. He was a legend."

Carter ran a hand over his chin. "He told me."

"Are you going to fix it up?"

"No. I'm selling it."

His father's eyes rounded. "You're not serious."

"Desperate times and all that." He studied his father. "Why are you *really* here? What do you want?"

His dad leaned back against Carter's workbench and sucked in air through his nose. "I'm sorry," he said. "I'm sorry for hurting you and Shauna. I was young, selfish, and immature when I left your mother."

"And us."

"Right. I know there is nothing I can say that will ever make up for what I've done, but I mean it when I say I want to be the father you deserve. I want to know my future grandchildren. I want us to be a family. I hope it's not too late."

Carter stared at him as he took in his words, which felt empty and worthless. "I don't think you could ever understand the depth of the pain you caused me."

"You're right." His dad nodded and sat down on a chair across from Carter. "I don't know how I can ever make up for that. Shauna told me what you went through with the transplant."

Carter crossed his arms over his chest and remained silent. His body began to tremble as his emotions crashed into each other—sadness, regret, grief, shame, and anger.

"I heard what you said last night, and you're right. If I had been here . . ." His voice was thick. "If I had been an actual father to you, I could have helped you—financially and emotionally."

Carter didn't respond.

"I want to make up for that. I want to help you now."

"The thing is, it is *too* late." Carter heard the harsh edge to his voice.

His father nodded, and sadness flickered over his face. "My uncle left me some real estate when he passed away. I sold it all. Got more than I expected, in fact. But I haven't spent a dime. I want to give half to you and half to Shauna. I would imagine it's enough for Shauna to pay off her house and plenty for you to get a new start. Then you won't need to sell your grandfather's car. I'm sure it means a lot to you."

Carter shook his head. "I don't want anything from you. And why now? Is it only because Shauna reached out to you and made you regret what you did to us?" His voice began to rise. "Don't try to tell me you've been looking for us, because we're not hard to find. Sure, Shauna's last name changed, but mine hasn't. I'm still living in the same town where you left me."

His father wiped his eyes with the back of his hand. "I've wanted to find you for a few years, but you're right. I was too embarrassed. Your sister had to open the door."

Carter's eyes narrowed as he studied his father. "I don't know why Shauna did that. In fact, I begged her not to."

"I deserve that." Dad's voice was soft, his expression full of shame. "But I want to make things as right as possible with you and with Shauna."

Carter shook his head as his tone hardened. "When I was a kid, I used to tell myself that you'd surprise me and show up for my birthday party. For years I waited for you, but you never came. *You never came*," he growled.

His father sniffed again. "I'm sorry."

"You say you are, but where have you been all these years? In Tennessee with your uncle enjoying your new life without us?"

"I moved around for a while, but yes, I finally settled in Tennessee."

"I don't care if you were living on the moon. All I know is that you weren't *here*, where we needed you." Carter pointed to the concrete floor. "Mom struggled to buy us clothes, food, shoes . . . She struggled to pay the power bill, the water bill. It was *always* difficult for her. I remember the nights she cried and the nights when Shauna cried. But you weren't there. You weren't!"

His father blanched as if Carter had struck him. "And that's the biggest regret of my life."

Carter snorted. "Sure it is."

Dad cleared his throat. "I was eighteen when I married your mother and when Shauna was born, and I was twenty-two when you came along. I was too immature and selfish to know how to be a good husband or a good father. When things got hard, I ran away, and I regret that. I wish I had fought for your mother, and I wish I had fought for you and your sister."

"But you didn't. We weren't important enough for you to fight for."

"I want to change that, Carter."

"Life is hard. How can I trust that you're not going to run away when it gets hard again?"

"I promise you that I won't, and I'm not just saying it. I'm going to show you and Shauna that I want to be here in Flowering Grove. This is where I've always belonged, and I regret that it took me so long to figure that out." Dad sighed. "You and your sister are my family, and I want to be and do better for you."

Carter crossed his arms over his chest. He couldn't allow himself to trust this man. He'd already caused too much damage.

Dad stood. "Thank you for letting me talk to you. I love you, son. I know it's hard to believe, but I do. You have no good reason to believe me, but I plan to work hard to earn your trust. I also hope someday you can find it in your heart to forgive me." He paused. "And I hope you'll let me help you rebuild your life. That money is yours, and I hope you'll consider taking it." He walked out of the garage, and his footfalls crunched on the rocks as he plodded toward the house.

Carter stared after him as confusion and heartache continued to take their toll.

* * *

LATER THAT EVENING DARCY AND THE REST OF THE WEDDING GUESTS WAVED crackling sparklers in the air. Haven and Derek had already changed into more casual clothes, and they exited the country club and climbed into a sleek black limousine that would take them to the airport. Darcy sniffed while watching her best friend and her new husband drive away, bound for a luxurious getaway in Cancún.

Darcy had no idea how she'd managed to get through the remainder of the reception after she and Carter had ended their relationship. She had rushed into the bathroom, broken down into tears, and sobbed in the far stall until she was able to get her emotions under control. She had considered calling her mother, but she didn't want to ruin their vacation. She also knew that if she heard her mother's voice, she would cry again and not recover. After fixing her makeup, she picked at her dinner until Liam made the toast.

When Haven and Derek had their first dance, Darcy had kept her emotions at bay. She'd danced half-heartedly with Liam, and Kaylen and Vince joined them on the dance floor. After that, she had done her best to keep a smile on her face and mingle with the other guests. After all, she was an expert at hiding her broken heart. She'd done it with Jace, and she'd do it with Carter too.

But when the DJ played "The Keeper of the Stars" by Tracy Byrd, Darcy had nearly fallen apart all over again. She had retreated to a bathroom stall once more and wept, remembering how Carter had held her close and danced with her at the concert. She covered her face with her hands and prayed no one would come in and find her.

When the song ended, she mopped up her face with tissues, fixed her makeup as best she could, and stayed as far away from Haven as possible. If Haven took one look at her, she'd know something was wrong—and Darcy was determined not to ruin her best friend's special day.

Darcy wanted to retreat to her house and curl up in the fetal position on her bed, but she had to make it through the night. She was grateful Haven was having the time of her life, too wrapped up in her happiness to notice Darcy dying on the inside.

Later in the evening, Haven threw the bouquet, and thankfully Kaylen caught it. Darcy had managed to dodge questions from friends who asked where Carter had gone, and when it was time for the cake cutting, she had remained at the back of the large room. She refused a piece of cake since her appetite had dissolved.

After helping dispose of the used sparklers, Darcy hurried back into the large hall and found her purse and phone. She couldn't help but glance at the screen, wishing for a text from Carter telling her he'd been wrong about what they both knew was true. She knew it was useless hope, but she couldn't help it.

The screen was blank.

She slipped her phone into her purse and scanned the room. She and Kaylen had ridden to the reception with Liam. Now she would have to ask someone to take her to her car, which was parked at the church. She had planned to ride back with Carter, but now . . .

"Darcy!" Kaylen hurried over to her. "Are you okay?"

She swallowed back her threatening tears. "Yeah." She conjured up a pleasant expression. "Do you think Liam would give us a lift?"

"Yes, of course." Kaylen took off after her brother. "Liam! Can you take Darcy and me to our cars?"

Liam nodded. "Just give me a minute."

Thirty minutes later, Darcy thanked Liam for the ride and hugged Kaylen before climbing into her Lexus. Finally alone, she allowed her heartbreak to hit her fully. The sounds of her sobs filled the car as agony and loneliness engulfed her.

She needed someone to listen, someone who would console her and tell her everything would be okay somehow—even though she was certain nothing would ever be okay again.

But her parents were on their way to Charleston, and she didn't want to interrupt their vacation. Haven was heading out to her honeymoon, and Darcy wouldn't dream of ruining the best day of her life.

Who else could Darcy call?

Pulling a tissue from her purse, Darcy mopped up her tears. Suddenly, Robyn's words from the night she'd visited with Darcy's parents filled her mind:

If you ever need me, text me. If it's four a.m. and you want to talk, I'm here for you.

She could call Robyn. After all, she and Robyn had gotten close over the past two months.

Even so, Darcy couldn't reconcile Robyn wanting to be close to her without trusting her enough to facilitate a relationship with her half-brothers. It just didn't make sense. And it hurt her—deeply.

Still, she needed someone to talk to, and despite how much that hurt, she trusted Robyn. Even with something this devastating.

She fished her phone from her purse and shot off a text to her biological mother.

DARCY: Can you talk?

A suffocating silence overtook the car as the seconds ticked by. Darcy felt her devastation creep in. She was alone and had no one to talk to. No one to hug her. No one who cared nearby.

Suddenly conversation bubbles danced across the screen, and she felt her heart lift a little.

ROBYN: Call me.

Darcy poised her fingers over the phone. She wanted to talk to someone face-to-face. This was too shattering to discuss over the phone. But would Robyn agree to meet her in person this late at night? Would Robyn truly be a mother figure to her now in her time of need?

DARCY: Can you talk in person?

Silence stretched once again, and Darcy sagged against the driver's seat. Robyn was going to let her down, and she couldn't blame her. Darcy was calling out of the blue, and surely Robyn was already dressed for bed . . .

ROBYN: Yes.

Darcy sat up. *Oh, thank goodness!*

Darcy texted: Can we meet somewhere?

Another pause, and Darcy cringed. Maybe it was too good to be true.

ROBYN: Want to come to my house?

Shock rocked through Darcy. Was she finally going to have a chance to meet her brothers? She wrote back quickly: Yes.

ROBYN: Great. Here's my address.
DARCY: I'll be there soon.

She started her car and headed for Concord.

* * *

THIRTY MINUTES LATER DARCY PARKED IN THE DRIVEWAY OF ROBYN'S two-story burgundy colonial in Concord. She glanced down the street and took in the warm yellow glow of the streetlamps. The clear night sky was peppered with sparkling stars—a stark contrast to her desolate mood.

She made for the front door, and her hands quaked as she knocked. Were her brothers home? Would she have a chance to meet them? Would they even want to meet her? If not, her spirit would be completely broken.

She ousted those thoughts from her mind when footsteps sounded from inside the house.

The door opened, and Robyn stood before her clad in gray yoga pants and an oversized purple t-shirt. "Darcy. What's going on?"

Darcy opened her mouth and tried to speak, but instead, a squeak escaped her throat. Then tears began leaking from her eyes and down her hot cheeks.

"Oh, sweetie. Come in." Robyn took Darcy's arm and led her through the foyer and into a large family room. "Sit," she ordered, directing Darcy to a gray sectional sofa. "Tell me everything."

Darcy took a deep breath and shared what had happened—beginning with her argument with Carter after the rehearsal dinner and ending with their breakup at the reception.

"So that's it," she said when she'd finished the story. "It's over between Carter and me, and I don't know how I'll ever recover. I feel as if my heart has been stomped on."

Robyn took Darcy's hands in hers. "Honey, I never met Jace, but I can guarantee you he wouldn't ever have blamed you for what happened to him."

"But if I had picked up my meds myself, Jace wouldn't be gone." She moved her hand over the arm of the sofa. "Now that I know he was Carter's donor, I'll see Jace every time I look at him. I'll relive that grief every day. And I can't . . . I just can't do that."

"Darcy, look at me."

She met Robyn's determined expression.

"It could have been you who was hit by that driver. It was an accident, Darcy. Don't let an accident define your entire life. You love Jace, and you always will, but he would want you to move on. He would want you to fall in love, get married, and live your dream of having a family. He wouldn't want you to be stuck in your guilt forever."

Darcy sniffed and stared at her lap.

"Listen to me," Robyn continued. "If the situation were reversed, would you want Jace to mourn you forever?"

Her brow wrinkled. "No. I would want him to find happiness."

"Do you love Carter?"

"Yes," she said without any hesitation.

"Do you want a future with him?"

"I do, but when I said I couldn't see him anymore, he agreed with me." Darcy sniffed as renewed grief rolled through her.

"Darcy, Jace saved Carter's life. He gave him a gift, and that shouldn't make you sad. It should make you happy."

Darcy stilled as Robyn's words took root in her mind.

A nearby staircase creaked, and a middle-aged man—whom

Darcy recognized as Graham from Robyn's photos—joined them in the family room.

"Darcy, this is my husband, Graham," Robyn said.

"Hi, Darcy." He was fit with short dark hair streaked with gray, and his brown eyes sparkled behind a pair of wire-rimmed glasses. He nodded toward the stairs. "I'm sorry to interrupt, but they're anxious to meet their sister. Would that be all right?"

Darcy sat up straight. Robyn had told her brothers about her? She'd waited so long for this day. She smoothed her hands down her dress and touched her hair, hoping she looked presentable.

Robyn gave Darcy a sheepish look. "Would you like to meet them?"

"More than anything." Darcy paused, and confusion whipped over her. "What made you change your mind?"

Robyn took her hand in hers. "I was overprotective of the boys, and I'm sorry." She looked toward the stairs for a moment, seemingly lost in thought before her eyes returned to Darcy. "I wanted to make sure it was the right time for them to meet you. When you reached out to me tonight, I realized that now is the time." She squeezed Darcy's hand. "I told them about you, and they were shocked at first. But then they both said they were ecstatic to have an older sister."

Darcy was overwhelmed once again. "I feel the same way about having brothers."

Robyn nodded at her husband, and he ascended the staircase. Muffled voices sounded before heavy footsteps pounded down the stairs.

When her two brothers appeared, Darcy clapped her hand to her mouth. Both were tall and fit like their father and were clad in sweatpants and t-shirts. She felt an instant connection to the teenage boys who had not only her sunshine-colored hair but also similar green eyes.

She stood, and a feeling of wholeness came over her. She felt as if she knew them—as if they already belonged to her.

They were part of her family.

The one with a baby face held his hand out to Darcy. "I'm Keaton."

"Hi, Keaton." She sniffed and shook his hand.

The second one had more mature features. He also shook her hand. "Brayden."

Darcy opened her mouth to greet him, but her throat closed and her eyes filled. She fought to get her emotions under control, but her stubborn tears began to fall once again.

Robyn appeared beside her and looped her arm around Darcy's shoulder. "It's late. Why don't we plan a time for you all to get together soon?" She lifted her chin toward the stairs. "Brayden, Keaton. Darcy and I need to talk alone, okay?"

"Sure, Mom." Keaton gave Darcy a warm smile. "See you soon."

Brayden nodded. "It's so cool that we have a long-lost sister."

"Having long-lost brothers is also very cool." Darcy wiped her eyes and managed a watery smile.

Her brothers retreated up the stairs, and Darcy felt the overwhelming need to tell Carter that she'd finally met her brothers.

Carter.

Her heart began to crumble once again. She'd lost him forever. How was she going to go on without him?

"Do you want a cup of tea?" Robyn asked.

Darcy hugged her arms to her middle as memories of Carter overwhelmed her.

Oh no.

More sobs threatened her. She had to get herself together. "No, I should let you get to bed." Darcy started for the door. "Thank you for talking through this with me."

Robyn hurried after her. "Hold on. You're in no shape to drive. Stay here tonight. We have a comfortable guest room, and you're more than welcome here. You're our family."

Darcy spun to face her. "You mean that?"

"Of course I do." Robyn touched Darcy's cheek. "You're my daughter."

Darcy's lower lip wobbled. "I miss Carter so much it feels like I can't breathe."

Robyn pulled Darcy into her arms again. "Honey, if you love him that much, go after him. Tell him how you feel. Find a way to make it work."

Darcy rested her cheek on Robyn's shoulder.

Her birth mother paused. "When I gave you up, I was shattered. It took me a long time to put one foot in front of the other. My heart seemed to stop beating the day I said goodbye to you."

Darcy sniffed as she took in the earnestness in Robyn's eyes.

"But I believed that somehow we would be reunited. And I'm so grateful that I have you now too." Robyn rubbed Darcy's arm. "Now I want to see you happy. Stop punishing yourself for what happened to Jace and look toward the future."

Her birth mother squeezed her hand. "Please listen to me, Darcy. I'm certain Jace would never blame you for what happened to him. Forgive yourself, sweetie, and start living again."

Darcy nodded as another wave of tears overtook her. She buried her face in Robyn's shoulder, hoping to find a way to revive her heart.

CHAPTER 31

SUNDAY MORNING CARTER FOUND SHAUNA SITTING ALONE AT THE kitchen table, scrolling through social media on her phone. He stilled in the doorway, recalling how angry he'd been with her and Gage. But after he'd spent another sleepless night staring at the ceiling, the need for someone to talk to pushed him toward her. He poured himself a cup of coffee and sat down across from her.

His sister looked up at him, and her eyes widened. "You look terrible."

"Thanks," he deadpanned. He sipped his coffee and set the mug down on the table. "Where's Gage?"

"He ran to the store for me." She studied her brother. "What happened to you?"

"I had a really bad day yesterday." He brushed his hand over the stubble on his chin. "A *really bad* day."

"What do you mean?"

He rested his hand on the mug. "Well, Darcy and I broke up." His voice rasped against his dry throat. "And then I came home and was ambushed by our dad."

"Whoa," she said. "You broke up with Darcy?"

He nodded as his eyes began to sting.

"Oh no." Her chair scraped across the floor as she scooted closer to him. "What happened?"

He blew out a deep sigh. "It's complicated."

"I'm listening. Tell me what happened."

He explained how they'd argued Friday night and how he'd called to apologize to her. "After we hung up, I started putting the pieces together. I realized I had received her late fiancé's kidney, and I knew that would tear us apart."

"Hold on." Shauna held her hand up like a traffic cop. "You received her late fiancé's kidney." She squinted as if working through it in her mind. "So I donated to the girl, her father donated to Darcy, and her fiancé donated to you?" She pointed to him.

"Right." He wiped his burning eyes.

She gasped. "Wow. What are the chances of that?"

"I managed to fall in love with my donor's fiancée. Just my luck. She's still not over his death, and I knew I would be a constant reminder of her deepest loss. And that's exactly how she feels. I told her what I'd realized at the wedding reception, and it was too much for her. So we broke up." He dabbed his nose with a paper napkin. "And now I'm gutted. I've lost everything."

"Carter, I'm so sorry."

"Yeah, me too." He looked down at his mug and then up at her sympathetic expression. His mind replayed his conversation with their father, and a muscle in his jaw jumped. "And I didn't appreciate that when I came home from the wedding, I had to deal with our dad too. I told you I didn't want him here."

"I'm sorry I didn't tell you he was coming," she said, "but I knew how angry you've been with him. I thought he would try to fix his relationship with you."

Carter frowned. "You had no right to do that, Shauna." He tapped the tabletop. "You treat me like a little kid."

"That's not true."

"Yes, it *is* true. You don't respect me. You knew I didn't want to see him, but you forced me to interact with him by allowing him into our home. That only proves that I don't belong here. This isn't my home."

Shauna sniffed and wiped her eyes with another napkin. "Don't say that. It *is* your home."

"No, it's *your* home and Gage's home, and it will be your children's home. But I'm rootless, Shauna. I don't belong anywhere." He took a tremulous breath.

Her brown eyes glittered with tears, and she touched his arm. "You belong here." She rubbed his shoulder. "I never meant to hurt you. I'm sorry you don't feel like this is your home. I'm sorry I didn't respect your wishes about Dad, and I'm sorry about Darcy. I'm sorry about everything, Carter. I really am." She sniffed and took a sip from her water glass. "There's got to be a way for you and Darcy to work this out. You love each other, and that's what matters most."

"It's not that simple, Shauna." He moved his fingers over his warm mug as his biggest fear came into clear view in his mind. "I don't deserve happiness. Every time it's within reach, it slips away. I've been rejected again. There has to be something wrong with me. I'm . . . Maybe I'm just broken. Or worthless."

"Carter, you're *not* worthless." Shauna sat up straight and glowered. "You think you are because of Dad."

Carter's eyes snapped to her. "What do you mean?"

She swiped her fingers over her eyes. "Carter, don't let Dad's mistakes dictate your future."

"I don't understand." His brow crinkled as he tried to comprehend his sister's words.

"You think you're worthless because he abandoned us. You think you're worthless because of *his* mistakes, but I'm begging you to wipe those horrible feelings out of your head. It's wrong, Carter. You're not a burden. Me, Gage, and his parents took care of you because that's what families are *supposed* to do."

He sniffed.

"Listen to me, Carter. You *are* worthy of love and a happy life." She cleared her throat. "You've gone through a lot of hard times, but it won't always be this way."

"It has been so far."

"Then change it. If you love Darcy, tell her. You've been given a second chance at life, so you need to grab it and go for it. Find what makes you happy and hold on to it."

Confusion whirled through him. His sister's words crept under his skin and into his heart, his soul. He stared at her, speechless.

He used the napkin to wipe his eyes and nose as his sister's words continued to soak through him. He stared down at his lap and tried to clear his fuzzy thoughts. Could Shauna be right? Could he and Darcy overcome what seemed like an unsurmountable obstacle? *Can I actually find happiness . . . and keep it?*

"Talk to me," she said. "What are you thinking?"

He looked over at her. "You've helped me realize something."

"What?"

"I don't want to be like our dad, and I'm not going to make the same mistakes he did. I don't want to let happiness slip through my fingers." He rested his hands on the table. "I love Darcy, and I'm going to fight for her."

Shauna smiled. "Good. I'm glad to hear it. Fight for her, Carter. Fight for love."

"I will," he said with resolve.

He just had to figure out how.

* * *

DESPAIR CONSUMED DARCY WHILE SHE STARED AT HER COMPUTER screen in her office Monday morning. After talking to Robyn late on Saturday night, she had taken her up on her offer and slept in the guest room. After breakfast Sunday morning, she drove home, pulled on Carter's hoodie, and curled up on her sofa with a blanket wrapped around her.

She had considered Robyn's words, and while she wanted to call Carter and ask him for another chance, she was still feeling weak and afraid—still feeling that invisible force holding her back from giving him her whole heart.

Although she hadn't slept more than a couple of hours last night, Darcy had somehow managed to push herself out of bed and make it to work on time. But she wasn't able to concentrate on any of her tasks. Instead, her mind kept replaying her last conversation with Carter. She longed to go back in time to tell him it didn't matter about the transplant or that Jace was his donor. She loved him and wanted to figure out a way to move past her pain.

But would she ever be able to look at Carter and not think of Jace? She'd grown so used to living with constant guilt over his death. Could she really put that behind her? Or was it more wishful thinking?

Closing her eyes, she recalled what Robyn had said Saturday night:

Forgive yourself, sweetie, and start living again.

"Start living again," Darcy whispered. She picked up her phone and began scrolling through the photos she and Carter had taken over the past few months. She stopped at a selfie of her and Carter sitting on their special bench in the park. She took in his coffee-colored eyes, handsome face, and gorgeous smile, and she moved her finger over the photo as the sound of his laugh filled her mind.

Her heart swelled.

After shutting down her computer, Darcy grabbed her purse and headed for the door. She knew what she had to do, and she prayed it wasn't too late.

* * *

CARTER TRIED TO CONCENTRATE ON REPLACING THE BRAKES ON THE GRAY Dodge Charger in his stall, but his mind kept wandering.

He had spent the remainder of Sunday out in the garage working on his grandfather's car, trying to comprehend what Shauna had said. Somehow, her words had started to make sense. Had he gone his entire life thinking he was a failure because of his father's abandonment?

Their father had stopped by again last night, and although Carter had managed to sit through a meal with him without getting angry, he avoided more conversations with him by excusing himself and retreating to his room.

He was grateful that Gage hadn't tried to cheer him up this morning and instead had just told him he was available if Carter wanted to talk. Carter had grabbed the first job he could and tried to bury himself in it, but his mind still whirred while his heart throbbed with grief.

When he felt something soft brushing against his leg, he looked down at Smoky purring. "Hey, buddy." He moved his hand over the cat's head. "It's always good to see you."

The cat continued to purr loudly and roll around on the concrete floor next to Carter, soaking up the affection.

The door leading to the showroom and office opened, and Glenda came into the shop. "Carter, you have a visitor."

"Who?"

Glenda motioned for him to follow.

He wiped his hands on a red shop towel and made his way out front. When he found Darcy standing by a display of tires, the air left his lungs.

She looked up at him, and he felt a stab to his heart. He took in the shadows lining her dull green eyes. Had she spent the past couple of nights tossing and turning too?

Darcy's pink lips formed a timid smile. "Can we talk?"

"Sure." He pointed to the hallway leading to the restrooms and the break room. "Follow me."

Carter tried to control his stampeding pulse as he led her into the break room, which was complete with a kitchenette, a refrigerator, and several cabinets. A worn mocha-colored table with four chairs sat in the middle of the room.

He came to a stop in front of the kitchenette counter and then faced her. "What's up?" he asked, trying in vain to sound casual despite the tremor in his voice.

"Well," she began, "I've been doing a lot of thinking the past couple of days, and something occurred to me." She paused, clasping her hands in front of her. "When I first met you in the parking lot, I felt something for you—something inexplicable. Something warm and familiar. It was as if I already knew you. I trusted you. That was why I didn't hesitate to accept when you offered me a ride."

He nodded and leaned back against the counter.

"I couldn't understand it because I didn't even know your name. But the more I thought about it over the weekend, it began to make perfect sense. People like us share a bond that no one else can understand."

Carter cocked his head to the side, trying to decipher her words. "People like us?"

"Transplant recipients. We're members of a club that no one wants to join. We know what it's like to be told we have a grave illness. We're faced with having to wait for a matching organ from a stranger to come available, and if we get that coveted call, we have to accept being reborn by receiving a kidney from someone who died. How can we celebrate a new life when someone had to die for it to become a reality?"

His eyes started to sting.

"And we know what it's like when our only other alternative, aside from a life chained to a dialysis machine, is to allow someone we love to risk major surgery and give up an organ so we can have a chance to be healthy." Her eyes studied his. "Did you want Shauna to donate for you?"

He scoffed. "Not at all. We argued about it for a long time."

"I bet she wanted to donate from the beginning, but you told her no. And that's why you were on dialysis for a year." She lifted an eyebrow.

"How'd you know that?"

"Because I know you, Carter." She took a step toward him. "I know your heart. You would never want anyone to sacrifice themselves for you, even though you'd do anything for someone you love."

He swallowed, unable to deny her observation.

"I also know exactly how you felt. I didn't want Jace to donate for me either. We argued about it for weeks, but he said he wanted to get me well and then marry me."

Carter looked down at the toes of his work boots. "I'm sorry I was his recipient."

"Don't be." She set her purse on the table beside her. "I'm not sorry."

His head jerked up. Had he heard her right?

"Your kidney disease—is it hereditary?" she asked.

"I don't know," he said, and her brow creased. "It's all a mystery. I had swelling in my legs. I went to an urgent care clinic, and a test showed protein in my urine." He ran his palm over the cabinet behind him. "Next thing I knew, I was in a nephrologist's office talking about dialysis. Shauna and I don't know of anyone in our family who suffered with kidney disease, so my doctor's best guess was that it was environmental. I could have come in contact with a chemical that did it. Maybe something in the shop. We really don't know what caused it."

He recalled their conversation in his truck Friday night. "And Robyn told you that her grandfather had kidney disease, right?"

She nodded.

His heart clenched for her. "I'm sorry."

"Me too."

They stared at each other for a moment, and he fought the urge to pull her into his arms right then and there and kiss her. He yearned to touch her, feel the warmth of her soft skin, and inhale the delicious aroma of her floral shampoo.

But she had made it clear Saturday that she couldn't see him anymore.

So why was she standing in front of him with her expression warm and open?

"Why are you here, Darcy?" His voice was soft, and he feared her answer.

"I'm here because Robyn helped me realize something. When I received this kidney, I was given a second chance at life—but I've been walking around acting like I'm already dead."

He swallowed as his throat thickened.

"I've blamed myself for Jace's death for so long that I've been stuck. I've been punishing myself for what happened to him, but Robyn gave me permission to forgive myself. Now I see that she's right." Her green eyes sparkled with unshed tears.

Carter ran his hand over the stubble on his throat, unsure of what to say.

"I've finally forgiven myself. Now I need to start living again, and I need to love again. And I want to love you."

"You mean that?" His voice was gruff.

"Yes." She sniffed and cleared her throat. "I'm so sorry I pushed you away, and I'm sorry I said I couldn't be with you. When you told me you received Jace's kidney, I took that as a sign that I wasn't supposed to be with you." She moved closer to him, and the aroma of her perfume filled his senses. "But the fact that Jace was your donor may be a sign that we *are* meant to be together."

She placed her hand flat on his chest, and tears streamed down her pink cheeks. "We both have been given this gift of life, and we need to embrace it, celebrate it, and enjoy it—together."

Although he wanted to respond, his words were stuck in his throat.

"I'm so sorry I hurt you, Carter," she whispered. "I'm here to tell you that I love you, and I want to be with you. I can't imagine living without you, and if you'll let me, I'm ready to love you for the rest of my life."

Carter shook his head. He was definitely dreaming. "How can you be sure that I can make you happy?"

Darcy rested her hand on his cheek, and he was so relieved to finally feel her warm skin against his again. "One of the greatest blessings in my life has been finding you. I'm completely and utterly in love with you. I will do anything and everything I can to make you my future."

"But you said that every time you look at me, I'll remind you of Jace."

"Carter, Jace saved our lives, and he would want us to be happy." She swiped her fingers across her cheeks. "I'm so grateful Jace saved you, that our transplants brought us together, and that you're part of my life now."

Carter couldn't believe the words he was hearing. Happiness twined through him as his heart expanded in his chest. "My sister pointed out to me that when I got sick, I closed myself off and pushed everyone away. That's why I lost touch with my friends from school. You're the first person who was able to break down the wall I built around my heart."

He took a deep breath. "I believed I was a loser. I thought I was broken and didn't deserve to have happiness in my life, but Shauna told me I believed I was a failure because of my dad's abandonment. I see now that I don't want to be like my dad. I'm not going to run away when life gets tough. Instead, I'll stay and fight for what I need, for what I love." He took her hands in his. "I'm ready to fight for you. I don't want to live without you." He dipped his chin, and when his lips caressed hers, his body was lit on fire.

Darcy wrapped her arms around his neck, and he stilled before stepping away from her. She stared up at him, wide-eyed. "What's wrong?"

"I'm a mess." He brushed his hands down his dirty clothes. "Covered in brake dust."

"I don't care." She pulled him close and deepened the kiss, and he drank in her taste, trying to commit it to memory.

He pressed his lips to her forehead and ran his fingers down her cheek. "Can you imagine a future with me?"

"Um." She tapped her finger to her chin, faking confusion. "I thought I made it clear that was my plan."

"A real future? A home? A family?"

She hesitated, and his smile flattened.

"Did I upset you?" he asked.

"You want a family?" she asked, and he nodded. "I know for sure that kidney disease runs in my family, but we don't know about yours. How would you feel about having children with me if there's a chance we could pass this disease on?"

"Well, we can take a chance or we could adopt."

Her smile returned. "Maybe we should do both."

"Darcy, as long as I have a future with you, I'm happy with whatever we choose."

She pulled her phone from her pocket and set it on the counter before swiping her fingers across it. Suddenly the opening of Tracy Byrd's "The Keeper of the Stars" began to play, and she grinned.

"What are you doing?" he asked.

"You didn't dance with me at Haven's wedding." Darcy's smile became mischievous. "So you owe me a dance."

"And you want to dance with me now when I'm in my dirty work clothes?"

"I want to dance with you anytime and anywhere." She held her hands out to him. "Dance with me, Donovan."

"Yes, ma'am." He took her in his arms, and they started to sway. He rested his head on her hair and inhaled his favorite flowery scent. "I love you, Darcy. I will do everything in my power to make you happy."

"You already have," she whispered.

EPILOGUE

SIX MONTHS LATER

Darcy smiled at Carter and squeezed his hand. Together they walked through the lush green grass as a cool breeze floated over them. The early April afternoon sky was bright blue and cloudless, and birds sang in the nearby trees.

Balancing a colorful spring bouquet in her arms, she looked over at Carter. Her spine tingled as she admired his chiseled profile and his relaxed posture. He had told her he was taking her somewhere special this afternoon, but they needed to make an important stop on the way. At his request, they had dressed up. She wore a little black dress and heels, and he looked stunningly handsome in a pair of khakis and a gray button-down.

She took a deep breath and considered the whirlwind she'd experienced since Haven and Derek's wedding. After reconciling with Carter, she had fully discovered how tightly she'd been holding on to Jace's memory. She donated her wedding gown to a charity, and she finally convinced Jace's mother to accept her engagement and wedding rings.

Ernie and Glenda Barton had decided to officially retire from their business. Gage took over as owner and asked Carter to be his partner, giving Carter a nice increase in salary. They hired two employees to help run the office while they continued to work as mechanics.

Shauna and Carter's father, Myles, moved back to Flowering Grove, and he was cultivating his relationship with them. While Carter was still dealing with some conflicting feelings about his father, Darcy was happy to see both him and Shauna sorting through their resentment in order to forge new relationships.

Myles was also learning how to be a supportive father, and although it took some coaxing, he convinced both Shauna and Carter to accept money from him. Carter was able to pay off his consolidation loan, and he found a two-bedroom house with a nice detached garage to rent in Flowering Grove. He had a fun housewarming party and invited his old friends from school, and Darcy was happy to see him finally reconnecting with them. Carter also had enough money to rebuild the engine in his grandfather's car, and he had been delighted to get it back on the road.

The family was overjoyed when Shauna and Gage's twins arrived a month ago. After a few weeks in the NICU, their beautiful babies—a boy and a girl—finally came home. Everyone was over the moon to finally hold them, and Shauna and Gage had named them Ian and Isabella. The entire family was overwhelmed with love, and Darcy couldn't wait to watch the little ones grow up.

Darcy continued to enjoy bonding with Robyn and her family. And Carter had also become a surrogate big brother to Keaton and Brayden, who frequently hung out with him in his garage. Together they lifted Brayden's 1986 Jeep Cherokee, and Carter was helping Robyn and Graham find a decent car for Keaton, who had recently obtained his driver's license.

Darcy had also started communicating with her biological grandparents, aunts, uncles, and cousins. She and Carter planned to go to Florida to visit her grandparents that summer, and she hoped to meet her other relatives too.

Most importantly, Darcy and Carter had become closer as they both learned to open up to each other. They held to their honesty pact, promising not to hold back any secrets. Darcy had finally given Carter her whole heart, and she fell more in love with him each day. She couldn't remember when she'd been so happy.

When they came to the end of the row near Jace's grave, Darcy rubbed Carter's bicep. "Are you sure you're ready?" she asked.

"Yes." Carter touched her chin. "Positive."

They approached the plaque in the ground that marked Jace Christopher Allen's resting place. Darcy placed the flowers in the grave's vase, then returned to Carter's side. She entwined her fingers with his.

"Jace, this is Carter," she said.

Carter rubbed his chin and glanced at Darcy. Then his focus returned to the plaque. "Jace, I wanted to thank you for saving my life." He paused and smiled at her. "I promise you I'll not only take good care of your kidney, but I'll also cherish Darcy every day I have left on earth." He lifted Darcy's hand to his mouth and kissed it.

Darcy's heart swelled with love for him. "Are you okay?"

"Yes. Thank you for bringing me to see him."

She gazed down at the plaque. "We'll be back soon to see you, Jace." When a colorful butterfly fluttered over and landed on the plaque, Darcy gasped. "Did you know butterflies are the symbol for organ transplants?"

Carter rubbed her shoulder. "No, I didn't. That's beautiful, Darce."

"It is." She smiled up at Carter. "I'm so glad I found you."

"I am too." Pulling her close, he kissed her. "Now for the surprise."

Together they started across the grass toward Carter's beloved Road Runner. "Where are we going now?"

"It's a secret."

They climbed into the car, and the engine roared to life. After a short ride, they were driving through Charlotte.

"Please tell me where we're going," she said, raising her voice so he could hear her over the thundering motor.

Carter gave her a sideways glance. "If I tell you, then it won't be a surprise."

She stuck her bottom lip out and folded her arms over her middle.

He chuckled. "You're adorable, but I'm still not going to tell you where we're going."

Soon he steered into the parking lot of the medical complex where their nephrologists' offices were located.

Darcy's brow creased. "Why are we here?"

Carter drove through the empty lot before parking in a space. "Isn't this where your car was when it wouldn't start?"

"I think so. But what are we doing here?"

He killed the engine. "Meet me at the front of the car." Wrenching the door open, he climbed out.

"Have you lost your mind?" she called after him.

"Possibly." Carter stood at the hood and beckoned her. "Please, Darcy. Come here."

Shaking her head, she unbuckled her seatbelt and then joined him. "Carter, what's going on?"

"What's today?"

"Saturday," she said.

"Right, but what's the *date*?"

"It's . . ." She paused and sucked in air. "It's April 3."

"Exactly. Three years ago today, our lives became intertwined, but we didn't actually meet until two years later." He smiled warmly. "Darcy, my life was forever changed when I walked past your car in this parking lot and heard it click." He took her hand in his. "You've not only healed my heart and taught me how to love again, but just as importantly you've taught me how to love myself."

He took a quaky breath. "You've shown me I'm worth loving. And you've also made me want to be a better man."

"Carter, I love you with my whole heart," she told him as her lip trembled. "Thank you for teaching me how to love again." She ran her thumb over the back of his hand. "You rescued more than just my car that day. You also rescued my heart."

He dropped down on one knee. "Darcy Jane Larsen, I am hopelessly and desperately in love with you, and I want to spend the rest of my life with you."

She pressed her hand to her chest, her eyes filling with tears.

He pulled a ring box from his pocket and opened it up, revealing a beautiful round diamond surrounded by smaller diamonds, all twinkling in a white gold setting. "This was my grandmother's ring, and I had it reset for you." He took a ragged breath. "Would you do me the honor of wearing it and agreeing to be my wife?"

"Yes, yes, yes!" she exclaimed.

He stood up to his full height, and she wrapped her arms around him and kissed him.

Carter slipped the ring onto her finger before he kissed her again.

Darcy closed her eyes and cherished the feeling of her fiancé's lips against hers. Never again would she waste a moment of this miraculous second chance.

ACKNOWLEDGMENTS

As always, I'm thankful for my loving family, including my mother, Lola Goebelbecker; my husband, Joe; my sons, Zac and Matt; and our five spoiled cats. I'm blessed to have such an awesome, amazing, and supportive family.

To my husband, Joe—thank you, thank you, thank you for putting up with my random text messages asking about cars. You're a saint for putting up with my crazy, especially when I ask you six times how to jump-start a car and you patiently text me step-by-step instructions so I won't get it wrong. I love you more than words can express.

Thank you also to my son Zac for answering my random questions about cars. I appreciate how you always love to help choose my characters' cool vehicles. I'm so blessed to have the two coolest sons on the planet!

To my super-awesome, amazing, fabulous, talented critique partner, Kathleen Fuller—I can't even find the words to properly thank you for your help with this book. I've learned so much from you, and I'm beyond grateful for your precious friendship. I look forward to working together on our future projects. You are the absolute best! I don't know what I'd do without your encouraging texts and phone calls.

Special thanks to my mom and my dear friends DeeDee Vazquetelles and Lori Wilen for proofreading the draft of this book and for believing in Darcy and Carter. I'm so grateful to have your love and support for each of my books.

To Candee Walker Elmore and Becca Butler—thank you for trusting me with your precious stories of adoption and searching for your biological parents. I am so honored and inspired by you, and I hope you enjoy Darcy's journey.

I'm so grateful to my wonderful church family at Morning Star Lutheran in Matthews, North Carolina, for your encouragement, prayers, love, and friendship. You all mean so much to my family and me.

Thank you to Zac Weikal for your help with my social media plans, my website, my online bookstore, and all of the other amazing things you do to help with marketing. I would be lost without you!

To my agent, Natasha Kern—I can't thank you enough for your guidance, advice, and friendship. You are a tremendous blessing in my life. I hope you enjoy your retirement with your family—especially your precious grandsons.

I would also like to thank my new literary agent, Nalini Akolekar, for her guidance and advice. Nalini, I look forward to working with you on future projects.

Thank you to my wonderful editor, Lizzie Poteet, for your friendship and guidance. I appreciate how you've pushed me and inspired me to dig deeper to improve both my writing and this book. I'm thrilled to work with you, and I look forward to our future projects together. I'm a better writer because of you, and I'm excited to keep learning from you.

I'm grateful to editor Jocelyn Bailey, who helped me polish and refine the story. Jocelyn, I'm thrilled that we're able to work together again. You always make my stories shine! And I love our fun conversations about the details. Your friendship is such a blessing to me. Thank you for being amazing!

I'm grateful to every person at HarperCollins Christian Publishing who helped make this book a reality.

To my readers—thank you for choosing my novels. My books are a blessing in my life for many reasons, including the special friendships I've formed with my readers. Thank you for your email messages, Facebook notes, and letters.

Thank you most of all to God—for giving me the inspiration and the words to glorify You. I'm grateful and humbled You've chosen this path for me.

DISCUSSION QUESTIONS

1. At the beginning of the story, Darcy dreams of finding her biological mother, but she's afraid to take the first step. When she meets Carter, she suddenly finds the courage to do it. What do you think inspires her to go for her dream?

2. Darcy lost her fiancé, Jace, in a car accident nearly two years before the story begins, and she struggles to move past her grief. Have you ever lost a beloved family member? If so, how did you cope?

3. By the end of the story, Carter finally believes he's good enough for Darcy, and their relationship is strong enough to go the distance. What do you think causes that change?

4. Carter is close to his sister, Shauna, and his brother-in-law, Gage. Do you have a special relative with whom you're close? If so, who is that relative and how has he or she influenced you and your life?

5. What has Carter learned about himself by the end of the novel? How does that influence his thoughts about a future with Darcy?

6. When Carter became ill and had to face dialysis, his girlfriend at the time, Gabrielle, broke up with him. Have you had your heart broken by someone close to you? If so, how did you handle that devastation, and what did you learn from it?

7. Carter's father, Myles, abandoned him when Carter was four years old. During the course of the novel, Carter's sister finds their father, and Myles returns to Flowering Grove to beg for forgiveness from his son and daughter. Do you believe Carter and his sister should forgive their father and try to forge a relationship with him? Why or why not?

8. Darcy and Haven have been best friends since college. They're each other's support, especially during rough times. Do you have a special friendship like that? If so, what do you cherish the most about that relationship?

9. Carter became a mechanic because he used to work on cars with his grandfather. Do you have a special hobby or interest that you share with a special family member? If so, what is it and why is it special to you?

10. Have you ever visited a small town like Flowering Grove? If you could go anywhere for vacation this weekend, where would you choose to go?

From the Publisher

GREAT BOOKS

ARE EVEN BETTER WHEN THEY'RE SHARED!

Help other readers find this one:

- Post a review at your favorite online bookseller
- Post a picture on a social media account and share why you enjoyed it
- Send a note to a friend who would also love it—or better yet, give them a copy

Thanks for reading!

CAN A SMALL-TOWN WAITRESS CAPTURE THE HEART OF A WORLD-FAMOUS HEARTTHROB?

Available in print, ebook, and audio

SOMETIMES TREASURE CAN BE FOUND WHERE YOU LEAST EXPECT IT.

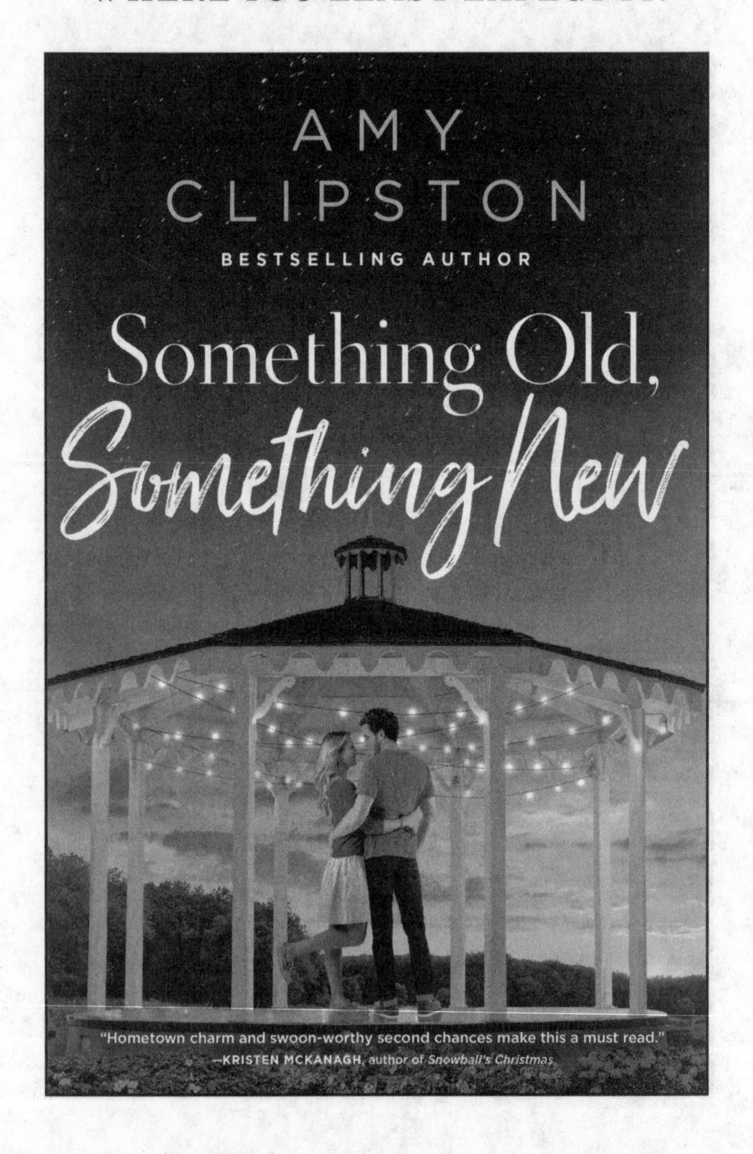

Available in print, ebook, and audio

ABOUT THE AUTHOR

Dan Davis Photography

AMY CLIPSTON IS AN AWARD-WINNING BESTSELLING AUTHOR AND HAS BEEN writing for as long as she can remember. She's sold more than one million books, and her fiction writing "career" began in elementary school when she and a close friend wrote and shared silly stories. She has a degree in communications from Virginia Wesleyan University and is a member of the Authors Guild, American Christian Fiction Writers, and Romance Writers of America. Amy works full-time for the City of Charlotte, NC, and lives in North Carolina with her husband, two sons, mother, and five spoiled rotten cats.

* * *

Visit her online at AmyClipston.com
Facebook: @AmyClipstonBooks
X: @AmyClipston
Instagram: @amy_clipston
BookBub: @AmyClipston